Rave reviews for Connie Mason from *Romantic Times*:

For *Promised Splendor*:

"The action never stops in this rip-roaring Western. Ms. Mason's engaging characters and vibrantly colored backdrop will satisfy fans of sensual, exciting tales set during the wild gold rush days."

For *My Lady Vixen*:

"*My Lady Vixen* is a delightful 'desire, deception and disguise romp' in the spirit of Brandewyne's *Desire in Disguise* and Jude Deveraux's *The Raider*."

For *Desert Ecstacy*:

"*Desert Ecstasy* is a story that sweeps across the desert like a raging sandstorm. This is an exotic 'frying pan into the fire' adventure that combines the atmosphere of Johanna Lindsey's *Captive Bride* with the sensuality of a harem romance. It's the stuff fantasies are made of."

INNOCENT FIRE

Moving with a will of its own, Dare's dark hand cupped a small, rounded breast, measuring its firmness. Her nipple rose against his palm as he stroked it to life beneath the smooth satin of her bodice, and her eyes flew open in dismay. In the dim light of the storeroom they turned a dark green, mysterious, utterly captivating. A shiver of arousal swept her from head to toe and a soft moan escaped her parted lips. The sound was all Dare needed to jerk him back from the brink of disaster into the cold dawn of reality. . . .

"You are remarkably responsive for one claiming innocence. Or were you referring only to the charge of murder? I think, Casey, that you are far from innocent. Either of murder . . . or anything else. Now, will you take off my mother's dress or shall I do it for you?"

BOLD LAND BOLD LOVE

CONNIE MASON

LEISURE BOOKS ⬛ NEW YORK CITY

Dedication

To
Aunt Ruth and Uncle Harry Schmidt
and
Dixie and Ted Clevenger
for
all their great support
and because I love them.
To
Marcia Mason,
my third daughter.

A LEISURE BOOK

April 1989

Published by

Dorchester Publishing Co., Inc.
276 Fifth Avenue
New York, NY 10001

Printed in the United States of America.

BOOK ONE

Bold Land
1807

CHAPTER ONE

Bending low over the steaming kettle of water, her ill-shod feet planted firmly in the mud-brown hard-packed dirt of Sydney, Casey O'Cain swiped a clammy forearm across her sweat-drenched face. Along with several other women convicts she labored behind the barracks of the 102nd Regiment, more commonly known as the New South Wales Corps but referred to as the "Rum Corps" for their devious dealings in that commodity.

Straggling tendrils of red hair clung damply to Casey's cheeks, the scattering of freckles all but obliterated by the angry red flush put there by the hot summer sun. Only her vibrant green eyes reflected her misery as she bent to the task assigned to her—washing dirty clothes for the men of the New South Wales Corps.

So engrossed was Casey in her own misery that she failed to notice the two men standing nearby talking to Lieutenant Potter whose avid glance rested on her more often than she would have liked. Potter was in charge of the women prisoners and normally the only time they saw him was when he issued orders or cursed their laziness.

"What did you have in mind, Mr. Penrod?" asked the lieutenant, eyeing the two men speculatively.

"Annie will be leaving in two weeks," the older of the two men replied. "She's served her time and is anxious to marry and settle on her thirty acres with her husband who's already been emancipated. I'm looking for someone to take her place."

Still handsome despite his fifty-two years, Roy Penrod quietly scanned the group of women toiling over various chores in the stifling heat. Beside him, his son Dare added his own perusal to the unlikely assortment, then looked away, frowning in barely concealed contempt.

"You've not much to choose from, Father," Dare ventured doubtfully. "Felons, thieves, whores, the lot of them look half-starved as well as infested with vermin. We were lucky to find a good woman like Annie but I doubt you'll find anyone like her in this sorry lot."

Slanting Dare a quelling look, Roy chided, "Nevertheless, we need someone to cook and clean, unless you or your brother would like to take over that chore."

"I'm afraid my duties at the station allow me little time for domestic chores," Dare drawled lazily, quirking a well-shaped dark brow.

Arriving in Sydney in 1792 at the age of fifteen, accompanied by his seven-year-old brother, Ben, and their ailing mother, Dare Penrod looked and acted as if he had been born and raised in the Australian bush. Yet he had lived in New South Wales but fourteen years, joining his father, a civil servant who had arrived with Captain Phillips and the first contingent of prisoners in January 1788.

Recognizing immediately the importance of settlers in this raw new land, Roy Penrod asked for and was granted 5,000 acres along with forty convicts to work his grant. His land lay on the Hawkesbury River near the newly constructed town of Parramatta, and he had fine success in raising wheat, corn and other grains. Following the example of Captain John Macarthur who had recently resigned from the New South Wales Corps, he imported sheep and was experimenting with different breeds. Though his flock nowhere equaled that of the mercenary Macarthur, Roy Penrod was considered a farmer of importance who supplied the settlement with meat and grain. Governor William Bligh thought highly of the Penrod clan, inviting them often to various functions at Government House.

Roy turned his rather amused countenance from his son back to Lieutenant Potter. "Are these the only women available?"

"Aye," grumbled Potter testily. "What did you expect? All the healthy ones were placed immediately, though you'll still find one or two here likely to meet your needs. Look them over, Penrod, and take your pick."

"What about that one, Father?" Dare asked, indicating a gaunt middle-aged woman struggling with a load of dirty laundry.

By now Dare had attracted more than his share of attention as the younger women preened and posed for his inspection, and even the older ones paused to take notice of the masculine attributes of the attractive young man. Dressed in bush attire of moleskin breeches that hugged and molded long lean legs and muscled thighs, knee-high boots and canvas jacket, Dare set more than one feminine heart aflutter, including Governor

Bligh's daughter, daughters of settlers, and female prisoners who avidly followed his passage.

His hair was black, so black it shone with faint
blue highlights under the brilliant rays of the sun.
Superbly fit and aggressively handsome, he surveyed his surroundings through thickly lashed
slate-gray eyes, cool and remote yet missing
nothing. He was tall, rawboned and beardless,
and his massive shoulders filled the jacket he
wore to perfection. He carried himself with a
commanding air of self-confidence, combined
with a touch of arrogance.

His face was bronzed by wind and sun, his lips
firm and sensual. The set of his chin beneath a
generous mouth suggested a stubborn streak.
Though his profile was rugged and somber, it was
softened often by laughter or pleasure. One recognized immediately the restless energy about
his movements, the power coiled within him.

Roy followed Dare's gaze to the woman in
question. She looked to be a rawboned country
lass of around forty. Dressed in rags and barefoot, she seemed capable enough to undertake
any chore. "What is that woman's crime, Lieutenant?" Roy asked, pointing to signify his
choice.

"That's Martha Combs," Potter revealed in a
bored voice. "Her record states she stole a ham
and three sausages."

"To feed her starving family, I presume," Roy
added with a hint of sarcasm, disdainful of
English justice.

"To the crown a crime is a crime and a thief is a
thief," shrugged Potter indifferently. "The woman stole something that did not belong to her and
was sentenced to transportation."

"Once she's cleaned up and fed, the woman should suit our purposes," Dare remarked, stifling a yawn. "At least she isn't a killer," he added absently.

Lieutenant Potter eyed Dare speculatively. "There are several younger women available," he hinted shrewdly. "With three healthy men in the family and women so scarce, you might prefer to choose another. Martha hardly seems the type to warm a man's bed. But there's no accounting for one's taste," he added disparagingly.

"Are you suggesting, Lieutenant, that either my brother, my father or myself would bed one of these . . . unfortunate creatures?" Dare asked, impaling him with a frosty glare. "There probably isn't one among them who isn't a whore, infested with God knows what disease."

"That's enough, Dare," Roy warned, well aware of his son's volatile temper. To Potter, he said, "We don't abuse our servants. If you value your hide you'll keep a civil tongue in your head. I can't vouch for my son's good humor with you spouting nonsense at him."

Flushing, Potter fumed inwardly, not at all pleased by the putdown. He never did like the arrogant Dare Penrod or his family, and now he had one more reason to hate the man. No one tangles with the New South Wales Corps and gets away with it. For one thing, the whole family was entirely too friendly with Governor Bligh and tolerant of the emancipists. For another, many of the settlers were beginning to look to Dare for leadership.

"If Martha is the woman you want I'll see to the transfer." He jerked out the words curtly.

Suddenly Dare was momentarily distracted by

a slim figure staggering into his line of vision
carrying a tubful of dirty water. Keeping her eyes
trained on the ground, Casey struggled with the
tub, intending to empty it in the narrow trough
dug for the purpose. Her steps led her close to
where the three men stood but she purposefully
kept her eyes trained on the ground, wanting
nothing to interfere with her duties or with the
heavy burden she carried. But fate willed otherwise.

Her frail body, already strained beyond its
meager strength, couldn't cope with her nearly
impossible task, and her arms simply failed her.
Stumbling clumsily, she tried desperately to hang
onto the tub but its weight proved too great for
her. It left her arms with a thud, spilling filthy
water all over Dare's spotless moleskin trousers
and boots, he being the closest to her.

"Bloody hell!" he howled, jumping back as
Casey lost her footing and followed the tub to the
ground. She wallowed helplessly in the resulting
mud while Dare looked on with barely concealed
disgust.

"You clumsy bitch!" Lieutenant Potter bellowed. "You did that on purpose."

Staring with dismay at his mud-splattered
trousers, Dare paid scant heed as the lieutenant
hauled Casey roughly to her feet, his hands biting
into the soft flesh of her upper arms. A snarl
curled Potter's thin lips as his right arm swung
back and then struck Casey with a blow that sent
her reeling. She would have fallen but for his
cruel grip. When he drew back to strike again he
found his wrist imprisoned in a viselike grasp.

"Are you crazy, Potter?" Roy admonished in a

stinging tone. "Can't you see the girl is too frail to survive severe punishment? Let her be."

Surprised by his father's outspoken defense of the girl, Dare turned his attention to the pitiful form struggling in Potter's hurtful grip. Much of her features were obscured by mud and filth but he could see that she was young. Strands of brilliant red hair straggled down her back and hunched shoulders to hang limply at her waist. Her clothes were no better than rags and she may as well have been barefoot for all the good her worn shoes did her. She was slender, too slender, but what there was of her was not displeasing.

Newly arrived in the penal colony of New South Wales, Casey awaited assignment to one of the area settlers, mostly farmers in need of a house servant or common laborer. It was no worse than expected, she reflected with a sad little sigh. She had taken a man's life and the law demanded its dues. Her mother was long dead, her father hanged for inciting a rebellion against the crown, so it mattered little that she was to live her remaining days in a wild country inhabited by natives, a handful of military and civil servants, too few settlers and hundreds of hardened criminals.

Then suddenly she looked up at Dare with eyes as green as sparkling emeralds, heavily fringed with indecently long dark lashes. Unable to help himself, Dare stared rudely back at her. Something about her disturbed him. He wasn't sure what it was but he was positive he didn't like the feeling. Why should one glance from a hardened criminal, and probably a whore, so completely unnerve him? he wondered distractedly.

Ill-clad in a heavy woolen dress stained beneath the armpits with perspiration and rendered nearly immodest by many rips and tears, Casey's slender figure belied the strength that had seen her through endless months of pure hell. It hadn't started that fateful day she boarded the prison ship to begin her six-month journey to the penal colony in Australia, but weeks earlier when her beloved father had been arrested in Dublin on a charge of instigating a rebellion against the crown.

The truth was that Seamus O'Cain, a teacher at the university, hadn't committed the crime he was accused of. He had done little more than advise some of the young men who were bent on fighting injustice visited on the Irish by the English—and his advice had been to bide their time and not do anything foolish. But somehow his name had been linked with the rebels and he was promptly arrested and tried, his trial a mockery of justice. Seamus O'Cain was a gentle man; a scholar and gentleman who loved his daughter and taught her more than most men taught their sons, more than was considered appropriate for a girl.

Casey's mistake had been in becoming involved, calling upon the judge in his private chambers to plead for her father's life. The judge, immediately taken with Casey's youth and beauty, offered to have her father transported if she would agree to certain conditions. Horrified, Casey listened to the judge's indecent proposals, shaking her head in disbelief. How could such a distinguished man of the court even suggest such things? Naive in the ways of men despite her twenty years, Casey had much to learn.

She was too shocked to offer a protest, and the judge mistook her silence for acquiescence. His lust for the shapely redhead aroused him to the point of panting to possess her. The moment he laid heavy hands on her young body, Casey reacted instinctively, struggling against his stocky form as he dragged her toward a settee, all the while tearing at her clothes and slobbering wet kisses on her pale face. She resisted furiously, but her struggles gained her nothing but bruises. Then Casey spied a large vase on a table nearly within her reach. Twisting until she was able to grasp it in her hands, she managed with herculean effort to bring it crashing down on the corpulent judge's head.

What Casey hadn't counted on was the man falling and banging his head on the edge of a marble-topped table and dying. Given the circumstances, explaining that she was merely protecting her honor proved a waste of breath. She was summarily jailed, tried, convicted of murder, and because she was a beautiful woman, sentenced to transportation instead of hanging. But far more difficult to accept was the fact that her father was hanged along with the leaders of the rebellion and all her good intentions had been futile.

Now, here she was, ragged and nearly barefoot, ravaged by the hardships suffered during the long sea voyage and laboring alongside other women who had yet to be placed into service. In this year of 1807 food was still scarce in the penal colony; cloth, tools, and livestock were so rare as to be nonexistent, except for the fortunate few with the means to purchase these necessities from trading vessels. For some reason the government kept sending more prisoners but did little to sustain them or make their existence more bearable. When a supply ship did drop anchor at Port Jackson the Rum Corps was there to buy and control the much needed goods, commanding their own price and acquiring much profit along the way.

"You've chosen the wrong person to defend, Mr. Penrod," Potter advised as Roy continued to glare at him. "She's a murderess. She killed a judge in Ireland. Her father led a rebellion against the crown and was hung for his crime. Besides that she's a whore. She tried to seduce the judge. When he refused to be influenced by her feminine wiles she killed him in cold blood."

Dare stared in dismay at the frail girl whose green eyes now blazed defiance and hatred at Potter. If looks could kill, the man would be dead. How this scrawny, bedraggled creature found the strength to openly defy anyone was beyond Dare's imagination.

"What's her name?" Roy asked curiously. Somehow the label of killer didn't fit the girl. Whore, maybe, but not murderess.

"Tell him, wench," Potter prodded. "Tell him your name."

Lifting her head to face the soft-spoken man who cared enough about her to leap to her defense, Casey said in a lilting Irish brogue, "My name is Casey, sir. Casey O'Cain."

"Is it true? Are you a murderess, Casey?" Roy surprised her by asking.

"I . . . I killed a man," Casey admitted, her chin tilted at a stubborn angle. "But I—"

Whatever explanation Casey was about to make never left her throat as Potter rudely interrupted. "Do you want Martha Combs or not? Leave this one to me. I'll soon take the sass out of her. It's unlikely anyone will want a servant who is a confessed killer. She's likely to slay them in their beds." His lascivious leer lingered overlong on the jut of Casey's breasts barely concealed by her threadbare gown, and Roy knew exactly how Potter intended to tame the girl.

"I'll take her," Roy shocked Dare by saying. "And Martha Combs, too. We could use another woman to help Meg with the chores."

"Father!" Dare exploded, staring at his father as if he had lost his mind. "The girl killed once, and is likely to do so again. Do you want that kind of woman in your household? According to the lieutenant, we won't be safe in our beds."

"Look at her, Dare," Roy scoffed with a careless toss of his head. "Casey doesn't look as if she could hurt a fly, let alone three strapping men. Besides, if she killed she must have had good reason. Isn't that right, Casey?"

Slowly Casey nodded, grateful for the first kindness she had known in months.

"Of course she's not going to admit to murder," Dare countered disgustedly. "You're too soft, Father. Don't be taken in by her sad green eyes. Forget her. Bring her home and she'll corrupt all our workers with her whoring ways."

Furious, Casey exploded. She had stood by long enough listening to these pompous asses talk about her as if she didn't exist. "I'm no whore!" she hissed indignantly. "I killed a man, but it was an accident. I never meant for him to die."

"So the cat has claws," Potter sneered nastily. "You didn't fool me one minute with your docile ways. I knew there was more to you than met the eye. Go back to your chores, wench, there's no place for you in a decent household."

"I said I'll take her," Roy repeated firmly. "Prepare the papers for both women."

Potter looked startled and opened his mouth to protest but thought better of it, nodding curtly and stomping back toward the barracks. Along the way he stopped to speak to Martha Combs. Once he was out of hearing, Dare rounded angrily on his father, completely ignoring Casey who stood nearby as if carved in stone.

"My God, Father, have you lost your mind? How could you take this . . . this murderess in our home? You know how impressionable Ben is. Do you want your young son seduced by this whore? Besides, we only need one woman to replace Annie, and Martha seems the sort to fit our needs. Meg can handle the household duties without help."

"Trust me, Dare. I have a feeling about Casey. Things aren't always what they seem. Look at your friend Robin. He was convicted and transported for a crime so minor it bordered on the ridiculous. And him only a lad at the time."

"Robin's crime didn't include murder. The girl admitted she killed a man. What more proof do you need?"

"I've never known you to judge so rashly, Dare," Ray chided crossly. "Normally you refrain from making snap judgments. What bothers you about Casey?"

Casey flinched under Dare's cold scrutiny but proudly stood her ground. Did this man think he was God to judge her so harshly? He was no different than the others who refused to believe her. But the older man, his father, somehow did seem different. Or was he? Was he all that he pretended or was he a man like the judge who wanted her for vile purposes?

"I . . . I have this crazy feeling we'll be sorry," Dare stammered lamely, unable to explain his animosity toward Casey.

"Time will tell," Roy replied. Then turning to Casey, he directed, "Go clean up, Casey. We'll be leaving soon. Tell Martha to gather her belongings. My name is Roy Penrod and this is my son Dare. We have a farm near Parramatta on the Hawkesbury River. I hope you'll be happy there."

"Anything is better than this, Mr. Penrod," Casey gestured gratefully. "I won't disappoint you, sir. And your son is wrong. I'm not a whore. You won't be sorry for employing me." Then she turned on her heel and left in a whirl of dirty skirts and dripping mud, slanting a baleful glare at Dare over her narrow shoulder.

Though Casey was female enough to note that Dare Penrod was shockingly attractive, she also marked him as being subtly dangerous, with a cold, careless air that intrigued and frightened at the same time. Those slate-gray eyes probed her relentlessly, peeling away the layers of protection until all her inperfections were exposed. Thank God it was the father she had to answer to and not the son, for surely no mercy existed in the dark chambers of Dare Penrod's heart.

Gray eyes narrowed speculatively. Dare watched Casey march away, noting the graceful sway of her body and the proud tilt of her head despite the filth and grime covering her from head to toe. Suddenly a dark thought entered his mind, one he could not quell no matter how hard he tried. Surely his father didn't . . . Once the notion piqued his curiosity he couldn't stop his wayward tongue. "Father, exactly why do you want Casey? You don't . . . don't mean to bed her, do you?"

The idea was so ludicrous Roy burst out laughing. But not for long. Only until anger replaced mirth. "If you weren't my son, Dare, I'd lay you flat for that nasty remark. What I feel for Casey is compassion and pity. You do me a grave injustice."

"I'm sorry, Father," Dare apologized sheepishly. "I know better than to suggest such a thing. It's just so unlike you to act so . . . so unwisely."

"And it's not like you to protest so vigorously without justification," Roy rejoined.

"Don't you consider murder ample justification?"

Roy searched Dare's face thoughtfully, wondering how one small girl could set off a reaction in his son that was totally out of character. Was he so wrong about Casey O'Cain? Was Dare correct in assuming the girl would bring disaster to his household? Or did Casey strike a responsive chord in Dare that he refused to acknowledge? One way or another, Roy was certain his home would not be the same after today. Right or wrong, he had made a decision, rash or otherwise, and come what may he would honor it.

CHAPTER TWO

The dirt track to Parramatta was rough, the heat nearly unbearable, and the bullock pulling the wagon so slow Casey could have walked faster. To date the only carriages in the colony belonged to the governor and high officials like Lieutenant Colonel Johnston, lieutenant governor as well as commander of the Rum Corps. Even horses were rare, but somehow Dare Penrod had secured one of the animals for himself, and rode it as if he were a part of his mount.

After cleansing herself of the coating of mud that covered most of the exposed parts of her body, Casey hadn't time to wash her only garment so she was forced to wear the grimy dress to her new home. Her meager belongings included a cherished brush and a locket she wore around her neck that had once belonged to her mother. Martha fared little better except that the odd assortment of clothing she wore was at least reasonably clean.

In her present condition Casey hardly considered herself attractive, and couldn't blame Dare Penrod for thinking her no better than the usual thieves and trulls sent to the penal colony. She vowed to keep out of his way during her years of servitude and wanted nothing to do with the arrogant settler, though she'd be blind not to notice his virile physique and handsome features. Too handsome and cocky, she decided disparagingly. Nothing like the honest lads from her own beloved Ireland.

Though popular and much sought after, Casey hadn't yet settled on one lad in particular. Though Timothy O'Malley had a clear edge on all the others. A braw, strapping lad, Tim had asked for her hand and it was understood they would marry one day, until the rebellion changed her plans and her life. Tim was jailed along with scores of other insurrectionists and was transported on the same ship as she. Though she had seen little of him once they left the ship, during the long journey they had encountered one another occasionally despite the strict segregation of men and women according to rules set by the English. If not for Tim she wouldn't have survived the voyage nearly so well.

"Mr. Penrod seems a kindly sort." Martha's voice startled Casey out of her reverie and she turned toward the older woman, smiling contritely for being too immersed in her own thoughts to pay her much heed.

"I'll reserve judgment until later," Casey hedged, unwilling to commit herself so soon. "Sometimes first impressions are deceiving."

"Still, I think we're lucky to be leaving Sydney. Especially with a fine family like the Penrods. It could be worse, you know. Whether you were aware of it or not, that Lieutenant Potter had his eye on you. If he'd had his way you would have ended up in his bed."

"Not likely," scoffed Casey, lowering her eyes. Actually, she knew full well what Lieutenant Potter had on his mind every time he leered at her. That's why he went out of his way to discourage others from hiring her.

From beneath lowered lids Casey studied the older woman. She was not unhandsome, but her bony frame was thin to the point of emaciation. Casey knew little of the woman's history beyond the fact that she'd been transported for stealing. Being thrown together as they were, they spoke occasionally but revealed nothing of a personal nature. Martha looked to be over forty with soft brown hair interspersed with gray. Weary brown eyes peered from a gaunt face that was no stranger to hunger or deprivation. Casey wondered what Martha would look like if provided with three square meals a day and attractive clothing.

"That young Mr. Penrod is some man," Martha remarked idly, her eyes drifting to Dare, who rode beside the wagon on his pure black stallion.

"If you consider arrogance attractive," sniffed Casey, daring a glance at Dare's broad back. "He treats us like the scum of the earth."

"Oh, no, Casey, I'm sure you're wrong," Martha replied, aghast. "He was nothing but kindness when he spoke to me while you were cleaning up. It's likely you two got off on the wrong foot. I'll admit splashing muddy water on him didn't endear you to him. Give him time, he'll come around."

"I doubt it," remarked Casey, slanting a baleful glare at Dare. As luck would have it, he happened to turn just at that instant.

"Did you wish to say something to me, Miss O'Cain?" he asked coolly, quirking a dark brow.

"N . . . no," she snapped, clamping her mouth tightly shut.

"I hope it wasn't my father to whom you were directing that venomous look," he returned with a cynical cluck of his tongue.

Before she could form a proper reply his horse bolted forward, leaving a cloud of dust in his wake.

"That man is an impossible bastard," Casey muttered darkly. "He's 'pure merino' through and through," she added, using the derogatory term often employed to describe English settlers.

Martha was astute enough to hold her tongue as she shifted her gaze from Casey to Dare, wondering at the animosity between the two.

Though the distance between Sydney and Parramatta was but fifteen miles, the rough track and slow-moving bullock ruled out a speedy journey. Looking ahead, Casey could no longer see Dare, or even the dust indicating his passage. Then, over the monotonous creaking of the wheels, strange sounds drew her attention to the tall trees growing beside the track. Returning her interested gaze were colorful parrots chattering and squawking. They looked like gems in flight in aqua, blue, sapphire, green and scarlet. This strange land never ceased to amaze her. This was Casey's first venture outside Sydney and her avid curiosity kept her enthralled.

From a tall eucalyptus tree came the cry of a magpie and the clatter of a kookaburra. Then another sound startled her. Several rough-looking men came rushing out of the bush on either side of the track whooping and hollering and waving clubs. Roy reacted instantly, reaching for his loaded weapon. He squeezed off a shot, but before he could prime and reload, two men leaped up to wrestle him to the ground.

"Bushrangers!" Martha cried, her eyes wide with fear. And with good reason. Bushrangers were escaped convicts who had taken to the bush and lived off the land, sometimes for years. Hiding in the foothills of the Blue Mountains, they came out to rob, steal and sometimes rape.

The two women clung together in the wagonbed, immediately recognizing their danger. These were desperate, hunted men intent on their own survival. And being women only increased their danger, for judging from the men's leering glances, they had been without women for a long time.

"Well, well, look what we got here, mates," said one man, obviously the leader, as he walked around to the back of the wagon.

"These women are my charges," Roy exclaimed, struggling with the two men who now had him pinned to the ground. "Don't touch them!" The leader barely spared Roy a glance.

"Gawd, Bert, look at all that red hair," another of the bushrangers gasped, gaping stupidly at Casey. "Ain't she somethin'?"

"That she is, Artie lad, that she is," agreed Bert. "Heave her outta the wagon while Sam and Whitey unhitch the bullock. Mayhap we'll find some use for the animal. As fer the woman, we all know what she's good fer." His salacious grin communicated to Casey exactly what duties she would be required to perform.

When Artie reached for her she reacted instinctively, catching him unawares as she pushed him aside and leaped from the wagon, racing through the brush and wattle to the safety of the trees. Behind her she could hear sounds of hot pursuit, but she dared not look back. Briers and burrs caught at her skirt and tore her tender flesh, but the pain was nothing compared to her fate at the hands of these desperate men.

"Run, Casey, run!" Roy called out in a strangled voice. His words of encouragement lent wings to her feet as she fairly flew through the brush.

Her lungs were on fire, her breath trapped in her throat, but in the end all her efforts were in vain. Due to her poor physical condition, she proved no match for her vigorous pursuer. She was just beyond the line of trees when she was jerked to an abrupt halt by a cruel hand that snatched at her long hair which trailed like a red banner behind her. She screamed in agony as Bert brought her to the ground, dragging her farther into the woods.

"I caught ya, wench," Bert gloated as he brought her to an abrupt halt.

"Let me go, you monster!" shrieked Casey, struggling in his grasp. "Don't you know I'm a convict just like yourself?"

Casey could have saved her breath, so little impact on Bert did her words have. "Yer a woman, ain't ya? An Irish lassie, if I'm any judge. I always was partial to red-headed wenches. Wild little thing, ain't ya?" He laughed.

Resisting wildly, Casey failed to hear the shouts and sounds of a scuffle coming from where the wagon had been ambushed. But Bert, accustomed to maintaining constant vigilance, heard and reacted instantly. Uttering a vile curse, he released his hold on Casey, immediately sensing danger to himself. No wench, no matter how tasty, was worth losing his life over.

"We ain't through yet, wench," he snarled, leveling a baleful glance in her direction. "I know where to find ya and ya can bet I'll have ya one day."

Thoroughly shaken, Casey could do little more than glare at Bert. Suddenly he turned and disappeared through the trees, the cry of the kookaburra laughing hysterically all but drowning out the sound of a horseman who came crashing through the bush.

Dare leaped from the saddle, landing beside the small, bedraggled form. "Miss O'Cain, Casey, are you all right? What did that scoundrel do to you?"

"I . . . I'm fine," Casey faltered, attempting to maintain her dignity. In her struggle with Bert and her headlong flight through the brush, her bodice had been ripped in several places, allowing tantalizing glimpses of skin. "You arrived in time."

Dare suddenly realized that her threadbare bodice had been rendered nearly useless. Stunned, he stared at her as if mesmerized. Never in his wildest imaginings did he think she would be so perfectly formed. Beneath the tears her body was white and smooth as alabaster. Her breasts were small but deliciously rounded and tipped with two pouting buds the color of ripe cherries. Though she was far too slim, Dare found everything about Casey O'Cain's small body pleasing. When finally he lifted his eyes to Casey's face, they glittered like polished silver.

Flushing angrily, Casey pulled at the ruined material to cover her exposed breasts but found her bodice beyond hope of repair. "Don't you know it's rude to stare?" she scolded tartly as Dare's eyes fastened on her breasts. "Give me your jacket."

Grinning impudently, Dare shrugged out of the garment and draped it over her shoulders, somewhat startled at the fragility of her bones beneath his fingertips. Casey gave an involuntary shudder at the unexpected heat of his hands as they lingered on her shoulders far longer than necessary. She felt a shock pass through her body at the brief contact and wondered if Dare felt it too. As if in answer, his hands flew away and a puzzled frown wrinkled his brow.

"Thank you," she murmured, hugging the jacket tightly about her, grateful for the protection against his heated gaze. She knew enough about men to recognize desire when she saw it. Instinctively she retreated a step. She hadn't escaped being raped by bushrangers to fall victim to a "pure merino." Especially one like Dare Penrod who considered her no better than the dirt he walked upon. It had been a struggle to preserve her virginity these past months and at the moment it was the only thing of value she possessed. No one would persuade her to give it up so easily.

Aware of Casey's stealthy retreat, Dare asked, "Are you afraid of me?"

"I fear no man," she declared defiantly. "But I'm no fool. I'm fully aware of my weakness and your strength."

Suddenly shamed by the surge of desire and sexual tension he had experienced from the moment he laid eyes on Casey O'Cain, a confessed murderess, Dare turned away in disgust.

"You need not fear me, Casey. I'm far too discriminating to avail myself of your rather questionable charms."

"Why, you . . ." But fortunately Casey's words died in her throat as another rider came plunging through the brush. "Dare, is everything all right?"

"Just fine, Ben," Dare assured the young man. "How are Father and Martha?"

"Father suffered a few cuts and bruises but is okay. They didn't touch Martha. What about . . . about . . ."

"Her name is Casey, Ben. Casey O'Cain," Dare supplied, noting the direction of his brother's admiring gaze.

Several years younger than Dare's twenty-nine, Ben possessed the rugged good looks of both father and brother. Except where Dare's gray eyes were often brooding and intense, Ben's sparkled with humor and gaiety. Tiny laugh lines radiated outward from the corners, and his mouth seemed to tilt upwards in a perpetual smile. Not quite so tall as Dare but nearly as broad, he wore his black hair tied back at the nape with a leather thong.

Ben's eyes widened appreciatively as he raked Casey from head to toe, obviously liking what he saw. Though Casey flushed under his steady perusal, she sensed no insult in his open gaze. "You never mentioned she was so beautiful, brother," he chided with mock annoyance.

"I hardly mentioned her at all," Dare flung back, for some obscure reason angered by Ben's interest in Casey. "Casey, this young pup is my brother, Ben. I came upon him on the track when I rode ahead. He and some of our workers were out hunting. When we heard the shot we rushed back to the wagon."

"Luckily we arrived in time," Ben continued importantly. "This is hardly the welcome you deserve, Casey, but I hope you'll be happy with us," he added, twinkling.

"Casey is not a guest who needs entertaining," Dare reminded his brother. "She is merely a servant. One of the convicts transported for committing a crime. Take her back to the wagon, Ben. I intend to search for the bushranger who assaulted Casey. What about the others? Did they get away?"

"All but two. Tom Healy and Buck Conroy are taking them back to Sydney. I'm sure the Corps will be more than happy to put them behind bars. Be careful, Dare. And don't worry about Casey, I'll take good care of her."

Scowling, Dare nodded as he swiftly mounted. "I'll see you back at the house. And Ben," he hinted meaningfully, "I'll talk with you later." Then he yanked on the reins and rode off into the bush.

Casey needed little imagination to know what Dare wanted to talk to Ben about. Of course Ben would be informed of her crime and warned to stay away from her. Too bad because she needed a friend and Ben seemed the sort one could trust.

"Don't mind Dare," Ben said, annoyed at his brother's brusqueness. "He tends to be some-what unbending at times but normally he's a grand bloke. Everyone likes him. His best friend is an emancipist. Most convicts assigned to set-tlers are treated kindly to encourage them to work, so you have nothing to fear. Father is not a difficult taskmaster."

"Thank you, sir," Casey murmured, warmed by Ben's friendly chatter.

"Call me Ben." The young man grinned impishly. "If you call me sir I'll think you're talking to Father. Now up with you, I'll take you back to the wagon."

With considerable ease he lifted her astride his horse and swiftly mounted behind her, clicking his tongue and snapping the reins.

The rest of the journey proved uneventful as Casey rejoined Martha in the wagon. Though somewhat battered, Roy managed the bullock with ease while Ben rode guard. But by now the bushrangers had melted back into the bush and no longer presented a threat. The party entered Parramatta before dark but did not stop. Casey noted that the town consisted of a small cluster of brick and timber buildings, erected by convict labor, lining both sides of the dirt track.

They reached Penrod station a short time later. To Casey it looked like an endless expanse of acreage mostly cleared of brush stretching west and south along the Hawkesbury as far as the eye could see.

Abruptly they came upon a large, rambling house surrounded by dogleg fences, green paddocks and grazing sheep on the hillsides. Chickens scratched in the yard, pecking at the dusty ground. A big gum tree offered dappled shade to the rectangular two-story house. Casey thought it grand and imposing, especially in this wild country where so few made a success of farming.

Ben helped the women down from the wagon and they entered the house through the front door. Casey noted that the central hall ran the full length of the house from front door to rear with three rooms on each side. No sooner had they walked in than a rotund, pleasant-looking woman bustled forward to greet them.

"I was beginning to worry, sir," she said, addressing Roy, "when you failed to return from Sydney at the usual hour. And I see you've brought back two women to take my place." Suddenly her startled brown eyes settled on Roy's bruised face. "Good Lord, what happened?"

"Bushrangers," Roy said tersely. "Bring some disinfectant so I can take care of these scrapes."

"Right away, sir. But . . . but where is Dare?" she asked, looking past Ben. "He's not hurt, is he?"

"I'm sure my brother will appreciate your concern, Annie," laughed Ben, "but he's fine. He remained behind to track one of the bushrangers who attacked Casey."

"The disinfectant, Annie," Roy reminded the woman. "When you come back I'll make the introductions." Nodding sheepishly, Annie scurried away, rejoining them a short time later in the parlor.

After introductions were made, Casey decided she liked Annie. About thirty-five, pretty and plump, she looked no more a criminal than Casey herself. After Roy's bruises were attended to, Casey and Martha were fed in the kitchen while the family ate in the dining room. Casey had no idea whether Dare had returned and was too tired to care.

Martha was given a room beneath the back staircase close to the kitchen, but Casey was led to the second floor and a small chamber at the far end of the hallway. Until Annie left in two weeks there were no other rooms available on the lower floor. The small cubbyhole off the kitchen was used by Meg, another convict about Casey's age whom she met briefly.

Meg did not strike her as a friendly sort. Brash, blond and buxom, she reminded Casey of a serving wench she had seen in an inn in Dublin. Casey could well imagine Dare's avid silver gaze following the girl, well-endowed and aware of her appeal, as she strutted between the kitchen and dining room serving the tasty dishes Annie had prepared. Not that it mattered, she told herself.

Too exhausted to do more than splash water on her face and hands, Casey removed Dare's jacket and flopped on the bed, falling asleep immediately. Her last conscious thought was of the bleak years of servitude stretching endlessly before her and of the handsome, arrogant Dare Penrod who most certainly would do all in his power to add to her misery.

CHAPTER THREE

"Wake up, Casey. Mr. Roy is asking for you. Martha has been up and about for hours."

Casey flopped over, cranking her eyes open to find Annie standing over her. "I didn't realize it was so late, Annie," she yawned, glancing at the light coming through the window. "Please tell Mr. Penrod I'll be down as soon as I'm washed and dressed." She reached for Dare's jacket lying at the foot of the bed.

"Mr. Roy told me to take you to the storeroom first," Annie informed her. "There are several trunks full of clothing belonging to his dead wife. He said to choose something decent to wear from whatever you find there. No one has been able to use them until you came along. Meg and I are both too plump and well-endowed in certain places, but they should be perfect for you with your petite figure."

"How thoughtful," Casey exclaimed delightedly. "I wondered how long I'd have to wear these rags. Tell me where the storeroom is and I'll go after I wash up. You won't need to wait around for me."

"The last door on the right at the far end of the

hall," Annie said. "Just past Dare's room. Choose what you need, then come downstairs for breakfast. You can see Mr. Roy after you've eaten."

At the mention of Dare's name, Casey tensed, her green eyes filled with a fear she could not name. "I . . . I'll hurry," she promised.

Misinterpreting her apprehension, Annie said kindly, "You've nothing to fear here, Casey. As long as you work hard and obey rules you'll get along fine." She hesitated, choosing her words carefully before continuing. "Meg said you killed a man. I don't know if that's the truth and it's none of my business, but everyone here with the exception of the Penrods are convicts. Some committed crimes worse than others but in the eyes of the law we're all the same.

"If you want to get along here do as you're told and the time will pass quickly. In two weeks I'll be a free woman. I stole to support my family and paid the price. Me and Matt, the man I'm going to marry, will combine our thirty acres each and make a new life for ourselves. You can do the same once you've served your time."

"I'll remember your words, Annie." Casey smiled. "And thanks for the advice. I certainly don't intend to cause any trouble. But tell me, I'm curious to know who informed Meg of my crime. Was it Mr. Penrod? Or one of his sons?"

"I believe it was Dare," Annie said somewhat embarrassed. "Meg is . . . er . . . a friendly sort, especially where Dare is concerned, if you get my meaning," she emphasized, rolling her eyes. "She probably had it out of him before he knew what she was about. I'd better leave now, the family will be wanting their breakfast. Don't forget, come down to the kitchen as soon as you're decently dressed."

Fifteen minutes later Casey found the store-room and was on her knees happily rummaging in the several trunks stacked against the wall. They held every conceivable garment a woman could need or want and Casey was ecstatic, for they seemed a perfect fit just as Annie predicted. Evidently Mrs. Penrod was slim as a girl. Idly she wondered when the woman died and how.

Careful to choose only the plainest and most serviceable clothing, Casey made a neat pile of her selections on the floor beside her when suddenly she came upon the most beautiful gown she had ever seen. It was fashioned of green satin with full, billowing skirt, short puffed sleeves and low scooped neckline, and Casey couldn't quell the urge to try it on. Annie said the family would be eating their breakfast now so she was reasonably certain she would not be disturbed. Swiftly shedding the robe that Annie had brought her last night, she donned the shimmering gown. Her only regret was that she couldn't see herself.

Suddenly she remembered the small mirror hanging over the washstand in her room. Gathering up the bundle of clothing, Casey turned and opened the door, intending to hurry to her room for a quick peek at herself in the mirror before returning the dress to the trunk. She walked directly into the arms of Dare Penrod who was passing on the way to his room.

"What the hell!" Dare thundered, reeling from the impact of her soft body colliding with his.

The neatly folded clothes left Casey's arms to spill in a bright array around her feet. A stunned expression formed on Dare's face and his eyebrows rose and fell with maddening insolence as his eyes raked her satin-clad body. She was ravishing. Never had Dare seen a lovelier sight. And she wore his mother's dress! Not to mention the entire wardrobe the little thief was in the process of stealing.

"What are you doing with my mother's clothes?"

Casey blanched. He looked forbidding, as if driven by the devil, and all the demons rode his coattails. "I . . . I . . ." she stammered before finding her voice. "Your father told me to take what I needed."

"You're a liar as well as a thief!" he accused hotly. "You aren't here a day and already you're helping yourself to whatever strikes your fancy."

Casey gulped, her aching throat working convulsively over words of denial. "I'm not a thief. Nor a liar. Ask your father if you don't believe me."

Suddenly Casey found herself being forced backwards into the storeroom, followed closely by a glowering Dare who shut the door firmly behind him. "Take it off!" he ordered brusquely. "My mother's things are too good for the likes of you."

Casey opened her mouth to protest his contemptible behavior, but courage fled on the wings of cowardice when she saw the implacable set to his jaw and his cold gray eyes.

"Get out first and I'll take off the dress," she retorted, eyeing him with misgiving.

"I've seen you before," he answered, a nasty smile etching his lips, "and you're far too scrawny for my tastes."

"I suppose Meg is more to your liking?" Why
did she say that? Casey wondered, dismayed by
her temerity. In truth, his preference in women
mattered little to her.

Flashing a lecherous grin, he admitted blandly,
"You might say that. At least Meg has killed no
one."

"Why do you dislike me?" Casey found the
courage to ask. "You've hardly given me a chance
to prove myself. I killed no one intentionally. I'm
innocent of murder."

She looked so appealing, so helpless, that Dare
nearly forgot she was a killer. And a whore. No
doubt she already made plans to seduce his
father, and perhaps his brother. It was up to him
to expose her, for obviously no one else in the
family saw past her youth and beauty. Perhaps,
he mused thoughtfully, he was going about it all
wrong. Maybe he should allow her to work her
wiles on him just to prove to everyone she was
exactly what he claimed her to be. If he feigned
interest she might leave his vulnerable father and
young brother alone, for he considered himself
the only family member able to resist should she
set her sights on one of them.

Warily, Casey eyed Dare through a halo of
fringed lashes, her curiosity piqued when a slow
smile replaced the cynical curve of his lips. "I
don't hate you, Casey. On the contrary, I find you
quite . . . intriguing, as well as delightful to look
upon."

They stood facing each other, nearly touching,
when his arm snaked out and circled her waist,
drawing her deep into his embrace. In an instant
of madness he lifted her chin and branded her
with the soft warmth of his lips. A riptide of

emotions swirled about her as his mouth covered hers hungrily, shocked at her own eager response to the touch of his lips. Blood pounded in her brain and made her knees tremble. Never had she been kissed in such a manner. When his probing tongue parted her lips and slipped past the barrier of her teeth, her world spun dizzily out of control.

Moving with a will of its own, Dare's dark hand cupped a small, rounded breast, measuring its firmness. Her nipple rose against his palm as he stroked it to life beneath the smooth satin of her bodice, and her eyes flew open in dismay. In the dim light of the storeroom they turned a dark green, mysterious, utterly captivating. A shiver of arousal swept her from head to toe and a soft moan escaped her parted lips. The sound was all Dare needed to jerk him back from the brink of disaster into the cold dawn of reality.

What had started out as an experiment had swiftly accelerated into a deadly game in which he could lose more than he bargained for. Casey O'Cain was a skilled seductress who nearly made him forget in a matter of seconds who he was and what he intended. She had used her body to lure him from casual interest to arousal so intense his self-control had been severely threatened. How he would enjoy forcing her to the floor and taking her. And judging from her response to his kisses she would welcome it.

He rudely shoved her aside, his mind churning with dismay that was carefully disguised behind a blank expression. It occurred to Dare that he was reacting to Casey like an untried boy. Somehow he had forgotten what he intended. How could one kiss so completely unnerve him? he reflected dismally. Never would he allow Casey to see just how thoroughly she had affected him. Surely he had more sense than to fall victim to the wiles of a criminal and whore.

Assuming a facade of polite disinterest, Dare said with cold deliberation, "You are remarkably responsive for one claiming innocence. Or were you referring only to the charge of murder? I think, Casey, that you are far from innocent. Either of murder . . . or anything else. Now, will you take off my mother's dress or shall I do it for you?" His lips formed a wolfish grin.

Casey bit her lip to stem the flow of bitter recrimination. Her eyes sparked with hatred and she silently cursed him for his cunning touch, his clever kisses and his damnable, deceitful ways. She wanted to lash out but feared reprisal. She was bound to these people until her sentence was either served or remitted. She could scarce afford to offend the son of her employer.

"What's going on here?" Enmeshed in their own battle of wits, neither heard Roy enter the storeroom.

Dare whirled to face his father, annoyed at being found in such a compromising position. "I told you bringing this woman home was a mistake, Father. I caught her stealing from Mother's trunks."

"You should have spoken with me first, Dare, before accusing Casey of theft. I gave her permission to choose what she needed. Her clothing was little better than rags, a fact you can well attest to, and your mother's things were just gathering dust packed away. I'm glad they fit her so well." To Casey he added, "I do think you should select something more serviceable, though. That gown is lovely on you but should be saved for special occasions."

Casey felt a rush of color rise from her bare shoulders upwards to slide over her cheeks. "I didn't intend to keep this gown, sir," she explained somewhat sheepishly. "It was so beautiful I couldn't resist trying it on. I've never seen anything so elegant. I'll return it immediately."

"No need, Casey, you may keep it, as well as anything else that strikes your fancy. Only save it for a more appropriate time."

"Yes, sir," Casey agreed, daring a glance at Dare's glowering features. He looked ready to explode and Casey made a hasty exit, stopping only to gather up the clothes she had dropped.

"After you've had your breakfast come to my study and we'll discuss your duties," Roy called to her departing back. "I've already spoken to Martha." Then he turned to his son, his face mottled with anger.

"Bloody hell, Dare, leave the girl alone! Don't think I haven't noticed how you badger her. What is it about her that sets you on edge?"

Dare glared defiantly at his father, and a little seed of uncertainty blossomed and grew into a tremendous doubt. He had questioned his father once about Casey but he needed to be reassured. "What are *your* plans for Casey, Father? You're still a virile man and there's no denying Casey's beauty."

Roy's gray eyes blazed with sudden temper. "Dammit, Dare, get your mind out of the gutter! This is the last time I'm going to tell you that I have no designs upon her person. I have a feeling

there is more to Casey than either of us realize. I
intend to find out why she killed, and when I do
I'm sure we'll both be surprised."

"I see the little witch has already worked her
wiles on you, Father," Dare snorted.

"I don't think I'm the one enthralled by the
girl," Roy remarked astutely. "Keep your hands
off her, Dare. She's not like Meg. So far I've said
nothing about your bedding the wench, because
she seems to want it. And as long as it's Meg's
choice I'll continue to overlook it."

"How noble, Father," Dare smiled blandly.
"Meg is a whore and so is Casey. But you needn't
worry, Casey doesn't appeal to me. Can you say
the same?"

"Bloody hell, Dare!" Roy exploded caustically.
"Keep your vile thoughts to yourself. I expect
you to treat Casey and Martha decently. You
have no trouble with Annie or Meg, so why
should Casey be a problem? I'm sure you have
duties, so if you'll excuse me I'll tend to mine."

Christ! thought Dare as he watched his father
walk stiffly away. What in the hell was the matter
with him? Since the first moment he laid eyes on
Casey O'Cain his nerves had been tied in knots.
And he cursed whatever perverse notion had
made him kiss her. Maybe he needed a woman.
Hell, if Meg wasn't available tonight he would
ride over to the McKenzie farm where he knew
Mercy would welcome him with open arms. Her
father hinted often enough that a match between
his daughter and Dare would not be frowned
upon. Mercy herself seemed to expect it. Maybe
it was time he married!

* * *

Dressed in a demure gray dress more in keeping with her station, Casey entered the kitchen to find Meg, Martha and Annie gathered around the large square kitchen table eating breakfast. She sat down to join them and Annie immediately rose to fetch a plate kept warm for her on the stone hearth. Smiling, she placed it before Casey.

"I see you found something suitable to wear," she said, eyeing Casey's choice with approval.

"Mr. Roy never offered *me* his wife's clothes," Meg sniffed sullenly.

"You couldn't get into them," Annie guffawed heartily. "Neither could I or Martha. Luckily Mr. Roy has several bolts of material tucked away and Martha can make herself something decent to wear just as you and I did."

"Nothing we make will be half as nice as what Casey is wearing," complained Meg. "It ain't fair."

"That will do, Meg," warned Annie crisply, using her hard-earned authority to uphold discipline. "You must all learn to work together without bickering."

Meg slanted Casey a covetous glance but said nothing further to antagonize Annie. Once Annie was gone, things would be run differently, she silently gloated. Then she would have no one but the Penrod men to answer to and she knew exactly how to get around them.

A short time later Casey knocked on the study door. "Come in, Casey," Roy called through the panel, expecting her.

Casey entered, finding Roy seated behind a hand-made desk in a small room that boasted rustic but attractive furnishings. In fact, all the furniture she had seen thus far had been fashioned by convict labor, as were the house and all the outbuildings. Luckily Roy Penrod had the capital necessary to run his successful farm, which was more than most settlers possessed.

Most Hawkesbury settlers suffered from numerous floods, too little capital and the constant harassment of the New South Wales Corps to purchase their land. Since William Bligh's arrival as governor in 1806, things slowly began to improve. But the Rum Corps had too great a hold on the economy, and the conflict between the government and personal interests sharpened. To his credit, Bligh tried to carry out British policy but was being slowly defeated by the New South Wales Corps whose leader, Lieutenant Colonel Johnston, in close association with John Macarthur, were implacably hostile to the convict settlers.

Roy motioned Casey into a straight-backed chair, a wistful look on his face. It had been many years since he had last seen his wife in the gray dress now adorning Casey's slim form. It had been different with the green satin, for he had never seen Clare in it since it was something new she had purchased to bring with her. But he had seen Clare wear the gray linen many times and it sparked long-forgotten emotions.

"You look very nice," he finally said. "I'm glad the clothes are finally being used."

"Thank you," Casey said sincerely. "Your wife must have been a slender woman, they fit me perfectly."

"Frail is a more apt description," Roy revealed, sighing regretfully. "Had I realized how frail I never would have asked her to join me here in Australia. She died before the journey ended and was buried at sea. Thank God both Dare and Ben survived. We've been alone ever since."

"I . . . I'm sorry," murmured Casey.

"Well," Roy said, clearing his throat, "that was many years ago. There's no time to look back. Shall we talk about your duties?"

Casey nodded warily. After the judge, she had learned to mistrust men and waited for Roy's next words with bated breath.

"Martha confessed she is a mediocre cook at best and would prefer other duties. Meg is even less inclined. That leaves you, Casey. Can you cook?"

Casey relaxed visibly, a wide smile dimpling her cheeks. "Father swore I was the best cook in Dublin," she said pertly. "He may have been exaggerating but he's not the only one who liked my cooking. Why, Tim managed to wangle an invitation to dinner nearly every Sunday." She paused for breath, then abruptly realized she was rambling. A rosy color stained her cheeks and suddenly Roy wished he were twenty years younger.

"Then it's settled," Roy said, pleased. "Martha can undertake the heavier chores and the gardening, which she says she prefers anyway. Meg can continue her duties as housekeeper."

Casey took his words as a dismissal and rose to leave, but Roy motioned her back into the chair. "Casey, if only to placate Dare and put to rest his fears that we'll be murdered in our beds, I think we ought to talk about your crime."

"You already know why I was transported," Casey said uneasily. "What more do you need to

know except that your son's fears are groundless
where I'm concerned?"

"I know that," Roy said. "But I have a feeling
there is more to your story than what Lieutenant
Potter told us. Do you want to tell me about it?
It's difficult to think of you as a killer."

"Let your son think what he will," Casey said
stubbornly. She'd be damned if she'd satisfy
Dare Penrod's morbid curiosity. If he couldn't
accept her for what she was he needn't accept her
at all. It served the arrogant bastard right to think
he might become her victim. The father seemed a
kindly man but she still remained wary of his
plans for her. She decided to reserve judgment
until she learned more.

"I appreciate your concern, sir," she said at
length. "But I'd prefer not to talk about it at this
time. Perhaps one day—"

"Casey, there's great opportunity for you here
in New South Wales. This can be as good a life as
you make it. Had you remained in England you
most certainly would be either rotting in prison
or hung for your crime. Since the war between
England and the colonies it's no longer feasible to
transport convicts to America, so England chose
Australia. Bide your time, lass, and like Annie,
one day you will be free to pursue your own life. I
hope you heed my words. If ever you want to talk
I'll be glad to listen."

"Thank you, sir," Casey replied, feeling somewhat more secure.

"Please call me Mr. Roy. It's what all our
workers call me. And Casey, a word of warning.
Keep out of Dare's way. He's normally a good-
natured fellow but for some reason you seem to
rub him the wrong way."

"I'll remember, Mr. Roy," Casey concurred wholeheartedly. Dislike seemed too weak a word to explain Dare's reaction to her. Yet, she mused thoughtfully, why had he kissed her as if he enjoyed it? It was too confusing for her to think about, she decided as she left the room to begin her duties. Whatever Dare's feelings, they were far too complicated to dwell upon.

Casey spent the following days becoming acquainted with her new home and duties. Annie taught her to prepare the family's favorite meals, and thus far all went well. She had successfully managed to keep out of Dare's way and rarely saw him. Ben, on the other hand, made it a point to visit her in the kitchen as often as his duties allowed.

Casey genuinely liked Ben. He was kind, funny, thoughtful, and nothing like his moody brother. She learned that Ben's duties pertained to farming while Dare managed their prosperous sheep business, experimenting with crossbreeding and wool. Roy saw to the family's finances and the employment of convict labor assigned to them.

It didn't take Casey long to discover that soil was richer on the Hawkesbury, and that most grains grew well there. Quite an improvement over the black sand of Sydney, whose land was nearly useless. Sydney was infertile, had no fruit, no meadows, but plenty of huge ants and mosquitoes whose bites were painful. Even around Parramatta, except for river flats, soil was poor and washed out. Then there were the floods caused by fast-flowing streams rushing down narrow valleys from the Blue Mountains. Beyond this narrow plain rose the Great Divide, stretching the entire length of the continent.

In this year of 1807, life in New South Wales was concentrated on a narrow strip of land fifty miles wide and one hundred and fifty miles long, shut in by the Blue Mountains on the west and the sea on the east. Though they were barely 8,000 feet high, no one had yet found a way across those imposing peaks. Men had been known to enter the Blue Mountains and never return. Not even the aborigines knew what lay on the other side of those lofty heights.

One morning several weeks after her arrival Casey was working in the kitchen alone. Annie had already left and Martha was busy in the garden. Meg, as usual, was nowhere in sight. Up to her elbows in bread dough, Casey did not hear the kitchen door open and shut. Nor the footsteps behind her. She started violently when a booming voice interrupted her reverie.

"So you're the woman who has Dare running around in circles. Now that I've seen you I can't say I blame him. I couldn't wait to meet you. Normally nothing ruffles my friend, but something is tying him in knots and I suspect that something is you."

Casey whirled, scattering flour across the spotless floor. "You . . . you startled me!" she scowled. "Who are you?"

"Robin Fletcher, at your service," he smiled, executing an exaggerated bow. "Ex-convict now the proud owner of thirty acres of prime farmland due north of here."

Despite herself, Casey found it difficult to remain angry at Robin Fletcher. His smile was so engaging Casey could not help but respond favor-

ably. There was something warm and enchanting
in his humor. He was tall and slim, and not
overly muscular, but she could tell at a glance
that he was tough, lean and sinewy. Sleek was the
word that came to mind. Sandy blond hair and
twinkling blue eyes lent him a rakish air, but
Casey thought his looks might be deceptive.
When circumstances demanded, she imagined
him a foe to be reckoned with.

"I'm Casey O'Cain," Casey offered with a shy
smile.

"I know," Robin replied. "An Irish lass with a
hint of old Ireland in her voice. A real beauty,
too. Welcome to New South Wales, Casey
O'Cain."

Wiping her hands on her apron, Casey asked,
"Would you like a cup of tea, Mr. Fletcher?
Though it's scarce, we still have enough on hand
to last until the next supply ship arrives."

"Nay, lass, but thanks. I imagine Dare knows
I'm here by now and is wondering where I've
disappeared to. He stopped by my place last week
and since then I've been itching to come over and
have a look at you. And my name is Robin. I was
a convict just like yourself, so no need to stand
on ceremony."

"You hardly seem the type found in London's
prisons," Casey blurted out before she could stop
herself. "What was your crime?"

"I could ask the same about you, lass. As you
well know, most of the convicts sent to New
South Wales are the sweepings of London and
provincial cities, but some were transported for
minor offenses. My crime was poaching in the
forest of one of England's great families. I was
but a lad at the time. Dare failed to mention your

own crime, though he hinted it was serious. Now that I've met you I believe he was exaggerating."

"It's true," Casey admitted slowly. "I'm surprised Dare didn't tell you I killed a man. He seems to delight in the telling."

A myriad of emotions passed over Robin's face, one of which was disbelief. "There must be some mistake," he refuted. "Though we've just met, I sincerely doubt you're capable of so terrible a crime."

"You always were a poor judge of character, Robin." Dare leaned negligently in the doorway, evidently there long enough to have heard part of the conversation. "The evidence against Casey was fully proven and documented, and as you just heard, she freely admits to killing a man. Is there anything else you'd like to know?"

"Sometimes you can be a son-of-a-bitch, Dare," Robin accused, slanting Casey an apologetic look. "Have you taken the time to listen to the girl's story? From my own experience I learned things aren't always what they seem."

"You sound just like Father," Dare scoffed. "I'm not totally without compassion. Naturally Casey will have the same opportunity afforded any other convict assigned to us. She will be given the chance to become rehabilitated and earn a pardon."

Casey impaled Dare with shards of green fire, the tension between them almost palpable. More than animosity flew between them, Robin astutely sensed as he watched the sparks ignite and blaze into something that both of them refused to acknowledge.

"You're being too hard on Casey, my friend," Robin said, seeking to defuse the volatile atmosphere. Casey looked ready to explode, and Robin knew that Dare would not hold back if Casey gave vent to her growing anger.

"Dare, let's find Ben and go hunting. You could use a day off and so can I. The Rum Corps has been out to my farm twice this week. They want my land, badly enough to keep harassing me to give up my grant. They won't be satisfied until they have control of every available acreage, no matter how small or how many settlers they have to swindle or badger to get what they want. What does Governor Bligh have to say about the Corps's unfair practices, Dare? Isn't there something he can do?"

Casey all but forgotten, Dare commiserated with his friend. "The governor is doing everything in his power to help the settlers, but the Rum Corps has been the reigning power far too long to break overnight. Originally they were enlisted in England as the 102nd Regiment to act as guards and as a police force in the colony."

"Now they are doing their utmost to obstruct Bligh's work by separation of interests," Robin spat. "On one side you have free men with privilege and money anxious to obtain control of convict labor on slave conditions, and of all commercial activities. On the other side is the government with a considerable measure of responsibility to see to the employment and rehabilitation of convicts. The problem is not easy to resolve. Poor farmers and convict settlers are being exploited daily by Macarthur and the Rum Corps. If only there were more concerned men like you and your father."

"It's a well-known fact that every member of the Rum Corps has become wealthy and power-

ful mainly because they had the power to misuse
or apply the law to their own advantage," Dare
went on to explain. "It's a damn shame they
gained a monopoly of import trade, particularly
rum."

"Rum," Robin said bitterly. "The bane of our
economy. The Rum Corps are the only ones with
gold or silver to buy it from shippers. I'm forced
to accept rum in payment for my farm produce,
and slowly but surely I'm being forced off my
land."

Suddenly Casey came to life after listening to
the shocking conversation. "But it's not fair!
Time-expired convicts have a right to the land
they earned."

Robin turned to her with a sad smile.
"Emancipists have little right to anything. If left
to the Rum Corps we'd remain slave labor. Right
now we are living in an 'exchange economy'
based on tyranny and rum."

Shortly afterwards Robin and Dare left to find
Ben, and Casey returned to her chores, her
thoughts consumed with the seemingly insur-
mountable problems facing this raw new fron-
tier.

Casey had already retired for the night when a
knock sounded on her door. Since Annie's departure she now occupied the cozy little room off the
kitchen. She found the room much to her liking
with its large window facing the Hawkesbury.
Thinking Martha had come to wish her goodnight, Casey didn't bother donning a robe but
answered the door in her prim white lawn nightgown that once belonged to Mrs. Penrod. It was a

logical mistake, for no one but Martha ever visited her room.

The door swung open beneath her fingers and when she recognized her caller she gasped in dismay. Casey was grateful for the semidarkness that hid the flush on her cheeks, but once she gained her senses, embarrassment turned to fury.

"You!" she hissed. "What do you want?"

Dare was not prepared for the sight that met his startled gaze. In the diffused glow of the lamplight shining behind Casey, her body glowed a pale ivory beneath the thin material of her gown. Every luscious curve, each hollow and plane, assaulted his senses and sent his blood soaring through his veins. His silver eyes turned to smoke as he felt flames of hot desire lick upward along his spine.

"I want to talk to you," Dare croaked, his throat suddenly gone dry. Without waiting for an invitation, he walked inside and closed the door behind him.

Squawking in protest, Casey reached for her robe, flinging it over her shoulders. "Couldn't it wait till morning?"

"No, I'm leaving for Sydney at first light. Robin and I hope to confer with the governor about the unfair treatment of emancipists by the Rum Corps. Bligh is a decent sort and I'm certain he'll help if he can."

"All right," Casey said grudgingly, "what is it that's so important it can't wait until morning?" Twisting her hands nervously, she glanced at the closed door, then back to Dare. "Please make it fast, I'm expecting Martha to stop by."

"Martha is already asleep, no light is showing

from beneath her door. Don't worry, Casey, we won't be disturbed.''

His words did little to allay the misgiving building within her. She did not trust Dare. And worse, she did not trust herself. He was too handsome, too sure of himself, and he affected her in ways she was not equipped to handle.

"Have I done something wrong?" Casey asked, wishing he would get to the point and leave. "Is my cooking unsatisfactory, Mr . . . Dare?"

"Dare will do just fine, Casey, you can drop the mister. And yes, you've done something wrong. You've made me want you so much, I can't sleep at night."

For weeks his yearning for Casey had simmered just below the surface and Dare had finally reached the point where nothing short of consummation would cure his malady. Tonight he had enough rum in him to confront her with his need.

"What!" gasped Casey, certain she had misunderstood. "What did you say?"

"I want to make love to you, Casey. Since the moment I set eyes on you something ignited between us. I mistakenly thought what I felt for you was intense dislike, but it wasn't long before I realized that dislike had nothing to do with my feelings. It went far beyond mere animosity. It took me into a realm I didn't care to explore. The longer I considered our mutual attraction, the more I realized the only way to break this strange hold you have on my emotions is by making love and getting you out of my system once and for all."

"You've lost your mind!" Casey gulped, frightened by the look of implacable determination on his face. "I have no intention of . . . of making love with you."

Her answer seemed to amuse him and a smile softened his set features. "Casey, you'd be lying if you tried to deny I affect you in the same way you do me. I don't know what it is, or even if this attraction has a name, but I do know I want you."

"That's impossible!" Casey denied vehemently. "You've shown me nothing but contempt since our first meeting. How dare you calmly state now that you want to make love to me. My God, Dare, what kind of man are you?"

"One who's obsessed with a beautiful, experienced woman. You've been here weeks now and have taken no man to your bed. Don't deny me this chance to exorcise you from my mind. I'll not disappoint you, Casey."

"You're . . . you're despicable!" spat out Casey, backing away. "Find someone else to ease your lust. I'm certain Meg would be happy to oblige."

"Aye, but I don't want Meg. I want you. You must have bewitched me to get me to admit so much. Robin's words today made me aware of what I want from you. I need to cleanse you from my blood, Casey. Free me from this spell so I can function again."

"Dare, I've cast no spells. And . . . and I don't want to . . . to make love. Please leave." Casey was positive this was some kind of crazy dream and she would soon wake up to find herself snug in her bed. Did all men run hot and cold like Dare? Or was he the exception? She knew he was unique in many ways but had not thought him mad until he burst into her room making impossible demands.

"I'll not be put off, Casey," Dare declared, suddenly reaching out to snare her around the waist. "I can make you want me. I'm not insensitive to a woman's needs. You seemed friendly enough with Robin, why not me?"

His arrogant words fueled the tiny flame of anger burning in her breast. Did he think her a whore? What she needed to do was set him straight immediately. "Dare, I'm not . . ." The words died in her throat as he pulled her against the hard wall of his chest, bringing his bold mouth down on hers in a kiss laced with the heady taste of rum. Yet his steady hands betrayed no sign of intoxication.

She gasped for breath as his searing kiss moved from her mouth along her cheekbone to a point just below her ear . . . it was as if every playful nip left a scar that would remain forever. Once again he claimed her mouth, forcing her lips apart. It was a grinding, scorching kiss, almost insulting, and she was defenseless against his forceful assault.

"Can you deny I stir you?" he asked when finally he lifted his face. When she refused to answer he gave her a little shake. "Tell me."

She disliked having to admit it, but despite her anger at his high-handed treatment and vile demands, he managed to stir her in a way she never dreamed possible.

"I . . . I cannot deny it."

His next kiss was probing, searching, one that awakened fires within her and left her clinging to him. A chuckle of satisfaction rumbled from his throat as he unbuttoned the neckline of her nightgown and pushed it off one shoulder, baring a small, perfect breast. He groaned aloud as the tender flesh swelled and its rose-hued tip flowered against his probing fingertips. With growing panic Casey felt the hard proof of his desire pressing against her belly.

"You may be a killer and a whore but I want you. I've fought my conscience long enough and I'm tired of being turned inside out." Desire flowed like liquid fire through his veins.

"You're drunk!" Casey accused, his words acting like a splash of icy water in her face. "You're saying things you'll regret in the morning. There is nothing between us but mutual hatred."

"Probably," agreed Dare, working to free her other breast from the thin cloth of her nightgown. He was so aroused that little of what she said made sense.

Summoning all her willpower in order to resist the magic of his hands and lips as well as her own rising ardor, Casey flung herself away, shoving against his chest with outstretched arms. "You'll not use me, Dare Penrod. You're wrong about me, dead wrong. I don't need a man, and if I did you'd be the last to know."

Caught off guard, Dare stumbled backwards, allowing Casey to slip past him and out the door before he could gain his wits. With no particular destination in mind, Casey raced through the kitchen and into the hallway, intending to lose herself outside in the shadows until Dare grew tired of looking for her. Just as she reached the front door it flew open, and Ben stepped through just in time to catch her in his arms.

"Casey, what the devil—"

In one sweeping glance Ben noted the disheveled red hair floating freely about her shoulders, her dishabille, the open neck of her nightgown ripped and exposing the tops of rounded breasts. Then he looked up, his startled eyes encountering Dare who came to a screeching halt a few feet behind Casey. Comprehension dawned and Ben's boyish features hardened into a frown of disapproval.

"My God, Dare, how could you?"

"Ben, I . . ." Words failed Dare as he saw himself in the same light as Ben did. And he didn't like what he saw.

"No, Dare, don't say a word," Ben warned, scowling furiously. "You've disappointed me enough for one night. A senseless explanation will only add to your shame." Placing a protective arm around Casey's quaking shoulders, he led her past Dare and back to her room. "Come along, Casey, I'll see you safely to your room. Don't worry about Dare, I'm certain he'll soon come to his senses and apologize."

Gratefully Casey leaned against Ben, certain that his insolent brother had never apologized to anyone in his life.

CHAPTER FOUR

Casey experienced a sleepless night fraught with thoughts and longings she dared not name. Throughout the long night she huddled in the dark beneath the sheets, her fevered mind vivid with images of Dare. In her dreams she relived the scene that had taken place in her bedroom that evening. The ferocity of his desire, his arrogant disregard for her feelings, her own unabashed passion in response to his kisses. Against her will she wondered what it would feel like to make love with Dare. She had never reacted to another man's kisses in such a wanton manner. It rankled to think she had nearly allowed him to have his way. To her bitter, unrelenting shame, she had demonstrated her willingness before coming to her senses. It stung to realize that every time he looked at her he would recall that brief instant of insanity when she had clung to him with abandon, responded to his touch. In the future she would make damn certain Dare didn't slip through her defenses.

The next morning Casey learned Dare had left early for Sydney. For some unexplained reason her anger soared when Meg sidled up to her while she was in the kitchen mixing batter for hotcakes and said, "I hate it when Dare goes away. He left so early I was too tired to give him a proper sendoff." She stifled an exaggerated yawn, her words meant to convey the message that Dare had awakened in her bed.

"Perhaps he won't be gone long," Casey replied with studied indifference. Her hand holding the whipping fork moved faster, and in her mind she beat more than just hotcake batter.

"Don't think you can take my place in his . . . er . . . affections," Meg warned, eyes narrowed shrewdly. "He's a handsome devil, one who knows how to please a woman."

"I assure you he can please you night and day for all I care. The man holds little appeal for me." Deliberately presenting her back, she added, "Doesn't the table need setting?"

Flouncing off, Meg tossed over her shoulder, "Dare has a woman, you know. Her name is Mercy McKenzie. Her father retired from the New South Wales Corps and settled on the Hawkesbury years ago. I imagine they'll marry one day." Though the reason escaped her, this revelation left Casey with a hollow feeling deep in the pit of her stomach.

Before she left, Annie had shown Casey and Martha the billibong, a widened place in a small creek behind the house where in wet years the swimming was good. And since this had been a wet year there was sufficient water in the billibong for bathing. The billibong was where Casey and Martha normally could be found after breakfast and morning chores had been completed. At that time of day the convict workers as well as the Penrods were occupied with their various duties and were nowhere nearby to interfere with the women's enjoyment of their baths.

Meg seldom felt the need to immerse herself in water, so Martha and Casey usually found themselves alone behind the house where the creek divided the plowed fields from the brush and wattle beyond. A bend in the creek shielded them from the house as well as from prying eyes. Roy had warned them to stay clear of the convicts, for most were hardened criminals who would delight in finding them alone and unprotected.

Several days after Dare left for Sydney, Casey and Martha found time one day to partake of a leisurely bath and made their way to the billibong. Disrobing to her thin shift, Casey entered the water and waded to the deepest part, which came only to her armpits. Martha entered more cautiously, having little liking for water. "It's not deep, Martha," Casey encouraged, "nor cold. In fact, it feels wonderful."

"Water makes me nervous," Martha admitted somewhat sheepishly. "The sea took my Jamie from me."

"Jamie was your husband, wasn't he?" Casey asked, curious yet not wishing to pry.

"Aye," sighed Martha regretfully. "And you'd be hard put to find a better man. He was a sailor and one day his ship failed to return. I later heard the *Lucy B* was lost in a fierce storm."

"It . . . it must have been difficult for you after that. Did you have children?"

"Aye, we had a son who lived barely a year. A frail little thing, but Jamie loved him dearly. Though we both wished otherwise, I never had another. And now . . . now it's too late. My Jamie isn't coming back."

"Have you no relatives?"

"Only my parents who are both too ill to work. Pa lost his health in the coal mines and Ma worked to support them until her own health failed. I helped all I could until I was caught pilfering a ham and three sausages from the wealthy household where I was employed. But they had so much I thought they'd never miss what I took. The wages I earned barely paid the rent on our little cottage, let alone fed us. Without Jamie's wages to sustain us, I was driven to thievery," Martha said sadly.

"What about your parents?" Casey asked, genuinely concerned. "Who is caring for them now that you're . . . unavailable?"

A look of despair spread over Martha's face, making Casey sorry she'd asked. "No one," she replied, a sob catching in her throat. "In all probability they are both dead. Who knows, perhaps they're the lucky ones. Look at me. I'm thirty years old and look forty. Jamie is gone, our child long dead. What do I have to look forward to?"

A look of amazement flitted briefly over Casey's expressive features. She had assumed Martha was over forty, and learning she was ten years younger came as a shock. She fell silent, her own misfortune paling in comparison to Martha's terrible loss.

Martha had already dressed and returned to the house while Casey lingered in the soothing water a few minutes longer, recalling all those happy hours spent swimming in the creek in

Ireland. Finally, unable to delay her return, Casey prepared to wade ashore when a strange noise caused hackles to raise on the back of her neck. It sounded like the cry of a wounded animal, coming from somewhere on the forest side of the creek. Yet the human quality was unmistakable.

"Who's there?" Casey called out sharply.

Peering into the thick, nearly impenetrable bush consisting of dozens of species of eucalyptus and undergrowth of wattle, vines and scrub, Casey heard nothing but the chattering and squawks of parrots and parakeets. Thinking her mind was playing tricks on her, she turned to wade ashore when the sound came to her again, more clearly this time. And it was definitely human.

Gathering her courage, she waded to the opposite shore, all her senses alert. Forgotten was the fact that her shift clung wetly to her body, clearly outlining every curve and valley. Climbing the grassy bank, Casey paused at the edge of the bush, prepared for a hasty retreat at the first sign of danger. But, curious by nature, she could no more have left her curiosity unappeased than she could stop breathing.

Straining her ears, Casey once again heard the feeble noise and came to the conclusion that somewhere in those woods a creature, human or otherwise, needed help. A series of moans indicating terrible suffering drew her forward. Someone was hurt, and her inquisitive nature demanded she investigate.

Moving quietly, her bare feet silent on the thick carpet of needles and leaves, Casey entered the forest. Cautiously she picked her way around tall eucalyptus and wattle. Suddenly a gray kangaroo hopped out of the woods to forage in tall, waving grass that grew beside the creek, and she jumped in fright, her heart thumping madly in her breast. She paused, panting to stem her growing panic until a groan of agony released her frozen limbs. This time she was able to tell from which direction the sound came, and resolutely she turned to the left, traveling but a few feet before nearly tripping over the body sprawled on the spongy forest floor.

Collapsed on his stomach lay a man, his clothes hanging in tatters about his emaciated form. From above, sitting in the crook of a tree, the wizened face of a koala calmly munching on leaves looked sadly down on him. A festering, blood-encrusted wound gaped from the flesh of his upper back, and if he hadn't groaned again Casey would have thought him dead.

Acting instinctively, she turned the man on his back, stifling a scream of dismay when she recognized the gaunt features. "Tim! My God, what have they done to you?"

Judging from the condition of his wound, Timothy O'Malley had been hiding out in the bush for several days. Where had he come from? Sydney? If so, he had traveled by foot fifteen miles while seriously injured. He was a strong man, for the loss of blood alone should have killed him. He appeared half-starved, and other scars on his body suggested he had been beaten often. If she were to save his life Casey realized she must act quickly.

Tearing off a section of her shift, she raced back to the creek, soaking the material in cool water. Returning immediately, she used it to cleanse the blood and gore from his wound. She groaned in despair when she inspected more closely the bullet hole that had been left unattended far too long. So long that it had festered and was oozing a yellowish pus. Even now his body burned with fever due to infection. It didn't take an expert to know the bullet would have to be removed if Tim was to survive.

Several times Casey returned to the creek to wet the cloth, bathing his face and neck in cool water and dribbling precious drops into his mouth. After a while he began to stir, moaning and thrashing about wildly.

"Tim, lay still," she whispered urgently. His struggles could only do him more harm and renew the bleeding.

The sound of her voice as well as the effects of the cool water served to bring him to his senses, and his eyes slowly opened. At first they appeared glazed and confused, but little by little sanity returned as he gazed up at Casey in disbelief.

"Casey? Is it really you, lass, or am I dreaming?"

"It's me, Tim," Casey assured him, her eyes damp with unshed tears.

Timothy O'Malley was as dear to her in his own way as her father. She loved him, not in a romantic sense, but as a beloved friend or brother. And Tim loved her. But his love was more complicated. One day they probably would have married and made a good life together. But fate had intervened and cast them adrift on separate courses in a country far from their native Ireland.

"Where did you come from?" Tim asked weakly.

"I might ask the same of you. What happened?

Why did you run away when you know there is no place to go?"

"You know me, lass. I'm as stubborn as a mule. Somewhere along the way I antagonized some high-ranking officers and as punishment was sent to New Castle to work the coal mines," Tim explained. "But, Casey, I couldn't take it. Working below ground in perpetual darkness was worse than a death sentence. After a few days of that hell I was determined to escape or die trying. And I nearly did. Die, that is."

"But where were you going, Tim?"

"To join the bushrangers. I heard they lived in the bush and fared quite well here on the Hawkesbury living off the land."

"But they are desperate, hunted men, Tim. Most of them are no better than animals," Casey contended, recalling the bushranger who nearly raped her.

"They're no worse than most members of the Rum Corps," countered Tim. "They treat us convicts like slaves."

"How were you wounded? Did you walk all the way from New Castle?"

"I was shot at by one of the guards while fleeing. Thank God for the darkness or I would be dead instead of merely wounded. Only I hadn't counted on the wound festering. I thought it merely a flesh wound and not life-threatening. I've been wandering in the bush for days. There's troopers following me. They have native trackers on my trail. They can't be far behind."

Casey's mind worked furiously. "I can't let you lay there and bleed to death or be captured. Yet I'm afraid to bring you back to the house. Mr. Roy is a compassionate man but I'm certain he'd

uphold the law should the authorities demand
your return. And Dare . . ."

"Mr. Roy? Dare?"

"My employer and his son. This is their land.
The house is across the creek and around the
bend."

"Emancipists or 'pure merinos'?"

"Settlers, from England," Casey said, unwilling to use the derogatory term. "Mr. Roy would
see to your wound, but Dare . . ."

"Casey! Where are you?"

"Oh God. Dare!" Casey started violently.
"He's back. I have to go, Tim, but I'll return late
tonight with food. Perhaps by then I'll think of
some way to help you. Please don't leave."

"Casey! Can you hear me!"

"Damn," Casey hissed. Why did Dare have to
return now of all times? And why was he looking
for her?

"Casey, who is Dare? You seem frightened.
Has he—"

"I told you, Tim, Dare is Mr. Roy's oldest son.
He . . . he and I don't get along," she revealed in
an effort to allay Tim's fears. In truth, her
relationship to Dare went beyond simple explanation. "I must go."

Bending low, she placed a quick kiss on his
forehead, then hurried through the bush to the
creek where she slipped into the water. By the
time Dare came crashing through the tall grass,
she was wading up the opposite bank.

"Are you all right?" Dare asked anxiously as
Casey came dripping out of the water.

"Of course, why shouldn't I be?" Casey retorted, puzzled at his evident concern.

"When you failed to return in time to start

lunch, Martha became worried and reported your absence to Father. I just returned from Sydney and volunteered to check on you."

Lord, had she been gone that long? She must have if Martha was concerned enough to inform Mr. Roy. "I hadn't realized it was so late."

"Are you alone?" Dare asked sharply, gazing suspiciously across the creek into the stillness of the bush beyond.

"Of course!" Casey retorted, suddenly wary.

"Dammit, Casey, how could you be so thoughtless?" Dare thundered, grasping her upper arms and shaking her until her teeth rattled. "Anything could happen to you out here. Don't you know there are snakes, crocodiles, wild animals and bushrangers lurking in the bush? Any one of them could easily take your life. You've upset the whole household. Think of someone other than yourself for once."

"I . . . I'm sorry, Dare, I didn't realize—"

"Are you sure you're alone?"

"I'm not meeting a lover, if that's what you're insinuating," Casey hurled back. "Please, Dare, you're hurting me." She hoped Tim wasn't watching, for he most certainly would become alarmed at Dare's threatening manner.

Dare's grip loosened, though he continued to hold her captive. Then, as the full measure of his anger abated, his gray eyes widened when finally he noted the skimpiness of her attire. Shiny silver turned to smoky ash as he raked her slender figure with a sweeping glance.

The fine lawn shift that once belonged to his mother had become nearly transparent, clinging wetly to rounded breasts, tiny waist and delicately curved hips. The reddish triangle crowning her thighs drew his gaze and held it captive. It took every ounce of Dare's control to keep from tossing her to the ground and taking his fill of her. What stopped him was the vivid recollection of how she had shamed him before his brother only days ago.

True, he had consumed more than his share of rum that night but he was far from drunk. He was simply a man in need of a woman. Not just any woman, but one special redhead who had teased his senses for too many days and nights. To have been spurned rankled enough. But far worse was Ben's scathing condemnation. Christ! What had gotten into him? Contributing to his embarrassment was the fact that he had allowed Casey a glimpse of the hunger that gnawed at him.

His body grew tense, his loins throbbed with desire as his silvery gaze roamed freely over Casey's thinly clad form. She had filled out during the past weeks and could no longer be called scrawny. On the contrary, well-rounded and delightful were the adjectives that came to his mind.

"You confuse me so, I don't know whether to strangle you or make love to you. I warn you, one day soon there will come a reckoning."

Casey watched warily as a spark of desire kindled in Dare's eyes and his head lowered as if he meant to kiss her. Distinctly she remembered how he had set her afire the last time their lips touched. She couldn't allow that to happen again. Mustering her strength, she slipped from his grasp.

"If you want lunch I'd best hurry back," she muttered, gathering up her clothes. Under Dare's hot gaze she hastily donned dress and shoes and

stockings, then ran all the way back to the house.
Dare followed close behind, a bemused smile
curving the corners of his mouth.

Casey sighed restively as she waited for the
household to retire for the night so she could go
to Tim. She prayed he had not strayed far from
the spot she had left him, for his wound was too
serious to be left unattended. Though it was pitch
black outside, the hour was not yet right for what
she must do.

Gazing pensively out the window into the
star-studded night, Casey never ceased to be
amazed at the strange way night arrived in New
South Wales. There was no long twilight as in
England. There was only day, and then night fell
like a slate-gray curtain stirred only by night
insects. And then the symphony began. Through
the darkness came a rhythm of clicks, croaks and
rasps in different tones, pitches and cadences,
with the added shrill of cicadas in nearby gum
trees. From the creek came the cry of the kookaburra with its hysterical laugh.

Pacing nervously, Casey waited until no noise
could be heard from the sleeping household, then
added two hours for good measure before quietly
leaving her room. She stopped briefly in the
kitchen where earlier she had hidden a swag filled
with food, antiseptic and bandages. Concealing
the swag beneath the cloak she hastily threw over
her narrow shoulders, Casey slipped through the
back door and into the moon-drenched night.
But as luck would have it, her passage had not
gone unobserved.

Dare stood at his upstairs window staring
moodily into the night. Sleep eluded him, his

mind in a turmoil, his body burning with fires only Casey could quench. How had he allowed the red-headed witch to totally consume his every waking thought and invade his dreams? Perhaps it was time to take a wife. Mercy needed but a single word from him to name the date. But she had neither red hair nor pixielike features with a sprinkling of freckles dancing across cheeks as soft and smooth as creamy ivory.

Abruptly Dare's thoughts scattered, his attention riveted on a slim, cloaked figure moving cautiously from the shadows of the house toward the creek. Definitely female. Too small for Martha. Probably Meg on her way to a tryst with a lover. He had paid Meg scant heed since Casey entered his life, and couldn't fault her for seeking solace elsewhere. Then, lustrous strands of fiery red caught and reflected the moon's glow. Casey! What in the hell was she doing sneaking out at this time of night? Had she taken a lover from among the convicts assigned to them? That terrible thought brought a rush of pain so sharp it was like a blow to the gut.

Dare's first inclination was to follow Casey to her lover's tryst, but he quickly discarded the notion, for such was his anger that he was likely to kill them both. No, he decided, he'd wait until she returned and then confront her. Perhaps she had a reason to be about this time of night, though for the life of him he couldn't think of one.

Casey hastened her steps and suddenly found herself facing the narrow creek. Sitting on the sloping bank, she removed her shoes and stockings, then stripped to her shift in preparation for crossing the narrow stream. She'd never been out so late before, and fear of the unknown made her clumsy as she struggled with the buttons on her dress. Finally she stepped into the water, grown chilly since the sun no longer warmed its surface. She held the swag aloft to keep it dry.

Unmindful of the dangers Dare had mentioned, Casey waded to the opposite shore at nearly the same spot where she had found Tim. "Tim," she called out softly. "It's Casey, I've come back." Nothing but the chatter of insects met her ears. "Tim, please answer me."

Suddenly from out of the bush stumbled an apparition that nearly drove Casey back across the creek. Until the gaunt, ragged figure spoke. "I'm here, Casey."

Weak from hunger and suffering from fever, Tim sprawled at Casey's feet and lay still. Dropping to her knees, Casey exhaled in relief when she saw he was still conscious though breathing heavily from his exertions. Raising his head, she reached into the swag, extracted a bottle of rum and held it to his lips. He took a healthy swallow, coughed, then greedily took another. When Casey set the bottle aside he managed to pull himself into a sitting position.

"Thanks, lass, I needed that," he sighed painfully. "Do you happen to have any food in that swag?"

Smiling, Casey reached into the swag again and set out roasted lamb, cold potatoes, bread and a fruit tart she had made for the family's supper. While Tim made short work of the meal, Casey spread a healing salve on his wound and bound a clumsy bandage around his chest.

"I'm no doctor, Tim, but that will suffice until

you get professional help," Casey remarked, slanting a critical eye at her handiwork.

"You're jesting, lass," Tim snorted. "Who would be willing to help me? As soon as I'm able I'll simply disappear into the bush."

"You'll die, Tim! You've lost too much blood, and you're too weak and feverish to manage on your own. That bullet needs to come out."

"I've no choice, Casey. I'm certain I heard native trackers in the distance today. They can't be far off."

"You're coming across the creek with me, Tim," Casey insisted stubbornly. "I've found a place where you can hide until your strength returns."

"No, lass, I can't let you place yourself in danger. What if your employer finds out? Helping an escaped convict is a serious offense. Don't concern yourself, lass, I'll just slip away in the bush."

Dawn was breaking before Casey managed to overcome Tim's resistance to her suggestion. She told him about the deserted hut located some distance behind the convict barracks. In all the weeks she'd been here she'd seen no one enter or leave. She learned from Meg that it had once been used as a jail of sorts to hold unruly convicts until the authorities arrived to collect them. But of late it had been used less and less as the workers came to realize that the life they lived on Penrod station was far better than they could expect elsewhere.

"Can you walk, Tim?" Casey asked anxiously as she helped him to his feet. "It will soon be light, and people up and about."

In Australia daylight arrived almost as dramatically as night. Dark changed suddenly to light as the sun made an unheralded appearance in the eastern horizon. In a matter of seconds indigo sky became azure.

Feeling better for the food he had consumed, Tim staggered to his feet. "You win, Casey," he sighed wearily. "I think I can make it." Leaning heavily on Casey, he entered the water, and together they managed to wade to the opposite shore without mishap.

After dressing, Casey led Tim to a hut with rough-hewn slab walls and roofed with wooden shingles. From earlier exploration she knew that the door would be unlocked, and she led Tim inside and settled him on a cot used by former occupants.

"There's enough food in the swag to last the day, Tim, and a bottle of water in addition to the rum," Casey said as she took her leave. "I'll be back again tomorrow night about the same time. Perhaps by then I'll think of a way to get you help."

"Casey, before you leave I want to know about that man, the one you called Dare. I don't like the way he treated you."

Casey flushed, unaware that Tim had seen her with Dare earlier. "I can handle him, don't worry, Tim. I really have to go."

Her skimpy explanation drew a frown from Tim but he did not detain her further. "Take care, love."

"I will, Tim, don't worry. Dare is—" How could she explain? "I can take care of myself."

"Ordinarily I'd agree, but that man looks dangerous. Be careful."

On that note Casey hastily departed. She reached the back door just as the sky burst into brilliant blue.

Needless to say, breakfast was late, but no one minded, except for Dare whose sharp reprimand drew an annoyed frown from his father and a snort of disgust from Ben. Nor could he resist offering an insult concerning her appearance.

"You look terrible, Casey," he jibed, referring to the purple smudges marring the tender skin beneath her eyes. "Didn't you sleep well last night?" His knowing smile nearly unsettled Casey but she managed to conceal her apprehension.

Dare's mood wasn't improved by the fact that he had fallen asleep in a chair facing the window before Casey returned from her tryst. Exhausted from his ride from Sydney, Dare had no idea how long she had remained with her lover. But he fully intended to observe her comings and goings again tonight. This time he would remain alert. And he knew exactly where and how he would confront her.

Casey thought the day would never end. Even Martha noticed her exhaustion and suggested she rest for an hour or two in the afternoon. The idea of a short nap held such great appeal that Casey decided no one would miss her if she followed Martha's advice. Collapsing on her bed, she fell asleep instantly, and did not awaken until Martha aroused her to prepare supper.

While Casey lay sleeping, Dare encountered Meg who had deliberately lain in wait for him when he returned from inspecting the sheep in the high pastures. With the onset of hot and searing dry weather, the sheep were woolly again and ewes and rams copulating vigorously. Soon it would be time for the drovers to drive them down from the pastures for washing and shearing.

Meg stepped down from the front porch at Dare's approach. His thoughts prevented him from noticing her until she placed a restraining hand on his arm. "Meg," he said, startled. "I'm sorry, I didn't see you. Is there something you wanted?"

"You've hardly noticed me in weeks, Dare," Meg accused petulantly. "Do you want me to come to your room tonight? Please, Dare, you know how well I . . . please you."

"Not tonight, Meg," Dare refused flatly. "I . . . I'm not in the mood."

"What's wrong, Dare? Normally you're always in the mood, but lately—" Meg's eyes narrowed as an unbidden thought entered her mind. "It's Casey, isn't it? You're bedding that little whore."

"That's ridiculous, Meg," Dare denied strenuously. "Besides, what I do and who I bed is none of your concern. Nor do you have the right to call Casey a whore."

"So it's true," Meg spat venomously. "That red-haired bitch has you tied in knots. If you haven't already bedded her it's only a matter of time until you do. You'll be sorry, Dare. She's a killer, for God's sake!"

"I strongly suggest you return to your duties," Dare advised tightly. "And Meg, I might have bedded you a time or two but that doesn't give you the right to dictate to me. You weren't virgin to begin with and if you hadn't invited my attentions I would never have touched you."

Meg fumed in silent indignation as she stared at Dare's retreating back. She felt certain Casey was behind Dare's chilly reception and vowed she'd find a way to pay her back. Or better yet, get rid of her. Until then she'd bide her time, watch, wait and remain alert. One day Casey O'Cain would make a mistake that would lead to her downfall.

CHAPTER FIVE

Retrieving the cache of food and water concealed in a cupboard, Casey left the house as stealthily as she had the previous night. And just as he had the night before, Dare watched from his upstairs window. Judging the time to be nearly midnight, Casey stepped carefully from the shadows and hurried around the convict barracks, heading toward the hut where she had left Tim. Behind her, Dare emerged from the house, straining his eyes for a glimpse of her small, neat figure.

He saw her slip around the corner of the convict quarters and hastened after her, keeping far enough behind so as not to arouse suspicion. But when he reached the place he had last seen her she had disappeared into thin air. Cursing his lack of luck, he paused, pondering his next step. Casey could have continued on to the creek, or circled around toward the river, or entered one of the many outbuildings in the immediate area. If the moon had been as bright as the night before he wouldn't be left guessing. Damn! What a rotten break. He had hoped to catch her before she and her lover . . . Suddenly a sly smile curved his sensuous mouth and a wicked gleam turned his eyes to liquid silver. Casey would not escape him this time, no indeed. Turning on his heel he retraced his steps back to the house.

As luck would have it, Dare wasn't the only one aware of Casey's midnight foray. Flattened in the doorway of the convict barracks, Meg did nothing to reveal her presence. Returning from a tryst with one of the convict workers, she saw Casey emerge from the house and her naturally suspicious nature cautioned her to remain concealed as Casey hurried by, too preoccupied to notice either Meg or Dare, who followed some distance behind. From her vantage point, Meg saw what Dare failed to notice. She watched with narrowed eyes as Casey entered the small hut sometimes used as a jail. She also saw Dare whirl and return to the house.

Leaving the shadows, Meg cautiously approached the hut, placing her ear against the door in order to hear the low murmur of voices coming from within. What she learned after a few minutes of eavesdropping brought a wide smile to her lips. Fate had placed a valuable weapon in her hands. Information that would aid her plan to eliminate Casey from Dare's life was hers for the taking.

Casey knelt at Tim's side, immediately aware that his fever had risen again. Fetching water she had brought along, she bathed his face, speaking to him in soothing tones. To Casey's consternation he appeared listless and barely coherent enough to respond.

"How do you feel, Tim?" she asked anxiously.

"Like hell," he groaned, slurring his words.

"You need to have that bullet taken out, and soon. Perhaps I should speak to Mr. Roy. I can't

let you die. He might turn you over to the
authorities, but at least you'll be treated by a
doctor."

"No, Casey, no!" Tim cried, his agitation
escalating as he attempted to rise but failed.
"Promise me! Promise you won't tell your employer. If he's a 'pure merino' I can expect no
mercy."

"You're wrong about Mr. Roy. I'm sure he'll
help you," Casey insisted, though not at all
certain she spoke the truth.

"No, Casey," Tim repeated weakly, "I want
your promise or I'll disappear the moment you
leave."

Grudgingly Casey agreed, realizing Tim
couldn't survive on his own in the bush in his
condition. She concentrated instead on cleaning
and rebinding his wound and feeding him the
lukewarm broth she had made for him. When she
left some time later she knew his life depended
on her making a decision soon. Promises meant
nothing when a man's life was at stake. Especially
when the man was as dear to her as Tim.

Her mind preoccupied by the dilemma facing
her, Casey quietly entered her room and locked
the door. In the time it took to walk to the house
she had decided, despite Tim's pleas, to tell Roy
everything first thing in the morning. Relieved to
have come to some kind of a decision, she slowly
began to undress, a single candle illuminating her
sensuous motions in its golden glow.

Her dress was the first to go as it slipped off her
hips to pool around her feet. Bending, she picked
it up and hung it on one of the hooks lining the
wall. Next she slipped off her shoes and stockings. Finally she shed her shift, hanging it beside

the dress. Absently she reached for the nightgown she had carefully placed at the foot of the bed hours earlier. But it wasn't there. Nor was it on the floor or hanging on a hook. A puzzled frown worried her brow and unconsciously she reached for the shift she'd hung up just moments before.

"Are you looking for this?" Dare stepped boldly from a shadowy corner, a flowing white garment dangling from his fingertips.

Casey blanched, whirling to find Dare's wickedly handsome face taking shape in the flickering candlelight. A scream rose from her throat but shock prevented all but a muted croak from escaping. Her hands fluttered helplessly in a futile effort to shield her nakedness from his knowing silver eyes. Then her gaze fell on the nightgown Dare held aloft. Desperately she lunged for it, only to have it jerked from her grasp, wadded up and tossed carelessly into a dark corner out of her reach. Stumbling clumsily, Casey fell into Dare's outstretched arms. Exactly where he wanted her.

Intense anger gave her back her voice. "What are you doing in my room!"

"Waiting for you, obviously," Dare drawled lazily. The feel of her satin skin beneath his hands scattered his thoughts. It took studied concentration to remember that he had come here for a specific reason. "Does your lover have a name?"

"What? I have no lover!" Casey returned hotly. "Take your hands off me."

Refusing to loosen his grip, Dare challenged, "What in the hell were you doing out two nights in a row if not to meet a lover?"

"You . . . you spied on me!"

"You could call it that," Dare admitted, not at all perturbed by her accusation. "Who is he?"

"No one! I'm telling the truth." Dare was the last person she wished to confide in.

"Then why the midnight outing?"

"I . . . I wanted to bathe in the billibong," Casey invented hastily. "It was hot and I couldn't sleep and . . . and I thought a swim might help."

"After my warning about the danger of being out alone?"

"Believe what you want, but it's the truth. Have you seen me speaking to any man since I've come here? Please, Dare, let me put on some clothes."

Dare's bold gaze raked her nude body insultingly. "Why? I like you this way. Your body is beautiful. But of course you know that. Your lovers must have told you the same thing many times." Suddenly, inexplicably, he was jealous of all the men who had held her, loved her, been loved in return.

"Dare, please, let me go."

Dare's avid gaze lingered on her breasts, sweeping downward over rounded hips to settle on the flaming triangle crowning her thighs. Perhaps she was telling the truth, he meditated. It was conceivable that she might have gone to the billibong to bathe.

The sheen of desire visible in Dare's eyes frightened Casey. With trepidation she looked up, and as their eyes met, a startling, sensuous light passed between them. His sexual magnetism drew her deeper and deeper into the seductive web she had tried to avoid all these weeks. She must resist now or surely be lost forever.

"Dare, I . . . I want you to leave . . . now."

"Casey, I want to be your lover . . . your only lover," Dare shocked her by saying. Shocked himself, if the truth be known. "I'm willing to give you the benefit of the doubt as to your reasons for being out these last two nights. Besides, I'm not your keeper. You have a right to bed whomever you please. But I want that man to be me."

His arms tightened as Casey renewed her struggles to leave his embrace, but Dare's determination made escape all but impossible. Unless she employed desperate measures . . . like screaming. Yet for some unexplained reason she did not wish to alert the household.

"Are you drunk again, Dare?" she asked, hoping to shame him into leaving.

"I'm stone-cold sober, love, and I want you. Let me love you, Casey. I'll be gentle. Strange as it may seem, I want to bring you more pleasure than any of your lovers before me. I . . . I've been told I'm a good lover."

His endearment shocked her. "Dare, there's been no—"

"Let me finish, love," Dare interrupted. "This thing between us has me turned inside out. I find myself consumed with a terrible hunger no one but you can appease, and I don't like it. Both Father and Ben have commented on my preoccupation with you. Becoming lovers will hurt no one, Casey, and we will both benefit. I'll make you happy, I swear it. Though it rankles to admit it, I need you."

No! This couldn't be happening! Casey silently screamed. The fact that Dare thought her a whore was made perfectly clear by his words. "I'm not a whore!" she blasted defiantly.

"It doesn't matter, Casey. After I make love to you you'll want no other man. You'll belong to me exclusively." For some strange reason the thought of Casey belonging solely to him was pleasing.

"Conceited ass," Casey muttered beneath her breath, bringing a chuckle to Dare's lips. "Why don't you find someone who will appreciate your endeavors?"

"No one else will do. Do you know what it's been like seeing you every day but not allowed to . . . to touch you? I intend to rectify that right now." His normally low voice was sharply edged with desire.

Her sensitive skin registered the slight roughness of his fingertips as they roamed across her bare back and buttocks, grasping the delightfully rounded mounds to press her body to his, letting her feel his need for her. Helpless to stop the yearnings that washed over her, Casey felt herself reacting violently to his magnetism. The male scent of him excited her and enticed her further into his web.

He tangled his hand in her hair, loving the soft feel of the gossamer strands. The fiery tresses falling though his long, slender fingers gave him a sensual pleasure he hadn't experienced with anyone else. Casey shuddered as his eyes grew dark, cinder-gray with desire. With a will born of desperation, she renewed her struggles. She'd be damned if she'd allow Dare the satisfaction of knowing how greatly he affected her.

"Casey, don't fight me!" Dare pleaded, his

voice a tortured croak. "I've been put off long enough by you." There was a warning in his tone, a gritty signal that his control was precarious at best.

Logic crumbled at her feet as his mouth lowered to capture hers. His tongue slid hungrily over her lips as he sought release from the torment she continually caused him. Drunk from the taste of her, his kiss deepened as his tongue searched and probed the warm recesses of her mouth. Casey trembled, her breath short and tremulous. Her heart thudded against her ribcage as the essence of him reached into her soul, speaking eloquently of his need.

Husky laughter rumbled in Dare's chest and his eyes danced with deviltry as he felt the beginning of her response. His hand cupped her chin, tilting her head to his, his thumb leisurely caressing the delicate line of her jaw. Tonight, he silently vowed, tonight he would assault her with a tenderness she would never forget. He would create a need in her no man but him could assuage.

With practiced ease Dare lifted her off her feet, placing her carefully on the bed. Leaning above her, he brushed his fingers over her bare breasts, his eyes glowing with silver lights as her soft nipples rose and tightened into aching buds. The sensation was so intense, so exquisite, that Casey experienced a rapture she never knew existed. And when his lips surrounded the swollen tips, drawing them into his mouth, her throat convulsed, her breath coming in short pants. The swirling torrent of fiery need grew intolerable when he bit down lightly on one nipple, kneading the other with his fingers. She clutched helplessly at his back as he moved to repeat the same loving act on the other breast.

A deep sound welled up in Dare's throat that resembled an animal's growl as he rose up and tore off his constrictive clothing before bringing his body's weight down on her with agile ease. His naked flesh against hers brought a sigh of pleasure and her roaming hands delighted in the erotic feel of his lightly furred skin.

While his lips sampled again the sweetness of her lips, he explored every feminine curve of her body. His straying fingers found the soft inner flesh of her thighs and he etched circles around that part of her that ached for his touch. Lingering on the mound of fiery red between her legs, Dare finally succumbed to the devils driving him as he sought the warm, tender folds of moist flesh. Casey gasped as his finger delved deeply, probing relentlessly as she writhed beneath him. No one had ever touched her in such a manner and Dare's invasion of her secret places left her mind reeling with shock.

Casey stared in awe at the bold proof of his desire. His magnificent maleness sprang from the dark forest of his loins like a shaft of delicately carved marble displayed upon a base of pure onyx. And then her thoughts disintegrated as he kissed her again, his hands probing the softness between her thighs, gauging her readiness by the hot wetness of her woman's flesh. A soft, uncertain cry broke from her lips as she arched to meet his touch.

"Dare!"

"Not yet, love, but soon," he breathed against her lips. "I don't want this to be a hurried coupling. We've hours to enjoy one another. When I leave your bed I intend to know your lovely body as intimately as my own."

In the glow of the flickering candlelight, Casey recognized the slumbering passion in his eyes, wondering if her own desire was as evident to him. Her half-formed thoughts scattered as once again Dare devoted himself to the budding flower of her sexuality concealed by the triangle of fiery curls. Gently his hands parted her pale, trembling thighs so his fingers could continue their slow, sensual tribute to that tender, secret place. He kissed and suckled her breasts, nipped at her waist, circled her navel with his tongue, all the while driving her wild with his loving manipulation from below.

Suddenly her body stiffened, all her senses alive as she hovered on the brink of her first taste of sexual fulfillment. Feeling her tense and tremble, Dare realized she was close to climax as she began thrashing from side to side. Exultation and pride caused him to intensify his efforts as he whispered words of encouragement in her ear.

"Yes, love, yes. Don't hold back. You're wonderfully responsive, just as I knew you'd be."

Casey heard but was beyond reply as reality fled, replaced by a need only this man could assuage. Nothing made sense but Dare's hands and lips driving her higher and higher as she searched for release from the exquisite torture he created in her. And then it came, sending her tumbling into an abyss, down . . . down . . . Dare's mouth swallowed the scream that left her throat at the moment rapture claimed her.

"Oh, Casey, I want you so badly I know I'll explode if I don't bury myself in your softness. I need to feel your warm flesh surround me," he groaned as he shifted his body to fit snugly between her slender, outstretched thighs. "Take me inside you, love. Let's journey together this time."

He slid full and deep into her welcoming softness, easing the throbbing of his maleness in the warm wetness of her body. Casey tensed, feeling herself expanding and filling with him. He lifted her hips, driving even deeper, and her eyes widened with shock and pain. She startled him by crying out and writhing to escape the torture being inflicted upon her. Mistaking her response for passion, Dare lunged strongly forward, burying his considerable length fully into her tight sheath.

He felt the membrane tear beneath his passionate onslaught at the same moment the scream of agony ripped from Casey's throat. "Oh God, no," he groaned, staring at her in stunned disbelief. "Why didn't you tell me?"

"I . . . I tried," she sobbed.

"It's all right, my sweet love. I'll make it all right. Relax, I won't hurt you again."

Steeling herself, Casey waited for the pain to renew itself. When it did not, she allowed herself to relax, waiting for the pleasurable feeling Dare had evoked earlier to return.

Though it taxed his control beyond human endurance, Dare remained motionless for several minutes in order to allow Casey time to become accustomed to the size and feel of him inside her. He waited until the slight movement of her hips expressed her willingness for him to continue. This time when he renewed the slow, seductive rhythm, Casey responded eagerly, matching his motion stroke for stroke. Her breathing grew labored and her head thrashed wildly from side to side as he worked skillfully and patiently to drive them both over the edge, extracting every sensation and emotion their union could provide. Abruptly, tenderness and care yielded to fierce, driving passion as Dare's control fled. With each forceful thrust, Casey's body began to pulsate with sweet, tormenting pleasure, until she was consumed by the unfamiliar sensation that rose from somewhere inside her.

Dare felt her body begin to vibrate and reveled in the knowledge that he had been the first to initiate her to the act of love and bring her fulfillment. Her reaction left him little doubt that the rapture she experienced was very real as she arched, cried out, then clawed at him. The moment Casey reached the pinnacle, Dare's restraint dissolved and he buried himself deeply into her quivering flesh, her ecstasy triggering his own as he emptied himself into her. Outside, the moon and stars fell from the heavens to brighten the world.

"Casey, I think it's time we talked," Dare said as he settled her comfortably in his arms. After they had made love, gloriously, exuberantly, they had fallen silent, each too stunned by the fierceness of their passion for coherent speech.

Neither made any attempt to untangle limbs or draw apart as their skin clung damply and their breath slowed to normal.

"Did you hear, love?" Dare repeated when Casey remained silent. His lips brushed her forehead in a tender gesture that startled her. She would have thought that once he had his way he would show nothing but contempt for her.

At length she replied, "I heard."

"Before I say anything else I want to apologize. It never occurred to me that you might be an innocent. The majority of women convicts transported to New South Wales are—"

"Whores," she supplied dryly.

"The sad truth is that if they aren't whores when they leave England, by the time they reach the colony circumstance forces them to take up the profession in order to survive. Life aboard a prison ship is hard, as you well know, and most women will go to any lengths to make their lot easier. How did you manage to arrive here intact?"

"A . . . friend protected me. We are from the same town in Ireland and well acquainted. We were transported together and ended up on the same ship," Casey revealed. "But for Tim I don't know what would have become of me."

"If ever I meet your savior I'll be sure to thank him for saving you for me," Dare smiled tenderly.

Casey did not reply, certain Tim would not appreciate Dare's words.

"Where is this man now?" Dare asked curiously.

"I . . . I don't know," Casey hedged, unwilling to say anything more on the subject.

"Let's talk about your crime, love. Tell me about the man you killed—if you really did kill him—and why."

Casey remained silent a long time, carefully choosing her words. "He was a judge, the man who sentenced my father to death. I went to him to plead for Papa's life. Papa was no insurgent. He was a teacher and a scholar. Somehow he became involved in the rebellion against his will, but only in a small way. To the authorities it made little difference. He was tried and sentenced to hang. I tried to reason with the judge. I begged him to change Papa's sentence to transportation as he did many of the others."

"I take it you weren't successful."

"The man was impossible. He . . . he said he might consider my request if I . . . became his mistress. His audacious proposal rendered me speechless. He took my silence for compliance and began tearing at my clothes." A small sob escaped her throat as she recalled the horror that followed.

"It was an accident, Dare! I never meant to kill anyone. I pushed him and he fell, hitting his head on the edge of a marbletop table. He didn't move, not a muscle. I was terrified." She began sobbing hysterically.

"It's all right, love, don't cry," Dare soothed, wiping the tears from her cheeks with his fingertips. "It's over with now."

"It will never be finished, Dare," Casey lamented tearfully. "I'll always live with it. I remember screaming, and people rushing in. It was so confusing. I was taken to jail, and a trial was held, then I was placed aboard a prison ship for transportation. While awaiting trial I learned Papa had been hung. It was worse than a nightmare, one I'll live and relive the rest of my days."

Dare's arms tightened around her as he grew angry with himself for his despicable behavior toward Casey these past weeks. She had enough problems without him acting like an arrogant ass. He realized now that all the while he was condemning her he was only denying his own feelings. He had no idea where this discovery would lead, but of one thing he was certain—no other woman affected him as violently as Casey. What was it about this special woman that made him want her above all others? How long would it last?

"I'm sorry for everything, Casey," Dare said sincerely.

Oddly enough, Casey wanted to believe him but her carefully erected defenses would not crumble. "Words come easily, Dare."

"You have every reason to doubt me, love. But if you'll allow it I'll make it up to you. These feelings are all so new it's going to take some getting used to before I . . . damn, Casey, I can't even think straight with you in my arms like this. It's too soon to offer promises that I might not be able to keep."

There was no time to ponder Dare's words as he lowered his head to kiss her, sending her senses reeling. A flicker of renewed excitement grew in her as he used lips and hands with such skill he soon had her gasping for breath. He teased, tasted and tantalized as he prepared her body once more for his passionate invasion. She answered his arousing strokes with hesitant touches of her own—across his chest, down his flat abdomen, to muscled legs and inner thighs, not brave enough yet to touch that place that brought her such pleasure.

Suddenly, in an agile move that left her gaping in horror, he draped her legs over his shoulders and kissed her there, between her legs. His hands kneaded her breasts while his mouth aroused her in a way she never dreamed possible. His tongue delved deeply into her velvety softness, making her forget everything but the way he made her body vibrate with a terrible need.

"Dare! No! You shouldn't."

"Please, Casey, I want to love you in every way possible. Every part of you is so beautiful."

Just when she thought she would die from the intense pleasure, Dare spread her legs and slowly entered, the petals of her womanhood closing around him. Instinctively she lifted her hips to feel the hot length of him slide full and deep. This time there was no pain and inside she felt like a torch flaming out of control, searing with exquisite agony all those secret parts of her.

"Casey, you're so warm and tight and feel so damn good," Dare groaned, straining above her. Fire sparked his silver-gray eyes.

His words made little sense as sunbursts of blinding white lights exploded in her head. Then ecstasy carried them away and eased the path to slumber.

Sunlight, dusty and hazy, trickling in warm, molten streams of gold through the window, drifted across Casey's face in a soft whisper, waking her. She lay still for a moment, suspended in a half-world between sleep and complete awareness. Her body ached, but pleasantly so, with some half-remembered pleasure.

Suddenly her eyes flew open and her hands searched the far reaches of the bed. She sighed in relief to find she was alone. Dare must have left sometime before daylight. How could she face him, she reflected, feeling the hot rush of blood to her cheeks, after acting like a wanton in his arms? He had only to touch her and she was all writhing passion and fire. Yet in her heart she knew no other man could affect her as Dare had. From the moment they met he had treated her with nothing but contempt. Yet he had made love to her as if he truly cared about her.

How could she describe her own feelings for the handsome settler? Certainly she was attracted to him, and she must care for him to allow him to make love to her without offering more than a token resistance. It was all too confusing, and far too soon to put a name to what she felt, Casey decided, stretching. Men were different from women. They took their pleasure where they might without care or consideration. Was Dare using her merely to ease his lust? Did he intend to continue their affair until he tired of her?

The more she thought about it, the angrier she became. She was not someone to be used and discarded. If that's what Dare intended, he would not find her so willing the next time, if there was a next time. Rising somewhat reluctantly, her body protesting its unaccustomed handling, Casey washed, dressed and hurried to the kitchen. She realized she was late and hoped no one would notice.

She found Martha bending over the hearth. Flinging Casey a grateful glance, Martha wiped the sweat from her brow, saying, "Thank God you're here, Casey. Mr. Roy is leaving for Sydney and wants his breakfast immediately. Dare already left. He grabbed a biscuit from the pantry and hurried out. What in the world kept you? Are you ill?"

"No, I—"

"Late nights and early mornings don't mix," warned Meg cryptically. She had entered the kitchen in time to hear Martha's question. "You should try going to bed earlier, Casey."

Casey paled, the skillet holding Roy's eggs suspended in her hands. What did Meg mean? Did she know about Tim? Or that Dare had come to her room last night?

"If those are Mr. Roy's eggs I'll take them in," Meg offered sweetly. "Ben is downstairs now and ready for his breakfast, too."

"What did she mean, Casey?" Martha asked curiously after Meg tripped from the room balancing the plate of eggs.

"I'll explain later," Casey hedged, busying herself with Ben's breakfast. "After I talk to Mr. Roy."

Thinking of Tim and the seriousness of his wound, Casey came to the inevitable conclusion that telling Roy about Tim was the only sensible solution. Her friend's life was at stake and there was a good chance Roy wouldn't turn him in to the authorities. Even if he did, there was too much at risk should Tim remain unattended much longer.

The moment the men finished eating, Casey hurried to Roy's office, hoping to catch him before he left for Sydney, only to find the room deserted. Rushing out to find her employer before he left the farm, she encountered Ben who happened to be passing the study.

"Whoa, Casey, what's the hurry?" Ben laughed, trapping her in his arms. She felt so good he made no effort to release her.

"I hoped to speak with your father before he

left for Sydney, Ben," Casey said in a rush of words. "It's important."

"It's too late, Casey. He rode off just moments ago. Word was received early this morning about a rebellion led by John Macarthur and carried out by the Rum Corps against Governor Bligh. Father left to see if he could be of help to the governor. Dare went to inform Robin and we're to wait here for word from Father."

"Why would Macarthur and the Rum Corps rebel?" Casey asked curiously.

Ben snorted derisively. "Macarthur is a pure type of predatory capitalist. He is a man of cold anger who uses others for his purpose and profit. He's hard, unscrupulous, and an ingenious plotter. Governor Bligh is in his way. Today the New South Wales Corps is the dominant financial power in Australia, and Macarthur is the brains behind the Corps. The governor poses a threat to their illicit dealings in rum, goods and convicts, therefore he must be removed. But if Macarthur succeeds, Casey, it will be a sad day for the colony."

"I've heard plenty about John Macarthur, Ben, and he sounds like a monster."

"Monster or genius, history will judge him, not I. His goal is to consolidate the land into huge estates, forcing the small farms owned mainly by emancipists out of existence. He was a captain in the New South Wales Corps who arrived in 1788 to garrison the colony. Evidently he saw great opportunity here and resigned from the Corps in 1794 to accumulate land at an amazing pace.

"He was sent back to England in 1801 and tried for dueling, but nothing came of it. He returned and began buying land and experiment-

ing in breeding for fine wool instead of meat. The
man virtually controls the economy. Why, last
year he was responsible for a large rise in the
price of mutton by withholding his wethers from
the market."

"Where does your father stand, Ben?" Casey
asked. "He's one of the few prosperous settlers in
the colony and a 'pure merino.'"

"I think Father secretly admires Macarthur,
but he deplores his methods. We're behind the
government and their efforts to rehabilitate the
convicts and employ them for the good of the
government. Already we are producing several
types of manufactured goods. And look at Parramatta. The city is an example of what could be
done by efficient utilization of convicts."

Casey turned thoughtful, apparently mulling
over everything Ben told her.

"Since both Father and Dare are gone, is there
anything I could help you with?" Ben offered,
recalling her request to speak with Roy.

"N . . . no, it can wait," Casey stammered,
deciding against involving Ben in her problem.
"When do you expect your father to return?"

"Tonight, if all is well in Sydney. If not, who
knows?"

Meg spent the better part of the day considering her discovery of the runaway convict and
how best to use her information. She could
inform the Rum Corps, but that still wouldn't rid
her of Casey. It wasn't until later, after Dare
returned to the house with Robin, that Meg
found a solution. A solution inspired by a conversation overheard between Casey and Robin.

As the day progressed, Casey's concern over

Tim grew. He had seemed so weak when she saw him last night. She prepared a swag with food, water and medicine to take to him later and had just hidden it in a cupboard when Dare entered the kitchen with Robin.

Dare's eyes sought Casey immediately, warmed by the sight of her flushed cheeks and red hair curling in disarray about her beautiful face. Vividly he recalled her response as she lay in his arms last night, all fire and hot desire. Behind those green eyes lurked a sleeping passion he'd just begun to unleash. His pleasure at finding her virgin remained a warm glow inside him. It had been a shock, but one that he welcomed. Now, just the thought of another man making love to her drove him wild with jealousy.

Having Dare appear so unexpectedly threw Casey into a state of confusion. Ever since arising this morning, she wondered how she would react when they met after their passionate encounter the night before. Would he return to the formidable, detached stranger she had come to expect? Or become the passionate lover of last night?

An awkward silence fell as they stared at one another across the space of the room. She started violently when at length Dare spoke, his deep voice striking a responsive chord in her heart.

"Neither of us has eaten this morning, Casey, do you suppose you could fix us something to tide us over till lunch?"

Shifting his pensive gaze from Dare to Casey, Robin frowned thoughtfully. It took little imagination to realize something was taking place between the two of them that he wasn't privy to. In Robin's earlier observation, Dare gave the distinct impression that he cared little for Casey, but he fooled no one but himself. Robin knew the day would come when Dare would recognize his own feelings. That day must have arrived, for he had never seen his friend so smitten. The sad part was that with Dare it was unlikely to last. The man seemed incapable of settling on any one woman. Not only was Mercy McKenzie panting after him, but Governor Bligh's daughter too. Not to mention that hot little piece, Meg. Robin hated to see Casey hurt, but becoming involved with Dare could lead to nothing but a broken heart. As much as he hated to interfere in his friend's business, he felt Casey must be warned. In fact, he had every intention of courting the girl himself.

Casey shrugged free of Dare's mesmerizing gaze as she finally found her voice. "There's some cold mutton and fresh bread, if that will suffice. Will you eat in the dining room?"

"We'll sit here," Dare announced, taking a seat at the square table bleached nearly white from constant scrubbings.

Dare and Robin talked quietly while Casey set out the food. "Do you think there's anything to this rebellion, Dare?" Robin asked.

"Decent settlers and civil officers are with Bligh, but the Rum Corps is succeeding in demoralizing the colony. And John Macarthur is behind it all. Every governor the colony has had tried in vain to run the colony according to the dictates of the government, but their efforts seriously interfered with Captain Macarthur and the Rum Corps."

"Where will it all end? Do emancipists like

myself have a chance to survive against such
overwhelming odds? It's not fair!" stormed Robin, banging his fist on the table.

The men fell silent as they finished their meal,
Dare's gray eyes following Casey as she went
about her chores. In his mind's eye he pictured
her lying naked in his arms, her wide-eyed innocence merely a smoke screen to disguise a passion he alone had awakened. Just thinking about
rose-tipped breasts swelling against his palms,
her secret flesh opening beneath his probing
fingertips, caused his loins to tighten painfully. If
he didn't leave now he'd shame himself before
his friend.

Rising abruptly, he said, "Are you finished,
Robin? I swear you'd sit there all day if I'd let
you."

"You go on, Dare, if you're in such a big hurry.
I haven't talked to Casey in ages. You don't mind,
do you, mate?" he challenged.

"Of course not," Dare replied gruffly, flashing
Casey an inscrutable glance. "Don't take too
long. I think we should ride over to McKenzie's
and talk to Thad about the rebellion. He's a great
friend of Macarthur and Lt. Col. Johnston and
maybe he knows something we don't."

"And perhaps see Mercy while you're there?"
teased Robin, unaware of Dare's dark scowl.

Casey couldn't help but overhear Robin's ref-
erence to Mercy McKenzie. If Meg could be
believed, Mercy McKenzie and Dare would marry one day. How stupid of her to think she meant
more to Dare than a temporary diversion. She
was no more important to him than . . . than
Meg. Many times during their enchanted night
together she heard him whisper that he wanted

her, yearned for her, even needed her. But not once did he tell her he loved her or cared a fig about her. Let him go to Mercy, she thought wretchedly. She had enough on her mind with Tim so ill and needing help.

Tim! Suddenly it came to Casey. She knew exactly what she must do to save Tim's life.

CHAPTER SIX

"How have you been, Casey?" Robin asked, startling Casey from her reverie. "Are you being treated well? If I know Roy he's the kindest of employers. And you've probably got poor Ben wound around your little finger. And Dare . . . Well, Dare is another matter. Are you two—"

"Everything is fine with me, Robin," Casey hastened to assure him before his questions became too personal. "I'm as happy as I can be under the circumstances."

"Good! If you have any problems, need anything, you've only to ask. I'm not all that far away."

Casey chewed over his words for several minutes before coming to a decision. Tim's life depended on her and if she had to confide in someone, Robin seemed the likely choice. "Robin, there is something," she said slowly, lowering her voice as she sank to the chair just vacated by Dare.

"Name it," Robin replied. "I'll do whatever I can if it's within my power."

"It's not for me, Robin, but for a friend desperately in need of help. A very dear friend."

"A friend?" Robin echoed, puzzled.

"He's wounded and not likely to survive unless he has medical attention. But of course I'll understand if you refuse. The penalty for helping an escaped convict is severe and I'd not ask you to do something against your principles."

"Your friend is an escaped convict? And he's wounded? Perhaps you should start from the beginning, Casey."

Hesitantly at first, then more forcefully once she gained courage, Casey explained how she found Tim two days ago in the bush. In detail she described the nature of his wound.

"How badly is he hurt?"

"The bullet is still in him. I don't think it hit anything vital but it's badly infected. He's been feverish since I discovered him the day before yesterday."

"Why did he run, Casey? I hate to ask so many questions but if I intend to involve myself in this I have to know all the details."

"I understand, Robin," Casey replied. "My only request is that you not report him to the authorities if you decide against helping."

"You needn't worry that I'll betray your friend, Casey. I've seen too many good men flogged at the whipping post or hung from the gallows on George Street."

"Tim is accustomed to roam free. He first attracted attention on the prison ship when he protected me from . . . others. He made enemies both aboard ship and among the guards in the colony. He was too rebellious, too contemptuous of authority. As punishment he was sent to work the coal mines north of Sydney."

"Christ! I don't wish that fate on anyone," muttered Robin irreverently.

"Tim couldn't handle it. He said he'd rather die than be buried beneath the earth day in and day out. He managed to escape but was shot in the attempt. It's a miracle he made it this far, but he'll die without proper care."

"Have you told any of this to Roy? Or Dare?"

"No," Casey admitted, her voice laced with panic. "I'm not sure about Mr. Roy, but I'm convinced Dare would turn him in. I want Tim to have a chance to live."

"I think you do Dare an injustice, Casey. I'm an emancipist, yet Dare has been my best friend. He has great compassion for his fellow men. So do Roy and Ben."

"But what about an escaped convict? It is punishable by law to aid one. No, Robin, I won't risk it. Either you help Tim or . . . or I'll think of something."

"Casey, I'll help your friend."

Tears of gratitude spiked Casey's sooty lashes and a long tremulous sigh escaped her parted lips. Robin thought her the loveliest woman he'd ever seen and vowed he'd not allow Dare to hurt her.

"I . . . I don't know how to thank you, Robin," Casey choked on a sob. "This means a lot to me."

"I know, Casey, that's why I agreed to help. That and the thought of what will happen to Tim if he's recaptured. But I want you to promise me something in return."

"Anything, Robin."

"Don't let Dare hurt you. Sometimes he's a bastard where women are concerned."

Startled, Casey's green eyes widened. What had Dare told him? Did Robin know that she and Dare . . . Good Lord! Was Robin trying to warn her about his friend? Aloud, she said, "In Dare's eyes I hardly exist. I see no possibility of him hurting me."

Robin looked skeptical. "I'm warning you because I care about you." When Casey remained mute, Robin shrugged and changed the subject. He had done his part, now the rest was up to Casey. Abruptly he asked, "Where is Tim now?"

"Hidden in the shed that sometimes serves as a jail. I can only visit him at night to bring food and water. I've changed the dressing on his wound but it's very bad. The bullet—"

"I'll see to it, Casey," Robin interjected. "There's an aborigine working for me who knows herbs and medicines. He can set bones and remove bullets. Don't worry, if anyone can cure your friend, Culong can."

"At least Tim will have a good chance of surviving in the bush once he's strong again. Wounded as he is, he wouldn't last a day on his own. What will you do, Robin? How do you intend to help him?"

"Tonight Culong and I will return after midnight with a wagon. We'll take Tim to my place. If I think the danger is too great at my house, Culong will hide him in his village."

"Thank you, Robin," Casey said sincerely, grasping both his hands in hers and tilting her head forward until red curls mingled with soft brown waves. "If there's anything I can do for you you have only to ask."

"I hate to interrupt so intimate a scene, but if you intend to accompany me to the McKenzie farm you'd best tear yourself away," Dare snarled acidly. His chilling glare pierced Casey and turned her to ice.

"Dare!" she exclaimed, jumping to her feet. "It's not—"

"It's none of my concern who you entertain, Casey. Obviously I've created a hunger in you and you thought to test your newfound—"

"Watch your tongue, Dare!" Robin warned, rising abruptly. "I don't know what's going on between you and Casey, but you have no call to talk to her like that. If you weren't my friend—"

"I have no argument with you, Robin," Dare shrugged. "And Casey knows well enough what I'm talking about. Come along, it's time we left." He stormed out the door, seemingly unconcerned whether or not Robin followed.

"I'm sorry, Casey," Robin apologized. "I don't know what's gotten into Dare lately. Normally he's a damn fine bloke and not a bit temperamental. But for some unexplained reason he seems to have changed these past weeks. I'd best go or he'll leave without me. And don't worry about . . . what we discussed, I'll take care of it." Then he hurried out the door after Dare.

Meg smiled smugly as she left her place of concealment outside the kitchen window. She had gone to the garden to gather flowers for the house when the sound of voices drew her attention. Sidling closer, she heard everything, and was now in possession of vital information to use against Casey O'Cain.

Stationed at the window overlooking the moon-drenched compound, Casey wished the yard wasn't so brilliantly illuminated. She knew it must be nearing midnight and expected Robin to appear at any moment. To eliminate the slightest chance of discovery she deliberately chose to remain in her room. Since all the men in the family were gone during the afternoon, she had sneaked out to visit Tim and told him about Robin. Still too ill to respond rationally, Tim nevertheless understood that he would be leaving the shed for a place less dangerous where he would receive proper medical attention.

Suddenly Casey froze, blood pounding through her veins at a furious pace. From behind the convict barracks a vague movement caught her eye. Slowly a shape began to emerge, and Casey breathed a sigh of relief. Robin had kept his word. Two shadowy figures crept toward the hut where Tim lay hidden. The wagon was nowhere in view, but she supposed Robin had left it out of sight where the creaking wheels would not give them away. Unaware that she was holding her breath, Casey strained her eyes as she watched the two men approach the front of the hut.

Why didn't Robin hurry, she silently implored, her stomach clenched in a tight knot. Then abruptly a vague sound outside her door drew her attention from the drama taking place beneath the stars.

The scratching at her door was loud enough for Casey to hear, yet undetectable to anyone else. Besides, her room off the kitchen offered a modicum of privacy. "Casey, it's Dare. I want to talk to you."

Dare! Dear God, what was he doing here? "Please leave, Dare, it's late and I'm tired," she hissed through the closed panel.

"I would have come earlier but it's taken me all

this time to reach a decision. If you don't want me in your room, join me outside. It's a warm night and no one is about to disturb us."

"No!" cried Casey, hot panic spurting through her. "Not outside. Wait a moment and I'll let you in."

Darting a glance out the window, Casey saw two shrouded forms leaving the hut supporting a third sagging figure between them. They were clearly visible in the diffused light of the moon. Flinging the curtains shut in an effort to conceal the damning evidence, she turned toward the door, hoping Dare found no reason to look out the window.

"Come in, Dare," she said, fidgeting nervously with the sash of her robe.

Dare stepped inside, closing the door quietly behind him. He stared appreciatively at Casey a few minutes before saying, "I've reached a decision."

Carefully maneuvering around Dare until his back faced the window, Casey asked warily, "What kind of a decision?"

"You've bewitched me, woman. I can come up with no other explanation for the way I feel about you."

"I'm no witch," Casey denied softly.

"When I came into the kitchen today and saw you and Robin so cozy I wanted to kill him. My best friend! One minute I want to take you in my arms and the next I could easily strangle you. Keep away from Robin, Casey. You don't want him."

"How do you know what I want?"

"Because you want the same thing I do. Admit

it, love, this powerful attraction we have for one another eats at you just as it does me. It drives me crazy to see you with another man. Even if the man is Robin. I'm selfish enough to want you for myself."

"What about my feelings? I . . . I don't want you."

"You make a terrible liar, love, and I'll prove it," Dare smiled wolfishly as he closed the space between them. "Let me make love to you, Casey."

She stared at him, astounded that he bothered to ask. From past experience she expected him to take what he wanted, with or without her approval. "Are you asking me?"

"I . . . yes, I'm asking. There's too much between us to be at odds with one another all the time. I want us to be lovers. One way or another I'm going to resolve these feelings I have for you."

"And if I refuse?"

"Then . . . then I'll probably take a walk to the creek for a midnight swim in the billibong. Perhaps the cool water will douse the fire you've created in me."

"No! I . . . I mean I don't want you to leave," Casey stammered helplessly. No matter what she had to do, she couldn't let Dare walk out of this room until Robin and Tim were well away from the farm.

Dare's eyes turned smoky with desire as he gently gathered Casey in his arms. "You won't regret it, love," he murmured in a husky whisper. "I leave for Sydney tomorrow and when I return I hope to have good news for you."

One reason for his trip to Sydney was to discover for himself the seriousness of the revolt against Governor Bligh. Another was to ask Bligh to remit Casey's sentence. It was within the governor's power to grant pardons as well as control all aspects of life, civil, taxes, appointments, grants and convict labor. Dare knew his father would agree wholeheartedly with his request even if he wasn't aware of the reason behind it. That, as well as his future plans, he would keep to himself, at least until he placed the pardon in Casey's hands.

Before Casey could question Dare's puzzling words, his large hand took her face and held it gently. His touch was suddenly almost unbearable in its tenderness. She could feel his uneven breathing on her cheek as he gathered her into his arms, holding her snugly. His kiss was slow, thoughtful; his tongue parting her lips sent shivers of desire racing through her.

With slow deliberation he slipped the robe and gown from her shoulders, pushing them past her hips until they lay in a puddle at her feet. In the flickering light he gazed at her for what seemed an eternity. The glow in his eyes spoke eloquently of his need.

Almost reverently he fondled one small globe before lowering his head and touching her nipple with his tongue, caressing the sensitive swollen bud. Casey shuddered. It seemed as if all her nerve endings centered on that place where his tongue worked so diligently. Then, so as not to show favorites, he moved to the other nipple, teasing it until it rose to its fullest.

Gently he eased her down onto the bed, sparing a moment to shed his clothes before settling down beside her. "You're the most enticing woman I've ever known, Casey," he breathed in her ear. His hand outlined the circle of her breast, then slid across her silken belly. "And sweet . . . so sweet."

"Dare!" she gasped, his name a plea on her lips.

He paused to kiss her, murmuring love words against her lips. With a will of their own her hands discovered the hard wall of his chest, the slim contour of waist and hips, the curve of rounded buttocks. Whatever devils drove her made her slip her hands around to grasp him, marveling at the hard smoothness of him, reminding her of sculptured marble. She never dreamed he would feel so warm and pulsating with life.

The moment Casey found him, Dare jerked violently, crying out in pleasure so intense it bordered on pain. "No, love," he gasped, removing her hands, "I don't want this night to end before it begins. Let me love you." The turbulence of his passion swirled around her and she gave herself up to the expertise of his hands and lips, dismayed at the magnitude of her own response.

"Dare, now," Casey sobbed, driven time and again to the edge of ecstasy and then denied the ultimate satisfaction.

"Soon, love, soon," Dare crooned, soothing her until she quieted. Then he began anew his slow arousal, until her impatience grew to explosive need.

"Dare!"

When he felt her on the brink of shuddering ecstasy, he lowered his body over hers, nudging her thighs apart. His hardness electrified her as she welcomed him into her body and his strong thrusts brought her the relief she sought. "I love you, Dare!" she cried out as ecstasy claimed her. And then she knew no more.

Immersed in the race to find his own reward, Dare did not hear Casey's stunning admission. And had Casey realized at the time what she said she would have been horrified.

Emerging from a sated slumber, Dare was shocked to see light coming in through the window. Bloody hell! He hadn't meant to sleep so long. If someone was in the kitchen they were bound to see him leaving Casey's room, and he certainly didn't want Casey thought of as a whore. She had been an innocent until he came along and seduced her, but no one need know what had happened between them . . . not yet, anyway.

Beside him, Casey felt Dare stir and opened her eyes, pinkening as she recalled her shocking behavior and the passion this man evoked in her. And then she saw the sun streaming through the window and jerked upright, alarm coursing through her.

"Dare! It's daylight!" she wailed, green eyes widening in silent appeal. "What if—"

"I know, love," Dare sighed regretfully. "I'm sorry. I hadn't meant to sleep so late. But don't worry, I'll crawl out the window if need be."

His eyes fastened avidly on the soft mounds of her breasts bared when she sat up so abruptly. What was it about this woman that made him still hunger for her despite the fact they had made love twice during the night?

Casey suppressed a giggle, imagining him squeezing his large frame through the narrow window. The sound brought an answering smile. "You should smile more often," Casey said, admiring the way his eyes crinkled at the corners and his mouth curved upwards.

"I would if I had something as lovely as you to look at all the time." Once again his eyes strayed to her pink-tipped breasts, alerting Casey to the fact that she was nude from the waist up. Hastily she made a grab for the sheet, but Dare stayed her hands.

"Don't cover them. You have beautiful breasts."

Casey recognized instantly the flare of desire in the tautness of Dare's body and in his molten silvery gaze. She drew her breath in sharply, feeling herself surrendering to the magnetism of his virile presence.

"Christ, don't look at me like that!" Dare breathed raggedly, bending down and seizing her lips with frantic urgency. He kissed her thoroughly and at length, until Casey regained her senses, reluctantly freeing herself.

"Dare, please! You must leave. We can't . . . not now. Surely someone is up and stirring by now. What if they see you leaving my room?"

Sighing regretfully, Dare pulled himself away with obvious reluctance. "One day, love, we'll . . ." No, he reflected, wisely holding his tongue. It was too soon yet to make a declaration he might be sorry for later. He had no idea what Casey truly felt for him. He had more or less forced her the first time they made love, never dreaming she would be a virgin. She was still too new to passion to make a coherent decision. After he obtained her pardon from Governor Bligh would be time enough to explore their feelings.

Casey looked at him askance, waiting for him to complete his sentence. When he didn't, she frowned and made an impatient gesture with her hands. "Please, Dare, what if someone sees you?"

Heeding her plea, he uncoiled his long length from the bed, unashamedly displaying his nudity. Mesmerized, Casey could not force her eyes from so perfect a specimen of virile maleness and masculine beauty. He was whiplash lean, yet the muscles of his shoulders, arms and thighs bulged beneath his hair-roughened skin. Even at rest his manhood was generously proportioned. When he turned his back to her she admired the twin mounds of his buttocks flexing with the exertion of pulling on his pants. Flushing guiltily, she lowered her eyes when he whirled to face her.

Dare smiled sardonically. He had felt her eyes on him and knew she wasn't totally immune to him. That thought pleased him. "Casey, when I return from Sydney we'll have a long talk about . . . about . . . us. Until then, will you trust me?"

Casey had no idea what Dare was talking about. Unless . . . No, she refused to think about that. Or about these strange emotions running rampant in her. He made her feel things she had only dreamed about. She knew now that had she married Tim she would have missed something very special. Something Tim could not provide however much she cared for him. Did that mean only Dare had the power to move her to wondrous heights? That no man but Dare could provoke such conflicting emotions?

Dare did not question her silence, for his own mind floundered in a turmoil of indecision. However, being of a practical nature, he chose to delve further into his feelings when he had more time to devote to the matter. More pressing was the need to slip unseen from Casey's room.

"I'll be in Sydney no longer than a few days, love," Dare said, turning back to Casey.

"Dare, be careful," she cautioned.

Inching the door open, Dare peered into the deserted kitchen, sighing in relief when he saw no one about. On the opposite side of the large room Meg's door remained tightly shut and Martha's small chamber was located farther down the hallway beneath the stairs. Closing the door silently behind him, Dare hastened through the kitchen, into the hall and up the stairs to his own room, secure in the knowledge that he hadn't been seen.

Meg's eyes narrowed dangerously as she watched Dare's stealthy exit from Casey's room. Having gone outside early to inspect the hut where Tim had been kept, she stood poised in the shadows beside the hearth, holding her breath lest Dare glance in her direction. It didn't suit her purposes to tell him at this time that she knew what he was up to. The moment he disappeared from sight, she let out her breath and stared balefully at Casey's closed door. Squaring her shoulders, a sly smirk tugging at her lips, she strode with malicious intent toward Casey's room.

Twisting the knob, Meg burst unannounced into the room, catching Casey standing in her shift preparing to dress for the day. "Open the window!" she flung out nastily, "the room reeks of sex."

"Wha . . . what!" Casey gasped, whirling to face her unwelcome intruder.

"You slut! You're as much a whore as I am, only I'm honest enough to admit it."

She knows! was Casey's first thought. Somehow she learned about me and Dare. Struggling to keep her face bland, she asked, "What are you talking about, Meg?"

"You should be on the stage, Casey, with your innocent act. But you can't fool me. I saw Dare leave your room a few minutes ago. How long do you think it will be before he tires of you?"

Given Casey's volatile temper, she could stand only so much of Meg's verbal abuse before exploding in anger. "How dare you judge me! What Dare and I do is none of your concern. Do you think he'll marry you? Are you jealous of me? Is that what this is all about? Even you are smart enough to know Dare would never marry a convict."

"In a few months I'll be emancipated," Meg crowed haughtily, "while you'll still have years to serve. Once I'm free, Dare will feel differently. He knows how well I please him."

"What about Mercy McKenzie?"

"Nothing has been settled between them. It's their fathers who hope for a match. I'm confident of my ability to take Dare from Mercy."

"You're mad!" Casey declared dismissively. But Meg was not so easily dismissed. She had more to say—much more.

Crossing her arms over ample breasts, Meg slanted Casey a measuring look, proud of her feminine allure. It was what had drawn Dare's notice when she first arrived at Penrod station. And no red-haired slut was going to steal him from her. The time had come to divulge her knowledge of the secret Casey had guarded so zealously. The evil smile that curved her full, sensuous lips boded no good for Casey, and she was astute enough to realize it.

"Did you tell Dare about the wounded man in the hut beyond the convict barracks?"

Casey froze as a wave of apprehension gripped her. Just the thought of Meg knowing about Tim shattered her. "Wha . . . what are you talking about?" she asked in a small, frightened voice.

"I don't believe I need to elaborate," Meg returned shortly. "You know as well as I the punishment for aiding an escaped convict. It might be enjoyable to see the skin flayed from your back. Or perhaps they'll hang you from the gallows on George Street."

She knows! Oh, God, Meg knew about Tim. Thank the Lord Robin had already taken him away last night and by so doing diffused Meg's vicious intention. "I think you'll find the hut empty," she bluffed with more confidence than she felt.

"Of course," Meg agreed sweetly. "Somehow you talked Robin into giving shelter to your friend. Poor Robin, he's already deeply in debt and on the verge of losing his farm. Should it be discovered he's helping an escaped convict he'll lose everything, including his freedom. The law is quite strict in that regard."

Casey was finding it increasingly difficult to breathe. Obviously Meg knew all the details and planned on using the information to suit her own purposes, whatever they might be. "Meg, I don't know how you learned all this, and it doesn't matter," Casey said. "What does count is that a man's life is at stake. Tim is no criminal in the ordinary sense. I've known him all my life. He's wounded, Meg, and Robin agreed to help. Have you no compassion? You're a convict yourself, for God's sake!" Her voice trembled with fear, not for herself but for Tim and Robin.

"Sergeant Grimes in Parramatta is a . . . er . . . good friend of mine. I'm certain he'll be interested in what I know. What good is compassion? No one felt sorry for me or offered help when I needed it. Besides, I hear there are high officers interested in Robin's land. Once Robin is jailed his property will be promptly gobbled up. So you see, Casey, a word from me will surely earn a generous reward."

"Meg, no, even you couldn't be so heartless. Robin is a friend of the Penrods', think how Dare will react if you do this." Casey was willing to beg in order to stop Meg from turning in Tim and ruining Robin's life. Pride flew out the window when human lives were concerned.

"Dare need never know," Meg smirked slyly, maneuvering Casey into an untenable position. "Who's to point a finger at me? You? You'll be long gone. However, there is one thing you could do to persuade me to overlook this whole matter."

"I'll do anything, Meg, anything," Casey rashly promised, "if you forget you know about Tim and Robin. I'll do your work, or—"

"There's only one thing I want from you, Casey," Meg interjected rudely.

"What is it?" Casey asked over her choking, beating heart.

Meg's voice was hardened and ruthless, with no vestige of sympathy. "You must leave here. Disappear without a trace. That is my price for silence."

"Surely you jest! Where would I go? What would I do?"

"You're resourceful," shrugged Meg indifferently. "You'll survive. In any event, it's no concern of mine. I want you gone—by tonight."

"If . . . if I leave, will you promise to tell no one about Tim?" Casey ventured, unwilling to trust the deceitful woman.

"You have my word," lied Meg deviously. "But you must leave today."

A tense, brittle silence filled the room as Casey carefully weighed her options. If she refused Meg's ultimatum, Tim and Robin would both suffer. And Robin had become involved only to please her. He didn't deserve to lose his land or his freedom because of something that was none of his concern. Then there was Tim to consider. Without expert care he would likely die. In the end there was no real choice.

"Well?" Meg demanded impatiently. "What will it be? Robin's future depends on your answer."

A glazed look of despair began to spread over Casey's face as she replied in a low, tormented voice, "I'll leave today."

CHAPTER SEVEN

Casey stared at Meg's departing back, misery churning her guts. A terrible regret assailed her at the thought of never seeing Dare again. In all likelihood she would die in the bush, for she was certainly ill-prepared to cope with this harsh land into which she was being set adrift without means to sustain herself. But leave she must in order to protect Tim and Robin.

Choking on the tears that clogged her throat, Casey barely had time to dash away the moisture gathering in her eyes before Ben bounded into the kitchen. Luckily he was far too excited to notice Casey's distraction.

"Casey, I'm going to Sydney with Dare," he informed her breathlessly. "We've decided not to remain here and wait for Father to send word on what's going on in town. We want to see for ourselves. When Dare told me he was going I insisted on accompanying him."

"Will you have time for breakfast?" Casey asked.

"No, that's why I'm here. Fix us a swag with

food to eat along the way, will you? Dare doesn't want to waste time sitting at the table for a formal breakfast. He seems to think we might be needed in Sydney. Will you women be all right on your own? Tom Healey will be left in charge of the workers. He's a good man and capable of carrying on in our absence. He's an emancipist who was run off his land by the Rum corps when he couldn't pay his debts."

"We'll be fine," Casey assured him as she promptly gathered food for their journey, carefully packing it in a swag.

"Take care, Casey," Ben called over his shoulder as he hurried out the door with the provisions flung under his arm.

"Good-bye . . . Ben . . ." Her words trailed off, painfully aware that this might be the last time she'd see Ben's smiling face.

Casey lingered in the kitchen hoping Dare would come to bid her good-bye, but when the sound of horses' hooves impatiently pawing the ground reached her ears, she knew her wish was not to be granted. Dare Penrod had ridden from her life forever.

It took little time for Casey to pack her meager belongings in a pillowcase and return to the kitchen to dig into the supply of staples stored in the pantry. As an afterthought she added a sharp kitchen knife, flint and a heavy man's cloak hanging on a hook behind the door. Glancing sadly around the room for a last look at the place she had come to think of as home, she turned to leave.

"Casey, where are you going?" When Martha saw Casey toting a heavy swag and carrying a cloak, she didn't know what to think.

Flushing, Casey whirled to face Martha. She had hoped to take her leave unobtrusively in order to avoid questions. "I . . . I'm leaving, Martha."

"Leaving!" Martha repeated stupidly. "Where will you go? What will you do? What happened, Casey? Did Dare or Ben——"

"No!" denied Casey vehemently. "This has nothing to do with them."

"Then what is it? This isn't like you at all, Casey. Please tell me what's wrong. Perhaps I can help."

"No one can help me," Casey lamented. "I have to leave, Martha. I'm involved in . . . in things you don't understand."

"What are you talking about? What kind of things? Are you in trouble?"

"Trouble? Yes, I suppose you could say that," Casey admitted wryly. "And I have no idea where I'm going except that it will be far from here."

Actually, Casey's immediate destination was Robin's house. She couldn't leave without warning him about Meg and her threat to expose them. Other than that she hadn't the vaguest idea where she would go. Into the bush to wait until Tim was well enough to join her, she supposed. Together they might survive.

Gulping back her tears, Casey slipped through the door, Martha's vigorous protests still ringing in her ears. As luck had it, no one was about and her passage went unnoticed by all but a thoroughly distressed Martha.

"Is she gone?"

Martha spun to face Meg who leaned lazily in the doorway. "What part did you play in this?"

she asked indignantly. Martha did not like Meg and made little secret of it.

Meg smiled deviously. "All I know is that Casey is in big trouble."

"What nonsense are you spouting, Meg?"

"I was in Mr. Roy's study cleaning and found the strongbox holding money and his dead wife's jewelry had been broken into. All of the money was missing as well as the more expensive pieces of jewelry."

"Are you accusing Casey of theft?" Martha glared hostilely. "She wouldn't do such a thing."

"She's gone, isn't she? What further proof do you need?"

Slanting Meg a quelling look, Martha brushed past her, not stopping until she stood before the strongbox in Roy's study. Just as Meg said, the lock had been pried off and the contents inside scattered. Martha could tell at a glance that nothing of value remained.

"Now do you believe me?" asked Meg from the doorway. Though the evidence appeared indisputable, Martha couldn't bring herself to accuse Casey. She wasn't the kind to steal Roy's valuables and run off. Much more was involved here than met the eye, and she was determined to get to the bottom of it.

"Where would Casey go? What good would the money and jewels do her?" Martha questioned sharply.

"They could buy her passage back to Ireland," suggested Meg slyly. "An unscrupulous captain wouldn't hesitate to aid an escaped convict who had the means to meet his price."

Martha's brow furrowed in concentration. Had Casey wanted to return to Ireland badly enough to steal? Did she know Casey well enough to say for certain she wouldn't do exactly what Meg accused her of? The evidence was indeed damning.

"You'll never convince me Casey is a thief," Martha resisted stubbornly.

"Let Mr. Roy be the judge," Meg returned, flouncing off. "If I were you I'd leave things just as they are until the men return," she threw over her shoulder.

In the privacy of her cramped room Meg locked the door, dropped to her knees and emptied the contents of her pockets into a small box hidden beneath the bed. She spent a few moments admiring the jewel-encrusted ring, broach and necklace before snapping shut the lid and shoving it all out of sight. What little money she found in Roy's strongbox was placed in her pocket with the intention of spending it in Parramatta. It had been a smart move on her part to rifle the strongbox to make it look like Casey had stolen the Penrod valuables.

Later that day Meg hastened to the stable, hitched the bullock to the wagon and headed down the dirt track toward Parramatta. She knew Sergeant Grimes would be interested to learn that Casey O'Cain and Robin Fletcher were involved with an escaped convict. She also intended to tell him about the theft. As it wasn't unusual for Meg to go alone to Parramatta to buy supplies for the household, no one questioned her leaving.

It was on just such a trip that Meg had first met Sergeant Grimes who was garrisoned in Parramatta with a company of men sent there to keep the peace. It was to Grimes's office in the new barracks that Meg headed when she reached the city.

Though Casey had never been to Robin's house, she knew enough to follow the Hawkesbury north until she reached his property. By cart or horseback the trip took less than an hour. Traveling on foot added considerable time to the journey. Not only was Casey hot and sweaty, but exhausted as well. After the first couple of miles the swag became such a burden she considered abandoning it, but wisely reconsidered when she thought of all the necessities it held.

It was late afternoon before Casey spied Robin's house. It was much less imposing than the Penrod farm, consisting of a stable, cowshed and convicts' huts clustered around a small house in a yard a foot deep in brown dirt.

The house, small by any standards, was constructed of split slab and rounded posts. The roof was made with sapling rafters crisscrossed at angles to support the overlapping bark that covered it. Other saplings had been laid across the top and tied down to hold the bark in place, making the house covering watertight.

Casey hurried past two men engaged in various duties. Curious, they stopped their work to stare at her as she approached the wide front porch and mounted the stairs. There was no need to rap on the door for it was flung open before she could so much as raise her hand.

"Casey, my God! What are you doing here? Did you come alone?"

"I . . . yes, I came alone," Casey stammered wearily.

"You walked?" Robin gaped in amazement, suddenly aware of the swag she carried as well as her obvious state of exhaustion.

"Come in, lass, come in," he motioned toward the cool interior behind him. He took the swag from her hand and led her to a chair. "Sit down, Casey, I'll get you a cup of cool water. Then you can tell me why you're here. Surely it's not because of your friend. I told you I'd take good care of him."

While Robin busied himself with pouring the water, Casey looked around the sparsely furnished house. What furniture there was seemed to be hand-carved and rather crude. Built on one floor, the main room appeared to be used for everything but sleeping. She assumed the two doors opening on either side of the main room led to bedrooms. Though far from luxurious, it suited Robin perfectly. She wondered where Tim was being cared for and would have asked if Robin hadn't returned with her water, watching as she drank greedily.

"Does Dare know you're here, Casey?" Robin questioned when the cup was drained.

Casey shook her head. "No, he and Ben left for Sydney this morning."

"I would have sent word if something had happened to Tim," he said with a hint of reproach. Then he looked pointedly at the swag resting beside Casey on the floor. "What's that for?"

"I . . . I have to leave Penrod station."

"Have to?"

"Perhaps 'forced to' is a better word."

"Forced? Why? Did Dare—"

"No! Dare has nothing to do with my decision to leave. It's because of Tim."

"Tim? I told you Tim is safe."

"Where is he? I'd like to see him before I leave."

"Tim was far sicker than either of us realized," Robin explained gently. "Culong suggested he be taken to his village where his sister lives. His sister is the tribe healer and more experienced in doctoring. I knew you'd want the best for Tim, so I agreed. Culong took him this morning and should be returning soon. Didn't you trust me to do my best for Tim?"

"Oh, no," denied Casey, "you don't understand. I came to warn you. Someone found out about Tim and knows he's been brought here. I don't want you to get in trouble for something that's clearly my responsibility. If Tim is able, I thought I'd take him into the bush and care for him myself. I won't have you punished on my account."

"That wouldn't be possible even if Tim were still here, lass, he's far too ill. Don't worry about me, I'm capable of seeing to my own welfare. As soon as you're rested I'll hitch up the cart and take you back home."

"No! You still don't understand. I can't return."

"Has someone threatened you?" Robin thundered, storm clouds gathering in his face. "Who found out about Tim?"

Casey hesitated but a brief moment before deciding to tell Robin everything. As long as it involved him he had a right to know. But before she could form the words there came a terrible racket at the door. It burst open revealing a short, stocky native with shiny ebony skin and unruly black hair.

"Soldiers come," he grunted breathlessly.

Gasping in alarm, Casey leaped to her feet. "We've been betrayed! Oh, God, we have to get out of here!"

"How long do we have before they arrive, Culong?" Robin asked, immediately seizing control.

"Culong run all the way from village when I see. They come soon."

"Is the injured man safe, Culong?" Robin questioned sharply.

"He safe with sister but much sick."

"We've been found out, Robin. What can we do? Where can we hide?" Casey cried, her voice thick with panic.

"Culong, take Casey to your village. She'll be safe there for the time being. Hurry, man, we can't let the troopers find her."

Nodding his understanding, Culong grabbed up Casey's swag and grasped her elbow. "Come," he urged, leading her toward the back door.

"Wait!" Casey resisted. "What about you, Robin? I'm not the only one who's in danger. Come with me."

"Go, lass. I'll keep them occupied while you make good your escape. Trust Culong." Despite Casey's violent protests, he shoved her out the door. She had no recourse but to follow Culong and pray for Robin.

Less than fifteen minutes later a squad of uniformed men rode into the dusty compound.

Robin met them on the front steps. "What can I do for you, Sergeant?"

"Where is he, Fletcher?" Sergeant Grimes demanded curtly. "We know you're sheltering an escaped convict."

Assuming a puzzled look, Robin replied, "There's no one here, Sergeant. You're welcome to search but you'll find nothing." Silently Robin prayed no traces of Tim or Casey remained, but he couldn't be absolutely certain.

"We intend to do just that," sneered Grimes nastily. Turning to his men, he snapped out terse orders, then dismounted. "Is the girl here?"

"Girl? You're talking in riddles. Someone has given you false information."

"My information is faultless, as well you know. My informant heard and saw enough to hang both you and Casey O'Cain."

"You'll need more proof than that," bluffed Robin, wishing Casey had taken the time to reveal the name of the person who had betrayed them.

"Sergeant, look here!" an excited voice called from inside the house.

"What is it, Larson?"

"We found these stuffed inside the stove but not yet set afire." A bundle of blood-soaked bandages trailed from his gloved hand.

Beneath his breath Robin cursed the hot weather that had kept him from burning the soiled rags after Culong had changed Tim's bandages. "They prove nothing," came Robin's feeble excuse.

"Have you been injured?" asked Sergeant Grimes pointedly.

Clamping his teeth tightly shut, Robin refused to answer. An injury to his person would be too easy to prove or disprove. The same held true for any of his workers.

"Sergeant, I just talked to two convicts who said a woman carrying a swag arrived by foot a short time ago and went into the house." This bit of information was offered by one of the soldiers sent to question the workers.

"Have you searched the house thoroughly, Corporal Larson?" Grimes asked.

"Yes, sir. If a woman was here she left before we arrived," Larson returned. "We searched every nook and cranny."

"Now search the outbuildings and grounds," Grimes barked. "I want that woman. Not only did she aid a dangerous criminal but she stole money and jewelry from her employer."

The sergeant's startling words caused Robin to start violently. Casey, a thief? Impossible! The person who betrayed her also made her out to be a thief.

"Where is she, Fletcher?" Grimes demanded to know. "We'll find her, you know, as well as the man she helped. We know the man was badly wounded. How long could an injured man and defenseless woman survive in the bush?"

"I know nothing about an escaped convict," Robin steadfastly maintained. Nothing or no one could drag Casey's name from his lips.

It was nearly dark when the search for Casey and Tim was halted by a disgruntled Grimes. Motioning toward Robin, he ordered crisply, "Tie him up and take him to Parramatta. It's about time we tried out the new jail." Immediately two men snapped to obey. "Hitch up the cart, Corporal Larson, I'm sure Fletcher doesn't own a horse. I'll notify Colonel Johnson tomorrow. He'll probably send someone out to see to the farm until a trial can be held. Certain Corps members have had their eye on this property for some time."

It did Robin little good to protest as he was seized, his hands tied behind his back, and led toward the stable. He spared one last glance at all he had worked and slaved for since his emancipation. The charges against him were serious and he could easily lose everything and end up exactly where he started when he was transported to this raw new land. But despite his loss he wouldn't hesitate to help Casey again. He held no ill feelings toward her for involving him in this mess and fervently prayed she would remain safe with Culong's people. But he knew that sooner or later Sergeant Grimes and his men would stumble upon the village if they took their search into the bush. Dare was Casey's only hope. Somehow he had to let Dare know about Casey's predicament so he could see to her safety.

Sydney was in an uproar. The streets were teeming with people and the distinctive uniform of the Rum Corps was in evidence everywhere. Dare and Ben forced their way through the crowds until they reached Government House, only to be turned away by members of the Corps who guarded the entrance. Nor were they able to learn a thing from dour guards. Questioning people in the streets proved fruitless for no one seemed to know exactly what was happening.

There had been a rebellion. That much they learned, and it had been instigated by John

Macarthur. Although he had resigned his commission several years earlier, he still controlled
the New South Wales Corps—particularly where
matters of trade, illicit dealings in rum, and the
acquisition of land were concerned. It was obvious that the power of the Corps officers in
carrying out Macarthur's aims was too great.
Governor Bligh posed a threat in his continual
championing of the "little men," and in attempting to run the colony by government rules.

Dare thought it was a scandal that the commu-
nity was virtually in the hands of a score of
farming officers who held the small grantees in
their power and continually found ways to ruin
them and then bought them out for a song. Even
the few "gentlemen farmers" who had immi-
grated from England eventually lost their land,
possessing too little knowledge of farming and
even less capital to run their grants profitably.
Except for a small force of settlers like the
Penrods who supported Bligh to the best of their
ability, the Rum Corps maintained their hold on
every aspect of life. They monopolized the supply of convict labor, mercilessly exploited the
poor, commanded trade and fixed prices. Their
officers sat as judges in criminal court.

Having learned nothing useful about the situa-
tion, Dare and Ben hastened to the home of
Drew Stanley in hopes of finding their father.
Whenever an overnight stay in Sydney was indi-
cated, Stanley, a settler who had arrived about
the same time as Roy, opened his home to them.
Not a farmer but a businessman, Drew, an
elderly bachelor, had become fast friends with
Roy. Both were staunch supporters of Governor
Bligh. But Roy was not there.

"Father is all right, isn't he, Drew?" Ben asked anxiously of the thin, gray-haired man. They sat around the kitchen table partaking of the meal Drew insisted they eat.

"To the best of my knowledge, your father is fine, Ben. He was at Government House with Governor Bligh at the height of the revolt. I assume he is still there."

"No one is allowed in or out," complained Dare, scowling. "Is Macarthur and the Rum Corps in control?"

"Haven't you heard? Bligh's constables arrested Macarthur. He's to be tried tomorrow for sedition."

"Ha!" laughed Dare disparagingly. "You and I both know the charge will never stick. His own men sit as judges on the court."

"What about the Judge Advocate? He's appointed by the governor, isn't he?" Ben ventured.

Before Drew could form an answer the door opened and Roy walked wearily into the room. "Father!" Dare exclaimed, leaping to his feet. "Sit down, you look exhausted. Can you tell us what's happening?"

"Dare, Ben, I'm glad you've come. The governor needs all the support he can get," Roy said as he sank into a chair.

"But I heard the governor had Macarthur arrested and he's to be tried for sedition," Ben contended.

"I wish it were that simple," sighed Roy, gratefully accepting the cup of tea set before him.

"Can you tell us what's taking place at Government House, Father?" Dare persisted.

"The Judge Advocate just resigned. He won't preside at Macarthur's trial tomorrow."

"Why would he do that?" Dare questioned.

"He was forced into it," revealed Roy, his voice laced with contempt. "It seems he owes a large debt to Macarthur. It was either resign or be ruined. Six military cronies of Macarthur's will preside at the trial."

A tense silence ensued, while each contemplated the outcome of the trial, if one could call such a travesty of justice a trial.

Just as the Penrods predicted, Macarthur's trial the next day proved nothing but a farce. The courtroom was so crowded they were forced to stand against one wall packed with curious onlookers. The verdict, which came almost immediately after testimony was heard, was in favor of Macarthur. He was released by the six military judges. Highly incensed, Bligh promptly had him arrested again by his constables, and pandemonium broke loose in the courthouse as well as in the streets among the people unable to find room inside. A second trial was ordered the next day.

Against Bligh's vigorous protests, Macarthur was again ordered freed. It was a slap in the face to Governor Bligh, who was powerless to retaliate further. No one was more disgusted than the Penrods. They remained in Sydney only long enough to speak with the governor before returning to the Hawkesbury. Dare in particular had reason to talk to Bligh. He hoped for a private audience for he wasn't ready to divulge his plans to his family. Two days elapsed before his wish was granted.

One morning while Ben and Roy were tending to some last-minute purchases, Dare was summoned to Government House for a meeting with

Bligh. After the fiasco of the past week the governor had retreated into the privacy of his own quarters, seeing virtually no one but close friends. Dare's knock was answered by Governor Bligh's daughter, Bess. Dare was well-known to the comely young woman, who promptly invited him inside. She showed him directly to her father's study though her sultry eyes hinted that she would welcome him later in the privacy of her room. Though Dare had sampled Bess's ample charms often enough in the past, they held little appeal for him now. A red-haired Irish lass had spoiled him for other women.

An hour later Dare left Government House, his face wreathed in smiles. Somehow he had convinced Bligh that Casey O'Cain had been falsely convicted and transported. Despite all the governor's problems, he promised to look into the case and remit her sentence if it was warranted. Murder was a serious crime, but if it had indeed been accidental and Casey was only defending her honor, then it was within the governor's power to grant a full pardon. Elated, Dare left in a state of euphoria, anxious to return to the Hawkesbury and tell Casey the good news.

Nearly a week after the Penrods left their Hawkesbury River farm, their return was heralded by a totally unexpected turn of events. Meg and Martha were both on hand to greet them. Dare thought little of Casey's absence until Roy said, "We're starved, Martha, ask Casey to prepare something to tide us over till supper."

"I'll fix it myself, sir," Martha offered, shifting her gaze to her feet.

"Is Casey ill?" Dare questioned sharply, sensing something amiss. "Where is she?"

"No . . . she's not sick," Martha hedged, fidgeting with her apron strings. Abruptly she turned to leave.

"Martha, wait!" The sharpness of Dare's voice brought an instant halt to Martha's steps. "What's the matter with Casey?"

"If something is wrong you'd better tell us, Martha," Roy added with authority.

"She didn't do it, sir! Not Casey! She's not a thief!" wailed Martha miserably, leaving them all bewildered.

"What in the hell are you blubbering about?" thundered Roy, growing impatient.

"You'll learn nothing from that twit," Meg sneered. "So I'll tell you. Casey is not only a murderess but a thief. She stole jewels and money from the strongbox in the study and then promptly disappeared."

"Casey? Disappeared?" Dare repeated stupidly. "I . . . I don't understand."

"Are you certain of this, Meg?" Roy questioned brusquely. "Couldn't one of the convicts have stolen the valuables?" He would have sworn Casey was honest despite her lurid past.

"Not likely," scoffed Meg. "Why would she leave so abruptly if she isn't the guilty party? There's no logical explanation but the one I offered. She certainly was treated well by the family." She paused, sliding an accusatory glance in Dare's direction. "Ask Martha, she can verify the fact that the strongbox was found broken into right after Casey left."

"Is that true, Martha?" Roy asked, frowning.

"I . . . yes, the strongbox had been broken into and the contents looted," admitted Martha reluctantly. It was obvious Martha was taking

Casey's leaving hard. "But that doesn't prove she—"

"She's guilty," crowed Meg, gaining immense satisfaction from Dare's stricken face. "Everything was left just as we found it in the study."

"When did all this happen, Meg?" Roy asked, still trying to sort out the facts.

"The same day Dare and Ben left for Sydney."

"That soon?" croaked Dare, recalling vividly the night of extraordinary passion they had shared. She had lost her virginity to him, but he had lost more than that. As much as he hated to admit it, he had lost his heart. The feeling was so new to him he still couldn't come to grips with it.

"I'm going to check the study," Roy announced, disappearing into the house.

"I'll go with you, Father," offered Ben.

Dare chose to remain in hopes of coaxing more information from Martha or Meg. "Do either of you have any idea where Casey went?" he asked, his gray eyes hard as cement.

"No," Martha shook her head. "I . . . I begged her not to go but she said she had to. Why, Dare? Why would Casey do such a thing?"

"I truly don't know, Martha, but I fully intend to find out."

"I'll tell you what I think," offered Meg complacently. "She wanted to return to Ireland. The jewels and money will buy her passage. Some unscrupulous captain will gladly accommodate her without asking questions. She probably made her way to Sydney and boarded the first ship bound for England."

Dare hated to admit it but Meg's theory made sense. Given Sydney's unsettled atmosphere this past week, Casey could easily have slipped unno-

ticed into the city and departed on one of the
supply ships anchored in the harbor.

"Why was she so eager to return to Ireland?"
he asked curiously.

"A man, why else?" lied Meg, carefully averting her eyes. "She mentioned someone once or
twice in conversation. Someone she cared
about."

Jealousy twisted through Dare's gut like an evil
serpent. "Do you agree with Meg, Martha?" he
asked, turning his attention to the older woman.

"I . . . I don't . . ." She hesitated thoughtfully.
"Well, I did hear Casey mention a man named
Tim a few times. She hinted he was someone she
might have married had things turned out differently. But I got the impression he was no longer
in Ireland." When Dare made no reply, merely
staring off into space, she asked, "Can I leave
now, Dare? I know you must be hungry."

Dare nodded distractedly and Martha scurried
off. Then he turned to join Roy and Ben in the
study, leaving a fuming Meg in his wake. She had
hoped he would turn to her immediately for
comfort but realized it would take time for him
to adjust to his loss. She had no idea he would be
so affected by Casey's sudden disappearance.
Did he care so much?

"Come in, Dare," Roy invited when he saw his
son standing in the doorway. He was poring over
the meager contents of the strongbox, and Dare
walked over to join Ben who stood nearby.

"Jesus!" Dare cursed angrily. "She didn't leave
much, did she?"

"Every valuable piece of your mother's jewelry
is missing," concurred Roy, stifling the sudden
spurt of anger. "Luckily I transferred all the cash

save for a few coins to another strongbox hidden in my room just before I left for Sydney. If I hadn't they would be gone, too."

"Then it's true," Dare muttered bleakly. "Casey is a thief."

"I don't believe it!" Ben exploded hotly. "I don't give a damn about the evidence. Casey isn't a thief. There's got to be some other explanation for all this."

"Will you notify the authorities, Father?" Dare asked.

"I should," Roy answered, staring blankly at the empty box.

"Don't," Dare advised. "At least not until I can find Casey and make some sense out of all this. Please, Father."

Roy searched Dare's face, translating accurately his dejection as well as deep concern. Was there something between Dare and Casey he wasn't aware of? he wondered curiously. Never had he seen Dare so upset over a woman. Intuitively he knew this was no time to question his son, for his emotions were too raw to expose.

"All right, Dare," Roy agreed. "Find Casey. I'd like nothing better than for you to prove her innocent. Truth to tell, I've grown quite fond of the girl."

"I'll help," Ben offered eagerly.

"No, Ben, I'm sorry," Dare refused. "This is something I . . . have to do myself."

"But where will you start? You haven't an inkling where she went. If she's hiding in the bush you'll never find her. What puzzles me is why Casey took the valuables if she intends to hide out in the bush. What good will they do her?"

"Precisely my thinking," Dare replied tightly. "Meg hinted she purchased passage to Ireland."

"But you don't believe that," Ben suggested astutely.

"No. I have every reason to believe Casey was happy here. I think she's still in the colony. And if she is, I'll find her. There's more involved here than meets the eye."

"How will you go about finding her?"

"First thing tomorrow I'm going to see Robin. He and Casey became quite friendly. Perhaps he knows something we don't."

Then Meg called them to eat and no more was said on the subject. But the ensuing silence suggested each man had his own opinion as to what made Casey O'Cain leave Penrod station without a word or explanation.

CHAPTER EIGHT

In a daze Casey clung to Culong as he melted into the bush, moving as silently as a wraith. She dared not look back, fearful lest the soldiers were hard on their heels. But nothing seemed to deter Culong who slipped from tree to tree, keeping well away from the beaten path leading through the tall grass and wattle. Only the chattering magpies broke the stillness. Once they surprised several gray kangaroos foraging on the rich foliage, sending them hopping for cover.

Still exhausted from her earlier trek to Robin's house, Casey found the going difficult. The thin soles of her inadequate shoes had nearly worn through, causing her to wince each time she stepped on a stone or thorny branch. Still she plunged on, her eyes glued to Culong's broad back. She was grateful to the native for carrying her swag, otherwise she would have disposed of it long ago.

Darkness settled abruptly, plunging the land into instant blackness. Casey could no longer see Culong ahead of her and panic seized her until he spoke softly in her ear. "Not far now. Give me your hand."

Nearly melting in relief, Casey offered her hand so he might lead her as one would a child. Shortly they came upon a clearing where several grass huts were clustered together for mutual protection. A huge fire burned in the center of the cluster, and Culong led Casey unerringly to a hut a little ways back from the others.

She hesitated briefly before the entrance until Culong urged her forward by tugging on her hand. By the light of a small fire inside the hut Casey saw Tim lying white and motionless on a pallet, and all reticence fled. "Tim!" she cried, dropping to her knees beside him. "Is he dead?"

"Much sick but not dead," Culong replied. While Casey fussed over Tim, Culong spoke softly to the woman who Casey had failed to notice sitting in the shadows. At Culong's urging she rose somewhat reluctantly to stand before Casey.

"This is Mantua," he said as Casey gazed at the small, shy woman whose skin shone like polished ebony in the firelight. "Mantua speaks no English. Mantua says your man will survive with much care and medicine she has prepared."

"Thank you, Mantua," Casey said sincerely. "I'm grateful for your help."

Mantua spoke to her brother in a language Casey did not understand, then waited for Culong to translate. "Mantua asks if this is your man?"

"Tim is . . . a good friend," Casey replied quickly. "He is like a brother to me."

Culong translated for his sister's benefit, waited for her soft reply, then said, "Mantua likes you and will make your brother well. The bullet is gone from his flesh and already his fever is less. You rest now. Mantua will prepare food for you."

Two days later Tim regained consciousness. Though still weak, he knew Casey immediately. During those two days Casey rarely left his side, taking her meals in the small hut and communicating with Mantua through Culong. Once she asked Culong if he thought they would be found by the troopers.

"In time they will think to look here," Culong said after much deliberation. "But do not fear, my people will keep watch. If come, we hide you."

"Casey." Casey whirled, uttering a cry of joy when she saw Tim awake and alert. His eyes were huge in his thin face as they hungrily followed her every movement.

"Tim! Thank God you're awake. Mantua said she'd make you well."

"Mantua?" croaked Tim. "Where am I?"

"Do you remember nothing?"

"Nothing after your friend Robin brought me to his house."

Taking a deep breath, Casey proceeded to tell Tim all that had taken place since he left Penrod station.

"Christ, lass, I'm sorry I've put you through this hell," Tim lamented. "And your friend Robin. If the authorities have him as you suspect, he's risked much to help us. I'm not worth it, Casey. You both have suffered excessively on my account. Robin could be hung for his part in this."

A distressed cry escaped Casey's lips. "Oh, Tim, surely not!"

"Don't cry, lass. What is this man to you?"

"A friend, Tim, just a friend. But a very good

one who risked all he holds dear for me. I feel so
guilty. Oh, Tim, what's to become of us?"

"I'll take care of you, Casey, never fear," Tim
promised tightly. "If I wasn't so damn weak——"

"You'll regain your strength soon enough.
Mantua is an excellent doctor."

"Mantua?"

"Culong's sister. She's the tribe's medicine
woman. They've all been very good to us. If
trouble comes they'll——"

As if on cue, Culong burst into the hut.
"Troopers come," he grunted excitedly. "We go
now."

"But Tim is in no condition to travel," Casey
protested.

"I'll manage," Tim groaned as Culong helped
him to his feet. "Damn this blasted weakness."
Then there was no time for words as they were
met at the door by another tribesman who supported Tim from the other side.

Mantua materialized out of nowhere to thrust
the swag into Casey's hands, the same one she
arrived with but newly replenished with fresh
supplies. She indicated another small bag, which
Casey discovered held a jar of medicine for Tim
as well as leaves and moss to be used as bandages.
Casey thanked her and hurried after Culong.

It took less than an hour to reach the place of
concealment Culong had chosen. Nestled in the
foothills of the Blue Mountains, the place seemed
perfect. It was a cave carved in the side of a hill.
The small opening was easily concealed by brush
and inside the ground was smooth and dry. The
space proved small and confining, but Casey
could stand without too much difficulty within
the single chamber which appeared to have but
one outlet. By the time Tim was stretched out on

a blanket, his meager strength was depleted and he fell immediately into a deep sleep.

"Will you return for us after the troopers leave, Culong?" Casey asked anxiously as the black man prepared to leave.

"Chief say it better you not come back to village," Culong said regretfully. "Troopers bring much trouble to our people. Your man soon well, no more need help."

"I . . . I understand, Culong," Casey replied, her voice catching on a sob. "I'm grateful for the help you and Mantua have given us. We'll manage."

To her chagrin Casey learned during the following days that the troopers hadn't given up their search for her and Tim. Cowering in the dank darkness of the cave, she heard sounds indicating that horsemen roamed at will throughout the area, keeping her confined to the small chamber. Only when the jerked beef, dried fruit and water Mantua thoughtfully provided in the swag was nearly gone did Casey venture from her safe haven. By that time Tim was well on the road to recovery.

Dare approached Robin's small house with a sense of foreboding he failed to understand. He saw at a glance that the convict laborers were performing their duties as usual, but neither Robin or Culong were in sight, which wasn't unusual for they could be anywhere on the thirty acres.

It was still very early morning but Dare had been so eager to question Robin about Casey he left at first light. Perhaps he'd even find Casey safe and sound with Robin, he reflected hopefully. However, he couldn't shake the vague feeling of unrest riding him, or the warning voice whispering in his head. With sinking heart Dare knew something indeed was amiss when the stout figure of a man he recognized but did not know personally appeared at the door. He knew the man as a speculator who had recently turned up in Parramatta and a friend of John Macarthur. Though they had never been formally introduced, Dare knew his name.

"What are you doing here, Lynch?" he asked gruffly. "Where is Robin Fletcher?"

Nate Lynch, a short, rotund, sly-faced man of middle years, wore his thin gray hair carefully arranged to conceal a balding spot atop his head. A speculator newly arrived in New South Wales, he quickly aligned himself with John Macarthur and the Rum Corps. Having met Macarthur in 1801 when the captain had been sent to England to face a court-martial for dueling his own senior officer, William Paterson, Lynch was convinced that riches existed for the opportunist in New South Wales.

After Macarthur resigned his commission and returned to the colony with plans to develop land and sheep farming, Lynch followed soon afterwards, leaving his wife behind but taking her fortune with him. Since his arrival he had been instrumental in forcing small land owners from their farms for the benefit of John Macarthur and men of the same ilk. Now, as he faced the storm-clouded gray eyes of Dare Penrod, he wondered if Macarthur hadn't met his match.

"Dare Penrod, isn't it?" Lynch asked, extending a hand which Dare blatantly ignored. "We haven't formally met, but I am Nate Lynch."

"I know all about you, Lynch," Dare sneered,

"and Australia would be better off without men like you and Macarthur. I asked what you are doing here on Robin Fletcher's property."

"I take it you haven't heard," Lynch said cryptically.

"Heard what? Has something happened to Robin?"

"You could say that. He's in jail in Parramatta. Sergeant Grimes brought him in nearly a week ago."

Astonishment touched Dare's bronzed face. What had happened? Everything had been well a week ago when he last saw his friend. Then a sudden, unbidden thought turned him to ice. Did any of this have to do with Casey's abrupt disappearance? "What has he done?" Dare asked. "There must be some mistake."

"The only mistake was made by Robin Fletcher," Lynch contended, openly contemptuous. "He helped an escaped convict."

"Who? I don't believe it!"

"Believe what you will, but the convict is a particularly violent man sent north to work the coal mines. He was wounded while escaping and somehow made his way here. Your friend treated his wound and then gave him sanctuary. You'll have to ask Sergeant Grimes for the details, for I know little more than what I've told you."

"I intend to do just that," Dare replied tightly, "as soon as you tell me what you're doing here."

"Someone has to see to the laborers and the farm," Lynch explained with a hint of sarcasm. "At least until Fletcher is brought to trial. Once he's convicted he'll lose his land, of course. Perhaps even his freedom. I'm only here to preserve his property for the crown."

"For Macarthur, you mean," spat Dare.

Lynch shrugged eloquently. "I'm but following orders. I suggest you talk to Sergeant Grimes. He's the one who made the arrest."

Deciding there was little more to be gained from talking to the obstinate Nate Lynch, Dare wheeled his mount and headed for Parramatta. Not only did he have Casey to fret over but Robin as well. He made but one stop on the way—to inform Ben and his father about Robin and the shocking turn of events.

"I demand you release Robin Fletcher, Sergeant Grimes," Dare insisted when he faced the trooper in his office later that day.

"You have no authority to issue orders, Mr. Penrod," Grimes returned shortly. "Especially in regard to Fletcher. Unless, of course," he hinted slyly, "you're involved in some way. The escaped convict was hidden first on your property, and if you weren't in Sydney at the time I'd be inclined to investigate your part in all this."

"What! What do you mean? Are you telling me the convict was found on Penrod land?"

"Exactly. But tell me, Penrod," Grimes smirked knowingly, "is one of your servants missing? Did you return from Sydney to find the convict, Casey O'Cain, missing along with your valuables?"

Dismayed, Dare struggled to maintain control of his emotions. How did Grimes know that Casey had run off? And what was her connection with the escaped convict? "If you know something about Casey, Grimes, you'd better tell me. Obviously this involves my family."

Sergeant Grimes stared at Dare, considering

his request. Suddenly coming to a decision, he grunted and nodded. "The man's name is Timothy O'Malley. A bad one; he continually disregarded authority and earned severe discipline. He was sent to the coal mines and escaped, making it all the way to your farm. I don't know if it was prearranged or what, but Casey O'Cain hid him until Robin Fletcher came for him. The two of them are guilty of harboring an escaped convict, which, as you are well aware, is a capital offense."

"Where is Casey now? What have you done with her?" Dare blazed. "Is she in jail?"

"Unfortunately the little slut got away," Grimes said. "So did her man, O'Malley. But we got Fletcher."

Dare winced when Grimes referred to O'Malley as Casey's man. "How do you know all this?" Though Casey was still missing, he was vastly relieved she wasn't at the mercy of a man like Grimes.

Grimes lowered his gaze, deftly evading Dare's question. "I have my ways," he hedged. "As for Fletcher, I had enough proof to put him behind bars."

"But you don't have Timothy O'Malley."

"We'll have him soon enough," came Grimes's surly reply. "As well as the girl. My men have orders to keep searching till they find them. If need be, Lieutenant Potter will send extra troopers to aid in the search."

"I want to see Robin," Dare said, his voice implacable. "I'm not completely convinced that he is guilty of anything. I'd like to question him myself."

"Oh, he's guilty, all right. So is the girl. There's

a witness. But I see no harm in a short visit with the prisoner. Mayhap you can get more out of him than I did."

A few minutes later Dare was ushered into the small building that served as a jail. The door closed behind him and he looked with distaste around the dim room that boasted not one amenity save for a cot and two buckets in the corner. One for fresh water and the other for waste.

"Dare! Thank God!"

When Dare's eyes adjusted to the meager light, he saw Robin sitting on the cot, his shoulders slumped in utter dejection.

"Robin, what's this all about?" he asked as Robin rose to his feet and the two friends embraced. "I find what Sergeant Grimes told me hard to swallow. Do you know what happened to Casey?"

"One thing at a time, Dare," Robin replied. "How much did Grimes tell you?"

"Only that you and Casey are accused of helping an escaped convict and that only you were caught. What in the hell is going on, Robin? Surely there is no truth in the charge."

"It's true, Dare, all of it," Robin admitted, lowering his voice so no one beyond the room could hear. Dare's shocked gasp caused him to add, "But wait and hear me out before you pass judgment.

"Timothy O'Malley is a man Casey knew from Ireland. He took part in the revolt against the crown, was tried, found guilty and transported. He couldn't cope with the coal mines and escaped. By an odd coincidence he made his way

here despite being badly wounded, and Casey
came upon him by accident. He was a friend, for
God's sake, she couldn't leave him to die or turn
him in!"

"Go on, Robin," Dare prodded, his face grim
and unyielding. "Tell me why Casey chose not to
tell either me or Father about this . . . friend."

"I think she was afraid you'd turn him in."

"This man must mean a lot to her," Dare
muttered.

"From what I gather they grew up together.
She did what she thought best," Robin continued. "Casey asked me to help because she knew
that I, being an emancipist, would be sympathet-
ic to Tim's plight. Of course, I agreed."

"Of course," Dare repeated dryly. "How did
the authorities find out? According to Grimes
there's a witness."

"Damned if I know," Robin said. "Casey
hinted she knew who the witness was, but before
she could reveal the name, Culong arrived to tell
us that troopers were only minutes away."

"Why did Casey steal my mother's jewelry?"
Dare asked.

"I don't think she did. It doesn't make sense.
And she never mentioned anything like that to
me. I'm afraid you'll have to ask Casey, though I
doubt she'll know what you're talking about."

"I will if I find her. Quickly, Robin, where is
she?"

"I want to tell you, Dare, because you're the
only one who can help her now. Will you, Dare?
Will you help Casey," Robin pleaded desperately.

"Christ, Robin, do you think I want to see

Casey punished for her part in this? I . . . I care for her," Dare admitted. "I don't want anything to happen to her."

Satisfied, Robin nodded. "Culong took her and O'Malley to his village. You know where it is. O'Malley was terribly ill and Mantua is caring for him. But it won't be long before the troopers think to look there. Go, Dare, find her. I'm worried."

"I intend to do just that, Robin, but I can't leave you here like this. No telling what they'll do to you once they get you in Sydney. I've got to get you out of here."

"Dare, listen to me. Nothing is going to happen. Not yet, anyway. There's still too much turmoil in Sydney, what with the revolt and all, for anyone to pay much attention to me. Macarthur is occupied with Governor Bligh, and the Rum Corps is busy keeping peace. It will be a while before they get around to me."

"Ben and I could easily break you out of here," Dare persisted.

"I won't have you involved more than you already are," insisted Robin. "You'll do us both a favor by taking care of Casey."

"You care for her, don't you, Robin?"

Robin hesitated. Of course he cared for Casey, but obviously so did Dare. And from what he had observed of the two of them together, Dare's feelings were reciprocated. At length he said, "Casey is my friend. I'll admit I . . . care for her but I fear friendship is all she'll settle for where I'm concerned. Can I count on you, Dare, to keep her safe, as well as see to that friend of hers?"

"Of course, Robin, but I still—"

"Time is up," interrupted the guard who had

opened the door of the jail for Dare and waited outside according to the Sergeant's orders.

Dare opened his mouth to protest but Robin quickly leaped into the void. "Go, Dare. There's only one way you can help me now."

"All right, Robin," Dare reluctantly acquiesced. "But I'll find a way to help you as well as . . . see to our friends." Then he was gone, leaving Robin to wonder where it would all end.

Darkness fell like a shroud over the land by the time Dare returned home where Ben and Roy anxiously awaited.

"Did you see Robin?" Roy asked.

"Aye, I saw him," replied Dare grimly. "In jail. He's been accused of helping an escaped convict."

"Well, is it true?"

"Did you learn anything about Casey while you were in Parramatta?" Ben chimed in.

"I'll tell you all I know," Dare sighed wearily. "But first have Martha bring me something to eat, I'm famished. After I wash up I'll dine in the study where we can talk without being overheard."

"I'll go," Ben volunteered, bounding toward the kitchen.

A short time later all three men were seated comfortably while Dare wolfed down his food, speaking between mouthfuls. "The convict's name is Timothy O'Malley. He's wounded and Robin felt compelled to help him."

Perplexed, Roy said, "You'd think he'd have more sense than to risk all he owns for an escaped convict. Because of his rash action he's likely to lose everything, including his freedom."

"He did it for Casey," Dare revealed, swallowing the last bite of cold mutton and pushing his plate aside.

"Casey!" yelped Ben, jumping to his feet. "What has she to do with all this?"

Dare told Roy and Ben everything he had learned about Casey, Tim and Robin. When he mentioned the fact that someone on Penrod station knew about Timothy O'Malley and had reported it to the authorities, Ben became livid with rage.

"Who? Who would do such a thing?"

"Robin has no idea. Casey never got around to telling him. But one way or another I intend to find out."

"Why did she steal from us?" Roy asked with a hint of reproach. "What is this convict to her?"

"That's a mystery I'll solve when I find Casey," replied Dare. "Robin told me where Casey and this O'Malley bloke are hiding, and I'm going after them. I'll leave at first light."

"Then Casey wasn't taken prisoner with Robin." Ben's relief was so great he nearly collapsed in his chair.

"No, both she and her friend were given shelter by Culong's tribe in the foothills. Troopers are out searching for them, but to my knowledge they haven't been found yet."

"I'm going with you," Ben insisted. "If searchers are out it could be dangerous."

"Ben—"

"He's right, Dare," Roy concurred. "Take your brother along. I'd feel better knowing you're not alone."

"Father . . ." Dare faltered, suddenly at a loss for words. "I can't explain, but it's imperative I find Casey. I could no more leave her to the troopers than I could stop breathing. I don't know what this O'Malley bloke means to her but I certainly intend to find out."

Roy stared intently at Dare, dismayed at the spark of passion visible in the gray depths of his eyes. Somehow during the past weeks Casey had come to mean a great deal to his son. He fervently prayed that Casey returned Dare's feelings and that they could surmount the prejudice that was certain to come between them. If, that is, Dare succeeded in saving Casey from the severe punishment she had earned by aiding an escaped convict. Roy had faith in Dare's ability to overcome all adversity, but with the governor in the midst of revolt, Casey's future didn't look too promising.

Aloud, Roy said, "I understand, son, and wish you luck."

"Thanks, Father," smiled Dare, clasping his father's shoulder. "There's one other thing. Don't breathe a word of what I've just told you. We don't know yet who betrayed Casey but it could be any of the house servants or convict laborers."

On that grim note Dare sought his bed, eager for the dawn that would bring him closer to finding Casey.

From the moment Meg heard that Dare went to visit Robin in jail she had been in a quandary. Had Casey told Robin who had betrayed them, and did Robin in turn reveal her name to Dare? When she thought of Dare's implacable anger she wanted to flee, yet could not, for she had much to gain if Dare remained ignorant of her plotting.

Dare was the prize she hoped to snare for herself.
So she remained, and when Dare returned and
she wasn't summoned instantly, she knew she
was in the clear.

Ever the opportunist, Meg instinctively realized she must press her suit immediately while
Dare was still vulnerable and hurt by Casey's
unexplained departure. She had no idea Dare
knew where Casey was, let alone the fact that he
fully intended to find her.

It bothered Meg not at all that she had promised to marry Sergeant Grimes the moment she
was emancipated. Using the jewelry she stole, he
intended to buy a farm for a pittance and become
rich raising sheep like John Macarthur. With
sufficient capital he could resign from the Corps
and begin buying out small farmers and
emancipists who were slowly being driven to
bankruptcy by the Corps's practices. But Meg
cared little for Sergeant Grimes's plans, for she
had better things in mind. Dare Penrod was
twice . . . no, ten times . . . the man Grimes was,
and she intended to have only the best.

It was well after midnight when Meg, wrapped
in a cloak, stepped stealthily from her room,
gliding noiselessly through the darkened house
and up the stairs. She paused outside Dare's
door, but only for a moment. Boldly turning the
knob, she slipped inside the silent room. A
stubby candle burned on the nightstand, and
Dare lay sleeping beneath a single sheet gathered
about his waist. His upper torso shone like liquid
bronze in the flickering light, and Meg sidled
closer, clearly mesmerized by the sight. When
she reached the bed she flung aside the cloak, her
voluptuous blond loveliness flushed with long-

ing. Lifting a corner of the sheet, she slid
effortlessly into bed, snuggling into the warm
curve of his body.

Never had Dare's dreams seemed so vividly
real. The soft warm body pressed so intimately
against his hardness could belong to no one but
Casey. Did he desire her so intensely that he
conjured her up out of thin air? Living out his
fantasy to the fullest, Dare gathered the apparition in his arms.

"Ah, my love," he murmured, nuzzling her
neck. "My sweet Casey."

Meg scowled, hating being called by another
woman's name yet afraid to break the spell she
was weaving around his senses. She hoped that
once he became involved with making love he
would be unable to stop himself. Using all her
considerable skill, she drew him inexorably into
her devious trap.

Plying both hands and lips with equal dexterity, Meg enticed Dare deeper and deeper into
passion's web while he remained oblivious to all
but his driving need to possess the woman who
had somehow captured his heart. His manhood
hard and throbbing, Dare loomed large above his
dream lover, ready to plunge deep into her
welcoming warmth. Opening his eyes in order to
see the expression on her lovely features when he
possessed her fully, his vision became obscured
by a cloud of blond tresses falling upon his
pillow.

"Hurry, Dare," Meg urged, panting as she
pushed her hips upward in mute appeal.

Eager to oblige, Dare nevertheless hesitated, a
nagging suspicion nibbling at the edges of his
brain. Then suddenly it came to him that this

was no dream and the woman in his bed couldn't possibly be Casey. Not unless her hair had changed overnight from red to blond. His raging passion died and shriveled as swiftly as it was born and he reared up, fighting the pull of Meg's grasping arms.

"Bloody hell, Meg, what are you doing here?"

"Aren't you glad to see me, Dare?" she purred seductively. "I knew you'd be lonely tonight and have need of me. I'll never leave you, Dare, not like . . ." Her sentence trailed off but she had no need to utter the name for Dare to grasp her meaning.

Rolling onto his back, Dare groaned, "Get out of here, Meg."

"Don't be foolish, Dare," Meg pleaded. "I'm where I want to be, where I belong. Forget about Casey. Make love to me. I'll soon make you forget everything except what I can do for you. I'll be emancipated soon and we—"

Lurching to his feet, Dare picked up Meg's cloak from the floor and threw it at her. "Put it on and leave. What you suggest is utterly ridiculous. You knew that from the beginning. I'll admit I enjoyed our few times together but so did you. It's not as if I used you, Meg. You sought my bed willingly, nay, eagerly."

"Don't be angry with me, Dare," she implored, scrambling into her cloak when she saw the ferocious scowl darkening Dare's features. How could things have gone awry? she wondered bleakly. She had been so certain Dare would turn to her once Casey was gone. How could she have so drastically misjudged the depth of Dare's feelings for the little witch? Nothing was going the way she planned.

She was halfway out the door when a terrible suspicion penetrated Dare's brain. "You haven't told me everything, have you, Meg?" he accused with cool deliberation. "About Casey, I mean. Who really stole that jewelry?"

"I . . . I don't know what you're talking about," Meg stammered. "I've told you all I know."

"Maybe, maybe not," said Dare cryptically. "Time will tell."

"Wha . . . what do you mean?" Panic rode her like a pursuing demon.

"Nothing. Except that once I find Casey the truth will come out."

"Find Casey?" Meg stared dumbly. She hadn't counted on that.

"I'm leaving in the morning and I'll not return without Casey."

"I hear she's wanted by the authorities?" Meg ventured.

"I'll cross that bridge when I come to it. At the moment nothing matters but finding Casey."

"Why, you truly do care for her," Meg said in disbelief.

"Goodnight, Meg," Dare bit out. "By the way, I trust you'll have no problem finding employment. We no longer have need of your services. I'll explain to Father why you found it necessary to leave." Dare would have slammed the door in her face if Meg hadn't slipped into the hall at that moment.

The next morning Dare and Ben rode to the aborigine village in the foothills of the Blue Mountains. They knew its exact location because their own native tracker, Burloo, came from the same tribe. Skirting Robin's property, they plunged into the bush, traveling west until the small group of huts came into view.

Recognizing Dare and his brother, Culong came to greet them. "You know why we're here, Culong," Dare said, his tone demanding instant obedience.

Culong nodded. "Woman and her man not here. Too dangerous. Troopers come looking many times but not find."

"Where are they, Culong? Are they safe?"

"Safe, I think. Man much sick, need care. Culong take them to cave."

"Exactly where is this cave, Culong?" Dare asked anxiously. "Have you been back to check on them?"

"No go back. Troopers watch, maybe follow."

"Tell me where. I'll find them."

With much gesturing and pointing while using his limited English, Culong gave directions to the cave where he had taken Casey and Tim, then pressed additional food and medicine on them to take to the two outcasts. Because of the dense forest they would be traveling through, they left their horses in the village under Culong's care. Culong's last words as he watched them walk off were those of warning, not only regarding the troopers who still searched the area but of bush-rangers camped somewhere in the vicinity.

CHAPTER NINE

As much as Casey dreaded leaving the safety of the cave, there was no help for it. Their water was completely gone and the cache of food desperately low. Familiar sounds indicated that water was close at hand and she assumed that a stream of some sort lay nearby. Perhaps she could spear a fish with the knife in her swag, or catch a small animal in search of water. At this point even berries and roots would be welcome. She also intended to replenish their supply of firewood before the rain came. Rain was a distinct possibility. By the looks of the thick black clouds roiling overhead when she dared a glance out the cave opening, it appeared that a storm was brewing. And though her stay in New South Wales had been of short duration she knew the storms could sometimes be fierce. Especially along the Hawkesbury which was prone to flood its banks in wet years and destroy hundreds of acres of farmland.

Tim sat propped against the side of the cave, still weak but obviously recovering. He watched Casey warily as she prepared to leave their hideaway. "Casey, lass, I don't like the idea of you going out by yourself."

"I wouldn't if it wasn't necessary," she replied, searching the swag for the knife she had taken from the Penrod kitchen. "I won't be gone long, and if I'm lucky we'll have something to cook for supper."

"Casey," Tim said, his voice cracking, "I'm sorry, lass. I never intended to put you through this. You've done so much for me."

"Don't be silly, Tim," Casey scoffed. "If need be I'd do it again."

"Now we're both outcasts."

"I know," she whispered tremulously. In truth, she had thought of little else these past few days. What would become of them? No doubt they could survive in the bush, but what kind of life was that? A life without Dare, for one thing. Not that she ever expected them to have a life together.

Their nights of love had been sheer ecstasy, but had proved nothing beyond his incredible knowledge and expertise at lovemaking. Once he tired of her he'd marry Mercy McKenzie, that faceless woman she'd heard about but never seen. What did Dare think when he found her gone? she wondered distractedly. Did Robin tell him why she left or had that poor man already been beaten at the whipping post or hanged on the gallows? Her mind in a turmoil, she left the cave despite Tim's weak protests that he was strong enough to go himself. Though recovering nicely he was in no condition to tramp through the bush. One consolation was the indication that the troopers no longer combed the vicinity for them, perhaps taking their search in another direction.

Otherwise she would be more cautious about leaving their sanctuary.

Following the sound of rushing water, Casey soon found the stream, crying in delight when she spied the enchanting waterfall spilling from the rocks above into a shallow pool. Her first concern was filling the water jug, which she did, holding it so as to catch the sparkling water flowing from above. It felt so refreshing she longed to shed her clothes and immerse herself completely in the cool stream. It had been days since she'd had a bath and the prospect was too delicious to resist.

Despite the lowering clouds and distant rumble of thunder, Casey threw caution to the wind and hastily shed her clothing, wishing the sunshine would return so she might wash and dry her dress and shift before returning to the cave. But sensing that was unlikely to happen, she decided a bath would suffice.

The water beneath the cascading falls barely reached Casey's waist as she splashed happily in the wet coolness. It wasn't until a streak of lightning split the dark skies that she recalled her reason for leaving the cave, and guilt consumed her when she thought of Tim's anxiety if she failed to return in a reasonable time. And she had yet to catch their supper or gather berries or wood.

Thoroughly refreshed from her bath, Casey waded ashore to the spot where she had left her clothes, but they were gone. Had some wild animal carried them off while she bathed? A shiver of apprehension swept through her, forming a tight knot in her stomach. Though she neither saw nor heard a thing, she could feel hidden eyes watching her every move. Another quick search of the area assured her that her clothes as well as the knife she had placed beside them were indeed missing. What should she do? There was only one choice as she turned to flee the unseen menace.

Then suddenly the choice was taken out of her hands when two men stepped boldly from the cover of wattle, one of them holding her clothing in grubby hands. "Be ye looking for these, wench?"

Casey gasped, caught off guard by the two men whom she recognized instantly. Bushrangers! "Give me those!" she cried, lunging for the garments the man held just out of her reach.

"Listen to that, Bert, the little lady wants her clothes."

"Sure, wench," Bert leered owlishly. "Just as soon as me and Artie are finished with ya. Sure was thoughtful of ya to get yerself all cleaned up fer us. Though a little dirt wouldn't have bothered us none, would it, mate?" Bert guffawed, punching his friend in the ribs.

"Naw, dirt won't hurt a thing," agreed Artie, grinning with salacious intent.

"What ya doin' out here all by yerself, wench?" Bert asked, his beady eyes widening as recognition dawned. "Say, I know you. Yer the wench I chased in the bush until them 'pure merinos' came along and ruined my fun. I told ya I'd get a second chance."

"I believe yer right, Bert," Artie concurred, his eyes narrowed in concentration as he studied Casey's slim form.

Her arms wrapped protectively around her nude body, Casey searched frantically for a means of escape. She lunged to the right, only to be cut off by Bert. Swerving to the left she found her way blocked by Artie's huge bulk. "I . . . I'm not alone," she warned, hoping to discourage them.

"Do ya see anyone, mate?" Bert asked slyly.

"No one but this purty little gal," Artie replied, rolling his eyes. "Ain't had nothin' but them black aborigine in so long I nearly forgot what a white woman looks or feels like."

"Well, look yer fill, mate, for ya'll see none purtier." Suddenly, without warning, Bert lunged, capturing Casey as easily as a wounded bird.

"No!" she screamed, struggling futilely in his hurtful grasp.

"Hurry, Bert, I'm about to bust my britches I'm so horny," Artie panted, reaching out to pat Casey's buttocks.

"Keep your filthy hands off me!" Casey screeched, kicking out with her bare feet.

"Help me pull her back a ways into the bush just in case she ain't alone," grunted Bert, perspiring from his effort to quell Casey's struggles. Together they wrestled Casey into the covering of brush and wattle.

Dare and Ben penetrated the bush in silence, their eyes trained on the terrain so as not to overlook the landmarks described to them by Culong. Any cave nestled in the foothills was difficult enough to find, but locating one particular cave was nearly impossible without following specific directions.

"There's the chimney rock!" Ben pointed excitedly. "Culong said to veer right until we come to a twisted wattle. The cave should be directly behind it in the side of a hill." Dare nodded mutely, too intent upon following the signs to answer.

The twisted wattle appeared just as Culong said and two pair of gray eyes searched the surrounding hills and rocks for the small cave opening. Dare located it first. But if the bushes hadn't been pushed aside revealing the small aperture they might not have found it so easily.

"I see it!" exclaimed Dare. Luckily they had left their mounts with Culong at the aborigine village, for the going was too rough to ride through the dense forest. "Let's go, Ben. Just be careful. From the looks of things someone has either just entered or left."

Loading and priming his pistol, Dare led the way, stopping just short of the gaping entrance. "Casey," he called out, his voice reverberating in the chamber within. "If you're in there, please come out! It's Dare." No answer was forthcoming.

Inside, Tim listened to the voice urging Casey to come forward. Was it a trick? he wondered desperately. Though he had heard Casey mention Dare Penrod many times during the past days, this still could be some sort of ruse. Should he answer? He was more than a little concerned because Casey hadn't returned yet from her search for food and water. Dare Penrod might present a threat to their freedom, but he needed help if Casey was in danger as he suspected. Struggling to his feet, he started toward the cave opening just as Dare, having grown impatient, burst through.

At first Dare thought the cave was empty, until he saw the gaunt figure move from the shadows and steady himself against the wall. Intuitively aware that the man was in no condition to pose a threat, Dare barked, "Are you Timothy O'Malley?"

"Aye," Tim replied shakily.

"Where's Casey?" was Dare's next question.

"She left some time ago to fetch water and food," Tim said, shuffling forward. "I'm Tim O'Malley."

"I know," Dare acknowledged tightly. "I'm Dare Penrod."

When the light from the cave's mouth fell on Tim, Dare's mouth fell open in shock. The man's appearance indicated he had been desperately ill; the flesh hung on his large frame and his eyes glowed dully with lingering fever. "Sit down," Dare ordered gruffly, "before you fall down." Without further urging, Tim complied. "Now, tell me where I can find Casey."

"I'm not certain," Tim replied, "but if there's a stream nearby that's where you'll find her. She said something about fishing, or trapping a small animal for our supper. We've eaten nothing but dried fruit and pemmican for the past few days. Our water is gone, too. I wanted to go myself but . . . damn this weak body! I'd appreciate it, Mr. Penrod, if you'd go and find her, for she's been gone far too long."

"I'll find her, O'Malley," Dare promised grimly. "She can't have gone far."

"Mr. Penrod." Tim hesitated. "You won't hurt her, will you?"

Startled, Dare stared at the big Irishman oddly, wondering what Casey had told him about their relationship. "No, O'Malley, I won't harm Casey."

"I'll go with you," Ben offered.

"No, stay with O'Malley," Dare responded shortly. "Fetch him food and water from our swag and see that he's kept comfortable. He still has a ways to go to full recovery."

Leaving the cave, Dare followed the sound of gurgling water, hoping the storm would hold off long enough for him to find Casey and seek cover before the deluge. Damn her for not trusting him! None of this would have happened had she come to him with her problem instead of involving Robin. Somehow he would have found a way to help her friend.

A flash of lightning split the sky, followed immediately by a clap of thunder, causing Dare to increase his pace. Abruptly he came to the stream, spying the discarded water jug Casey had filled. A quick perusal of the area told him Casey was nowhere in sight. Why would she leave without the water she had come to fetch? And then he spied the dress and shift carelessly abandoned on the ground. Alarm bells rang in his head and an icy chill shook his body. A feeling deep in his bones told him something dreadful had happened in this place to Casey.

Then over the rumble of thunder came a sound that set his heart thumping in his chest. A scream. A wounded animal? No, this sound was human, followed by sounds of a struggle and yet another cry. Searching the line of wattle and brush edging the stream, Dare noticed that something had disturbed the tall grass, leaving an uneven trail. It took little skill to follow that trail into the dim forest. Employing extreme caution, he soon came upon a sight that froze the blood in his veins and stopped his breath.

Casey, nude and struggling, was being dragged

deep into the bush. Her outraged screeching provided the catalyst that released Dare's frozen feet. That and the horrifying thought of Bert touching Casey in an obscene manner.

A red haze blurred Dare's vision as he drew his pistol, loaded and primed, aimed and fired. As it happened it embedded itself in Bert's buttocks. "You bastard!" Dare roared as Bert bellowed in pain and shock.

Not waiting for Dare to reload and turn his attention to him, Artie squawked, flopped his hands in distress, and took off at a run. Instantly releasing Casey, Bert followed close behind, clutching his bleeding flesh.

Turning to Casey, Dare slipped off his coat and placed it around her quaking shoulders. "My love," his voice cracked with emotion, "what have they done to you?"

"Dare—I can't believe you're here," Casey wailed, clutching frantically at his shirt front. "Thank God you arrived before those men . . . before they—"

Gathering her in his arms, he crooned, "It's all over, love, I'm here now. I won't let them hurt you."

Around them the wind howled through the trees and the downpour that had threatened all day unleashed with fury. But to the man and woman kneeling in the dirt there was no storm, no rain; nothing existed but the two of them wrapped in a cocoon that allowed no interference.

"Casey, if anything had happened to you I don't know what I'd have done."

Their eyes met, and clung, Dare's mute appeal answered in the emerald green pools staring back at him. The look he returned was soft and gentle, almost a caress. As if his body thirsted for hers, he drank greedily of the vision of her. Dare could no more halt what happened next than he could stop breathing.

Unmindful of the raging elements, he began raining kisses on her cheeks and mouth, her throat, the sensitive spot where her neck met her shoulders. The rain pounded, keeping time with Casey's heart as he continued plying her with exquisitely tender kisses, becoming more frantic at the thought of nearly losing her.

Their mouths came together in dazzling passion, intensified by the thrill of danger and the heightening storm. Casey trembled, not in fear but from intense longing.

"What if I lost you?" Dare groaned, the thought instantly sobering him.

Her answer was lost on the wail of the wind. Except for the sounds of falling rain and roaring thunder, they were sealed in a perilously sensual world where nothing existed but the two of them. With a flash of lightning cutting across the sky, the realization came to Dare that he wanted this woman. Desperately. Not just for a little while, but forever.

Every nerve ending seemed to come alive as his skillful hands teased and touched and his mouth burnt into hers like a hot brand, naming her his for all time. His kiss probed the depths of her mouth, demanding, dominating, delighting. One hand cupped her soft breast, catching the nipple between his fingers, stroking it into taut promise.

His name was warm on her tongue and his need became hers as with a will of their own her fingers worked frantically at the buttons on his wet shirt, pulling it from his upper body and flinging it in the mud. For a moment confusion dulled his response, but Casey's murmured pleas soon released him from his stupor.

"Casey, love, are you sure? You've been through so much."

"Dare, please, I . . . I need you to cleanse the loathsome touch of those . . . those bushrangers from my body. Please love me."

Casey neither felt nor heard the elements raging around them as Dare's warm lips caressed her open ones, claiming the hot, moist depths as his tongue slipped inside, darting, teasing, promising, stroking the innermost reaches. She gasped at the sensation. Then he left her mouth to begin a foray of her upper body, lingering maddeningly at her nipples, lapping up the raindrops that gathered in rivulets in the valley between her breasts.

His caresses were exquisite torture and she urged him to continue, telling him of her need, moaning his name over and over. Dare responded by shrugging out of his remaining clothes and renewing his exciting stroking until Casey throbbed with white-hot desire.

There was not an inch of her body that did not yield to the delicious torment of his touch, not a corner of her soul that did not welcome him with overwhelming joy. His caresses trailed along her inner thigh, and she shivered beneath his probing fingers. Unmindful of the wet ground beneath them, they sank to the spongy earth as with one accord.

He was kissing her all over, moving slowly down her body until his tongue flicked her navel, moving lower until his lips brushed her soft thighs. Tantalizing fingertips stroked the insides of her thighs, spreading them apart as his questing tongue moved closer, closer. . . . Casey gasped as he grasped her spread thighs, pulling her to his seeking lips. She trembled at the warm moistness of his mouth caressing, stroking, her breath coming in painful pants. Then his tongue was a hot, wet blade driving deep in her depths and she groaned, clasping the back of his head and pulling him still deeper. And then he freed her in a burst of dazzling lightning that rivaled the display overhead.

And when he finished with her he slid up to kiss her mouth. She could taste the essence of her on his lips and it excited her all over again. Then suddenly they were combatants rather than lovers, each fighting for supremacy, each demanding the other's surrender. She gasped in intense pleasure at the sensation of his forcing his huge length into her, tilting her small hips up for his deeper penetration. Over and over they rolled in the wet earth, their breaths hot and ragged. The ground beneath them shook, and the air around them reverberated with the sounds of the storm and the fierceness of their loving. Then she sighed in surrender, yielding to his superior strength as she brought her legs up to clasp his hips. She could feel him throbbing deep within her and imprisoned his hips, her insides quivering, convulsing, trying to hold onto his hardness.

The rain pelted them, rivers of water ran over and under their bodies in its downward course, soaking their hair, splattering them with mud as they moved wildly together. The storm around them was no less violent than the storm within.

Like a raging torrent the tension built as rain sloshed between their driving bodies, fusing them into one. All doubts, all inhibitions were washed away as Casey urged him on with low murmurs of encouragement. His strong thrusts proclaimed his ownership in the most primitive way and she rose up greedily to meet him. Then Dare felt the power of her climax, the wild shuddering of her body, and he cried out, burying himself deep inside her, withdrawing, then plunging again as he began his own tumultuous journey.

They fell to earth with a crash, reality intruding in the form of pelting rain as sharp as needles stinging their naked flesh. Casey shivered, causing Dare to curse his lust. How could he allow his passion full rein after the harrowing experience Casey had been put through? Her clammy flesh served as a harsh reminder that they had just made love on the wet ground at the height of a fierce storm! And he had experienced the greatest pleasure he had ever known!

Swiftly he rose, gathered up his wet clothes, and searched frantically for a place of refuge to weather the storm. He spied what he was looking for in the form of a narrow ledge with an overhang that promised a modicum of shelter. Scooping Casey up in his arms, he sprinted the few yards and scooted them both under the protective cover, the earth warm and dry beneath them.

"I'm sorry, love," Dare whispered in her ear. I shouldn't have made love to you in the pouring rain, but I couldn't control myself. I'll never forgive myself if you fall ill because of my lust. I don't know what I was thinking of."

"Don't blame yourself, Dare." Casey smiled sheepishly. "I wanted you just as fiercely."

His answer was lost in a loud clap of thunder, but Casey was content to settle against the curve of his body and soak up their combined heat. She roused herself to murmur, "I'm glad you found me, Dare."

After that she must have dozed for she awoke a short time later to the thrill of Dare's hands stroking and touching her sensitive flesh. His eyes, soothing as warm liquid, flowed down her trembling frame, over curves and planes that ached with renewed ardor from his sensuous touch.

"You're perfect," he murmured. "Every inch of you is pure poetry." He placed his hands on her shoulders, then leisurely moved them down to grasp her hands, their bodies fusing together.

"You're beautiful, too," Casey whispered, running her hands down his muscled length, stroking his massive chest, testing the dark hair there, following the thin line until it was lost in the dark forest below.

Dare gasped, his eyes glazing over. "Men aren't beautiful."

"You are," she teased, her hands suddenly still.

"I'm glad I please you."

"You do. I can't describe how good you make me feel. I wish—"

"What do you wish, love?"

"That you'd make love to me again," she improvised. It would be presumptuous of her to voice her fervent wish that she and Dare might be together like this for always. Not only was she a convict with many years left to serve, she was also wanted for aiding an escapee from the coal mines. Her position placed her outside of Dare's reach.

"I can deny you nothing," Dare teased, drawing her into the warmth of his arms.

The driving rain soaked the earth beyond their snug haven, lightning split the sky, and thunder echoed off the hills rising above them, but the lovers heard nothing but the beat of their hearts, saw nothing but naked desire reflected in each other's eyes.

His mouth was on hers again, his tongue taking its softness at the same time his manhood took her sheath, the first heat of their coming together already slaked on the wet ground in the driving rain. With slow, wonderful abandon their bodies met and meshed, gradually building to a wild crescendo. It was like nothing Casey had ever known. Deliberately pacing himself, Dare waited until he felt her first tremors before unleashing his own passion. Together they surmounted the swirling black clouds to soar far above the place where mere mortals dwell, floating gently back to earth on the wings of euphoria.

"Casey."

"Ummm . . ."

"Why didn't you trust me enough to tell me about O'Malley?"

"I . . . I was afraid," Casey admitted. "Your family are strict upholders of the law. I couldn't take the chance that one of you might turn Tim in."

"Just what does O'Malley mean to you, love? I understand you knew him in Ireland. Do . . . do you love him?"

"Love?" Casey repeated thoughtfully. "I suppose I do love Tim." Her words brought an instant scowl to Dare's features and a coldness to his gray eyes. "I've known him all my life and we probably would have married and done well together had . . . things turned out differently. But now . . ." Her words trailed off.

"Now?" Dare prompted hopefully.

"I'm glad we never married. Tim is more like a brother to me than a lover."

Outside their snug haven the storm abated, the rain slackened to a light drizzle. But none of that mattered to Dare as Casey's words brought a ray of sunshine into his dismal existence. A brother! How sweet the sound. She loved O'Malley like a brother! What better time to tell her what was in his heart.

"Casey, love, there's something—"

"Dare! Casey! Where are you?"

"Bloody hell!" cursed Dare, hastily shrugging into his damp pants. "Of all times for Ben to come looking for us. I've been gone so long he probably became anxious, especially since we failed to return after the rain stopped."

"Ben is here? Oh, Dare, I can't let him see me like this."

"I'll take care of it, love. Stay here. I'll find Ben and send him back to the cave and then retrieve your clothes. They'll be soaked but better than nothing."

Scrambling from beneath the overhang where they had weathered the storm, Dare jammed on his boots, pulled on his shirt and then stooped to drape his jacket over Casey's nude form. He walked out to meet Ben who came rushing frantically through the brush waving his pistol in the air.

"Put that damn thing away, Ben," Dare snapped as he stood waiting for his brother. "I thought I told you to stay with O'Malley."

"Damn it all, Dare, when you didn't return I naturally assumed the worst. I couldn't wait until the storm abated so I could look for you. Where is Casey?" he asked, surprised to find Dare alone. Abruptly his gray eyes filled with panic. "You found her, didn't you?"

"Casey is safe, little brother," Dare assured him. "We sought shelter from the storm and would have returned soon. Go back, Ben, we'll follow shortly."

"Something happened, didn't it, Dare?" Ben asked suspiciously, noting the condition of Dare's clothing. "Casey is all right, isn't she?"

"For God's sake, Ben, I told you Casey is safe. Something did happen and I'll tell you about it later. Go back to the cave before the skies open up again and you'll be as drenched as I am."

Aware of the strange undercurrent in Dare's voice, yet at a loss to understand, Ben turned to retrace his steps back to the cave where Tim anxiously awaited word of Casey. In the meantime Dare found Casey's clothes on the creekbank and made his way back to their skimpy shelter. Upon his return he was so quiet and thoughtful that Casey assumed he regretted having made love to her. Rather than hear him voice those very words, she chose not to question him, busying herself instead with wringing the excess water from her dress and shift before donning them.

"Are you ready, love?" Dare finally asked as if aware of her presence for the first time.

"As ready as I'll ever be." Casey sighed, frowning at her wet and rumpled clothing. Vaguely she wondered why he insisted on calling her his love when nothing could be farther from the truth.

"Then let's go."

They stopped briefly to retrieve the water jug Casey had left by the stream and then continued to the cave. From his joyous welcome it was obvious that Tim was vastly relieved to see Casey as he enfolded her in a bear hug that brought a furious scowl to Dare's face.

"Thank God," Tim breathed. "Ben and I thought something terrible had happened to you. You're soaking wet, lass."

"It's raining," Casey reminded him, gently disengaging herself from his arms.

For the first time Tim became aware of more than Casey's wet clothes. Her red hair was matted and tangled and there were leaves and small twigs snarled amidst its thick strands. Scratches covered her face and arms and a purple bruise discolored her left temple. Outrage filled Tim's heart. An outrage directed primarily at Dare, for he knew of nowhere else to place the blame.

"Sweet Jesus, Penrod, what have you done to her?" he challenged hotly. His huge fists clenched in barely suppressed rage and he would have swung at Dare had he the strength.

"Tim, Dare did nothing!" Casey defended vigorously. "He saved my life."

"Saved your . . . What happened, Dare?" Ben jumped in.

"Remember those bushrangers who attacked Father when he was bringing Casey and Martha to the farm?"

Ben nodded, his eyes widening. "Is that the reason Casey failed to return to the cave earlier?"

he asked, his voice trembling with anger. "Those bastards! Did they hurt you, Casey?"

"Two of them stumbled upon me while I was . . . drawing water." She refrained from telling them she had been bathing and caught naked. "They dragged me into the bush and . . . and . . ."

"Jesus! I'll kill them!" Tim roared in a voice loud enough to raise the dead.

"No, Tim, you don't understand," Casey added quickly. "Dare arrived in time. They didn't . . . hurt me. Except for a few scratches and bruises, I'm unharmed."

Both men swung their gaze to Dare, waiting for him to corroborate Casey's story. "I managed to wound one man and would have killed him if rage hadn't spoiled my aim. Casey said I got to her in time and I believe her."

"Then what in the hell took you so long to get back?" Tim scowled furiously.

"I . . ." Casey hesitated, dropping her eyes and leaving it to Dare to explain in any way he saw fit.

"By that time the rain was coming down so hard I sought shelter for us rather than drag Casey all the way back here. We were preparing to leave when Ben found us."

While Dare spoke, Casey moved to the center of the cave where Ben had started a fire. He had gathered wood before the rain began and set some meat on sticks to cook. She knelt before the small blaze, spreading out her skirts to dry, sniffing the mouthwatering aroma of sizzling fat.

Evidently Dare's explanation sufficed, for soon all three men joined her around the fire, waiting for the meat to cook.

"I killed a wallaby," Ben said proudly, patting

the boomerang all Australians carried. It was an effective weapon when used correctly.

While they relaxed around the fire, Ben kept glancing curiously from Dare to Casey. He still wasn't completely satisfied with Dare's explanation of why they hadn't returned to the cave sooner. And Casey had not confirmed his rather condensed telling.

Sensing Ben's confusion, Casey jumped into the rather tense void. "I'll make damper to go with the meat," she offered, rummaging in the swag Ben had set next to the fire. Along with boiled, salted beef, damper was a mainstay of hunters, explorers and settlers. It consisted merely of dough made from flour, salt and water and was placed in hot ashes to bake. Usually it was washed down with steaming hot billy tea.

Dinner was a veritable feast after the uninspiring diet of dried fruit and jerky the past few days, so conversation was at a minimum. Dare especially seemed preoccupied, too immersed in his own thoughts to engage in small talk. His mind was fertile with ideas, discarding some, accepting others. Deliberately he refrained from speaking until things became clear in his head. Only then did he reveal his thoughts.

"Have you given any thought to the future, Tim?" he asked carefully, slanting an inscrutable look in Casey's direction.

"What future?" laughed Tim. "I have no plans outside of surviving off the land for as long as possible. If need be, I can join the bushrangers."

"Tim, no, not those despicable creatures!" Casey cried.

"What else is there for me, lass?" His eyes gentled and filled with love when he turned his gaze to her. "Mayhap Dare can help you but there's little he can do for me. I can't ask you to share the life of an outcast, but if things were different—"

"There's no need to worry about Casey," Dare stated curtly. "I'll take care of her."

Casey inhaled sharply, forbidding herself to tremble. What did Dare mean? His words so stunned her she could provide no comment to his surprising statement.

"Because it means so much to Casey I've decided to help you, O'Malley," Dare continued, ignoring Casey's astounded expression.

"How, Dare?" Ben asked, curious. "What have you come up with?" Whatever Dare decided, Ben felt confident his brother would succeed in any endeavor he attempted. If Dare wanted to help Casey's friend, then he could do no less than offer his wholehearted support. "What can I do to help?"

"Why would you help me?" asked Tim uncertainly. "You being English and all."

"I'm doing it for Casey, O'Malley, not you," Dare returned shortly. "For some reason she thinks highly of you. Besides, I understand you're the one who protected her on the prison ship. He is the one, isn't he, love?" he addressed his question to Casey.

Thunderstruck by the endearment he casually let slip, Casey could only nod dumbly. Only during their most intimate moments had he called her his love. What would Ben think, not to mention Tim?

Tim's eyes narrowed thoughtfully as he became aware of much that had escaped his notice these past days. Though Casey had spoken many times of Dare, often with a strange tenderness, until this moment he had failed to realize her true feelings. Obviously she harbored tender emotions for her employer's son. Perhaps he had been too ill before to notice the inflection in Casey's voice when she spoke of Dare. Watching them together now, seeing Dare's tender glances, his concern, Tim knew that no hope existed for him where Casey was concerned. He could only hope that Dare's intentions were honorable, for if not there wasn't a damn thing he could do about it.

"What's your plan, mate?" Tim asked slowly. "I'll agree with anything as long as Casey is protected."

A meaningful glance passed between Dare and his brother, for Ben now realized the full extent of Dare's feelings for Casey. Never one to display his emotions, until now Dare had kept his sentiments strictly to himself and Ben experienced a pang of resentment. But that did not prevent him from agreeing to any plan hatched by his brother.

"Ben will leave here in the morning," Dare said, lowering his voice despite the fact that they were completely isolated from the world.

"Alone?" Ben protested. "What about—"

"All in good time, Ben, just listen," Dare advised sternly. "You're to return with two full sets of men's clothing. One for me and the other for Tim. I'm taking him to Sydney."

"What!" exploded Casey, aghast. "Dare, you said—"

"And I meant what I said, love. How many people in Sydney would recognize Tim? Very few, I'd wager. Dressed in decent clothes and his hair dyed black with berry juice, not even his own mother would recognize him."

"What then, Dare?" Ben asked eagerly, warming to the subject.

"Then we boldly walk through Sydney and buy Tim passage to . . . France or America. I'm certain he'd not want to return to Ireland. He can make a whole new life for himself."

"As simple as that?" questioned Tim with a hint of irony.

"Exactly," Dare nodded complacently. "Right now there's so much unrest in Sydney we should encounter little difficulty."

"How do you know there's a ship in port?" Tim asked.

"You forget I was in Sydney a short time ago. There were two ships in port at the time and neither was planning on leaving for a week or two."

"Do you really think it will work, Dare?" Ben asked.

"I wouldn't have suggested it if I wasn't confident it would work."

"What about me and Casey? What are we to do while you're in Sydney?"

"You'll both remain here."

"In this cave?" squeaked Casey.

"It will only be for a couple of days," Dare promised. "I think it's unwise to show yourself until Tim is safely gone. There's always a margin for error. Or a chance of discovery." Suddenly a thought came to him. "Speaking of discovery, Casey, do you know who turned you and Robin in to the authorities? Robin didn't seem to know."

"It was Meg," Casey said bitterly. "Somehow she learned about Tim, and about Robin's involvement."

"I suspected as much," Dare muttered, his face grim. "You didn't really steal Father's valuables, did you?"

"Dare!" came Casey's shocked reply. "How could you accuse me of such a thing? True, I left, but I took nothing of yours with me."

"I'm willing to bet Meg is behind the theft," Ben ventured astutely. "Wait until I get home. She'll—"

"She's already gone, Ben. I sent her packing."

Dare's impenetrable expression gave Ben second thoughts about questioning him further. Instead he said, "Good riddance. Shall I tell Father about your plans?"

"I think you should. What we do involves him as well. But I will use my money to buy Tim's passage. You know where it's kept, Ben. Bring it along with the clothes.

Two men walked unhurriedly through the crowded streets of Sydney. Both were dark-haired, tall and reasonably well dressed. If one man seemed exceptionally pale and unsteady on his feet, no one noticed, being too involved in their own affairs to pay heed to two men on foot.

Tim O'Malley still refused to believe he would leave this hellhole so easily. Nothing in his life so far had come easily. His one regret was leaving Casey behind. When he challenged Dare to allow Casey to leave with him, the man became belligerent. But despite all, Tim's heart told him Casey would be well taken care of, that her future lay with Dare Penrod. When he spoke privately with

Casey, she adamantly refused to leave the colony. And Tim knew that Dare was directly responsible for her decision.

"Hang on, O'Malley, we're almost there," Dare cautioned, anxiously watching Tim's pale face for the first sign of collapse. "You've done remarkably well so far for a man who was knocking at death's door only days ago."

"Never fear, I'll make it," Tim gritted from between clenched teeth. "Just get me on that ship."

Only one ship remained in port when they reached the harbor. An American trading vessel.

"How do you feel about going to America?" Dare asked as they gazed at the sleek clipper anchored in the bay.

"Suits me," Tim replied tersely. "I hear there's great opportunity in America. Especially since the war has freed the colonies from England's yoke."

At the waterfront Dare hired a small vessel to row them to the *Gallant Lady* and soon he was haggling with Captain Guy Flint over passage. If the good captain was suspicious of the man wishing to leave the colony so precipitously, he gave no hint of it as he accepted Dare's coin. In truth, it mattered little if the man was an escaped convict or an emancipist for he felt great compassion for the poor wretches forced to endure conditions akin to slavery—another institution he held in contempt. The *Gallant Lady* was strictly a trading vessel which occasionally carried passengers, and he decided to accept Mr. Timothy Nolan, if that be his name.

"I'll never be able to repay you for this, Dare," Tim said soberly. "My thanks will have to suffice." He paused briefly before continuing. "About Casey, be good to her. I dearly love the lass. Always have."

"I'll take care of Casey, Tim." Dare promised. "I really do care for her, you know."

"I was sure of it!" Tim grinned gleefully. "Just as certain as I am that Casey loves you."

"I hope you're right, Tim, for I'm staking my future on it," Dare replied as they shook hands in parting.

Setting foot on shore again, Dare stood for a long time, waiting until the sails unfurled and the *Gallant Lady* gracefully slipped from the harbor. Only when he was certain Tim had gotten away without mishap did he turn and leave. He wanted to be able to assure Casey that Tim was safely out of the colony. With that cleared from his mind there was only one thing left for him to do before returning to the Hawkesbury. He had to make certain he and Casey had a future together.

CHAPTER TEN

Dare walked through the city, shocked at the rumors he heard from men gathered on nearly every street corner. Several times he stopped to join in and add a word or two of his own, but mostly he listened. What he learned was gravely distressing.

The putting down of the revolt against the governor had solved little. John Macarthur was still hard at work behind the scenes to incite and instigate. He and the Rum Corps wanted Bligh gone and were prepared to go to any lengths to accomplish their goal. If gossip could be believed, Macarthur was trying to convince Lieutenant Governor Johnston, commander of the Rum Corps, to arrest Bligh for "oppressive behavior." It looked as if poor Bligh was in the midst of another revolt.

But Dare did not let the unrest in the city dissuade him from his mission as he directed his steps toward Government House. His future with Casey depended on seeing Bligh and enlisting his help. From past experience Dare knew Bligh to be a humane man who worked tirelessly for the benefit of the convicts, emancipists and honest settlers. It was only the unscrupulous and dishonest speculators who earned his wrath. The foremost of which were members of the New South Wales Corps.

"Dare, what brings you back to Sydney so soon?" Governor Bligh's daughter, Bess, greeted as she opened the door to Dare. "I was disappointed when you left town without so much as a good-bye. But now that you're back . . ." she brightened perceptably.

"I'm here to see your father, Bess, on urgent business," Dare explained, smiling lamely. For he had no valid excuse to offer Bess for his past rudeness. None that he'd care to divulge, anyway.

Bess's face fell as she valiantly hid her regret. Older than Dare by four years, and a widow, Bess was still a lovely woman though long past the first bloom of youth. Warm-hearted and generous, she was attracted to Dare from the moment of their first meeting. It wasn't long afterwards that they naturally gravitated into an affair. Even when Dare started seeing Mercy McKenzie seriously they still enjoyed one another upon occasion. Good men were few and far between in the convict colony in 1807. Bess never considered marriage to the handsome settler for she had no intention of settling down in Australia. And Dare would consider nothing else.

At length Bess said, "I'll see if Father will see you, Dare. Things aren't going well for him these days." Simply put and grossly understated.

Dare paced the entry hall until Bess returned to say her father would see him. Dare's relief was so great he rudely pushed past Bess to enter Governor Bligh's office.

"Sit down, Dare," William Bligh said, motioning him forward. "I'd hoped you'd return before . . ." His words trailed off and he stared distractedly out the window.

"Is it true, Governor, what they're saying on the street?"

"I don't know exactly what they're saying but I suppose most of it is true. My time here is limited. The New South Wales Corps has wanted me out for a long time and will stop at nothing to gain their ends. I've thwarted their self-interests and greed at every turn, but one day they'll go too far. I only wish I could be here when that day arrives."

Short, stocky and partially bald with a fringe of gray hair circling his head, William Bligh had survived being set adrift in an open boat on the high seas after the mutiny on the *Bounty*. Exhibiting great fortitude, he had drifted a remarkable 4,000 miles before reaching the island of Timor in the East Indies. And now he faced a challenge nearly as great. His worry as well as his weariness was clearly evident in the lines creasing his face and the deep purple shadows under his eyes.

"I'm aware you've had little time to . . . consider what I asked concerning Casey O'Cain, Governor, but it's imperative I have your answer. Is . . . is it within your power to grant Miss O'Cain a full pardon?"

"Today it's within my power," Bligh shrugged, "but tomorrow, who knows."

"And what have you decided?" Outwardly calm, his heart thudded erratically in his chest.

"What does this woman mean to you, Dare?"

"I . . . I care for her, Governor."

"Care for her?" scoffed Bligh. "You care for your horse."

Dare had the grace to blush. "I love her, dammit! I've loved her from the moment I saw her."

Bligh smiled. "That's what I wanted to hear. Oh, I know there was a time when I thought you and my Bess . . . But Bess would never agree to remain in the colony. She's a good girl, Dare, I want the best for her."

"She deserves the best, Governor," Dare concurred, wondering how they had gotten off the subject of Casey.

"Harumph! Yes," Bligh coughed, somewhat embarrassed to have exposed his tender sentiments. "But back to your young lady. I've given it some thought and was torn between granting an outright pardon or a ticket of leave. And I'm still undecided. Much depends on your response to my next question."

"I'll answer to the best of my ability," Dare replied hopefully.

"What will happen to Miss O'Cain if she's freed? In other words, what are your intentions for the girl?"

Dare hesitated for the space of a heartbeat. "I'm going to marry her if she'll have me, and I have reason to believe she will."

"You realize, Dare, that until I knew for a certainty what you intended I couldn't pardon the girl and turn her loose in this town of cutthroats. I understand she's beautiful, and if what you told me about her crime is true, she's guiltless as well. Then there's the New South Wales Corps to contend with. She's still wanted for questioning about the escaped prisoner, Timothy O'Malley. I've been told he's still at large despite an extensive search. And to my knowledge Casey O'Cain is still missing."

"Governor Bligh, the man was badly wounded. By now he's either long dead, lost in the bush or devoured by wild animals. Casey knows nothing of this man," he lied.

"There was a witness," Bligh pointed out.

"A jealous convict who sought to discredit Casey in my eyes because we were becoming too close. Meg's jealousy drove Casey away and inspired her to lie about many things."

"It's a known fact that Miss O'Cain has disappeared."

"Not really. I know where she is. So does my father."

"What about the jewelry and money she stole?"

"Lies," spat Dare. "I've good reason to believe Meg took the valuables and deliberately placed the blame on Casey. It's somewhat complicated but boils down to the fact that Meg thought she'd fare better in my affections with Casey out of the way. I'm afraid she was badly mistaken, for Meg means absolutely nothing to me. I've since sent her packing."

"Do you wish to press charges against the woman?" Governor Bligh asked.

"No," Dare said. "I don't want Casey to be hurt by all this any more than she already has been. I wish Meg joy of her ill-gained bounty. I'm sure Father feels the same."

"Well, Dare, I've decided to pardon Casey O'Cain, though I can't vouch for the actions of the Corps when they learn of this. My days are numbered, my boy. This may well be the last official document I sign. Wait outside, Dare, while my clerk draws up the pardon for my signature."

"Governor Bligh, about Robin Fletcher—"

"Don't press your luck, Dare," Bligh warned sternly. "The woman is one thing, but the Corps would raise all kinds of hell should I do the same for Fletcher. I'm afraid they won't back down from this. Obviously someone in high office wants Fletcher's property and there's little I can do about it. Especially given my precarious position. The day after tomorrow is Christmas and I'm certain the Corps will do nothing about him until after the new year. That's all the hope I can offer in Fletcher's case. That should also allow sufficient time to complete your plans concerning Miss O'Cain."

"Christmas!" Dare exclaimed. "I've hardly given it a thought. Merry Christmas, Governor, and thank you. I appreciate all you've done for me and Casey."

Though he longed to stay and plead for Robin's release, Dare realized that Bligh's power extended only so far, and judiciously withdrew.

A myriad of thoughts absorbed Dare's mind as he rode through the streets of Sydney on his way back to the Hawkesbury. The most important of which was Casey's pardon folded neatly in his inside pocket. But in view of the governor's tenuous position he was uncertain whether the document was enough to ensure Casey's freedom. Not until they married and he gave her the protection of his name would he breathe easier.

When he and Tim had reached Sydney earlier that day they had left their mounts at the house of Drew Stanley. Now he rode north on his own horse while leading Ben's, which Tim no longer had use for. Dare's plan was to stop first in Parramatta to see Robin and tell him all that had transpired. Robin would be relieved to learn that Casey was safe and now a free woman. It rankled in Dare that he had succeeded only in obtaining Casey's pardon while Robin still languished in jail. Dammit! He hated the thought of Robin being tried by unscrupulous members of the Corps and convicted of a crime that was none of his doing. Whoever wanted his land was willing to obtain it through whatever devious means necessary.

When Dare reached Parramatta, Sergeant Grimes told him it was too late to see Robin. Frustrated, he made his way home, where Roy anxiously awaited word of Dare's success or failure in Sydney.

Roy listened without comment until Dare finally ran out of words. Then he asked, "Do you really intend to marry Casey?"

"Are you disappointed, Father? I know you and Thad McKenzie thought I'd marry Mercy one day."

"I suspect if you really wanted to marry Mercy you'd have done so long ago," Roy said, smiling. "I like Casey and will happily welcome her into the family. You do love her, don't you?"

"I . . . yes, I love her."

"Does she love you?"

"I think so . . . I hope so."

"Then you most certainly have my blessing."

"Father, you realize the family may be shunned by the exclusionists if I marry Casey. Many of our friends will be outraged. You know how the McKenzies feel about emancipists."

"Son, it won't make a bit of difference to our real friends. Now get some sleep so you can go after Casey tomorrow. I imagine Ben is growing anxious. And doubtless Casey is concerned about her friend."

"I wish I could have seen Robin first, but that bastard Sergeant Grimes insisted it was too late."

"If it will make you feel better I'll go to Parramatta myself tomorrow and see Robin," Roy promised.

Christmas Eve, Dare thought as he rode toward the foothills the following morning. Ben's mount trotted patiently behind on a leading line. What a terrible time for Robin to be incarcerated without the slightest hope of reprieve. But at least Casey is safe, he reflected gratefully—as long as Governor Bligh is in power, that is. Hopefully he will put down this revolt just as he did the previous one.

Leaving the horses in the aborigine village and continuing on foot, Dare reached the cave, eager to see Casey and tell her she was no longer a convict. As yet he hadn't the opportunity to ask her to be his wife and he hoped to correct that oversight immediately. Her agreement was the only Christmas gift he wanted or needed.

Dare was dismayed to find the cave deserted, and immediately thought the worst. Rushing outside, he began calling frantically, and was rewarded by Ben's response. Within seconds the young man came striding through the brush. But his brother was alone.

"Where is Casey, Ben? What's happened to her?" Dare's questions came in quick succession.

"Casey is fine, Dare, don't get excited," grinned Ben with more than a hint of amusement. "She's down at the stream . . . bathing. I'm keeping watch."

"What are you watching? Casey or for intruders?" Dare remarked dryly.

"Come, brother, you know me better than that," Ben leered owlishly.

"That's precisely why I asked, I do know you."

"All joking aside, Dare," Ben said, turning serious, "how did it go in Sydney?"

"Exactly according to plan. Tim O'Malley is on his way to America."

"And Casey? What's to become of her?"

"I'm going to marry her. Governor Bligh saw fit to grant her a pardon. Hopefully my name will protect her from further harm."

"Marriage!" Ben gasped, startled. "What about Mercy?"

"I don't love Mercy, it's Casey I want."

"In the back of my mind I've always known you wanted Casey, Dare, but I never thought . . . that is . . . I assumed you only desired her."

"I do desire her, Ben," Dare admitted in a rare show of emotion, "but forever, not just as a mistress."

They chatted a few minutes more, mostly about Robin's situation, then Dare said, "Go back to the farm, Ben. I'll bring Casey home. I left your horse with Culong."

"But Dare, why—"

"I need time alone with Casey, Ben. There's

much I need to explain. Our marriage plans are
likely to come as a shock to her. You understand,
don't you?" Dare's gray eyes twinkled devilishly.

An answering spark ignited identical gray orbs.
"Aye, brother, take your time. Christmas dinner
will wait until you and Casey return."

Standing beneath the waterfall Casey tipped
her head back, her flaming tresses caressing her
hips as sparkling water spilled over her. She was
grateful to Ben for allowing her this time for a
much needed bath and felt at ease knowing he
stood guard nearby. But at the moment Ben did
not occupy her thoughts. That honor belonged to
Dare.

In the few weeks she had known him he had
become an obsession. At their first meeting he
had been arrogant, demanding and thoroughly
detestable. And then he had made love to her. A
hot flame seared her body and her senses swam
with remembered delights as she began to relive
the rapturous heights and sensations he had
evoked in her. Casey sighed deeply, nearly suffocated by the pressure of her emotions. Did Dare
feel the same about her? He enjoyed making love
to her, she knew, and at times he acted as if he
truly cared for her. Didn't he come looking for
her and offer to help Tim? If only he loved her as
much as she loved him.

"Foolish girl," she scoffed aloud. "I'm a convict, there is no future for us." Even if it were
possible, he and his family would become objects
of contempt to his exclusionist friends, she reasoned in silent contemplation. They would be
shunned by decent folk and she couldn't bear
that.

Immersed in her thoughts, Casey heard nothing over the roar of the waterfall save for the thumping of her heart. Dare . . . Dare . . . Dare . . . it seemed to say. She loved the sound of his name. A bold name for a bold man. And at the height of her ecstasy she heard her own name, transformed by his demanding lips into a velvet-edged caress.

"Casey."

At first Casey imagined she had conjured up Dare's voice from the depths of her longing. Until a pair of strong hands circled her waist. Gasping, she turned in his arms, brilliant green eyes sparkling in welcome. He stood beside her beneath the falls, his bronzed chest glowing a dull gold in the sunlight.

"Dare, thank God you're back. I've been so worried."

His gray eyes dark with desire, Dare found it difficult to concentrate on her words, so appealing did she look standing in the circle of his arms. Ruby-tipped breasts, perfectly molded of the creamiest alabaster, left indelible pinpoints of flame on his bare chest, and of their own accord his hands roamed freely over soft, enticing contours of hips and buttocks. Tightening his hold on those fleshy mounds, Dare pulled her flush against his flanks, making her all too aware of his raging desire.

"You fit me perfectly, Casey," he groaned, his hardness pulsing with life. "I could make love to you day and night and never tire."

"Dare, wait!" Casey resisted while she still had the strength. "What happened in Sydney? What about Tim?"

"Tim is on his way to America," Dare replied

impatiently as he lifted Casey until her feet
dangled helplessly in the water. "I'll tell you
about it later . . . much later."

Her reply was lost in the splash of the water
foaming around them as he claimed her mouth,
his tongue surging between her lips, exploring the
velvet warmth in a way that sent her pulses racing
and filled her with tingling excitement. When
finally he lifted his head she found herself snared
forever in the web of his intoxicating gaze, sealing her fate for all time.

As she threw her head back to allow him
access, Dare trailed fiery kisses along her lovely
neck to hover over each rosy tip crowning her
breasts while his bold caresses stroked her hips
and thighs. When he lifted her astride his lean
flanks a savage cry of sheer delight ripped from
Casey's throat. Her legs clung naturally to his
hips as Dare's throbbing manhood probed between her thighs for the opening. Aided by the
buoyancy of the water, he slipped easily inside,
her warm sheath contracting around him in
welcome. Hands planted firmly on her buttocks,
he moved her to meet his strong thrusts as
Casey's green eyes widened in surprise. She was
still too new at the game of love and unaware of
the various and diverse ways of giving and receiving pleasure. Dare took note of her expression
and smiled.

"I will teach you all the ways to love, sweetheart," he whispered, his voice rich with promise. "We have a lifetime ahead of us. Ah, love,
you feel so good. You're tight and hot and soft as
velvet." His last words were uttered on a groan.

"I never thought making love could feel so

wonderful," Casey gasped, by now nearly beyond speech. "Oh, Dare, please, please—"

"Soon, love, soon," Dare promised, bracing his feet on the sandy streambed as he reacted vigorously to her pleas.

Within moments her wish came true and she clutched desperately to his wide shoulders as bolt after bolt of white-hot ecstasy jerked and spasmed through her slender body. Lost in the throes of her climax, Casey was scarcely aware as Dare's own moment reached its zenith and he cried out.

Once the storm within subsided, Dare waded ashore, gently laid Casey down on the tall grass, and made love to her again. Only this time less urgently, leisurely, with great care and exquisite tenderness. When it was over, her eyes shimmered with moisture, aware that Dare had just made love to her as if actually *in* love with her. Afterwards they dressed and huddled close together while they spoke of all the things they had not had time for before their explosive joining.

"Dare, where's Ben?" Casey asked, suddenly aware that he might have been watching their passionate interlude. That notion brought a rosy flush to her face, and Dare thought she never looked more appealing.

"Put your fears to rest, sweetheart," he grinned roguishly, correctly interpreting her thoughts. "I sent Ben home."

"Oh," she breathed on a relieved sigh. "Tell me about Tim, Dare, was there much danger involved?"

"All went smoothly," Dare revealed with a hint of pride. "There was so much going on in

Sydney no one grew suspicious of two men
walking toward the harbor. At any rate, the Rum
Corps hardly expected a wanted man to show up
in their midst. Besides, they were far too busy
keeping peace and carrying out Macarthur's orders.

"As luck would have it, an American trading
vessel was preparing to depart and the good
captain offered no objection to taking a passen-
ger. If he suspected anything he didn't say, and
shortly afterwards the ship slipped unchallenged
from the harbor. By now Tim is well on his way
to Boston."

"Thank God," Casey breathed with undis-
guised joy. "And thank you, Dare. I'll always be
grateful. Tim means a lot to me."

Casey's words brought a dark scowl to Dare's
face until he remembered that Tim O'Malley was
too far away to challenge him for Casey's affections. "You've already repaid me, love," he
grinned with devilish delight. "Twice over, in
fact."

A becoming scarlet tinged her cheeks when she
recalled her wanton behavior just moments ago.
"I . . . I have little restraint where you're concerned," she admitted shyly, averting her eyes.

"It's nothing to be ashamed of, love," Dare
said, cupping her chin and lifting it upwards.
"Don't ever deny what you feel. You do feel
something for me, don't you?"

"Does it matter?" she fenced deftly, warming
and tingling all over.

He was regarding her now with eyes that
crinkled in amusement, silver orbs that seemed
to peer right into her soul, while his lips twitched
in a crooked smile. "It matters a great deal. I'd

like my wife to be at least moderately fond of me."

"Your . . . your wife! Dare, what are you saying?"

"I've just asked you to marry me."

"Why? Why would you propose to a convict with years left to serve out her sentence? If it's because . . . because you took my innocence, forget it. Given my circumstances it was bound to happen sooner or later."

"Dammit, Casey, did it ever occur to you that I might love you?" Dare blasted, exasperated.

"I . . . no! Oh, I knew you desired me, but men like you don't marry women like me."

"Bloody hell! Give me some credit, Casey. How do you know what kind of man I am? Listen to me, you stubborn wench. I love you! Do you hear? *I love you!"* Each syllable was pronounced clearly and firmly, leaving Casey trembling with happiness.

Still, she was astute enough to realize there was no future for a convict and a pure merino and she told him so.

"You're not a convict, love," Dare replied, confounding her. "Your pardon is in my pocket. Governor Bligh granted it before I left Sydney."

"Oh Dare, Dare, do you mean it? Am I truly free? How did you do it?" Her joy was contagious as Dare hugged her exuberantly.

"Yes, love, you are now an emancipist and free to marry."

Abruptly Casey's happiness turned to concern. "But your friends," she countered, not entirely convinced, "what will they say? And . . . and your family. Oh Dare, we couldn't . . . we shouldn't."

"We can and we will, love, let me worry about the consequences. Besides, my family approves and no one else matters. What I really want to know is what you feel for me. I've bared my soul to you, will you not do the same?"

"There's nothing to hide, Dare," Casey confessed shyly. "My heart has always belonged to you. Even when I thought you were an arrogant, conceited ass." She laughed at the look of dismay her words brought. "You have to admit there was little about you to love when we first met. You took great pleasure in tormenting me."

"Guilty as charged," Dare flushed. "It was my way of fighting the growing attraction between us. I didn't want to love you, but somehow you found your way into my heart. Now I can't imagine life without you. You will marry me, won't you, Casey?"

Across the narrow distance, their eyes locked, and a wordless commitment that would span time and space bound their souls forever. "When?" Casey asked, smiling tremulously.

"Oh my love, soon. As soon as possible after the new year. Did you know tomorrow is Christmas? You've given me the best gift possible."

Claiming her lips, he crushed her to him. Crying out with happiness, she returned the kiss with reckless abandon, secure in his love. Drinking in the sweetness of her lips, Dare urged her to her feet.

"Come, love, it's growing dark. Let's go back to the cave."

"Aren't we going home?"

"Not tonight. I'm selfish enough to want you all to myself tonight. Once we return to the farm we must act in a more circumspect manner until our wedding."

"Why?" Casey teased archly. "It never mattered before."

"Minx," Dare laughed delightedly. "You're my intended bride now and I want everything perfect. I'm going to make damn certain my rascal of a brother won't have a thing to tease us about once we're married. As much as it pains me, we'll not be able to be together like this till after we're wed. So come along, love, we've the whole night ahead of us and I don't want to waste a moment of it."

Later, Dare killed a wallaby and Casey made damper, washing the feast down with billy tea. Sharing it with the man she loved made it taste like manna from heaven and Casey vowed she'd never eaten a finer meal. But what came after was pure rapture. Time after time Dare brought her to shuddering ecstasy, teaching her the many ways to love and be loved, to enjoy and be enjoyed. It was a night to savor, a night to remember. And while they pledged their love in the way of all lovers since the beginning of time, neither were aware of the dark forces working to tear them apart.

BOOK TWO

Bold Love
1808 – 1809

CHAPTER ELEVEN

Ben rushed out to greet them when Casey and Dare entered the yard astride Dare's horse. "It's about time you two showed up," the exuberant youth shouted with a hint of reproach. "If Father hadn't stopped me I would have ridden out to the cave at first light."

Crimson crept up Casey's neck as she was aghast at the thought of what Ben would have found had he barged in on them early this morning.

"Thank God for Father's good sense," muttered Dare, rolling his eyes heavenward.

Roy strode from the house to join the trio. "Welcome home, Casey." He smiled, grasping her hands. "Are you all right? You haven't been harmed in any way?"

His obvious concern warmed Casey's heart, and she replied, "I'm fine, Mr. Roy, truly. Especially now that Dare and I . . ." She slid a loving glance in Dare's direction.

"What Casey is trying to say is that she has agreed to marry me," Dare proclaimed proudly.

"How wonderful!" Ben cried. "If you had waited any longer I'd have asked her myself."

"Casey needs a man, not a pup," quipped Dare.

"Now wait a minute, brother," Ben puffed up indignantly. "I'll have you know—"

"Boys, boys," interjected Roy, laughing. "No arguments, please. Today is a happy occasion. Not only is it Christmas but an engagement party of sorts. Martha is in the kitchen now coping singlehandedly with a celebration meal, and I'm certain Casey wishes to go to her room to change her clothes."

"Oh, yes," Casey agreed, anxious to shed the clothes she'd spent days in. "And as soon as I'm finished I'll give Martha a hand with the dinner."

"Casey," Dare advised, "there's no need."

"Yes there is, Dare. Martha can't possibly manage everything by herself. Besides, I want to help."

She turned to leave, but a hand on her arm stayed her. "Welcome to the family, Casey," Roy said, kissing her cheek. "I wish only the best for the both of you."

Suddenly Casey grew thoughtful. "Mr. Roy," she began hesitantly, "about the jewelry. I didn't—"

"I never thought you did, my dear. Let's forget all that, it's unimportant. I have a good idea who took them. And please drop the mister. You are no longer a servant."

Nodding happily, Casey made her way to her room. For the first time in months she felt truly secure. There was nothing Meg or anyone could do to harm her now, she reflected. Soon she'd be Dare's wife and need no longer fret over what life had in store for her.

* * *

Working in the kitchen beside Martha, Casey experienced more joy than at any time since her father's death. Martha's welcome had been nearly as exuberant as Ben's, and they chatted happily as they went about their chores, chewing over the latest news. Mostly they talked about Casey and Dare and the love they shared.

"I'm so happy for you, Casey," Martha said, wiping a tear from her eye. "It's wonderful about your pardon. You and Dare are perfect for one another."

Casey thought so too until unexpected guests arrived to partake of Christmas dinner. Thad McKenzie and his daughter Mercy turned up just as everyone was seated at the table and Casey was in the process of serving the roasted leg of mutton.

"Dare, darling," Mercy gushed, rushing through the door Ben had opened and straight into Dare's arms. "I felt certain you'd come to see me today of all days. When you failed to arrive I talked Papa into bringing me here."

Dismay followed by irritation marched across Dare's face as he stared numbly at the beautiful woman filling his arms. Perversely, Ben thought it served Dare right for stealing the hearts of the two loveliest women in New South Wales. But when he noted the expression on Casey's face he regretted his rash thoughts. Immediately Roy took charge, hoping to defuse the potentially volatile situation.

"You're just in time for dinner, Thad. Will you join us?"

"Aye," Thad agreed heartily, eyeing the leg of mutton. "And if the storm that's brewing outside lets loose, you may have us longer than you expected."

Carefully placing the roast in the center of the table, Casey stared resentfully at the beauty resting so comfortably in Dare's arms, as if she had all the right in the world to be there. And until Dare told her differently she would continue to assume he belonged to her.

Privately, Casey thought Mercy a ravishing beauty, all peaches and cream. She possessed a rare combination of alabaster white skin and pale blond hair, enhanced by ruby-red lips and innocent, cerulean blue eyes. She was daintily fashioned of tiny proportions, reaching barely to Dare's chest. Yet she was amply endowed, evidenced by high, round breasts and full hips likely one day to turn to fat.

Disengaging himself from Mercy's clinging arms, Dare suppressed a groan. Why did she have to turn up now of all times? He hadn't seen her in weeks, nor thought about her, for that matter. He realized he owed her an explanation and intended to apprise her of the current situation at his earliest opportunity. Perhaps it was fate that brought her here on this special day, he reasoned. Now she could see for herself how it was between him and Casey. A love like theirs was difficult to disguise.

His thoughts in a turmoil, Dare said unthinkingly, "Casey, set two more places at the table, the McKenzies are staying for dinner." What he failed to realize was how much it sounded like a command given to a servant rather than a request to the woman he loved.

Slanting Dare an affronted glare, Casey replied tartly, "Yes, sir, *Mr.* Dare." Then she turned and stomped away.

"Obviously your servants need a woman's touch to keep them in line," Mercy sniffed. "Is she one of the women convicts you recently acquired in Sydney? A plain little thing, isn't she?"

"Casey is . . ." Dare faltered, wisely deciding to withhold explanations until a more propitious time.

Just then Casey reentered the room with plates and silverware, saving Dare from responding. Roy rescued the situation by saying, "Set all the food on the table, Casey, then you and Martha join us."

"What!" Mercy gasped, startled. "You let your servants eat with you? Why, everyone knows these women are all whores."

Dare leaped to his feet, ready to defend Casey and give Mercy the tongue lashing she so richly deserved, but Roy motioned him back into his seat. "Let it go, son. This is Christmas and the McKenzies our guests. After explanations are made, I'm sure Mercy will better understand the situation. Let's all enjoy our dinner."

Disgruntled, but aware of what Roy was trying to accomplish, Dare sat down. It didn't help matters when Mercy continued blithely, unwilling to let the subject drop, "When I'm mistress here this unorthodox procedure will come to a halt."

Absolute silence reigned, and when Dare did nothing but grit his teeth, Casey said, "Martha and I prefer to eat in the kitchen." She flounced from the room, mustering all the dignity she possessed, with Martha in loyal pursuit.

Frustration consumed Dare. He wanted to

rush after Casey but forced himself to remain seated. He felt he owed it to Mercy to tell her gently about Casey, and he intended to get it over with the moment the meal ended.

After everyone had eaten and an uncomfortable interlude ensued, Dare rose, inviting Mercy outside for a walk before the rain began. Noting the loud rumble of thunder rolling across the black sky, he expected a deluge at any minute.

"I hope you two lovebirds set a date soon." Thad smiled knowingly as they left the room. "I'd like grandchildren before I'm too old to enjoy them."

"Papa!" chided Mercy, blushing prettily for Dare's benefit.

"Well, it's true, girl," the older man persisted. "You've been waiting for Dare long enough. I had to speak my piece."

Dare wished the floor could have opened up and swallowed him. His decision to marry Casey was likely to alienate Thad as well as hurt and anger Mercy. But there was no help for it. Casey was the woman he loved and intended to marry. The others had been mere distractions along the way to true love.

"Father, perhaps you'll speak to Thad while Mercy and I are gone," Dare suggested meaningfully, urging Mercy toward the door with a hand at her back.

"Of course, Dare, if that's what you want," Roy agreed cautiously.

"What was that all about, Dare?" Mercy asked once they stepped onto the wide porch.

"Mercy, we need to talk," Dare said.

"Of course, darling," beamed Mercy, "we need

to set a date for our wedding. You heard Papa, I've waited a long time and my patience is running out. I've been wondering when you'd get around to it."

"Mercy, I never meant to hurt you, and at one time I truly did consider making you my wife."

"At one time! What are you talking about?"

"I've met someone. Someone I love very much. I've asked her to marry me."

Suddenly Mercy's blue eyes lost their wide innocent look, replaced by a murderous glare. "Who is she? Who is the bitch who stole you from me? Is it Governor Bligh's daughter? She's much too old for you, darling."

"It's not Bess, Mercy, it's Casey," replied Dare, knowing of no easy way to cushion the shock. Though he hadn't actually proposed to Mercy it had been understood that one day they would wed.

"Casey? Casey who?" Mercy spat, feigning ignorance.

"You've already met Casey, she served our dinner."

Mercy's face turned deathly pale and Dare thought she might faint, until she suddenly came to life with a burst of anger. "A convict!" she screeched. "You let a convict whore come between us? You despicable cur! I suppose all the little slut did was shake her tail and you panted after her like a cat in heat. Did she open her thighs for you?"

"Mercy, it's not like that," protested Dare, his temper hanging by a fragile thread. "I love Casey."

"Love, bah! You love what's between her legs.

Can't you just take what she offers and forget her? I won't hold it against you, darling. All men have a wild streak in them."

"Mercy, I won't have you talking about Casey that way. She's the woman I'm going to marry."

"How noble, Dare, but you obviously forgot something. Casey is a convict."

"No longer. Governor Bligh granted her a full pardon just days ago. She's an emancipist and soon will be my wife."

"Will nothing I say change your mind?"

"Absolutely nothing."

"I'll never forgive you for this, Dare," Mercy said tightly. "You've ruined me for other men. Who will have me now?"

"If you're talking about your virginity, Mercy, it didn't exist. You lost it long before I bedded you."

"Don't be crude, Dare. I'm referring to your . . . lovemaking. No one can compare with you."

"I'm flattered, Mercy, but I'm certain you'll find a man worthy of your love one day."

Her answer was lost in a roar of thunder as lightning streaked across the sky and rain came pelting down on their heads. Though Dare wasn't too happy about the situation, it looked as if Mercy and Thad would be forced to spend the night.

The house had finally quieted down, and a difficult evening it had been with both McKenzies turning decidedly cool once they learned Dare was serious about marrying Casey. Though Casey had reluctantly agreed to join the family and guests in the parlor after dinner, she was so ill at ease that she soon pleaded weariness and excused herself. Dare fretted because he hadn't had a moment alone with her since their return earlier that day nor an opportunity to present her with his surprise gift. But hopefully, once everyone was sleeping, he could sneak undetected to her room for a short visit.

Pacing restlessly until just past midnight, Dare slipped a small package into his shirt pocket and strode purposefully toward the door. Only to have the panel open before he reached it and a small shrouded figure step inside.

"Casey?" he whispered joyfully, enfolding the soft form in his arms. "You surprise me, love. I didn't expect you tonight."

The small figure stiffened, then drew away with a jerk, placing herself close enough to the flickering candle to reveal her identity.

"Bloody hell! What are you doing here, Mercy?"

"Don't be angry, darling," Mercy pleaded. "I've come to remind you how good we are together so you'll forget this crazy notion of marrying a convict; a woman you know nothing about."

"Go back to your bed, Mercy, I love Casey. It's unlikely I'll change my mind."

"Perhaps I can convince you," she purred seductively as the concealing cloak slithered down her body to lay in a dark pool at her feet.

Dare gasped as the meager light revealed pale porcelain flesh resplendent in glorious nudity. Erect pink buds cresting milky mounds and the shimmer of gold nestled between supple thighs sent a jolt of desire coursing through his veins.

No man alive was capable of indifference when presented with such overwhelming feminine allure.

"You want me, Dare," Mercy murmured throatily. "Take me. Forget that little slut downstairs, she's not good enough for you. Obviously she's bewitched you. But I'll forgive you. You need a wife like me, someone from your own class."

Her words provided the catalyst needed to release Dare's frozen senses as he calmly retrieved the cloak from the floor and placed it over her shoulders. "I never meant to hurt you, Mercy," he said evenly, holding himself to blame for her outrageous behavior. "Once Casey entered my life no other woman meant a thing to me. Goodnight, Mercy, it's best we both forget this ever happened."

While he spoke he guided her firmly toward the exit, and before she knew it she found herself standing in the hall facing a closed door. Fuming with impotent rage, she stomped off to her own cold bed.

The moment the door closed behind Mercy, Dare exhaled sharply, shaking himself to clear his head of the lingering aroma of roses she had left in her wake. Then he left his room, patting his pocket to make certain his gift to Casey still rested there. He found her door unlatched and slipped inside as it opened on noiseless hinges. The room was in total darkness and Dare waited a moment until his eyes adjusted to the meager light before drawing a flint from his pocket and lighting a candle. Casey came awake instantly.

"Dear Lord, Dare, you scared me half to death!" she panted, clutching her throat.

"I'm sorry, love, I just had to see you," Dare murmured, perching comfortably on the edge of the bed. "I want to apologize for today. Mercy isn't usually so disagreeable, but I've hurt her terribly."

Casey grunted, thinking that "disagreeable" was hardly an appropriate term for Mercy McKenzie's rude behavior. "Perhaps I'm not the right woman for you," she ventured, allowing him the opportunity to rescind his offer of marriage while he still had the chance.

"You're the *only* woman for me," he countered. "That's the reason I'm with you now. I have a gift for you."

"A Christmas gift? Oh, Dare, I've nothing for you," Casey wailed.

"You've given me yourself, love. That's more than enough." Then he reached in his pocket and retrieved a small box which he lovingly placed in her hand. Casey stared at it a few seconds, then at Dare.

"Open it, love," he urged.

Quivering with anticipation, Casey opened the lid and let out a startled yelp. Nestled in velvet folds reposed a square-cut emerald surrounded by diamonds. It was breathtaking. "Oh, Dare, it . . . it's absolutely stunning! But it's far too valuable, I couldn't possibly accept something that cost so much." Though farmers might be well-to-do, it was a well-known fact that capital was so scarce that goods usually were bartered or traded.

"It belonged to my mother, love. Now it belongs to you."

"But I thought all your mother's jewelry had been stolen."

"Not everything. This piece was given to me to give to my future bride. The reason it wasn't stolen is because it wasn't with the other pieces. I want you to have it."

Reverently he lifted the ring from its nest and placed it on her finger while Casey looked on with awe. "I've never seen anything so lovely."

"Nor have I." Dare smiled, his gray eyes never leaving her face.

"Thank you, my love, thank you," Casey said, covering his face with kisses.

Laughing delightedly, Dare disentangled her arms from around his neck and reluctantly forced himself to his feet. "I'd better leave, sweetheart, or neither of us will get any sleep. And after last night we both could use a good night's rest."

Casey blushed, distinctly recalling the previous night when ecstasy had claimed them again and again. The thought that she could experience that same feeling night after night once they were married sent goosebumps down her spine.

"Goodnight, my love," Dare said wistfully, allowing himself no more than a chaste kiss upon her brow. "Sleep well."

As if she could sleep after all the excitement tonight!

The McKenzies left early the next morning, a friendship of long standing shattered. But Casey was so happy she spared the haughty Mercy no more than passing consideration in the days that followed. Roy had presented her with his dead wife's wardrobe, and she and Martha spent every free minute altering clothing and fashioning a suitable wedding dress. They finally settled on a sprigged dimity not too out of fashion and cool enough to withstand the hottest day.

Casey and Dare had not been together as lovers since that night in the cave and the strain was beginning to tell. Seeing each other daily with nothing but a kiss or two to ease their passion wreaked havoc on their emotions. Dare felt ready to explode and Casey hovered on the brink of collapse. She was overjoyed when Dare announced the first week after the new year that he was leaving for Sydney to find a preacher. During the last year a preacher had made his way to the colony and Dare hoped to bring him to the farm to perform the brief ceremony uniting them. Casey was ecstatic. In a few days she would be Mrs. Dare Penrod. She would be the best wife possible, she promised herself. Nothing but good things would happen to them from now on. There would be children—lots of them—and love—and laughter—and . . . Her mind worked overtime imagining the happiness and long life she would share with Dare, forever and ever.

Ben insisted on accompanying Dare, and the day they left was the second happiest day of Casey's life. The first would be the day the preacher pronounced them man and wife. She expected Dare and Ben back the next day. When they failed to return she grew frantic with worry. Her anxiety affected Roy, who became concerned when another day passed with no word from his sons. Too many things could have happened along the track to Sydney. Bushrangers were still reported in the area. Or perhaps something was amiss in town.

* * *

"What in the hell is going on?" Ben asked as they rode into Sydney.

The 102nd Regiment was assembled in the streets, most if not all of the Corps drunk and roistering noisily. It seemed that the regiment was headed for Government House.

"Bloody hell!" exploded Dare, dismayed. "They're going after Bligh! Come on!"

Drawn by the crowd, they converged with the masses that followed in the wake of the marching Corps. The rebellious forces rolled to a drunken halt before Government House and within minutes had broken down the front door and swarmed inside. Except for the civil constable, the only law-enforcement body in New South Wales was the Corps, and their revolt, led by Lieutenant Governor Johnston and inspired by John Macarthur, left Governor Bligh totally defenseless.

"What can we do, Dare?" Ben asked, itching to jump to the governor's defense.

"What can we do against the entire Corps?" Dare returned realistically.

"Perhaps some of the crowd will join us if we defend Bligh?" suggested Ben.

"Ha," scoffed Dare. "Look at them, Ben, the scum of Sydney." He nodded at several drunken revelers. "Do you want *them* fighting at your side?"

Ben's answer was lost in the racket caused by men of the Corps bursting from Government House dragging a wildly protesting Governor Bligh into the street. Someone had rolled the governor's carriage up to the door and Bligh was unceremoniously thrust inside. At that moment John Macarthur appeared, taking the reins of the

carriage himself, and along with his friends and
Corps members proceeded to parade through the
town with Bligh in tow while the louts and clods
of Sydney got uproariously drunk on free rum.
Ben and Dare could do little more than stand
helplessly by and watch. Until Bess Bligh appeared screaming at the door of Government
House and took off at a run after the carriage
carrying her father.

Bess, convinced that the Corps would kill her
father, ran panting beside the carriage in the dirt
road begging for his life. At the sight of that
courageous woman jumping singlehandedly to
the defense of her father, something snapped in
Dare, and he spurred his horse through the
crowd, followed closely by Ben. Dare grew livid
with rage when he saw Lieutenant Potter riding
beside the carriage blatantly ignoring Bess's
pleas.

"Let her inside with her father, Potter!" Dare
yelled above the din. "What kind of man are
you?"

Swiveling his head, Potter glared murderously
at Dare. "Keep out of this, Penrod. It's too late to
do anything for the governor. The colony is in the
hands of the Corps. We make the rules from now
on."

Near exhaustion, Bess heard Dare's voice and
turned her ravaged face in his direction. "Help
me, Dare, please help me! They'll kill my father."

Fury rose in Dare like a searing flame, and
unmindful of the consequences he took matters
into his own hands. Jumping from his mount, he
tossed the reins to Ben and moved swiftly to
Bess's side. At the end of her endurance, she now
clung desperately to the door handle, dragged

along by the carriage as the riotous parade continued down George Street at a slow pace. Throwing caution to the wind, Dare grasped Bess by the waist, flung open the door, and boosted her inside with her father in one fluid motion. It all happened so quickly neither Lieutenant Potter nor anyone else had realized Dare's intent.

The damage already done, Potter did not bother with Bess but immediately bellowed to his men, "Arrest that man!" pointing to Dare. Instantly three men were upon Dare, wresting him to the ground. When Ben made to intervene, Dare warned him off.

"Don't do it, Ben!" His voice sounded strained as he was quickly hustled off to jail. "They can't hold me long. Wait at Drew Stanley's house until I'm released." Then he was wrestled through the crowd, leaving a stunned Ben staring helplessly after him.

But at least Dare's sacrifice hadn't been in vain, for Bess was allowed to accompany her father in the carriage. And after a rather lengthy triumphant parade through Sydney the governor was taken back to Government House where he was placed under house arrest until he could be sent back to England. The colony of New South Wales now existed at the mercy of the unscrupulous Rum Corps.

The next day, Macarthur, having won his ground, immediately prepared to defend it. With the cunning of a fox, he had himself arrested for sedition and was immediately acquitted by a court of his friends. He used his mock trial to make a case against Governor Bligh, and evidently his words found fertile ground. To further malign Bligh's character, he circulated the story that Bligh had been dragged by the Corps's members from hiding beneath a servant's bed, a vicious blow against the personal honor of a man renowned for his courage.

While all this took place, Dare fumed helplessly in jail, his fate left to the Corps. If they so desired, he could easily be made an example of and held for as long as they saw fit. But he failed to reckon with Ben's powers of persuasion. Mustering all the charm at his command, Ben went directly to Lieutenant Governor Johnston to plead Dare's case, citing his brother's chivalry as the cause for his actions. Dare never could stand to see a woman in distress. Johnston's jubilation over the Corps's victory made him inclined to be lenient, and he ordered Dare's release. Lieutenant Potter was far from pleased as he released Dare.

"It's against my better judgment to let you go, Penrod," Potter grumbled. "You thwarted me once but it won't happen again. It's only a matter of time before the O'Cain girl is brought in for punishment."

"You can't hurt Casey, Potter, she's a free woman," Dare said. "Governor Bligh granted her a pardon shortly before Christmas. It's on the records, if you care to check. She'll soon be my wife."

"Like hell!" Potter growled, splaying long fingers through thinning hair. "You might have convinced the governor, but it's the Corps who'll have the final say now. Besides, it's too late."

"Too late for what?"

"The girl's status matters little. She committed a crime when she aided an escaped convict and must be made to pay. If she's an emancipist as you insist, she'll be tried and sentenced. While you're here playing Sir Galahad to Bess Bligh, your . . . intended," he snickered lewdly, "is being seized by Seargeant Grimes. I hope you enjoyed her before you left, for it will be the last time. Once she's convicted I've arranged for her to be assigned as my servant. I always did have a yen for the little baggage. If she refuses to give us the information we seek, a whipping might loosen her tongue."

"You bastard!" howled Dare, lunging for Potter, who stepped several paces backwards to escape Dare's rage. If Ben hadn't rushed forward to restrain his brother, Potter wouldn't have had a prayer against Dare's superior strength.

"Dare, for God's sake, don't let Potter provoke you! You won't do Casey any good sitting in jail. And that's what's likely to happen if you attack the son-of-a-bitch."

Recognizing the wisdom of Ben's words, Dare gritted his teeth, clenched his fists, and with great effort backed off from further confrontation with the smug lieutenant. "Come on, Ben, let's go home and find out if this bastard is lying," he growled, glaring venomously at his adversary.

Before long they were thundering back along the dirt track to Parramatta. "What happened to Governor Bligh?" Dare asked as he drew alongside his brother.

"Under house arrest," Ben said tersely.

"And Macarthur?"

Ben told him in as few words as possible what Macarthur had done to defend his actions. "Talk is that Macarthur will leave for England soon to defend himself. It looks like we're at the mercy of the Rum Corps for some time to come, for it will be at least two years before word gets to England and another governor is appointed."

"God help us all," muttered Dare as he urged his horse into full gallop. "And God help Potter if Casey has been harmed."

CHAPTER TWELVE

Sitting and waiting for Dare to return no longer satisfied Casey. He and Ben should have returned long before now. She threatened to take the wagon into Sydney herself, but Roy was adamant in his refusal.

"Perhaps the preacher had some unfinished business to attend to before he could come out here," Roy temporized, more worried than he let on.

"If that were so, Ben would have returned alone to tell us of the delay," Casey said stubbornly. "No, Roy, I just know something dreadful has happened."

"Mayhap you're right," he allowed with a frown.

"If I can't go to Sydney, then you go, Roy," Casey pleaded. "I can't explain, but the feeling persists that something terrible has happened or is about to happen."

Finally persuaded by Casey's anxious pleas, Roy agreed to ride to Sydney. "Will you and Martha be all right by yourselves until I return?" he asked, his better judgment telling him to remain until one of his sons showed up with an explanation. "Tom and the men are in the south field driving sheep to the creek to be washed in preparation for shearing. You'll be alone here."

"What danger can exist for us here on the farm?" Casey scoffed. "Martha and I will be safe enough until you return. Please hurry, Roy."

Fifteen minutes later Casey heaved an enormous sigh when Roy rode out of the yard and down the track toward Sydney. A half hour later, shortly after Roy left Parramatta behind, Sergeant Grimes, accompanied by four troopers, lit out for the Penrod farm just minutes after receiving a directive from Lieutenant Potter in Sydney ordering the arrest of Casey O'Cain at Penrod station.

Casey sat on the porch steps in hopes of catching an errant breeze, her stomach churning with anxiety and frustration. In the hottest time of the year, the stifling heat only added to Casey's distress. What had happened to Dare and Ben? she agonized. Had bushrangers attacked them? Or had they encountered trouble with the Corps? Any number of things were possible in a town like Sydney. Perhaps someone had found out that Dare had been responsible for Tim's escape from the colony. All manner of dismal thoughts occupied her brain as Casey stared absently into space.

When she first became aware of a cloud of dust rising in the distance, she hoped it might be caused by a breeze. Then came the vague knowledge that the dust was caused by approaching horsemen. "Martha!" Casey called, excitement coloring her words. "Come quickly. I think the men are returning." Her first thought was that Roy had met his sons on the track and all were

returning together. Of course the preacher would
be with them.

Martha joined Casey on the porch to wait in
eager anticipation. Shading her eyes against the
sun's glare, Casey grew increasingly worried. As
the horsemen drew near, a warning voice whispered in her ear and set alarm bells ringing.
Something was wrong, dreadfully wrong. She
knew it the moment she recognized the distinctive uniform of the Corps.

"Lord help us," Martha whimpered, her face
draining of all color. "It's troopers."

Amazingly, Casey did not consider her own
safety but thought only of Dare and his family.
The arrival of troopers fortified her belief that
Dare had encountered some kind of difficulty.
She watched with trepidation as Sergeant Grimes
and four troopers rode into the yard. All five men
dismounted, but only Grimes approached the
women. His leering grin and bold eyes surrounded Casey in a black blanket of fright, and
she groped for Martha.

"What do you want?" she asked when Grimes
stood before her. She had never met the man but
assumed he was the trooper posted in Parramatta
to keep the peace. She was also aware that he was
the man who had arrested Robin and led the
search for her and Tim.

"I'm Sergeant Grimes. Which one of you is
Casey O'Cain?" He looked from Casey to Martha, knowing full well the redhead was the woman he wanted, but waited for confirmation.

"I'm Casey O'Cain," Martha said and stepped
forward, slanting Casey a warning glance. "What
do you want with me?"

"I'm the one you want, Sergeant," Casey said,

grateful to Martha for the sacrifice but unwilling to accept it.

Smiling smugly, Grimes said, "I thought you were the one, with that red hair and all. You're under arrest for giving aid to an escaped convict."

"How can that be? I was just recently granted a pardon by Governor Bligh."

"I don't suppose you've heard yet, but there's been a revolt in Sydney. Governor Bligh is under house arrest and the Corps is in control of the colony."

"Dare," Casey whispered fearfully beneath her breath. So that's what kept him in Sydney. Aloud, she said with more bravado than she felt, "You can't arrest me, I told you I was pardoned."

"It makes little difference whether you are a convict or an emancipist, what you did was unlawful," Grimes informed her. "There's a witness who swears you helped an escaped prisoner. I'm to take you to Sydney for trial."

"No!" cried Martha, clinging to Casey. "You can't take her. Not until Mr. Roy and his sons return."

Grimes smiled slyly. "You alone, are you?"

"N . . . no," Casey lied, truly frightened by the hungry look in his greedy eyes. "Tom and some of the workers are close at hand."

A glance around the deserted yard easily disproved Casey's words and Grimes chuckled nastily. "Nice try, Miss O'Cain." Turning to his men, he barked, "I'm taking the woman inside so she can pack a few of her belongings." He nodded to Martha. "Keep this one outside and . . . don't follow us inside no matter what. Is that clear?"

"No!" cried Casey, sheer black fright squeezing the breath from her lungs. It didn't take a wizard to know what Grimes intended. "I . . . I don't need anything. I'm ready to go now."

"Come along, wench. All women need a thing or two of their own, be it a brush or bar of soap." Grasping her firmly by the elbow, he turned her around and shoved her through the door. "Where's your room?" he growled, his beady eyes glittering with lust.

It shouldn't matter to Lieutenant Potter if the girl was returned slightly used, Grimes reasoned gleefully. Meg never told him Casey O'Cain was a raving beauty with all that red hair and white skin. She looked so fresh and innocent. Nothing like the whores he was accustomed to. He thought Meg was exceptional with her fine figure and unmarred features, but Casey O'Cain had her beat by a mile. And every other woman in the colony, too. The moment he saw her he knew he had to have her before Lieutenant Potter claimed her. He'd take his fill first, then go on to Sydney with none the wiser. Finding the women alone was a bonus he hadn't expected. But no one ever accused Linus Grimes of being too stupid to take advantage of a golden opportunity when he saw one. He wanted the enticing wench, and God-damn, he'd have her!

"Where's your room?" he repeated when Casey refused to answer. "Dammit, girl, we haven't got all day."

Gut-grinding pain seized Casey when Grimes, growing impatient, brutally twisted her arm behind her back, and an agonized cry ripped from her throat. "Your room! Where is it?"

"Off the k . . . kitchen," sobbed Casey, gripping her shoulder to ease the pain.

"Now you're showing some sense," Grimes chuckled, dragging her through the house. "Believe me, it's not going to take long. I'm already hard as a rock."

If Casey had any doubt as to his intentions before, they were now quickly laid to rest. He meant to rape her before taking her to jail. Oh, Dare, she silently lamented, why aren't you here to protect me? Where are you, my love?

Dare, followed closely by Ben and Roy, thundered into the yard. From a distance they had spied horses tethered in front of the house and several troopers milling about. Skidding to a halt, Dare took in the situation at a glance. Martha stood on the porch wringing her hands and crying while four troopers formed a ring around her. Casey was nowhere in sight. Neither was Sergeant Grimes. Beads of perspiration dotted Dare's wide brow and a frisson of fear gnawed at his innards. Casey! Where was she?

Dare leaped from his mount to confront the troopers who guarded the front door against intrusion. "Where's Casey O'Cain?" he thundered, glowering dangerously.

"You mean the little redhead?" snickered a loutish corporal. "I reckon she's flat on her back spreading her legs for the Sergeant about now. I wouldn't mind a piece of that myself."

Dare lunged for the door. "Here now," growled the corporal, blocking the way. "The sergeant said no one was to interfere." Immediately three men seized Dare from behind, preventing him from brushing past the corporal and into the house.

"What is the meaning of this?" Roy leaped to

Dare's defense. "This is my home, and my sons and I have a right to enter. Release Dare!"

"The sergeant says no one's to go inside while him and the girl are . . . um . . . gathering up her belongings. She's under arrest and we've orders to take her to Sydney."

"Like hell!" Dare blasted, renewing his struggles to free himself.

Just then a shattering scream reverberated through the house, bursting into Dare's brain like an exploding bomb. The saliva in his mouth turned to cotton, nearly choking him, and nothing human could have prevented him from leaping to Casey's defense. In short order three men took flight as Dare, employing superhuman strength, hurled them through the air. Suddenly free of restraint, he burst through the door, leaving Ben, Roy and Martha to see to the troopers. Within seconds he flung open Casey's bedroom door and hurtled inside. The sight that met his eyes turned him into a raging bull bent on mayhem and destruction.

Sergeant Grimes was attempting to wrestle Casey onto the bed, and just as wildly Casey was resisting. Then suddenly Grimes was flying across the room and she felt herself clasped in strong, comforting arms.

"Casey, love, it's Dare. You're safe now."

Certain she was hallucinating, Casey squeezed her eyes shut, then slowly opened them. At length the mist began to clear and Dare's beloved face took shape. "Dare! It *is* you! Thank God. That man—that terrible Sergeant Grimes tried to—"

"I know, love," Dare smoothed, glancing down in disgust at Grimes's crumpled form.

Dare had flung him from Casey with such force that the man now lay on the floor in a daze. "Did he hurt you? If he did I'll kill him and the consequences be damned.

"No," Casey replied tearfully. "You arrived in time. But had you delayed one more minute . . ." She shuddered, and Dare held her tightly, afraid to think what would have happened. When he and Ben had met their father on the track and learned Casey was alone, he nearly killed his horse to reach her in time. And he'd almost failed.

Suddenly four troopers burst into the room, followed by Ben and Roy. "What have you done to the sergeant?" the corporal asked, helping a wobbly Grimes to his feet.

"Nothing he didn't deserve," spat Dare belligerently. "His superiors won't be pleased to learn he was attempting to rape a defenseless woman."

"Get out of here, Grimes," Roy ordered curtly. "You've done enough damage for one day. How did you know Casey was here?"

"I'm not leaving without the girl," Grimes growled, finally gaining his senses. "My orders are to take her to Sydney. It was Lieutenant Potter who learned about her. The governor's clerk told him about the pardon and he rightly assumed we'd find her here. His orders are to bring her to Sydney for questioning."

"Did your orders include rape?" Ben asked hotly.

Choosing to ignore Ben's accusation, Grimes turned to his men. "Take the girl. We're expected in Sydney before dark."

Four men moved forward but Dare thrust

Casey safely behind him, refusing to give her up. "You'll take her over my dead body," he boldly challenged.

"That can be arranged," smirked Grimes.

"Dare, please," pleaded Casey, finally finding her voice. "Don't interfere. I think it best for all concerned if I go along with the troopers. I . . . I don't want to cause trouble."

"No!" Dare bellowed, enraged. "Grimes is an animal, I won't have him . . ." His words died in his throat as Grimes's imperceptible nod was correctly interpreted by one of the troopers who stealthily stepped behind Dare and clubbed him with the butt of his pistol. He dropped to the floor with a thud.

"Dare!" screamed Casey, scrambling to her knees.

With murder in his eyes, Ben lunged forward, but found himself forcibly restrained by Roy. "Let go, Father! Look what that bastard did to Dare!"

"There's nothing we can do for Casey now, Ben," Roy said between clenched teeth. "We'll have better luck going to Sydney and petitioning the court. I'm certain they'll understand once everything is explained to their satisfaction."

"Listen to your father, Ben," Casey advised desperately as she examined the lump rising on the back of Dare's head. The steady rise and fall of his chest told her he wasn't seriously injured and she heaved a sigh of relief.

"All right, girl, get your things," Grimes ordered gruffly. "Just enough to fill a small swag, mind you."

"Leave the room while I change," Casey said

in daring defiance. "Thanks to you, this dress is . . . is scarcely decent."

"So you can escape out the window?" bit out Grimes, openly derisive. "No, indeed."

"Have you no decency, Grimes?" Roy chided angrily. "Allow Casey the privacy she deserves."

"I promise I won't try to escape," Casey added. "But I refuse to budge until I've changed."

"Change your clothes," relented Grimes, muttering obscenities beneath his breath, "but make it quick." Then, glancing down at Dare's limp form, he ordered, "Get him out of here." Both Ben and Roy hastened to comply while everyone but Casey filed out of the room.

"I'll be right outside the door so don't try anything funny," Grimes warned, slanting a glare over his shoulder.

Ten minutes later Casey walked through her bedroom door, a swag with a few necessities flung under her arm. She was vastly relieved to see Dare, somewhat wobbly and pale, standing on his own two feet.

"I'm ready," she said, her voice quivering as tears as large as boulders lodged in her throat.

Grasping her arm, Grimes herded her toward the door, pausing briefly as Dare's voice, shaking with emotion, issued a threat that left Grimes more shaken than he cared to admit.

"Harm one hair on Casey's head and you're a dead man. I will personally see you in hell."

CHAPTER THIRTEEN

Steeped in misery, Casey paced the small cell. Six paces from end to end, six paces from side to side. One small window high up provided the meager light during the day, and at night she was allowed one candle. She could barely stomach the slop that passed as food and during her two weeks behind bars she had lost considerable weight. A pile of straw covered with a moth-eaten blanket served as a bed.

Whether or not she was deliberately being denied visitors, Casey had no idea, but in two weeks she had seen no one, not even Dare. Knowing the Penrods as she did, Casey strongly suspected they were being turned away. The one person who seemed to have unlimited access to her cell was Lieutenant Potter. Though he was still a young man, neither grotesque nor unpleasant to look upon, Casey cared little for his brooding features or hungry eyes. Nor did she appreciate his insolent remarks or the way his leering glances raked her body from head to toe.

Where was Dare? she wondered dispiritedly. She had no way of knowing that all three Penrod men were still in Sydney staying with their friend, Drew Stanley. They had arrived at nearly the same time Casey did, having followed Sergeant Grimes and his men into the city in order to ensure Casey's safety.

They had set to work immediately, using whatever influence available to them to free Casey. But to Dare's chagrin and despair, it appeared to be a hopeless cause. The Rum Corps, now in full control of the colony under the direction of John Macarthur and Lieutenant Colonel Johnston, thought to make an example of Casey to impress upon others the dire consequences of aiding convicts, who now fared little better than slaves under their cruel regime. Governor Bligh, still under house arrest, was of no help at all to Dare who, driven by desperation, had been reduced to begging. The fact that he expressed a desire to marry a convict offered little inducement.

As she slumped dejectedly in the soiled straw that served as her bed, Casey's mind drifted back two weeks to the ride to Sydney following her arrest. How she despised Sergeant Grimes, who had forced her to travel the entire distance seated in front of him on his horse. All the while he whispered obscenities in her ear, his bold hands drifting continually over her breasts, hips and thighs. She still carried bruises on her tender flesh from his cruel fumbling. But to her vast relief his abuse went no further, due no doubt to Dare's grim warning as well as the fact that the Penrods could be seen traveling a short distance behind.

Upon her arrival in Sydney, Lieutenant Potter immediately took charge, placing her in the cell she still occupied. Since then Potter had returned frequently to taunt her with threats about her uncertain future. Immersed in misery, Casey started violently when the cell door clanged open and admitted her nemesis, grinning smugly.

"I thought you'd like to know your trial has been set," Potter informed her. "Day after tomorrow. The Judge Advocate and Corps members will decide your fate."

Casey said nothing, staring at him with bleak eyes. Surely they wouldn't hang her for helping Tim, would they? She knew that hangings took place regularly on the gibbet erected on George Street, and occasionally women were led up the scaffold. But dear Lord, she didn't want to die; didn't deserve to die for so slight an offense! Vaguely she became aware that Potter was speaking to her.

"I'm not without influence, you know," he hinted slyly. "You can help your cause by being nice to me."

Casey blinked, not certain she understood. "Are you suggesting that I . . . that we—"

"You're not stupid, Casey, you know what I'm talking about," spat Potter nastily. "I've wanted you from the moment you were placed in my custody. You're no innocent. Surely three lusty men like the Penrods made good use of what you offered. I'm as good as they are. Spread yourself willingly for me and I'll see that you're given a light sentence."

Red dots of rage exploded behind Casey's brain. "Go to hell!" she said violently. "You can force me, but everyone in the colony will know of it when I'm brought to trial. I'm certain your pride and integrity will suffer when I'm finished with you, unless you consider yourself on the same level with Sergeant Grimes who tried to rape me."

His blue eyes turned flinty and his hands clenched into tight fists. "You little bitch! Just wait, I'll have you yet!" he promised menacingly. "And it won't be so pleasant as it would have been had you complied willingly." Turning on his heel, he stormed from the cell, leaving Casey shaking in fury as well as fright.

Though Casey prayed fervently for just one glimpse of Dare, her wish was not granted. And two days later a sullen Lieutenant Potter escorted her to Government House where her case was being heard. No one was present except for the Judge Advocate and three judges, all Corps members who would act as jury and decide her punishment. As if in a daze she listened to the charges against her, remaining mute during the reading. An unexpected shock came when Robin Fletcher was led into the room, looking hollow-eyed and gaunt from his long weeks in jail. It appeared they were to be tried together for the same offense. They were given no opportunity to communicate, but the looks he sent her held sympathy as well as encouragement. Casey took heart, until a smirking Meg was called into the room to provide witness.

Bending Casey a look of pure hatred, Meg, in a high, clear voice, condemned and accused as she told all she knew about Tim, and about both Casey's and Robin's part in his successful escape, which was considerable. When she finished there was little for Casey to say except to vehemently deny she stole valuables belonging to Roy Penrod. As to the charge of aiding an escaped convict, her guilt was all too obvious. Robin's defense was no defense at all. Their guilt was undeniable.

When pressed to reveal the whereabouts of
Tim O'Malley, both refused to answer, except to
say he had probably died in the bush of his
wounds. Then Meg, having no further information to offer, was dismissed. Casey's knees
quaked as the stern-faced Judge Advocate
frowned down on her.

"Miss O'Cain, the charge against you is a
serious one," he said in a censorious tone. "A
crime obviously committed willingly on your
part. I have no choice but to—"

Suddenly a racket arose outside the closed
door and a tremor went through Casey as Dare
burst in, the restraining hands of two troopers
having little effect upon his determined progress.
"What's the meaning of this?" the startled judge
barked.

"Miss O'Cain is my fiancée," Dare proclaimed
loudly. "I demand you release her!"

"You demand!" shouted Lieutenant Potter.
Until now he had stood quietly in the back-
ground watching as the trial progressed. "The
woman has committed a serious crime and must
be punished." He was more than a little dismayed to hear Dare refer to Casey as his fiancée.
That a pure merino would marry such a woman
was beyond imagining.

"I believe I am the judge here," the Judge
Advocate said coolly, looking down his long nose
at the disruption. "Lieutenant Potter is correct in
saying a crime has been committed and punishment due. It is the judgment of this board that
Miss Casey O'Cain be given a penalty of seven
years' labor to be served in the colony under the
direction of Lieutenant Potter."

"But she's been pardoned!" Dare cried, his

temper exploding. "Governor Bligh emancipated her and we are to marry!"

"And I have just revoked that status by invoking a new penalty," the judge glared, not pleased by Dare's startling announcement about his marriage plans.

"Then I request that Casey be assigned to Penrod station to fill her old position as cook," Dare persisted.

"It's too late," Potter said, stepping forward. The crafty smile playing about Potter's mouth filled Dare with foreboding. "I've already asked that Miss O'Cain be assigned to me. I recently bought a house and am in need of a housekeeper."

"A bedwarmer, you mean!" blasted Dare, snarling in disgust. "You touch her and I'll kill you!"

"Enough!" roared the judge, rising from his seat. "Take him out of here. Restrain him if need be but don't let him near the woman. I believe placing Miss O'Cain with Lieutenant Potter is in her best interest. Under his able guidance she will be completely rehabilitated at the end of seven years."

Cursing, resisting all the way, Dare was forcibly evicted from the room, leaving Casey in shock. She was to live in the same house with Lieutenant Potter! She knew exactly what would come of that. One way or another he meant to have her. Abruptly she became aware of the judge's voice and forced her attention on his words.

"Robin Fletcher, your pardon is also revoked. I'm imposing a penalty of seven years at hard labor and the confiscation of all property held in your name. You are to be transferred to the coal mines where you will serve the entirety of your sentence."

Robin sagged, his frame seeming to crumble. It was tantamount to a death sentence. No one could survive seven years in the coal mines.

"I'm sorry, Robin," sobbed Casey tearfully. "It's all my fault. I never meant this to happen."

Robin's answer never reached her for he was hustled out before the words left his mouth. But his ravaged face effectively proclaimed his anguish, which only served to reinforce Casey's tremendous guilt.

Released into Potter's service, Casey dragged her feet as she followed him from Government House, aware that Dare was lost to her forever. Each of the Penrods watched with stricken eyes as Casey emerged from Government House.

"Wait," cried Roy before Casey could be led off. "I'd like to speak with Casey."

"Have your say and be quick about it," Potter growled, his surly expression conveying his displeasure.

Roy frowned, angry that he wasn't to be allowed a private moment with Casey. However, he and Dare cautiously approached her under Potter's wary eye. Their words, meant to inspire courage, served only to intensify her longing to return to the Hawkesbury with them. While they talked in low voices, Ben, who had somehow escaped Potter's notice, sidled inconspicuously to Casey's side. She stiffened, then relaxed when she felt Ben slide a cold, hard object into her hand. Curling her fist around the blade, Casey hid it within the folds of her skirt, conveying her thanks with her eyes.

Dare's words of encouragement still echoed in her ears when Lieutenant Potter led her into his small house not far from the center of town. "Take heart, love. One way or another I'll get you out of this." What was meant to instill hope only plunged her deeper into despair. She had already cost one man his freedom and couldn't bear seeing the man she loved being led down the same path.

Casey glared sullenly as Potter shoved her through the door of the small dwelling he had recently purchased. The narrow entry led directly to a parlor furnished sparsely with crude furniture. A bedroom and dining room opened off another narrow passageway leading from the parlor. The back rooms consisted of a kitchen, study and tiny servants' room. The house was small by any standards, and far from luxurious, but sufficient for a bachelor's needs, which Potter was quick to point out.

"Your duty will be to cook, clean and see to my . . . needs," Potter hinted broadly. "You will do well to please me, for I can be generous when well satisfied. Seven years sounds like a long time but I think you'll find I'm not a difficult taskmaker."

Seething with impotent rage, Casey knew exactly what it would take to satisfy Potter. "I'll perform my duties to the best of my ability," she bit out between clenched teeth. "The *household* duties only." Her terse words left him little doubt that he would find her unwilling to perform more personal tasks.

"You'll do whatever I ask," Potter ground out, eyes glittering dangerously. "And you'll start now. I've waited a long time for you."

Before Casey realized his intent, Potter grasped her around the waist and bodily forced her into the room that was to be hers, tossing her unceremoniously on the hard surface of the bed, skirts awhirl. Leering greedily at the lovely length of exposed limbs, Potter threw himself atop her, his hands settling on her breasts. An oath burst from his lips as his fingers encountered numerous buttons on the front of her dress, effectively hindering him from plundering her bare flesh. Suddenly his patience gave way and, hooking his fingers in the neckline, he ripped her bodice from throat to waist, baring those luscious fruits to his hungry gaze.

"Jesus! That's the prettiest pair I've ever seen," he groaned, grasping a tight, pink bud between his teeth and biting down painfully before drawing it into his mouth.

Struggling, crying out in pain, Casey realized with a start that she still clutched the knife that Ben had slipped into her palm earlier. Somehow she had managed to keep it concealed all this time in the folds of her skirt. Her situation was so desperate that committing murder seemed preferable to submitting to Potter's base desires. Cautiously she brought her hand forward until the point of the blade pressed against the soft flesh of his stomach. Consumed by lust, Potter did not realize Casey's intent until the knife tip pierced his flesh, and he yelped in surprise, abruptly jerking backwards.

"What the hell!"

"Let me go or I'll drive the blade home," Casey hissed, her green eyes ripe with hatred.

"You little bitch!" Potter spat angrily. "Where did you get the knife?"

"None of your business," Casey replied tightly. "Just remember, I've killed once and feel no compunction about killing again. They say it's easier the second time."

"I could easily disarm you," Potter smiled nastily. "Your meager strength is no match for mine."

"Of course you're stronger than I am," Casey agreed sweetly. "But rape me and I swear some way, somehow, when you least expect it, I'll strike. You might take my weapon but there will be others available. Perhaps I'll attack while you're sleeping, but then again I might pounce on you as you come into the house, or . . ." She shrugged. "The possibilities are unlimited."

"I should have known better than to take a murderess into my home," Potter complained. Convinced that Casey was entirely capable of carrying out her threat, his ardor quickly shriveled against his stomach. Shifting his weight, he rose unsteadily to his feet. "I ought to beat you."

"Go ahead," Casey boldly challenged, lifting her chin defiantly. "But it won't change a thing. Leave me be and I'll perform my duties efficiently, but touch me . . ." Her words trailed off but her threat was implicit.

"You little whore!" Potter spat. "What makes you think you're special? All women have the same thing between their legs, some probably better than yours. Heed my warning, Casey O'Cain. I can be driven only so far." Casey shuddered, his words hanging in the air like autumn smoke.

The following weeks crawled by with grim regularity. The days weren't nearly so bad, for Casey had her chores which she performed to the

letter, allowing Potter no cause for complaint.
The fact that Potter had his own duties during
the day helped immeasurably to ease her woes.
Though he had not tried to molest her again, his
narrowed gaze followed her everywhere. She kept
as much to herself as possible, since it was
blatantly obvious that Potter still wanted her in
his bed. And just as clear that he was a coward,
fearing to turn his back on a murderess whose
threats successfully kept him at bay.

When Potter returned in the evenings, Casey
made certain his meal was prepared and served
immediately. After cleaning up she promptly
sought the safety of her room. Sometimes he
taunted her cruelly; other times he remained
sullen and uncommunicative, probing her relentlessly with hooded eyes. It was those occasions
Casey feared most, especially when he turned to
drink. But thus far he had kept his distance, for
which Casey was eternally grateful. She wasn't
certain she could kill a man, no matter what the
provocation.

It was in the privacy of her tiny room that
Casey felt most threatened. Not by Potter but by
her own thoughts and yearnings. Dare! Memory
merged with dreams as she conjured up his
beloved face, and like a candle that burned
brighter and hotter in the presence of the wind,
she burned with remembered pleasure. Their
shared passion had been real, an emotion so
strong she could not suppress it any more than
she could deny her love. Her body rebelled at the
revolting thought of another man possessing her
as Dare had, touching her in places only Dare
knew. Reason as well as instinct warned her that
there no longer was the remotest possibility of

their marriage taking place. What man, no matter how strong his love, would wait seven years for a woman?

Where was Dare now? Casey wondered bleakly. Was he back on the Hawkesbury with his family, immersed in his work? Did he occasionally think of her? Casey would have been shocked as well as vastly pleased to know that Dare's thoughts and yearnings closely paralleled her own.

Dare could not bring himself to leave Sydney immediately following Casey's trial. How could he continue his everyday existence while the woman he loved faced danger at every turn? He easily learned the location of Lieutenant Potter's house and began watching it closely, hoping for a glimpse of Casey. But to his chagrin, she never appeared. He had no idea she was forbidden use of the front door and was allowed only in the rear yard protected by a high fence. To his knowledge, Casey did no shopping in the government store, for Potter brought home food and supplies on a daily basis. No one else entered or left the house.

Dare had not been idle these last weeks. He had petitioned John Macarthur, Lieutenant Colonel Johnston, and every high-ranking officer in the Corps, all with disappointing results. His pleas went unheeded. He made so many calls at Government House he was finally forbidden entrance. Exhausted from his efforts, worn down by despair, Dare came to the inevitable conclusion that there was nothing further to be done at this time for Casey. His only recourse was to return to the farm to gather his wits and carefully plan his next course of action. A chance conver-

sation overheard in the street drastically altered
his plans.

Two troopers lounged outside Government
House gossiping, and Dare paused in passing
when he heard Potter's name mentioned.

"Are you joining Lieutenant Potter's patrol
tomorrow, Moore?" asked one of the men, a
brash-faced private.

"Aye, and you, Smith?" came Moore's reply.
He had hoped to spend the night with his favorite
prostitute instead of chasing escaped convicts.

"Aye, I'm going, for all the good it will do,"
Smith complained. "These convicts have a way
of disappearing in the bush never to be seen
again. Unless it's to rob decent folk of their
valuables or steal sheep. Bushrangers are a menace to the colony the way they flaunt authority. I
can't blame the Corps for wanting them hunted
down and disposed of."

"You're not the only one complaining about
this patrol," Moore snickered lewdly. "Lieutenant Potter seldom ventures from his house since
the O'Cain girl was assigned to him. To hear him
talk, she's so hot for him they spend all their
spare time in bed. I wouldn't mind a hot little
thing like that spreading her thighs for me. No
wonder he's afraid to let her out of his sight."

"Looks like he'll have no choice this time,"
Smith guffawed. "He's likely to be gone several
days. What will that sweet little thing do without
him? Mayhap she'll try to seduce Corporal Frederick, the man Potter is leaving behind to . . .
protect her."

For some unexplained reason that remark produced a burst of laughter as both troopers ambled
off in the opposite direction, leaving Dare with

the terrible urge to kill Potter. Could what the troopers said be true? he wondered glumly. Had Casey willingly become Potter's doxy? No! He refused to consider such a thing. In order to retain his sanity he had to believe Potter was not possessing Casey in the same way he had. Despite the danger, he knew of only one way to learn the truth. He had to see Casey for himself. Only then would he decide whether or not Potter should continue to live.

The following day passed so slowly Dare chafed with impatience. From a distance he watched as Lieutenant Potter led his patrol out early that morning. Dare hoped the escaped convict would lead them on a wild chase through the brush consuming several days. He needed time, lots of it. In the meantime he lingered near Potter's house, waiting until darkness to make his move.

When a black blanket settled over the land, Dare cautiously made his way toward the back of the house. The fence posed no problem as he easily scaled it and dropped noiselessly to the ground. A lamp burned in the kitchen and through the window Dare saw Casey set a dish of food before a trooper whose gestures were decidedly effeminate. Despite the man's burly build, Dare sensed immediately the cause of Troopers Smith and Moore's mirth when referring to Corporal Frederick. Lieutenant Potter had picked the best man at his disposal to guard Casey, one who had no interest in her as a woman yet was brawny enough to protect his property.

Dare waited with bated breath as the corporal finished his meal and wandered into the parlor.

Casey quickly completed her chores and disappeared into a room off to the right. That was all Dare needed to know as he easily located her window, waiting until the light was doused before slipping noiselessly through the opening.

Casey had intuitively realized the first moment she laid eyes on Corporal Frederick that he would pose no threat to her as a woman. She had heard about men like him but expected them to be of slight build and to possess feminine traits. Instead, Corporal Frederick was rather handsome, in a surly way, and brawny enough to be a prizefighter. Only his eyes and certain mannerisms betrayed him.

Corporal Frederick's duty was to guard her, but escape was furthest from her mind. Where would she go? Certainly not to Dare. She had already ruined one man and couldn't bear the thought of bringing disaster to another.

Undressing quickly, Casey slid beneath the sheet, the intense heat making her cotton nightgown unnecessary. Her nakedness was a luxury she wouldn't have allowed herself had Potter been in the house. Tossing restlessly, she did not hear the soft patter of footsteps whisper cross the floor. At first she thought the strained words wafting through the darkness nothing but the echo of her longing. But then she felt a warm breath brush her cheek and smelled the familiar, tantalizing odor that never failed to arouse her. No other man in the world had that power over her.

"Dare." The word came tumbling from her lips in a strangled murmur.

"Casey, my love."

"Oh, Dare, if only you were real."

"I am real, sweetheart. Wait, I'll strike a light so you can see for yourself." He fumbled in the dark before a flickering flame spread its meager glow. "There," he said, turning to face her. "Now do you believe I'm real?"

The bedsprings groaned as he slid down beside her, drawing her into his arms. Then his mouth slowly descended on hers, hot and hard and hungry as desperation to experience her sweetness once more drove him. She opened to him and welcomed him, driven by the flames of overwhelming love. It felt so warm, so right to be in Dare's arms again as she melted into his embrace. Abruptly he broke contact, backing off and drawing the sheet away from her slim form.

"Dare, what is it?"

Her skin was soft and smooth, unmarred and flawless. Dare could only stare in fascination at her lovely nude body. Slowly his hands moved, stroking over belly and tops of her thighs and back to rose-tipped breasts.

"He hasn't harmed you, has he?" Dare asked tightly. "Has that bastard forced you? I see no marks on your flesh."

"He hasn't touched me, Dare," Casey was quick to assure him. "The man is a coward. I threatened him with the knife Ben gave me and told him I'd find some way to kill him if he laid a hand on me. Surprisingly, he believed me."

"Thank God the man is a fool as well as a coward," sighed Dare gratefully.

Ignoring the danger from Corporal Frederick who was within hearing distance if he was awake, Dare swiftly undressed, and Casey felt the shock of warm muscle and sinew settle against her softness.

Then he was kissing her. Ravenous kisses that made her head spin and her senses reel. Fiery kisses that awakened in her an answering fire; wonderful kisses, magical kisses that made her forget all but the here and now. Reluctantly abandoning her lips, Dare found an aching nipple, suckling her like a babe. She responded by moaning his name. Then he found the most magnificent things to do to her with his fingers, rubbing and caressing her until her legs spread wide and she was writhing with pleasure.

Using tongue and hands with consummate skill, he prepared and stimulated her beyond endurance. Until hunger stormed her body and demanded feeding. "Now, Dare," she urged as her small hand found his manhood; a warm column of burning steel sheathed in velvet.

"No, love," Dare denied her, panting raggedly. "Let me touch you. It's been so long. I want to explore every inch of your delicate flesh. Let me . . . Let me . . ."

A heavenly, wonderful feeling began to build as his fingers explored her soft wetness and searched for her moist depths. Then his mouth found her and his tongue probed where his fingers had been only moments before, reducing her to a kind of senselessness, all feelings and emotions. Then ecstasy seized her and spun her away into a mindless void.

Coming slowly to her senses, Casey felt his thigh slide between hers, hair-roughened and hard. The sensation was exquisite, and once again she allowed him to fill her senses and carry her away. He thrust himself inside her, pushing his hard length until she feared she would split in two, but she didn't care, her need was a delicious agony driving her.

"Oh, my love, you're so warm, so tight, so wet. I've dreamed of this for weeks," Dare groaned hoarsely as his hips worked at her with powerful, determined thrusts.

Grasping her buttocks, he easily reversed their position, allowing her to set their pace. Lustrous strands of red hair tickled his chest as Casey strained over him, slowly at first, then gaining momentum as she became accustomed to the position. Joyfully meeting her downward thrusts, Dare hung on the brink for a breathless moment before reversing their positions once again, placing Casey beneath him.

"Hurry, love," he urged breathlessly. "I can wait no longer. This is as close to heaven as I can expect to get."

His sensual words drove Casey over the edge as she exploded . . . and exploded . . . and exploded. The moment Dare felt her body tense and her insides tighten around him, he gave in to his own raging need, shuddering and groaning with an ecstasy bordering on pain.

"I love you, Casey," he whispered as they floated in an ocean of euphoria. "Never doubt my love, no matter what may happen."

Casey snuggled against his warmth, too content to pay heed to anything but his declaration of love. "I've always loved you, Dare, and always will," she pledged.

Weariness laced her voice, but before sleep could claim her Dare poked her awake. "Don't go to sleep, love, we must be far away before daylight."

"Far away?" Casey repeated groggily. "What are you talking about?"

"I'm taking you away from here. It tears me apart to leave you at the mercy of a man like Potter. Do you know what he's saying? He's telling everyone that you . . . you share his bed. And that you . . . enjoy it."

His words startled Casey awake. "But, Dare, that isn't true!"

"I believe you, love, but I still can't bear to leave you with him. Get dressed, we're leaving."

"Where will we go? There's no place in the colony where we'll be safe."

"We can hide in the bush and live off the land," replied Dare with grim determination. "We'll be safe for the time being at the cave."

Casey shook her head regretfully. "No, Dare, I can't and won't ask that of you. I refuse to drag you down to the same level as myself. You've too much to give up, too much to lose. "No," she objected strenuously. "I won't leave with you."

"Bloody hell, Casey, do you enjoy living here with Potter?" Dare exploded. "Are his stories about the two of you true?"

"Dare! How could you? It's you I'm thinking of. And Ben, and your father. Will you have the Corps confiscate all that Roy has worked for years to accumulate, all he possesses and loves? Being responsible for such a travesty would haunt me for the rest of my life."

"What would you have me do?" Dare agonized.

"Forget me," Casey pleaded, choking on a sob. "I don't have the right to ask you to wait seven years for me."

"I love you. You have every right in the world

to ask anything of me, except to leave you here. One day Potter will call your bluff and take you by force. You know it and I know it. Please, Casey, don't argue, just hurry and dress."

Thinking he had put an end to her objections, Dare rose and hastily threw on his clothes, surprised to find that Casey had not done the same. "Casey—"

"Go, Dare, before you're discovered," she urged. They were the most difficult words she had ever uttered. "Please."

"Who's in there?" a voice outside the closed door demanded. "Who's with you, girl?"

"No one! There's no one with me," Casey answered, feigning drowsiness. "You woke me up, Corporal. What is it you want?"

"I swear I heard voices coming from your room," he grumbled, openly skeptical. "I'm coming in."

"No! Wait! I . . . let me cover myself first!" To Dare she hissed, "Go, Dare, please."

Left with no alternative, Dare gave an exasperated grunt and stepped through the window, turning back once to promise, "I'll be back, love. Somehow I'll convince you that nothing matters to me but your safety. I'll gladly sacrifice all I own for you."

Leaving Casey behind was the hardest thing Dare had ever done in his life. Then he was gone as swiftly and silently as he had appeared.

A few seconds later Corporal Frederick burst through the door and found Casey alone, sitting in the center of the bed with the covers pulled up to her chin.

CHAPTER FOURTEEN

Lieutenant Potter returned late the next day. The hapless convict was captured before he could melt into the bush and disappear. Potter was in a jovial mood when he walked into the house, having returned his prisoner in record time. The aborigine tracker employed by the Corps demonstrated his fantastic skill by leading them directly to the man. In making his escape, the convict had killed a man and was to be hung for his crime within the next few days.

With Potter's return, Dare realized there was virtually no possibility of taking Casey from under his nose, for the man watched her like a hawk. Why wouldn't she go away with him while the opportunity existed? Dare agonized. Did she doubt his ability to protect her? Didn't she know he'd sacrifice everything for her? Maybe she didn't love him enough. No! he scolded himself sternly. Those thoughts were unworthy of the love they shared. It was Casey's fears over his safety that kept them apart. There was nothing to be done now but return to the farm as he originally planned and devise some other method to free Casey. Given time, Dare realized with a pang of terror, Potter would put Casey's threat to the test, and she hadn't the physical strength to resist.

For a week after Dare had returned home, neither Ben nor Ray were successful in dispelling the gloom that gripped him. He drove himself relentlessly until exhaustion claimed him. After a quiet supper shared with his family he usually disappeared into his room with a bottle, passing the night drinking and pacing. If he slept at all, Ben wasn't aware of it for he heard his brother's footsteps through the thin walls no matter what the time of night.

Ben was deeply concerned over his brother's shattered emotions, sleepless nights and morose disposition. So worried, that he conferred often with his father about it. "Is there nothing we can do to ease Dare's suffering, Father?" he asked one day when they were alone. I don't know how much longer he can go on like this."

"Lord only knows I've talked to everyone who will listen," Roy replied, shaking his head in defeat. It's as if all doors are closed to me. The Corps have all the exclusionists thinking as they do. They consider emancipists second-rate citizens with no rights at all and convicts no better than slaves. They believe in strict segregation of classes, and Dare has broached those boundaries by openly declaring his intention to marry a convict."

"Dammit, Father, love has no boundaries!" Ben exclaimed, wise beyond his years. "Casey and Dare love one another and have the right to be together. We both know Casey isn't capable of murdering anyone. Her conviction was a mistake. I feel so damn helpless."

"So do I, son."

"What about Thad McKenzie? He resigned
from the Corps years ago but retained some
pretty influential friends. He and Lieutenant
Colonel Johnston have been close for as long as I
can remember. Thad is also a fervent advocate of
John Macarthur."

"Since Dare dropped Mercy and declared his
love for Casey, Thad hasn't spoken to me. He
holds me responsible because I brought Casey
into our household. Besides, he's a confirmed
supporter of the Corps and their policies. No,
Ben," Roy allowed with painful resignation,
"there's no help there, or anywhere, as far as I
can tell."

Their conversation ended on that note, but
their concern did not.

Dare stared morosely into the distance. He
loved this rich, rugged land scrubbed bare by
winds and parched by summer sun. It was a
strong land, unyielding and unforgiving, yet
upon the low sloping hills grew brush, now
seared dry, eucalyptus and thorn bushes. It
wasn't totally desolate, for with the rains came
lush grass and flowers of every hue. This was his
home. Yet he would willingly sacrifice all to have
Casey with him. He watched appreciatively as
the sun sank below the hills in a spellbinding
display of red and gold and darkness settled over
the land. It was time to go home. Time to retreat
to the solitude of his room where his only solace
these days lay in strong spirits.

When Dare entered the house he found a
surprise waiting for him. Seated in the parlor
with Ben and Roy were Thad McKenzie and

Mercy. The tension in the room was thick enough to slice, and an inexplicable foreboding seized Dare. The men wore deep scowls, but Mercy's smile struck him like a ray of sunshine in the gloomy atmosphere. She reminded Dare of a kitten who had just lapped a bowl of cream.

"Thad, Mercy," he greeted, looking from father to daughter. "What's going on here?"

"I'll let Mercy explain," Thad said, obviously not too pleased with whatever had brought him here. "I just want you to know I don't entirely approve of what my daughter proposes, but I'd do anything to see her happy."

"What's this all about, Mercy?" Dare asked warily.

Suddenly Thad rose from his chair. "Let's leave the young people to hash this out. Come along, Roy, Ben. I want to try some of that good brandy of yours. Perhaps in a little while we'll have something to celebrate."

"Dare," Ben began hesitantly, "I—"

"Come along, Ben," Thad advised sternly. "The decision is not ours to make." Reluctantly Ben turned and followed Thad and Roy from the room, but not before he slanted Dare a pitying look.

"Sit down, Dare," Mercy coaxed.

"Mercy, I don't know what this is about but if you don't tell me soon I'm going to throttle you. All this mystery is setting me on edge."

"You always were impatient, Dare. In more ways than one," she hinted broadly. "So I'll be direct."

"That's a novelty," Dare mocked with provoking rancor. "Get on with it."

Gulping, Mercy said, "Let me begin by saying

I'm sorry about your friend Robin. Even though he was guilty the punishment was unnecessarily harsh."

Dare acknowledged her words with a curt nod but said nothing.

Suddenly her words came tumbling out one after another. "Dare, I can help you. Not only can I arrange a ticket of leave for Robin Fletcher to work where he wants, but I can obtain a full pardon for Casey O'Cain."

Dare's silver eyes showed the tortured dullness of disbelief. A tumble of confused thoughts and feelings assailed him. "Why?" he asked, his voice trembling with emotion. "Why would you do that? And how? I know Father has exhausted every avenue of appeal."

"I love you, Dare, what better way to prove my love?"

"You're aware, of course, that once Casey is free I fully intend to marry her. What satisfaction would you derive from your 'good deed'? And what makes you so certain you can deliver what you promise?"

"I'll answer your last question first," Mercy smiled coyly. "Papa has already spoken to Colonel Johnston. They're old friends, you know. And the lieutenant governor owes Papa a favor. At Papa's urging he has agreed to emancipate Casey. But all he would guarantee for Robin was a ticket of leave. You have to admit that's a vast improvement over the coal mines."

"Why would your father take it upon himself to help Casey and Robin?" asked Dare suspiciously. "His feelings toward convicts and emancipists are well known."

"For me, Dare. Because I asked him. Papa loves me and wants me to be happy."

"It would make you happy to see me married to another woman?" Now Dare really was confused. Mercy never did anything without a motive.

"You know me too well, Dare," Mercy temporized. "I wouldn't do this if there wasn't something in it for me. You're the prize, darling. Casey gets her freedom, Robin is released from the coal mines, and . . . I get you."

"Bloody hell! Make sense, will you!"

"Darling, Papa isn't too keen about this whole thing, but it's what I want. He knows I love you and he's willing to use his clout with the Corps to fulfill my wishes and give me what I desire. I desire you, Dare. As a husband. The moment you say, 'I do' Casey O'Cain will be a free woman."

"My God, Mercy, that's blackmail!" Dare exploded, astounded by her gall. "Do you know what you're asking?"

"I think so," Mercy stated shrewdly.

"How could you want me knowing I love another?"

"I'm counting on your love for Casey to win you over. I know how you feel about her living with Lieutenant Potter. I'm staking my future on the premise that you'd do anything to gain her freedom. Even marry me."

"I can't believe what I'm hearing," Dare said, trembling with fury. "I'd make you a lousy husband."

"I'm willing to take my chances," Mercy said wryly. "We were good together once, darling, and we could be again. You would have married me if Casey hadn't come along when she did. Marry me, Dare, and you'll gain more from our union than I will. But I'm a gambler at heart. I'm willing to bet in time you'll come to love me as much as I love you. I'm counting on that, darling."

Love Mercy? His voice hardened ruthlessly. "You're deluding yourself, Mercy. If I marry you, and I stress the word 'if,' it will be to help Casey and Robin and for no other reason."

His contemptuous tone sparked Mercy's anger. "Be careful, darling, or I'll withdraw my offer. Think it over carefully before you refuse."

Assuming a thoughtful look, Dare nodded and walked to the window to stare morosely into the darkness. Could Mercy really deliver all she promised? he reflected glumly. Somehow he believed she could, given her father's warm friendship with both Johnston and Macarthur. The next question he asked himself was whether he was willing to spend the rest of his life with a woman he cared nothing about in order to set Casey free and help Robin. The answer was a resounding "yes." No sacrifice was too great for the woman he loved.

Whirling abruptly, Dare barked, "How do I know you'll keep your word?"

"I'll bring you the pardon and Robin's ticket of leave on the day we marry. Father will hold the papers until the ceremony is performed, after which he'll hand them over to your father."

"You're certain your father can accomplish all this?" Dare questioned skeptically. "After all, my own father is not without influence and he has had no success."

"I wouldn't be here now if there was the slightest doubt. All that stands in the way is your pride. But somehow I think you're smart enough to realize I'm Casey's only hope."

All the fight seemed to leave Dare as his shoulders slumped dejectedly. Then a derisive grin turned up the corner of his mouth as he bowed with exaggerated mockery. "Mercy, will you do me the honor of becoming my bride?" The words tasted like bile on his tongue.

Mercy suppressed a shudder, the look on Dare's face causing a twinge of regret deep in the recesses of her heart. But it was too late. For better or worse she was committed. And if the cold, unyielding glare in Dare's eyes was any indication of their future, her life was about to undergo a drastic upheaval. Was being with the man she loved enough to compensate for his contempt? No man enjoyed being forced into marriage.

Confident of her ability to bring Dare to heel, Mercy purred seductively, "I'll make you happy, Dare. I'm determined to make you love me. Shall we tell the others our good news?"

Roy and Ben exchanged worried glances as Dare sat in silent contemplation, brooding, his eyes blank. He had retreated into silence, sucking moodily at a mug filled with rum ever since the McKenzies left. His mood differed greatly from their guests' obvious jubilation. But then, he had little reason for celebration.

"You don't have to go through with it, Dare," Roy advised. "Think of the years ahead of you married to a woman you don't love."

"A love match in this day and age is rare," Dare remarked absently.

"How do you think Casey will feel when she learns of your sacrifice?" Ben ventured.

Suddenly Dare came to life, his eyes blazing with an inner fire. "You're not to tell her, Ben, do you understand? Nor you, Father. Casey is guilt-ridden enough over involving Robin in all this.

Knowing that I'm going into this marriage for
her sake alone will only add to her guilt. She's not
to know. Tell Casey anything, but not the truth."

"Dare, when Casey learns of your marriage
she's likely to hate you unless she's made aware
of the truth. Do you want that?"

"Perhaps it's best she *does* hate me," said Dare
bleakly. "I've nothing to offer Casey once I
marry Mercy. I wouldn't want her to go through
life loving me when there is absolutely no hope
for us." His expression was one of mute wretchedness, his misery like a steel weight bearing
down on him.

"So you truly intend to see this through," Roy
remarked, his heart bleeding for his son.

"In two days Mercy McKenzie will be my legal
wife. The ceremony will be performed by the
Judge Advocate at Government House. After
spending a few days at McKenzie station following the ceremony I intend to return home. Mercy
can accompany me if she wishes. I don't give a
damn what she does. But I refuse to live anyplace
but on Penrod station."

"What about Casey? How will she support
herself once she's free? Have you thought about
that? We can't turn her loose in a town like
Sydney," Ben argued. "She'll be fair game to men
like Potter and Grimes."

Dare's anguish peaked to shatter the last
shreds of his control. "Bloody hell!" he raged. "I
won't set her free only to throw her to the wolves!
Father, bring Casey back to the farm. Tell her
she's to be a guest in the house, anything, only
don't let her remain in Sydney."

"Can you handle it, Dare? Having Casey in the
same house, I mean. I would think seeing her

every day will only increase your torment. Not to mention the vigorous objection Mercy is likely to voice."

"Casey will probably hate me so much she'll refuse to speak to me. As for Mercy, she'll have no choice but to accept Casey as part of our household. Needless to say, every day of my life will be a living hell with Casey so close."

Privately, Roy thought Mercy would raise a terrible ruckus when she returned from her honeymoon and found Casey living on the farm. Things certainly wouldn't be dull around here. That is if he could convince Casey to return to the Hawkesbury with him. A not inconsiderable task.

Once Dare left Sydney, Casey's circumstances changed drastically. Inexplicably she was allowed to leave the small house to purchase food and supplies with the meager coins doled out by Lieutenant Potter. But she was no fool. She knew that if Dare returned she would once again be confined to the house and back yard.

The days following Dare's nocturnal visit were particularly trying ones for Casey. She wondered if he was angry with her for refusing to run away with him. Didn't he realize she loved him far too much to turn him into an outcast?

Memories of their stolen night together were all she had to sustain her in the long days and nights to come. No man but Dare could bring her to the pinnacle of ecstasy. His hands, his lips, even his eyes made love to her with an ardor that was uniquely his. Her nighttime fantasies often carried her to the realm of intense longing where she imagined him lying beside her. Unconsciously she'd reach for him, then, not finding him, lay awake for hours aching for him and his touch.

One night about two weeks after Dare left Sydney, Lieutenant Potter came into the house roaring drunk. That in itself was so unusual that Casey immediately became apprehensive. What made her even more wary was the way Potter stared at her as she served his meal. He had something to say, she knew, for the calculated gleam in his eye gave him away. Yet he chose to torment her with his silence. If he didn't speak soon she'd go crazy. The hell with him! she decided irritably. Why should she stand around and become the object of his perverse amusement? Without a word of warning she whirled and sought the relative safety of her room.

To Casey's horror she soon learned there was no safe place in the small house to hide from Potter. With a strength born of lust and strong drink, the door to her room burst open on shattered hinges and Potter reeled in the doorway, leering at her.

Instinctively Casey reached for the knife always kept in readiness on the nightstand, and found it missing. Panic seized her as she scrabbled frantically amid the contents atop the stand, then dropped her eyes to the floor, searching . . . searching.

"Are you looking for this?" Potter asked, slurring the words. The knife rested in the palm of his hand. Staggering to the open window, he tossed it out into the night. "I took the liberty of removing it while you were preparing supper. I didn't want it anywhere in sight when I told you my news."

"News?" repeated Casey warily.

"The whole town is celebrating the big wedding. Free rum for everyone."

"You're drunk," Casey spat disgustedly.

"Mayhap," hiccupped Potter, "but how could I refuse to toast the bride and groom? A bloody fine show. Old man McKenzie knows how to marry off his daughter in style."

"You mean Mercy? Mercy McKenzie got married today?" Bells of warning sounded in her brain and Casey suddenly felt ill.

"The Judge Advocate performed the ceremony and the happy couple left immediately for her father's farm to begin their honeymoon while the drinks flowed like water," Potter informed her gleefully. "I have to admit I'd rush the girl off to bed just as Penrod did. An enticing bit of fluff. Penrod must be pleased with himself. Her old man is loaded and quite influential."

"Penrod!" Casey gasped, gaping in disbelief. "Ben married Mercy McKenzie?"

Potter's derisive laughter gave Casey the first inkling of what was to come. "No! No!" she cried, refusing to accept the news that Potter seemed so eager to impart.

"Oh, yes, my sweet," he sneered. "Your lover married another woman. Can you blame him for refusing to wait seven years for you? So much for love. Now there's no one but me to take care of your needs. See to mine, Casey, and I'll ease yours."

Caught off guard by the sudden shock of Dare's marriage, Casey reeled, unable to speak or react as Potter advanced on her. Only when his hands grasped her shoulders and his lips slobbered wet kisses on her face did she regain her senses.

"No!" she objected violently, shoving him

away with all her might. "Don't touch me, you're disgusting."

"Disgusting, am I!" laughed Potter lewdly. "I'll show you I can be a better lover than Dare Penrod. I'm through with your nonsense, Casey," he growled. "I want you, and by God your puny threats don't scare me. I must have been stupid or crazy to believe you could harm me."

But once again fate intervened at a crucial moment. A loud clamoring of voices at the front door brought a vile curse to Potter's lips. He sought to ignore it, renewing his efforts to subdue Casey. But the loud voices demanding entrance were too authoritative to ignore. Letting loose a string of expletives, he stormed from the room, slamming the door behind him. "I'm not finished with you, bitch," he threw over his shoulder in parting.

Huddling in the center of the bed, Casey could hear little beyond the closed door except a murmur of voices raised in anger. Then suddenly something inside her snapped. She'd be damned if she'd lie here meekly and await Potter's return like a lamb brought to slaughter. Despite her shock over Dare's sudden marriage, she'd not allow herself to be abused by her employer. Nor would she wallow in self-pity. With Potter otherwise occupied, she could escape out the open window and disappear under the cover of darkness.

Rising swiftly and setting her clothes to rights, Casey hastily began gathering a few belongings necessary for survival. Though she had advised Dare to forget her and make a life for himself without her, his betrayal left her in a state of shock. She hadn't expected him to desert her so soon. What kind of a man was he to flit from woman to woman so easily? Her own heart was not so fickle. Once she gave her love it was for life.

Abruptly the voices outside her door ceased and Casey reacted quickly, grasping her swag and heading for the window. Fear hurried her steps. What would Potter do if he caught her attempting to escape? Would he have her tied to the whipping post and beaten? Or would he do it himself? Poised in the open window, one leg swung over the sill, Casey groaned in terror when the door burst open.

"Casey! Thank God!"

"Ben!" Casey was so astonished she lost her balance and fell to the floor with a painful thud.

Ben's eyes narrowed angrily as he helped Casey to her feet, her pale face and terror-stricken eyes speaking eloquently of her ordeal. Whatever happened in this room had obviously driven Casey to take her chances on the streets of Sydney or in the bush.

"What happened, Casey?" Ben asked, scowling furiously as he drew the sobbing girl into his arms.

"I can't believe you're here," she wept, clinging to his wide shoulders.

"Casey, answer me! Did Potter hurt you?"

Gradually gaining her senses, Casey shook her head. "N . . . no, he's a coward. He might have hurt me if you hadn't arrived in time. He'll try again once you leave. I no longer have strength left to resist. I . . . I was going to run away."

"There's no need now, Casey, I'm taking you home," Ben soothed, leading her toward the door. "Father is here, too."

"But . . . but, Ben, I can't go," wailed Casey. "Lieutenant Potter will never allow it."

"You don't understand, Casey," Ben smiled, "you've been pardoned."

"I . . . what? How can that be?" Casey stammered, refusing to believe herself so lucky. "How . . . how did all this come about?"

"Suffice it to say highly placed officials were persuaded to review your case and decided that a pardon was in order," hedged Ben, refusing to meet her eyes. Damn Dare, he cursed silently, for extracting his promise to withhold the truth.

"Did your father arrange all this?" Casey probed. If Dare knew that Roy was working to have her freed, why did he marry Mercy on the same day her pardon had been granted? she wondered. The weight of the answer nearly crushed her. Dare had never loved her! His words were nothing but senseless mouthings meant to coax her into his bed.

Picking up her swag, Ben said, "Finish packing, Casey. Father is keeping Potter out of the way, so he'll not interfere. We'll talk later."

Lieutenant Potter had to be forcibly restrained when Casey was taken from his house. Though Roy was twice Potter's age, his superb condition lent him the strength to keep the lieutenant at bay, especially in his drunken state. Mouthing foul threats, Potter refused to believe that Casey had been emancipated despite the physical presence of a pardon legally signed and executed by Lieutenant Governor Johnston.

Existing in a void brought on by shock and betrayal, Casey clung to Ben, uttering no protest when he settled her in the wagon they had driven to Sydney earlier to witness Dare's wedding. "Where are we going?" she asked numbly.

"We're staying overnight at Drew Stanley's house," Roy answered kindly. "We'll return to the farm tomorrow."

Casey's next question came tumbling from her lips, the words spilling out one after another. "Is it true? Did Dare really marry Mercy McKenzie? Why would he do such a thing?"

Only the tightness around Roy's lips betrayed his anguish. "Yes, Casey, it's true. But it's not . . . you see, Dare . . ." He stuttered to a halt, bound by his promise to his son. The hopeful look illuminating Casey's face soon turned to one of bitter disappointment.

Casey's heart hardened and her green eyes turned cold as icy emeralds as she thought of Dare and Mercy together. Suddenly she recalled Roy's words concerning their destination. He intended to take her back to the Hawkesbury! Impossible! Being privy to Dare's happiness with his wife was one agony she needn't endure, not as long as she had a breath left in her body. She was a free woman and the choice was hers to make.

"No," she objected stubbornly, shocking both Ben and Roy. "I'm not going back to the farm with you."

Her pride was at stake. As difficult as her future might be, it would not include Dare Penrod. She would go her own way and make a life for herself. What she failed to take into consideration was the Penrods' determination to protect her no matter what the cost to her pride.

CHAPTER FIFTEEN

Dare lingered in the McKenzie parlor long after Mercy had left to prepare herself for her wedding night. Her seductive smile and teasing tone spoke volumes about what was expected of him, but he felt little desire for his wife. Wife! Bah! The word tasted bitter on his tongue. It should be Casey sharing his name and his bed. His feet seemed unwilling to move in the direction of Mercy's bedroom. How could he expect his body to respond in the appropriate manner when he felt no spark of desire for her? His thoughts were totally consumed with Casey, anxious for her safety and worried over Roy's ability to bring her to Penrod station if she balked at the suggestion.

Reeling from the chair where he had sat consuming still more of the potent alcohol he had partaken of so freely following the ceremony, Dare went in search of another bottle. If he had to make love to his wife he wanted to be too drunk to remember it afterwards. And judging from the clarity of his mind he still had a ways to go. Better yet, he thought with perverse satisfaction, why make love to her at all? Being forced into marriage was hardly conducive to romance.

Thus he remained rooted to the spot, his mind anywhere but on his bride. It was no wonder he was startled to look up and find Mercy's shimmering form poised dramatically in the doorway, every luscious curve of her voluptuous body clearly outlined beneath the thin confection of lace and satin she wore. From the design and golden hue of the aged cloth, it could have been a garment worn by her mother on her own wedding night.

"Dare," she purred huskily, "please come to bed, darling. Haven't you had enough to drink for one night?"

Dare slanted her an oblique look, deciding to be brutally frank. "I have no intention of sleeping with you, Mercy. I may have been forced into this marriage but I never promised to share your bed. Your body holds no appeal for me. Frankly, I don't desire you."

"But I want you, darling," Mercy murmured, her low voice laced with promise. "And we both know I'm experienced enough to *make* you desire me."

Sidling up beside Dare, she ran her hands boldly over his body, smiling to herself as she felt him tense. The muscles in his shoulders rippled beneath her fingertips; the hard wall of his chest expanded as her feather-light touch caressed and fondled, moving lower to brush the pillar of his manhood. Under her expert handling his involuntary response brought an instant hardening to that part of him she longed for most.

"I carried out my part of the bargain and I demand you consummate our marriage," she stated, her chin tilted at a stubborn angle. "I delivered all I promised. Casey is free and Robin has been released from the coal mines. You owe me this night." Boldly she stroked his manhood where it strained against the tight material of his trousers. "Make love to me, Dare, you're as eager as I am."

Without tender wooing, he grasped Mercy by the waist and bore her down to the floor. The lovely nightgown meant to inspire romance was ripped from her body. To add insult to injury, Dare merely released himself from his own constrictive clothing without undressing.

"Dare, wait! I'm not ready!" Mercy wailed, writhing beneath him.

Driven beyond restraint by Mercy's merciless teasing, experiencing a lust far removed from love, Dare plunged into her receptive body, feeling her muscles tauten in an automatic response despite her words to the contrary. Long legs circled his waist and her nails found purchase in the exposed flesh of his neck, bringing a roar of pain from Dare. It sickened him that his brutal entry served only to bring her surging to the peak of ecstasy as she gasped and panted, meeting him thrust for thrust. He strained above her, caring little for her pleasure, seeking his own as quickly as possible. He had no idea Mercy reveled in his roughness, thrilled to his lust despite the fact that his ruthless taking in no way resembled the act of love. It came as something of a shock when Mercy reached a shattering climax only seconds before his own. To Mercy's chagrin Dare managed to retain his senses as he withdrew to spill his seed uselessly on the carpet beneath them.

"What are you doing?" she cried once she realized what he had done. She had counted on bearing Dare a child in order to earn his love and secure her position. But it wouldn't happen if he continued to withhold his seed.

"It's obvious, isn't it, Mercy? I want no child by you," Dare replied, rolling to his feet and staring down passionlessly at his wife's nude body.

"You're still thinking of *her*, aren't you? Don't you realize Casey is lost to you? You've pledged yourself to me."

"You might have my name, Mercy," came Dare's unyielding reply, "but that's all you'll ever have. You knew from the beginning where my heart lies, and I only give my love once. It might very well be too late for me and Casey, but you'll not have my child. Our marriage has been consummated. That's as much of me as you'll ever have, for we'll never share another intimacy."

His cold words stunned Mercy. She never expected Dare to be so unyielding. He must love Casey far more than she imagined. But time was on her side. With Casey out of the way she expected Dare to relent. He was a man, and Mercy had every confidence in her ability to lure him to her bed.

"We'll see." She smiled coyly. "We'll see."

No matter how many plausible excuses not to return to the farm that Casey provided, either Ben or Roy returned a convincing argument to the contrary. She couldn't live in Sydney without protection; she had no money or means of support; she was ill-prepared to exist on her own in the wild environment of the penal colony. All these and more made good sense but did little to solve Casey's problem. It went beyond human endurance to face Dare and his bride day after day. How could they ask that of her?

Neither Ben nor Roy were insensitive to Casey's dilemma, fully aware that Dare faced the same struggle to survive daily contact with the woman he loved while married to another. Yet they could see no other solution to the situation. They had promised Dare to see to Casey's safety, and bringing her back to the Hawkesbury was their only answer to his plea.

After Casey had been delivered from Potter's lecherous clutches she was taken to the home of Drew Stanley, where she spent a sleepless night alternately hating Dare and longing for his touch. The next morning found her hollow-eyed and wan, facing an adamant Roy and equally persuasive Ben over the breakfast table. Drew Stanley, a kindly, compassionate man, had conveniently excused himself.

"It's settled, Casey." Roy shrugged aside her protests. "Your home is with us."

"Can't you see how painful it would be for me?" Casey objected. "Think of Dare and . . . and his wife." The word nearly choked her. "It would be best for everyone concerned if I remained in Sydney and found employment."

"Employment!" scoffed Ben, brutally frank. "As what, a whore? With convicts providing all the labor necessary in the colony, whoring or marriage are your only choices."

Casey's face drained of all color, crushed by Ben's brutal remarks no matter how true they might be.

"Don't be crude, Ben," Roy chided. "I think Casey is well aware of her choices."

"There is another," Ben ventured tentatively. When Casey's attention sharpened, he added, "Casey can marry me. Then there would be no question about her right to live in our home."

The heavy gold lashes that shadowed her cheek flew up, caught off guard by Ben's astounding offer. One she had no intention of accepting, though it served to endear him to her forever.

"Ben," she smiled through a mist of tears, "you have to be the sweetest man alive. But I can't accept. I've ruined enough lives without adding you to the list. I love you, true, but as a sister loves a brother. And I'm certain your feelings for me are the same. Someday you'll meet a woman you will love enough to marry, and it won't be me."

A blush ran over Ben's cheeks, realizing that Casey was astute enough to recognize his gallant gesture. It was true he loved Casey like a sister, and had she agreed to their marriage he would never have touched her in desire or lust. She belonged to Dare and he would have protected her and kept her safe for his brother's sake. Ben felt great compassion for Dare and Casey and would have sacrificed his own future happiness for his brother, who he knew would do the same were the situation reversed.

At length Ben said, "Casey, my offer is genuine. I'd be pleased to have you as my wife."

Roy sucked in his breath, waiting for Casey's reply. It amazed him that Ben would unselfishlessly give up so much to see Casey kept from harm. But one disastrous marriage in the family was enough. Though he had come to love Casey like a daughter, any fool could see their union would be a mistake, undertaken for the

wrong reasons. He released his breath loudly
when Casey's answer dispelled his fears.

"I'm sorry, Ben, I can't marry you. I appreciate your offer but we both know that Dare . . .
that Dare and I . . . well, it's impossible, that's
all. But your offer has made me realize that you
and Roy really do have my best interests at heart.
I can no longer thwart your efforts to protect me.
I'll go back to the farm with you."

Elated, Ben leaped up, thumping his father on
the back.

"On one condition," Casey added with firm
resolve.

Abruptly Ben sobered. "What condition?"

"I can't accept your charity," Casey insisted
stubbornly. "I want to work for my keep. You'll
provide room and board and a small monthly
stipend in return for housekeeping and cooking
duties. And I will be free to leave whenever I
choose."

Ben left it to his father to provide an answer,
which was swift in coming. Anything was agreea-
ble as long as it brought Casey to the farm.
"Agreed." Roy nodded, rising from the table.
"Let's go home. Robin has been issued a ticket of
leave and probably will join us in a few days."

"Robin?" Casey choked in disbelief. "My
God, Roy, what did you do to bring this all
about? First me and now Robin."

Roy flushed guiltily, looking to Ben for help.
What could he say? Certainly not the truth after
he promised to keep Dare's secret.

"Suffice it to say that someone very highly
placed obtained your freedom," Ben replied
cryptically. "The how, when or why don't matter."

Before Casey could satisfy her curiosity with more questions, Roy intervened. "Come along, children, I'm anxious to get home."

The rutted, dusty trek to Parramatta proved tedious and fatiguing but uneventful, leaving Casey free to contemplate her surroundings and the harshness of this new land. Bordering the parched road, the outcroppings of rust-red boulders looked thousands of years old, and the brush climbing the shallow hills and gullies appeared dry and lifeless, yet continued to exist on too little water and too much sun. Casey's skin felt like sandpaper peppered with red silt that the wind stirred up and blew with abandon. How she missed the green of her own Ireland. Yet there was an austere beauty in this land that promised greatness. So far no one had found a way across the Blue Mountains, but one day someone would, for it was obvious the colony would soon outgrow the fifty-by-one-hundred-fifty-mile length and breadth of the present colony.

Casey's random thoughts took many courses, but finally settled on the one subject she wished to avoid. Dare. Thank God he wouldn't be returning with his bride to Penrod station for several days. Thad McKenzie had thoughtfully remained in Sydney to allow the newlyweds the privacy of a honeymoon. Perhaps Dare and Mercy would decide to remain on McKenzie station, Casey thought hopefully. After all, Mercy's father would be alone now. That thought held a modicum of comfort as the wagon pulled into Penrod station. To Casey's astonishment, she felt as if she had come home.

Refusing to occupy the upstairs guest room

Roy offered, Casey settled in the pleasant little
room off the kitchen she once occupied and
where she felt completely at ease. Martha's greeting was exuberant and heartfelt, leaving Casey no
doubt as to her welcome.

Casey was astounded by the change in
Martha's appearance. Where once near starva-
tion had rendered her gaunt to the point of
emaciation, an improved diet had worked mira-
cles on her tall form. Gently rounded curves
replaced sharp angles, lending her a soft, feminine appeal.

No longer did Martha look the forty or more
years Casey had attributed to her. Though she
would never be beautiful in the classical sense,
her comely features were now more in keeping
with the thirty years she claimed. The awkward-
ness that Casey first noted had disappeared with
Martha's newfound self-worth attained under
the benevolent eyes of her employer. Her hair,
now a shiny brown, possessed a new vitality as
did her soft brown eyes, and Casey couldn't have
been happier. Martha's friendship meant a great
deal to her, for in all of New South Wales she
could call no other woman friend.

Somehow the days passed with boring regularity as Casey settled into the routine of household
duties she had willingly undertaken. During the
weeks she'd spent in jail and with Lieutenant
Potter, Martha had become a fairly decent cook,
finding she enjoyed the challenge of creating
different meals daily. But Casey didn't give up
entirely the cooking duties she enjoyed so much,
taking it upon herself to teach the older woman
all she knew about the art of cooking. They both

pitched in to help with the laundry and worked
together on the heavy household jobs. During
that time Casey tried desperately not to dwell on
Dare or the day he would return, praying for a
reprieve. But in the end her prayers went unanswered.

In deference to Thad McKenzie's wishes, Dare
remained at McKenzie station with Mercy for
several days before suddenly announcing, "I'm
going home."

He'd had enough of spending every day riding
in the searing heat until he was drenched in a fine
sheen of perspiration that numbed his brain and
exhausted his body. Afterwards strong drink
dulled the ache that consumed him night and day
due to the pain of losing Casey. Frantic, Mercy
used every wile at her disposal to coax him from
the moodiness that marred every aspect of their
honeymoon.

Honeymoon! Bah! It had taken but a few days
for Mercy to realize how mistaken she had been
to assume Dare would forget Casey so easily.
What had seemed like a wonderful idea now
tasted like ashes in her mouth. But defeat was a
word Mercy did not accept. She hadn't lost yet.
She had years ahead of her to capture Dare's
love.

"What about me?" she asked on the heels of
Dare's abrupt announcement.

"Do what you want," Dare shrugged indifferently. "Penrod station is my home, I've wasted
enough time on stupid pretense. Our honeymoon
is a mockery."

"Sometimes you can be an obstinate bastard,

Dare," Mercy gritted out. "My place is with you and I will leave when you do. How soon should I be ready?"

"Suit yourself," Dare said curtly. "Be ready in an hour. Pack only a few necessities. Your father can send the rest later." He turned to leave.

"Dare, wait!" He paused but remained with his back to her. "Can't we at least be friends? We've a lifetime together. Must you treat me so callously in front of our families? Can't you appreciate what I've done for your two friends instead of hating me for forcing you into marriage? You could have refused me, you know."

Mercy's words brought a thoughtful frown to Dare's face. True, she had accomplished a near miracle. And he hadn't been forced to agree with her plan. But neither did it mean he had to love Mercy, or bed her. However, she was his wife and deserved a certain amount of respect, especially in their dealings with their families. Besides, if he wanted Casey to believe he had married Mercy of his own free will he had to modify his behavior toward his wife.

"You have a point, Mercy," Dare allowed grudgingly. "I owe you something for what you did for Casey and Robin." Intense joy suffused Mercy's face, only to be shattered by Dare's next words. "I'll try to treat you decently but I've not changed my mind about sharing your bed."

Then he calmly exited the room, Mercy's screech of fury following him out the door.

Wielding the broom with brisk strokes, Casey failed to hear the front door open or the footsteps pause behind her. Roy and Ben had left the house early leaving Casey and Martha free to scrub and sweep to their hearts' content. Wearing her oldest dress, her red hair bound up in a turban, Casey attacked the dirt vigorously.

"Have your servant take my bag upstairs to our room, darling." Mercy's petulant voice brought Casey to an abrupt halt as the broom clattered from her hand.

At first Dare failed to recognize the petite figure in faded clothes, thinking Roy had hired another convict to help Martha in the house. The first sign of recognition came when the woman's small shoulders stiffened at the sound of Mercy's voice. Something in that proud carriage looked hauntingly familiar.

"Bloody hell!" he exploded in a fit of anger. "What do you think you're doing, Casey?" He never meant for her to be a servant in the house.

Casey whirled, staring at Dare and his bride with something akin to horror. Her first instinct was to turn and flee, until her better judgment took over. She had assumed that Dare and Mercy would both be surprised to see her at Penrod station, but she couldn't have been more mistaken. Mercy was the only one shocked by the turn of events.

"I'm just performing my job, sir," Casey retorted, her voice laced with bitterness. "I'll take your . . . wife's bag upstairs. I imagine she's exhausted from her ride over here and . . . everything," she added, boldly appraising Mercy's appearance.

"What in the hell is she doing here?" Mercy screamed in an unladylike manner. "This was never part of our—"

"Careful," Dare warned, slanting her a baleful look. "We'll talk later. Go upstairs and freshen up while I speak with Casey."

"Send her away, darling," Mercy coaxed.

"This house belongs to my father, Mercy, and he has a right to hire whomever he chooses. Now do as I say. I'll be up in a few minutes."

Glaring murderously at Casey, Mercy picked up her bag and flounced past, careful to sweep aside her skirt so that no part of it touched the other woman.

The moment Dare heard the door to his room close he rounded on Casey. "Whatever was Father thinking of? You were to be a guest in this house, not a servant."

His words caused Casey to flounder. Was Dare aware that Roy intended to bring her back to the farm? Obviously the knowledge didn't extend to Mercy, for her reaction had been one of total shock. Nor was she pleased with the situation.

"Did you expect me to live off your father's charity?" Casey shot back. "I made the decision to work for my keep and a small monthly wage. Once I've accumulated a nest egg I'll leave. I realize having me here offends your . . . wife, but I had noplace else to go. Your father was kind enough to offer honest employment."

Her sharp retort cut Dare deeply. How he longed to take her in his arms and kiss away all the hard feelings and resentment she harbored in her small body toward him.

"Casey . . ." It tore him apart to see her hurting.

"If you don't mind, sir, I have work to do."

"I'm sorry, Casey, truly sorry." The words meant to soothe only fueled her anger.

"Don't be. I was a fool to believe you cared for me. Too many things stood between us. I can't fault you for wanting someone of your own class. But," she choked on a sob, "did you have to lie to me? Was it necessary to tell me you loved me? I hate you for deceiving me, Dare Penrod. Nothing you can say will change that."

Dare hung his head, unable to look Casey in the eye lest he break down and reveal the truth. His intuition told him it was best for all concerned that the love she once bore him wither and die. And yet . . . yet, the urge was strong to confide in her, to beg her to remain his despite his marriage, to allow no other man the right to savor her love. But in his heart he knew that Casey deserved better than to be cast in the role of mistress. In the end he said nothing, watching with stricken eyes as she reclaimed the broom and brushed past, a mist of tears clinging to long golden lashes.

It would have shocked Casey to know that shortly afterwards Dare faced a thoroughly incensed Mercy in the privacy of his room. His suggestion that she occupy the guest bedroom was met with stony silence and outright hostility. Though Dare's room was definitely too masculine for her tastes, she hoped to alter it to suit her own personality. Not once did she consider moving to a guest room. She eyed the bed wistfully, wondering if she and Dare would ever make love in it. And then she thought of Casey living in the same house and anger rose in her like waves of vomit.

"What is that little slut doing here, Dare?" she challenged hotly. "You said we'd talk, and I'm anxious to hear what you've got to say. The possibility of Casey living here was not mentioned in our deal."

Dare managed to keep his voice below a roar. "Keep your vile tongue to yourself. Father makes the decisions here. Any more discussion?"

"Yes, ask your father to send her packing. I'm your wife and it's an insult to live with your doxy in the same house."

"If you don't like the arrangements you can always leave," Dare suggested hopefully.

Mercy's eyes blazed with defiant fire. "You'd like that, wouldn't you?"

"It's your choice."

"Damn you, Dare! You could at least try to make this marriage work."

Disdaining an answer, Dare turned to leave, remarking with exaggerated politeness, "Excuse me, *wife,* but I must find Father and Ben. I'll see you at dinner." Then he was gone.

Fuming in impotent fury, Mercy paced the room, planning her strategy now that Casey O'Cain was thrust back into her life. Soon an idea took shape in her brain and a sly smile curved her full lips. Surely Casey must feel a certain amount of animosity toward Dare now that he'd married another woman. Why not stoke those emotions into full-fledged hatred by providing the fuel?

Anxious to set the wheels in motion before Dare got wind of it, Mercy rushed from the room, only to bump into Casey who had come upstairs to sweep the hallway. "Oh!" Mercy exclaimed, righting herself. "Watch where you're going, clumsy."

Gritting her teeth, Casey muttered, "Sorry."

"Well, as long as you're here you might as well make yourself useful," Mercy said haughtily. "Papa has promised to select a maid for me in Sydney. I imagine she'll arrive here with my trunks in a day or two. Meanwhile I'll have to make do with you. Come along." She motioned Casey into Dare's room.

"What is it you want?" Casey asked sullenly, glancing around the room to see if anything was amiss.

"I want you to make room for my things," Mercy directed imperiously. "I'll need half the wardrobe and several drawers. You know how helpless men are at such things."

"Are you certain Dare has given permission to move his things?" Casey asked skeptically.

Tossing her blond curls, Mercy snapped, "Dare expects me to share his room—and his bed. Whatever I decide is fine with him. He's very indulgent where I'm concerned," she added coyly. "Start with the wardrobe."

Casey did as she was bid, automatically sorting through Dare's clothing to make room for Mercy's. It nearly tore her apart picturing Mercy's things in intimate contact with Dare's, suggesting more private intimacies it hurt to think about.

"Dare is so handsome," Mercy enthused as she watched Casey work. "Our honeymoon was so romantic." Aware that Mercy was deliberately goading her, Casey bit her lip to keep from flinging out a scathing retort.

"Perhaps one day you'll have a lover as expert as Dare," Mercy continued blithely, watching Casey's reactions closely. "But then again, I

doubt there's another man to compare with
Dare. He's so virile, so powerful, he makes me
feel—"

"Enough!" shouted Casey. Mercy's cruel
taunts finally succeeded in destroying her self-
control. "What you and Dare do in the privacy of
your bedroom is no concern of mine. I don't care
if Dare is the best lover in the world."

"Oh, he is," sighed Mercy, the sound a soft,
seductive purr. "But I forgot, you already know
that, don't you? Dare is anxious for a child.
Mayhap one is already growing. If not, it's certainly not from lack of trying."

That's it! thought Casey, slamming shut the
wardrobe door with such force the whole room
vibrated. "I think Dare should move another
wardrobe in here for your things," she bit out
tightly. "This one is too small to share. I have
better things to do than stand here and listen
while you describe your husband's lovemaking."
Whirling on her heel, she marched purposefully
toward the door.

"Oh, Casey, one more thing."

Casey paused without turning to face her adversary, waiting.

"Henceforth you are to address me in a more
respectful manner. You may call me either Mrs.
Penrod or ma'am. And I prefer you address Dare
as Mr. Penrod or sir. Is that understood?"

"Perfectly—ma'am." The way Casey said it
made it sound like an insult.

Martha served supper that night, sparing
Casey that final indignity. From Martha's description it was a somber affair. Only Mercy
appeared in good humor, spurring the lagging

conversation with witty remarks until the lack of response drove her to silence. Mercy retired to her room immediately after the meal, the look she slanted Dare full of promise. According to Martha, Dare deliberately ignored his wife's blatant invitation, choosing instead to join his father and brother in the study. Casey had no idea when Dare finally sought his bed or his wife's arms, nor did she care. Or so she tried to tell herself.

Casey would have been surprised to learn that Dare spent the night in the guest bedroom. Before he left the next morning, the bed was neatly made up so that not a trace of his occupancy remained. The nights that followed continued the same pattern, driving Mercy into a frenzy. So many nights wasted when she had so much to offer Dare! It just didn't make sense. He continued to resist her at every turn despite the fact that Casey avoided him like the plague.

It was no secret that Casey went out of her way to avoid Dare, performing her duties silently and efficiently but disappearing the moment he walked into the house. She tried to convince herself she hated him, and for a while she did. But on those rare occasions when she was forced to accept his presence, he followed her every move with hungry gray eyes filled with such remorse she was at a loss to understand. Wasn't one woman enough for him?

Shortly after the men left for their various duties one day, a commotion at the back door drew Casey's attention. Her lips curved upwards in a delighted smile when Robin's tall frame appeared in the doorway.

"Robin!" she squealed, throwing herself into

his welcoming arms. "You finally got here!" The way he hugged her proved that Robin was just as happy to see her.

Finally releasing her, Robin said, "I was given a ticket of leave, Casey, and knew it must have been due to Roy's influence. I'm free to accept employment wherever I choose so I made my way directly here. Thank God I had good boots, for I walked all the way. But tell me about yourself. Were you given a ticket of leave also?"

"I don't know how it was accomplished, but Roy wrought a miracle. I was emancipated. Come, sit down," she coaxed, leading him to a chair. "Are you hungry?"

"Starved," Robin admitted, patting his sunken middle.

Martha, who'd been in the kitchen when Robin appeared, said, "I'll fix you a bite. There's fresh bread hot from the oven, cold mutton and berry pie left from last night's supper."

Robin turned, seeing Martha for the first time but failing to recognize her. Then something in her shy smile alerted him to her identity. "Martha? My God, woman, what have you done to yourself? I'd hardly take you for the same person." Though the thin, angular woman hadn't turned into a swan overnight, the transformation was amazing. There was much about her he considered attractive, even pretty.

Martha flushed becomingly, pleased but unaccustomed to praise. Though she had loved her Jamie dearly, he had been a man of few words, rarely handing out compliments.

Sensing her confusion, Robin said, "I'll be glad to sample your bread, Martha, and cold mutton and berry pie sounds like a feast to a man dying of hunger." The flustered woman bobbed her head and then set about filling a plate. She considered him far too thin for his large frame.

Eyeing Robin critically while he ate, Casey also thought him too skinny. The flesh seemed to have melted from his bones since last she saw him. His face was drawn and his brow etched with permanent lines of exhaustion. It was obvious that these last weeks hadn't been easy for him. His once healthy tan had faded to a dirty yellow and his sallow skin possessed an unhealthy glow. No wonder Tim had hated the coal mines and risked life and limb to escape.

Robin sighed contentedly as Martha set a juicy piece of pie before him. "You'll spoil me, lass," he grinned with a hint of the old Robin.

"I'm sure Dare will be happy to see you, Robin," Casey said as Robin dug into the pie.

"I'm just as anxious to see him," Robin said, chewing thoughtfully. "With you as his wife I imagine he's one happy man. I know I would be." Though his words were congratulatory they were laced with regret. Why couldn't he be the one to have captured Casey's love?

Casey tensed, suddenly realizing Robin had no way of knowing about Dare and Mercy. "Robin, I'm not . . ." Her words died in her throat as the door flung open and Dare burst through.

"Robin! By God, it's good to see you! Burloo was in the yard when you arrived and couldn't wait to tell me. Did Martha and Casey take care of you?" he asked, eyeing the pie appreciatively. "You wouldn't happen to have another piece of that pie, would you, Martha? And a cup of tea, if it's not too much trouble."

"Coming right up." Martha grinned cheekily.

Though Dare spoke to Martha, his eyes lingered hungrily on Casey, aware of her penchant for avoiding him and not blaming her. Noticing the direction of Dare's gaze, Robin smiled a secret smile. Obviously Dare was deeply in love with his wife, and though he might be a tad envious, he didn't begrudge his friend the happiness he so richly deserved.

"Martha has turned out to be quite a cook," Robin allowed. "And I suppose congratulations are in order, mate. When you visited me in jail you told me of your plans to marry Casey. When did the happy event take place?"

Dare flushed, wishing they were alone so he could explain to Robin in private. He hated to speak with Casey present and add to her hurt and bewilderment. "Robin," he began hesitantly, "Casey and I, we're not—"

"I thought I heard voices out here," Mercy said breezily as she sailed into the kitchen. "Why, Dare, darling, what are you doing home this time of day? Oh," she gasped, her eyes falling on Robin. "I see you finally arrived."

Approaching the table where the two men sat, Mercy stopped before Dare, bent down and kissed him full on the mouth. Robin's mouth flew open and his eyes blinked repeatedly, unable to believe what his eyes told him. Dare and Mercy? Looking at Casey for an explanation, he saw that she had quietly slipped from the kitchen after Mercy's grand entrance. He turned to Dare, his eyes accusing. Noting Robin's confusion, Mercy sought to enlighten him as quickly as possible, leaving the convict no misconception concerning her position in Dare's life.

"Dare, have you told Robin our good news?"

"I was going to, Mercy, when you interrupted," Dare bit out impatiently.

"Good news?" Robin asked, looking from one to the other. "You and Mercy?"

"Dare and I were married nearly a month ago," gushed Mercy before Dare could form an appropriate reply.

"Mercy," Dare said tightly, "I'm certain you have things to do. Why don't you leave the explanations to me? Robin and I have much to discuss."

"Very well." Mercy pouted, slanting Dare an aggrieved look. "I'll see you at supper tonight, darling." Skirts twitching enticingly, Mercy swayed from the room.

"Bloody hell, Dare, I hope you have a good explanation," Robin blasted. "I thought you and Casey . . ." Dare's warning frown brought his words to a halt.

"Let's go outside, Robin," Dare suggested, rising. "We're keeping Martha from her duties." Nodding, Robin followed Dare from the room.

The moment they cleared the door, Robin's staccato questions flew at Dare. "Is it true? Are you really married to Mercy? I thought you loved Casey. If Mercy is your wife, what is Casey doing here? Surely she's not a servant! What in the hell got into you, Dare?"

Weeks ago Dare had decided to keep the truth about his marriage strictly in the family. That meant keeping Robin as ignorant as Casey regarding the facts surrounding his hasty marriage. Knowing Robin, that knowledge would feed his guilt just as it would Casey's. His only recourse was to hope he could retain Robin's friendship without divulging too much of the truth.

"I owe you no explanation, Robin," Dare said shortly, "except to say I am married to Mercy. And Father convinced Casey to return to the farm with him despite her misgivings about the situation. Wisely she realized she could not exist on her own in Sydney. Father intended her to be our guest but she insisted on working for her keep."

"Did you marry Mercy before or after Casey was pardoned?" Robin asked tightly.

Flushing, Dare said, "On the same day."

"Why? Jesus, Dare, couldn't you wait? Casey loves you and I know you loved her. What kind of man are you?"

Dare winced. "No matter what you think, Robin, things aren't always what they seem." After imparting those cryptic words, Dare launched quickly into a description of Robin's duties. "You arrived just in time. Tom saved enough money to buy his own small farm and left two days ago. Your duties will consist mainly of overseeing the convict laborers. I'd like to offer you a room in our house but at the moment there are none available. Tom's quarters will have to suffice for the time being. But you are to take your meals with us."

"Yes, sir," Robin spat derisively.

"Robin," Dare began, hurt by the bitterness in Robin's curt reply, "think of Penrod station as your home. Ours will be no convict-and-master relationship. You're my friend."

Robin was suddenly ashamed over the way he had spoken to Dare, and his face softened. "Thank you, Dare. Your family has been like my own. And if Casey can accept your marriage to Mercy in good grace, I can do no less."

CHAPTER SIXTEEN

Though both Ben and Roy did their utmost to make things easier for Casey, no one could ease the ache of knowing Dare was so close yet as unattainable as the moon and stars. Casey's fragile heart broke each time Mercy walked up the stairs at night, knowing that Dare would soon be making love to his wife in the privacy of their room. Not even Robin's frequent visits to the kitchen served to lift her spirits. As the days passed it became increasingly evident that Robin's interest in her had sharpened dramatically now that Dare was no longer a contender for her affections.

Late one night after chores, Casey wandered into the yard to cool off. Listlessly she paused beneath a huge gum tree, staring into the darkness and listening to the noisy serenade of night insects. She started violently when Robin came up silently behind her to whisper in her ear.

"Casey, you look so beautiful with the moonlight turning your hair into living flame."

"Robin, you frightened me," Casey gasped, whirling.

"I was on my way to the barracks when I saw

you standing there. Do you mind if I join you?
It's been some time since we've talked privately."

"I don't mind." Casey smiled, grateful for the
diversion. "I've not had the chance to thank you
properly for your part in helping Tim. You've
been a true friend to me, Robin."

"I'd like to be more, Casey, if you'd allow it,"
Robin confided. "But I won't be free to offer
marriage for seven years. I don't expect you to
wait for me."

Startled, Casey replied, "Robin, please, don't
talk like that. I . . . I'm fond of you but I don't
love you."

"It's Dare, isn't it?" Robin challenged. "You
still love him even though he betrayed you by
marrying Mercy."

"I . . . I can't help it," Casey admitted, her
voice breaking on a sob. "I try to hate him but
can't find it in my heart."

She began to weep and at that moment Robin
could have gladly killed his friend. Wanting only
to offer comfort, Robin opened his arms to her,
cradling her head against his chest as she stepped
into his embrace. It was only natural that he
should kiss her. Not with passion, for now that he
knew there was no hope for him, solace was all he
could provide. He made soothing noises in his
throat as he tenderly pressed kisses to her cheeks,
her eyes, her mouth, until she quieted in his
arms. Then he reluctantly set her aside.

"Thank you, Robin," Casey said with a watery
smile. "I . . . I don't know how much more of
this torment I can take. I'm seriously thinking of
leaving soon to find work in Sydney." Leaning
forward she kissed his cheek, then turned and
walked away. With a twinge of regret, Robin

watched her walk out of his life. He was completely at a loss to understand Dare or his reason for marrying Mercy when Casey loved him so much. The newlyweds certainly didn't strike him as being the happiest couple in the world.

Suddenly a figure detached itself from the shadows and approached on silent feet as Robin waited, his body tense as Dare's scowling face reflected darkly in the moonlight.

"Dare! What in the hell are you doing skulking around in the dark?"

"I'd ask you the same but it's obvious what you were doing," Dare replied with the intensity of one long denied. "Keep away from Casey, Robin, she's not for you!"

"Casey is no longer your concern," Robin retorted, finding it difficult to control his anger. "I'd advise you to concentrate on your wife. I've seen the way you look at Casey when no one is watching. If you want Casey so badly, why did you marry Mercy? I've never known you to harbor prejudice against emancipists but I can think of no other reason for your hasty marriage to Mercy when obviously you desire Casey."

"Robin, I don't want to argue with you, nor do I owe you an explanation," Dare defended staunchly. "Regardless of my motives, a relationship between you and Casey is impossible. You're not free to offer marriage and Casey deserves no less. I won't have you dallying with her affections."

"Sometimes you can be a real bastard, Dare. Casey doesn't want me. I was only offering comfort, nothing more, nothing less. She's hurt and confused, thanks to your callous treatment. Have you spoken to her at all? Explained your-

self? She deserves that much, Dare. You may be
my employer and friend, but I won't stand for
you taking advantage of Casey. And that's exactly what will happen if I read you correctly."

"You do me an injustice, Robin," Dare
scowled furiously.

"Mayhap, but I'm warning you anyway. Perhaps Casey is right. Leaving here will free you
from temptation."

"Casey is thinking of leaving? How do you
know?"

"She told me tonight she was going to find
work in Sydney."

"Bloody hell! You know as well as I what's
likely to happen to her if she leaves here."

"Do you think I'm stupid?" Robin contended
hotly. "Of course I know. But Casey has a mind
of her own. I suggest you think carefully about
what I've said. Goodnight, Dare."

Eyes narrowed thoughtfully, Dare watched
Robin disappear into the darkness. He should
have known that Casey's pride would prevent her
from remaining in the same house with him and
Mercy. As far as Casey knew, he shared Mercy's
bed each night, which was as far from the truth as
her assumption that he loved his wife. Though
Mercy teased, cajoled and used every feminine
wile known to man, Dare chose celibacy over
making love to the woman who had forced him
to abandon his true love.

The thought of Casey's leaving was abhorrent
to him. She needed the Penrod protection, such
as it was, and if it meant the difference between
Casey's staying or leaving, he'd leave the farm
himself before allowing Casey to do so. It was

something he'd been thinking of for some time. His mind made up, he returned to the house, entering through the back door. Deliberately, he paused before Casey's small room off the kitchen, noting a sliver of light beneath the doorjamb.

Aware that Casey would refuse him entrance if he asked first, Dare tried the knob and found the door unlatched. Fearing lest he alert Martha, who now slept in Meg's old quarters across the room, Dare pushed open the door and slipped quietly inside, closing the door behind him. Not one squeak gave him away.

Overwrought and unable to sleep after her talk with Robin, Casey had made ready for bed, washing and slipping into a clean shift instead of donning the high-necked, long-sleeved nightgown much too warm for this time of year. Then she pulled a chair to the window and sat down to brush her hair, hoping the tedious chore would provide a distraction from her glum thoughts.

Was it possible to both love and hate a man at the same time? she wondered bleakly. She felt herself tottering dangerously on that fine line separating those two emotions, and if she remained at Penrod station much longer her sanity would be sorely tried. Not once during the past weeks had Dare offered an explanation for his rash marriage to Mercy on the same day she gained her freedom. Why? Certainly Dare was no coward who feared criticism for taking an emancipist as a wife. Both Ben and Roy remained mute on the subject, steadfastly refraining from making mention of Dare's marriage. Though both men dealt politely with Mercy, neither exhibited the warmth due a family member. It was all terribly confusing to Casey and only served to fortify her determination to leave.

Engrossed in her musings, Casey did not hear Dare enter the room. Something else alerted her to his presence. That special feeling, all tingling excitement; the overpowering sense of being drawn to something beyond her control, all combined to bring her senses into sharp focus as she turned her head and saw him.

Dare halted but a few steps from where Casey sat brushing her hair, candlelight and moonlight combining to turn her into a fairy being, too beautiful to be mere mortal. Her long red hair provided a perfect frame for delicately carved features, full lips and high, exotic cheekbones. Soft, ivory shoulders sloped gently to enhance jutting breasts and narrow waist. She was slender, reedlike, willowy, and he loved her with an intensity that would follow him to the grave. If he couldn't have Casey he would die without ever making love to another woman.

Casey slowly rose to face Dare. He stared mesmerized at the ethereal creature bathed in moonlight, mysterious lights glowing in vivid green eyes. Limned in a golden glow, her delicate, shift-clad body appeared wraithlike as dancing light gilded her shoulders and kissed the sweet, rounded lines of her hips. Long, flowing hair cascaded down her shapely back to brush her waist in a bright, enchanted halo that dazzled the senses.

For a long, sweet moment they stood gazing at one another, the air charged with tension and longing. And then they were in each other's arms, the yearning, the need, the ravening desire that

raged in them like wildfire robbing them of the
last vestiges of self-control. Neither meant for
this to happen, but nothing could have prevented
it. Fate had decreed their explosive coming together, driven by an urgency bordering on madness.

All the sweetness of her body was flowing
toward Dare as he whispered her name, wanting
her, needing her, yearning beyond imagining to
hear her voice, touch her skin, drown in the green
depths of her expressive eyes.

Casey could move nowhere but into Dare's
arms, her hands resting lightly on his shoulders
as she searched the fathomless depths of his gray
eyes suddenly turned dark with desire. She observed no coldness there, no reserve separating
them, just warmth, and a gentleness that brought
tears to her eyes.

What was Dare doing here? Casey wondered,
unwilling to break the tender silence. Endless
questions and wild conjectures crowded her
mind, creating a sickening whirlpool of confusion. Had he come to her seeking satisfaction his
wife failed to provide? Or to explain why he
chose to marry Mercy? Suffocated with the pressure of her emotions, suddenly it no longer
mattered. Feelings that only Dare could arouse
rose from the depths of her being to totally
consume her.

He cupped her face in his big hands, kissing
her forehead, her eyelids, her nose, her lips in a
flurry of soft, sensuous kisses. Casey shivered in
delight as he stroked her back and hips. Without
volition they strained toward each other, captured by their longing, caught in the yearning that
penetrated the barriers of flesh to join them in

spirit and soul. Unbidden, her hands roamed his body, warm to her touch, pulsating with the strength of his maleness. A strangled groan escaped his lips.

Desiring only to worship her, perhaps for the last time, Dare carefully removed her shift and dropped to his knees, kissing and nipping along her ribcage and abdomen as his hands stroked and caressed her back and hips. She closed her eyes against the dizziness and then opened them to see his head slipping lower. He cupped her buttocks, arching her to him, as he buried his searing mouth in the fiery curls between her thighs. His lips and tongue tasted her hungrily, feasting on her sweetness long denied him. She trembled all over, sharp pinpoints of acute rapture tingling through her as his teasing, flicking tongue searched and explored· her innermost core. The sensation was exquisite, wonderful, setting her aquiver, stopping her breath and spinning her away.

For the first time since Dare entered the room Casey spoke. "Oh, Dare! Dare, please!" She made soft sounds deep in her throat as she began to move with a natural rhythm against the onslaught of his mouth. A sharp intake of breath warned Dare that her internal explosion would soon be impossible to control and reluctantly he slid his mouth upwards, blazing a path back to her mouth.

"Not just yet, love." His voice, an agonized whisper, shook with powerful emotion. "I want you to experience more joy tonight than you've ever known. I want you ready for me as you've never been before." For this will be our last time, he thought but did not say.

How was it possible to be aroused to a higher degree than she already was? Casey wondered distractedly. He had but to look at her and she melted. Under his deep kisses and the probing touch of his hands, lips and mouth, she had been driven beyond mere arousal. Hot tongues of desire licked at her; she was warm and moist, driven almost mad with wanting him. It no longer mattered that Dare had a wife, tomorrow would be soon enough for guilt.

Lovingly her fingers traced the lines of his face, committing him to memory for the long, lonely days to come. Her lips tasted his, the kiss bittersweet, filled with the knowledge that tonight would be the last time they could be together like this. She could offer him her body, give him her heart, but he would never belong to her. Nothing but death could free him to claim her despite this crazy desire they felt for one another. If tonight was all they were granted, she vowed to make it a night to remember.

Their passion rose like the wildness of a summer storm, hungry mouths clashing, feverish hands touching. She tore at his clothes, soon rendering him as naked as she. There was no yesterday, no tomorrow, only today, this room, this man, and love. With a single graceful motion he swooped her off her feet and laid her tenderly on the bed, the springs protesting as he eased his weight to lie full length beside her, his arms pulling her to him, shaping their bodies together.

Flames lashed at him, bodies touched, mouths fused. Yearning for her touch, Dare whispered hoarsely, "Touch me," taking her hand in his and moving it downward along the hard length of his body. She allowed her hand to follow his, comb-

ing past the thicket that surrounded the eager
pillar of steel between his thighs. Hesitantly, her
fingers explored him, moving upward to touch
the smooth tip, drawing a drop of moisture, like a
glistening raindrop. His member was incredibly
sensitive to her touch, and she drew pleasure
from his sharp, indrawn breath as she traveled
the amazing length. She closed her hand over
him again, relishing the masculine hardness of
him and feeling it throb in anticipation of his
possession of her.

"Oh, God," he groaned, his hand closing over
hers. "Yes, like that. Don't stop, love. Oh God,
yes . . ." A deep rumbling sound vibrated in his
chest, unable to withstand her sensuous onslaught a moment longer.

Grasping her waist, he rolled her beneath him,
bringing his mouth to hers. Her lips parted,
allowing his tongue to dart inside to tease and
caress. His head lowered, flicking teasingly over
her breasts, drawing first one rosy tip in his
mouth and then the other. It felt wonderful.
Warm and wet and intensely erotic.

He entered her with slow, sensuous strokes and
the caressing roll of his hips. He inspired her to
take him deep within her, move with him, helping her ease the sweet ache at the center of her
being. Then he was thrusting inside her, at first
slowly and sensuously, then boldly, urgently,
masterfully, their bodies joined in that age-old
rhythm of love, their hearts pounding in unison.
Fire sparked where their flesh joined, but it was
only kindling compared to the raging conflagra-
tion of their souls. Upward they spiraled until
they teetered on the brink. And with one powerful, deep thrust, they were soaring to the stars.

When their lips met again, they tasted the salt of tears, each certain it was their own.

They slept in one another's arms, but only for the length it took to recover from the incredible journey they had embarked upon. There was so much Dare wanted to say and so little time. "Are you awake, love?" he asked, brushing his lips against her temple.

Reluctant to break the spell, Casey took her time in answering. Finally she said, "I'm awake, Dare."

"I'm sorry, Casey. I didn't mean for this to happen. Hurting you is the last thing I want to do."

"I didn't want this to happen either."

"Whenever I'm alone with you I lose all restraint. I meant only to talk to you tonight, to tell you it's not necessary that you leave. But all my good intentions flew out the window the moment I set eyes on you. It was the same with you, I could tell."

Casey lowered her eyes, acknowledging the truth. "That's exactly why I must leave, Dare. What's between us is too volatile, too explosive to deny. But you made your choice when you married Mercy and I have no right to interfere. I won't be your lover. I can't spend my life waiting for you to decide which night you'll come to me and which belongs to your wife. I won't share you. My pride will not allow it. What took place tonight must never be repeated."

"I know, love," Dare agreed, a haunting sadness in his voice. "You deserve better. But you can't leave here. Your safety means too much to me. Though I can't legally claim you I can protect you in other ways. That's why I've decided to leave. I know how painful my presence is to you and I can't bear your suffering."

"Dare! No! This is your home. If anyone leaves, it will be me. You can't abandon your family. What about Mercy?" Suddenly she remembered something Mercy said to her. "What if she is carrying your child?"

A bitter laugh escaped Dare's throat, startling Casey. "That's impossible."

A puzzled frown wrinkled her forehead. "How can you be certain?"

"Believe me, Casey, Mercy will never bear my child."

Throwing caution to the wind, Casey asked, "Don't you love Mercy?"

"Love? My feelings for Mercy are many and varied, none of them remotely related to love."

"Why did you marry her?" Suddenly she flushed, the answer all too clear. "No, don't tell me, I already know. I'm not good enough to marry. I'm an emancipist, a convicted murderess, and you are a pure merino. Obviously you had second thoughts about taking a woman like me to wife. I understand. Love had nothing to do with it."

"You're wrong, love," Dare objected vigorously. "My marriage to Mercy was part of a bargain we'd struck. She delivered her part and I felt duty-bound to fulfill mine. She demanded marriage and I obliged, though I strongly suspect she has finally come to realize her mistake. My name is all she'll ever have of me."

Aware that he had already revealed more than he meant to, Dare clamped his mouth tightly shut. "You'll just have to trust me, love, when I say I didn't marry Mercy by choice. I don't love her and I don't sleep with her, though she'd have it otherwise. You're the only woman I've ever loved."

Casey longed to believe Dare, but it was difficult to visualize him being forced into anything against his will. Did he think confessing his love would ease her pain? She didn't regret their lovemaking tonight. On the contrary, she welcomed it, rejoiced in it, but it could not happen again.

"I'm sorry, Dare, I find it impossible to believe you. Can you blame me? I'm grateful for what your family did for me, and if it's any consolation, I wanted you tonight. If you hadn't made love to me I would have been terribly disappointed. It's something I'll cherish for the rest of my life." She paused to catch her breath, then said, "I'll leave tomorrow."

"No, Casey," Dare returned shortly. "I already told you I'm leaving. I learned about an expedition forming in Parramatta to explore the Blue Mountains. There's not enough land available in New South Wales to satisfy the sheepmen. Men like Macarthur look west for expansion, in hopes of driving their flocks to greener pastures. They're financing the exploration and I've decided to join them. There's still plenty of time before winter arrives to find a route across the mountains and return."

"Dare, I've heard of men becoming hopelessly lost in those mountains," cried Casey growing alarmed. "Think of the hardships, the danger. Other men have tried and failed."

"My mind is made up, Casey. I'll lose my sanity if I remain here with Mercy. I've been thinking of a walkabout for some time."

"Have you told your father? Or . . . or Mercy?"

"I've already spoken to Father. He isn't exactly thrilled with my decision but understands my need. As for Mercy, I intend to tell her immediately."

After his confrontation with Robin tonight, Dare realized he couldn't remain on the farm. The thought of another man touching Casey drove him wild with jealousy. Yet, as Robin so aptly pointed out, he had no right to interfere, no right to demand her love no matter how willingly given.

"Dare, I wish . . . I wish—"

"Don't say it, love," Dare admonished gently, "for I can't bear the thought of being unable to grant your wish. There's still tonight. Let me stay with you."

Casey hadn't the will to deny him, nor the inclination as his eyes beseeched her. Eyes a changeable silver which could take on the azure of a summer's sky, the gray of a storm-tossed sea, or the dangerous glint of fine Toledo steel. "Love me again, Dare. Give me memories for the empty years to come."

His head lowered, tasting her lips as his hands stroked and caressed her thighs until she moaned, her loins aching for his touch, then sighed in delight as his expert fingers began to work their magic. His hands traveled upward from her ankles to the inside of her legs, lingering in the bend of her knees. Gently but firmly he parted her legs. His head dropped and she felt the moist roughness of his tongue.

"Dare," she moaned, flinging her head back in utter abandonment. Broad hands cupped her buttocks and his tongue teased knowingly at the hard bud of desire hidden in soft folds of swollen flesh. The first sweet tremors of ecstasy pushed her to the edge of madness.

Frantically she clutched at his shoulders. But Dare only tightened his grip, his face buried in tender flesh. On the fringe of awareness, Casey felt Dare slide upward as his manhood claimed her. Gentleness had no part of this mating as Casey's arms and legs held him tight, lifting her hips to meet his probing thrusts, again and again, harder, faster. She clung to him desperately as explosions rent her body, feeling the violent shudders of Dare's taut body beneath her fingertips as they scaled the peak of ecstasy.

CHAPTER SEVENTEEN

Daylight burst upon the land with an abruptness that never failed to move Dare. He had awakened only moments ago and lay quietly watching Casey sleep, knowing he had exhausted her utterly and loved her thoroughly. Even in sleep she had the power to move him deeply. Each curve of her body was eloquently fashioned, the roundness of breasts with their pink, swollen crests, the slender arc of her hips that narrowed in long, lean legs, the golden hue of her skin gleaming softly beneath the fine sheen of perspiration.

"Bloody hell!" he cursed softly beneath his breath. He'd never be able to leave if he lingered a moment longer. Reluctantly, employing great care so as not to disturb her, Dare removed his arms from Casey's warm body and arose, dressing in silence. As an afterthought, he removed the signet ring he wore on his finger and placed it in her hand, closing her palm around it. She stirred but did not awaken.

He stepped out into the kitchen unaware that Martha and Robin sat quietly at the table enjoying a cup of tea before beginning their day. It had become a habit with Robin, relishing the early morning camaraderie with Casey, who for some unexplained reason had failed to appear at her usual time. The moment Dare slipped from Casey's room, the reason for her unaccustomed sloth became only too clear. Intent upon his own thoughts, Dare would not have noticed them but for Martha's stifled gasp.

Astonishment turned Dare's face ashen as his attention focused on the couple seated at the kitchen table. Shock left him speechless and he groaned inwardly at his bad luck. Martha quickly averted her face, but Robin's bold stare communicated his contempt. Words were unnecessary and Dare offered none, merely nodding before making a hasty departure. Not for the world did he wish this to happen, but it was too late for remorse, long past the time to repair the damage he had wrought.

Mercy was still asleep when Dare burst into the room they had never shared as man and wife. Jolting awake, she was astounded to see him flinging open drawers and chests that still held what clothing he hadn't already removed to the spare bedroom where he spent sleepless nights yearning for Casey.

Rising to a sitting position, Mercy settled the pillows behind her, watching Dare through slitted eyes. When he made no attempt to explain himself, she took matters into her own hands. "To what do I owe this pleasure, Dare?" she purred, her anger tight beneath the surface of her soft words. "This is the first time we've occupied this room together. Does this mean you've finally come to your senses?"

"As you can see, I'm gathering my belongings,"

Dare tossed over his shoulder, refusing to engage in verbal sparring. "I'm leaving Penrod station."

"Leaving! Where are you going? What about me?"

"I'm joining an expedition to the Blue Mountains. With any luck I'll be back by July. But don't count on it. If we do find a way across I may remain to help form a new colony."

"My God, Dare, men have tried before and never returned from those blasted mountains!" Mercy objected. "You can't go!"

"My mind is made up, Mercy," Dare returned, whirling to face his wife. "I can't live like this. Our marriage is a farce and we're both miserable. So is Casey."

"Then send Casey away, darling," Mercy implored, teetering on the edge of panic. "Once she's gone we can work things out between us. I know things could be better if you'd give us a chance."

"I'm sorry, Mercy. In one way I'm grateful for all you've done to free Casey and ease Robin's life. But another part of me hates you for the lives you've destroyed when you insisted on this loveless union," Dare said bitterly.

"No! Don't say that!" Mercy cried, jumping from bed to throw herself at him. "Don't leave me."

Removing her clinging arms from around his neck, Dare callously set her aside. Mercy's narrowed gaze sharpened as she studied him carefully, noting the dark smudges under his eyes, the purple stubble shadowing his chin, the same rumpled clothes he had worn the day before. He looked as if . . . Wrinkling her nose, she accused hotly, "You've just come from *her*, haven't you? You reek of sex! Instead of spending your last night in my bed where you belong you were with Casey. You bastard!"

"I was where I wanted to be," Dare said cryptically.

"What about me? What am I supposed to do while you're gone?"

"Whatever pleases you," Dare shrugged indifferently. "Perhaps your father will enjoy having you for an extended visit," he suggested. "But should you choose to remain here, Father will see that you are adequately provided for—as long as you behave," he added sternly.

Mustering the pride inherent in her nature, Mercy squared her narrow shoulders, refusing to break down in his presence. Once her face was composed into stoic lines, she said, "Good-bye, Dare. I wish you luck. Though you probably will disagree, I've always had your best interests at heart. Maybe one day you'll appreciate me."

Casey stretched lazily, every muscle protesting the strain of the strenuous night she had shared with Dare. A splendrous night, the most fantastic night of her life. He had made their parting something special with his tenderness, his caring, his careful attention to bring her as much joy as humanly possible. She no longer doubted his love, for no man was that good an actor.

From the moment she opened her eyes, Casey intuitively knew that Dare was gone. Not just from her bed but from the house and from her life. She felt the emptiness in her heart and the pain in her soul. Realizing it was long past the time she normally began her day, she made haste to arise, suddenly aware of a hard object resting in the center of her closed palm. Carefully releasing her fingers, she stared in awe at the circle of gold Dare had placed in her hand. Lifting it to the light, she saw it was the signet ring Dare constantly wore on his finger. In fact, he was seldom without it. His wanting her to have it was an undeniable expression of his love. If only he had trusted her enough to explain his reason for marrying Mercy instead of merely hinting at things she did not understand.

A short time later, Casey entered the kitchen to begin her day, unaware that Martha and Robin had seen Dare leave her room earlier. Robin had already departed but Martha stood at the hearth stirring a pot that was to be part of the evening meal. Roy and Ben had already eaten and left.

"I overslept," Casey said sheepishly, lowering her eyes. Had she been looking she would have seen Martha slant her a look laced with compassion.

"It doesn't matter, Casey," Martha replied. "Everyone deserves a day off once in a while. Sit down and have something to eat. Roy and Ben left for the fields hours ago and Dare—"

"Dare is gone," Casey said dully, her voice catching on a sob.

"I'm sorry."

"No one said life was easy. I've never found it so."

"I saw Dare leave your room early this morning," Martha revealed, lowering her voice. "I thought I'd best warn you that I wasn't alone. Robin was with me." Casey's gasp caused Martha to add, "Don't worry, Robin won't say anything. But he was terribly upset with Dare. Angry enough for a confrontation if Dare hadn't left so abruptly. He told me he'd warned Dare once about taking advantage of you."

"I'm sorry you were both on hand to witness our . . . indiscretion. But I love Dare. Nothing will change that. Not his marriage or his leaving."

"If it's any consolation, neither Robin nor I hold you accountable for Dare's actions. Robin doesn't understand Dare or his reluctance to discuss his hasty marriage," Martha admitted in a hushed voice. "Another thing puzzles me. Did you know Dare has been sleeping in one of the spare bedrooms? The other day he asked me to change the bed linen. It looked as if he's been occupying the room for some time. Does that sound like a man in love with his wife?"

A look of incredible joy transformed Casey's tired features. Dare wasn't lying! He wasn't sharing Mercy's bed or making love to her as she'd assumed. "I wish Dare had seen fit to confide in me before he left," Casey mused aloud. "I might never learn why Mercy and Dare became husband and wife unless Mercy chooses to tell me."

Martha snorted derisively. "That's highly unlikely. Do you think Roy or Ben know?"

"Probably," mused Casey thoughtfully, "but they're just as secretive as Dare."

"Speaking of Ben, he was terribly upset when Dare refused to take him along on the expedition," Martha said. "He threatened to run off and join on his own, but Roy finally convinced him he was needed on the farm in Dare's absence. I'm certain Ben begrudges Dare the adventure he is undertaking."

"A *dangerous* adventure," Casey stressed, Dare's safety uppermost in her mind.

"Dare can take care of himself, Casey," Martha replied, hoping to ease Casey's mind. Then both women turned back to their work.

But Casey was far from satisfied. Somehow, some way, she fully intended to learn for herself Dare's reason for marrying Mercy when obviously it was not what he wanted.

Ben remained sullen for days after Dare's departure, angry over being left behind while his older brother courted adventure and danger. But Casey was happy to note that his good nature soon reasserted itself and he settled down into his daily routine. The nip of fall was in the air, especially the nights, which were greatly appreciated. Casey was about to experience her first Australian winter. She learned from Ben that July was the coldest month but rarely severe. Little if any snow fell, except in the highest reaches of the Blue Mountains, and though the temperatures remained moderate on the coast, inland on the Hawkesbury severe frost could and did occur, often late enough to destroy spring crops.

On one of his trips to Sydney to sell his crops and mutton to the government store, Roy returned with warm cloaks for both Martha and Casey. Casey looked forward with relish to the cooler days and pleasant nights when sleep came easier.

Yet Dare's continued absence continued to plague Casey. Night after night she tossed restlessly, experiencing in her dreams the magic of Dare's hands and lips on her body, bringing her time after time to the brink of ecstasy—and back. Never again would she know the joy of his lovemaking. For when he returned—if he returned—she must leave, no matter how persuasive Dare's arguments to the contrary.

Beginning with the day Dare left, Mercy's attitude toward Casey changed dramatically. No longer demanding or argumentive, she seemed almost friendly. It was so out of character that Casey grew suspicious, trusting her not at all. In the past the woman rarely had a good word for anyone, so why should Dare's leaving change all that? It was a question Casey asked herself often when Mercy began making friendly overtures.

But as time passed, Mercy became the least of Casey's worries. There had been no word from Dare in weeks, not that she expected any, but still the hope existed. It was nearly two months after Dare's departure that Casey knew for a certainty that he had left a part of himself behind. She was pregnant. The first time she missed her monthly flow she thought little of it. But by the time the second month rolled by, all signs indicated that their union had produced unexpected fruit.

Why now? Casey silently lamented. Nothing happened the other times she'd been with Dare. What was so different about the last time? Did the exquisite joy Dare brought her make her womb more receptive? Whatever the reason, in seven months she would bear Dare a child in shame and degradation. No! Casey objected, not in shame, but out of the love she bore him. The one thing she wouldn't do was embarrass Dare's family, not after all they had done for her. Sometime before her pregnancy became noticeable she'd take her meager savings and leave to seek employment elsewhere. Surely someone in New South Wales would be willing to employ her.

Casey's dilemma became acute when, one

crisp fall day, Ben began making plans for Dare's return. It was nearly July and already snow could be seen on those lofty peaks of the Blue Mountains. That was the day Mercy sought out Casey for a private conversation. She found Casey alone in the vegetable garden gathering the last of summer's bounty.

"Casey, can we talk?" Mercy asked lightly.

"I can't imagine what we have to discuss," Casey returned, in no mood for a confrontation. She had lost her breakfast just minutes ago and her knees felt wobbly.

"Come inside, it's much too cool out here for my liking. No one is home so the parlor should do nicely." Brooking no refusal, Mercy turned abruptly and led the way inside. Frowning in exasperation, Casey followed.

"That's better," Mercy said crisply, moving directly to the hearth which had been lit to ward off the chill. "You're aware that Dare will be home soon, aren't you?" Casey nodded warily. "And you must know how uncomfortable it's been here for him living with you in the same house."

"Don't mince words, Mercy. What are you getting at?"

"Only that it's time you moved on. You owe me, Casey. I'm calling in your debt."

"What debt? I owe you nothing that I'm aware of."

"Didn't Dare tell you? I was certain he had. If not, then it's time you knew," Mercy stated, her voice hardening. "Obviously my husband had . . . other things on his mind when he was with you. He's a marvelous lover, isn't he?"

"Oh," Casey gasped, turning a bright red. Did

Dare tell Mercy about . . . about their wonderful night of love?

"Did you think I didn't know?" Mercy goaded maliciously. "Regardless of what you think, I'm no fool. Dare is an extremely virile man and celibacy isn't one of his virtues. He wasn't in my bed so I assumed he was in yours. Your interference in our lives has prevented our marriage from succeeding."

Privately, Casey thought their union doomed from the beginning. But rather than argue the point she changed the subject. "You mentioned earlier that I owed you. Just what is it I owe you?"

"Your freedom," Mercy responded frankly. "To please me my father arranged your pardon and Robin's ticket of leave. Lieutenant Governor Johnston owed Papa a favor. They've been close friends for years. For my sake Papa agreed to ask Johnston for your freedom and for Robin's release from the coal mines."

The play of emotions on Casey's face was all that Mercy hoped for. She didn't think she was being excessively cruel. She only wanted what was rightfully hers. As long as Casey remained at Penrod station there was no future for her and Dare.

Casey's mouth dropped open. "Your . . . your father arranged for my pardon? You're certain?"

"Absolutely."

"And Robin's ticket of leave?" Why was she repeating all this? "Why didn't Dare tell me?"

"You'll have to ask Dare."

Suddenly comprehension dawned as the truth crushed down on Casey like a lead weight. Marrying Mercy was part of the deal Dare hinted at.

Casey's freedom for Dare's name! My God! Dare wasn't lying. Her freedom and Robin's ticket of leave were the direct result of his marriage to Mercy. It hurt terribly to realize that none of this would have happened but for her, starting with finding Tim and enlisting Robin's help. Had she known the sacrifice Dare was making in her behalf she would never have allowed it. Was that the reason Dare failed to tell her? Abruptly Mercy's words made sense. She actually did owe Mercy a tremendous debt. One she could only repay by leaving Penrod station and removing herself from Mercy's life. Besides, wasn't her pregnancy already reason enough to leave?

At length she said, "You're absolutely right, Mercy. I owe you more than I can repay. Had I known the truth from the beginning I would never have allowed Ben to talk me into coming here. And believe it or not, I already decided to leave before Dare returned. I'll do so immediately."

Mercy's brows rose several notches. She found it difficult to believe that Casey would leave of her own accord. Just to make certain she wouldn't change her mind, Mercy sweetened the deal. "I'm not entirely heartless, Casey. I want Dare to love me, and with you here that's impossible. To show you I mean you no harm or ill-will I want to help you. Would you like to open a small shop of some sort in Sydney? I'm in a position to provide you with the means to do so. We're both women and I know you'll be at a disadvantage on your own in Sydney with no means of support. Dare would hate me forever if something dreadful happened to you."

"You're too kind," Casey remarked dryly. "I

don't want your money. I can take care of myself."

"I insist," Mercy said with firm resolve. "It's the least I can do."

"No . . . I . . ." Casey faltered, assailed by second thoughts. Why shouldn't she accept Mercy's assistance? Soon she'd have a child to support. He or she deserved a chance in life. Without funds to support herself, what would become of her and her child? Asking the Penrods for help was out of the question, for they had already done more than enough. More than she had a right to expect.

"If you truly feel the need to offer help, Mercy, then I accept," Casey allowed, swallowing her pride. "Your request that I leave is a legitimate one and I owe you that much for my freedom. Now maybe you and Dare can . . . can make something of your marriage."

"You're wise, Casey. Smarter than I gave you credit for. I hold no grudge against you for . . . for loving my husband, and should you ever require assistance in the future you've only to ask. Now," she announced happily, "we've only to collect the funds I promised. Tomorrow you can accompany me to McKenzie station. Papa is holding money left to me by Mama."

That night was the most difficult Casey had spent since Dare's departure. She wondered if Robin was aware of Dare's sacrifice on his behalf. Probably not, she decided, for like herself, he would never have allowed it. Her own guilt was enormous, which was exactly the reason Dare failed to tell her, she surmised. Life was so unfair. She knew Dare loved her, for all the good it did her. If it had not been for Mercy's timely intervention she would be a captive to Lieutenant

Potter's lust. The woman deserved a chance to earn Dare's love. Casey's one consolation was Dare's child growing beneath her heart. No one could take that from her, she reflected, cradling the slight bulge of her stomach.

In the wee hours of the morning she slept despite her churning emotions. During the long hours between midnight and dawn she decided not to tell Ben or Roy about her leaving until the day of her departure, allowing them little time for argument. Meanwhile, she'd accompany Mercy to McKenzie station in accordance with her wishes. After that her life would be in her own hands.

Martha protested vigorously when Casey announced her intention the next day to go with Mercy to McKenzie station. "The woman hates you, Casey. I don't trust her. Take Robin with you if you must go."

"I think we've misjudged Mercy," Casey remarked, stunning Martha. "She . . . she has reason to hate me. She's spoiled and accustomed to getting her own way, but her life's been far from easy since Dare brought her here."

"Are you daft? The woman delights in tormenting you. What has she done to gain your confidence?"

"I . . . I can't explain, Martha. Regardless of what you say, I'm going with her."

"You and Mercy shouldn't go anywhere alone," Martha persisted. "Only last night Ben told about bushrangers roaming the area. Nearly every day someone is robbed."

"You worry too much," chided Casey as she grabbed her wrap and headed for the door. "We'll be back before you know it."

CHAPTER EIGHTEEN

The dull gray sky and low-hanging clouds did little to dispel the gloom in Casey's breast as Mercy expertly drove the wagon along the dirt track skirting the Hawkesbury River to McKenzie station. The knowledge that she was responsible for Dare's marriage to a woman he didn't love and his ultimate unhappiness was a knife thrust in Casey's heart. The guilt would follow her for the rest of her life. Thank God she'd have Dare's child to remind her of the love they shared. Mercy's money would be used to good advantage to establish herself in Sydney and support her child.

"Casey, pay attention," Mercy said sharply. "When we reach McKenzie station, wait outside in the wagon while I speak privately to Papa. It shouldn't take long."

Casey nodded dully. The day Dare left, so did her zest for life. If it weren't for the child she carried . . .

The track they traveled was deserted, bordered on one side by the Hawkesbury and on the other by dense forest, brush and wattle. Though Casey was anxious to get this over with, the lumbering

bullock would not be hurried. With growing
dismay she felt fine misty rain fall chillingly from
the leaden skies to dampen her skin and add to
her misery.

"Damn!" Mercy muttered. "It would have to
rain now. If I could prod this animal into moving
faster we might . . ." The words died in her
throat, replaced by a yelp of fright.

Starting violently, Casey followed the direction of Mercy's terror-stricken gaze. Her hands
flew to her mouth to stifle her scream as several
bearded, unkempt men emerged from the bush
and surrounded the wagon.

"Well, well, look what we got here, mates?"

"No!" Casey cried, recognizing the scruffy
bushranger as the man who twice attempted to
rape her. And would have if not for Dare's timely
intervention. The same man Dare had shot on
their second encounter at the cave.

"I see ya recognize me," Bert grinned in a
parody of a smile. "I've been waitin' a long time
fer ya, wench."

"Do . . . do you know this man, Casey?" Mercy asked, clutching her in panic.

Breathing in shallow, quick gasps, Casey nodded. "This . . . this man and his friends attacked
us on the track between Sydney and Parramatta.
They overpowered Roy, but Dare and Ben arrived in time to . . . to prevent them from harm-
ing me and Martha. Then another time—"

"Quit yappin' and climb down," Bert ordered
gruffly, reaching up to grasp Casey's arm.

Clumsily she stumbled to the ground, Mercy
following as Bert's partner, Artie, hauled her
roughly from the wagon.

"What's the meaning of this?" Mercy sputtered indignantly, struggling to free herself. "Don't you dare touch me. I'm Mercy McKenzie Penrod, Dare's wife."

"Feisty little bitch, ain't ya," snarled Bert, his upper lip curling derisively. "Stuck-up, too. Pity yer husband ain't here. I owe him fer what he done to me. I couldn't sit down for weeks."

"I don't know what you're talking about," Mercy retorted.

"The redhead does," Bert grinned lasciviously, feasting greedy eyes on Casey as he addressed his next words to her. "I thought ya were Penrod's woman. Ain't ya good enough fer the man? Or does he need more than one woman to satisfy him? Why did yer lover marry Miss High and Mighty McKenzie?"

"You don't know anything," Casey defended hotly.

"I hear talk," Bert replied sullenly. "Artie was in Sydney when yer trial was held. He heard young Penrod tell everyone ya were his intended. Next thing I know he's married to old man McKenzie's daughter. The bastard don't know how lucky he is to have two beautiful women to screw."

"How dare you say such vile things!" Mercy blasted, eyes spitting blue fire.

"A real spitfire, ain't she, Artie? Yer welcome to her, mate. The redhead's mine. Of course we'll have to share with the others but there's enough to go around."

"What about Big John?" asked Artie, licking his lips in anticipation. "He'll be joinin' us at the meetin' place accordin' to plans."

Bert frowned. "Bugger him! The women will be ruined if that big son o' bitch gets 'em first."

"I ain't no coward but I sure as hell don't want to mess with that giant bastard. I say we take the women before he gets here."

"I'd like nothin' better than to screw them here and now, but one of us has to keep a cool head. It's too dangerous to lay 'em right here on the track where passersby can come upon us. Besides, we're too close to McKenzie land fer my likin'. We'll take the women with us. Let's go, mates," he called to his comrades.

"What about the wagon?" someone asked. "And the bullock."

"Leave 'em. The wagon's no good in the bush and the bullock's too tough to eat." His next words were directed at Casey and Mercy. "Git movin', yer comin' with us."

Clinging together for mutual support, the women refused to budge, too shocked to believe this could be happening to them. Bert's cruel prodding released Casey's frozen senses.

"You're crazy!" she gasped, twisting from Bert's grasp. "I'm not going anywhere with you and neither is Mercy. If you think you've got troubles now, wait until the Penrods and Mr. McKenzie find out what you've done!"

"Casey's right," chimed in Mercy, finally finding her courage. "Colonel Johnston and Papa are good friends. The Corps will be out scouring the bush in force once they learn about this."

"The bitch has a point, Bert," Artie allowed, scratching his chin beneath his shaggy beard.

"Ain't nobody can find us where we're goin'," scoffed Bert. "They ain't found us yet and they won't now. Ever since Big John and his mates joined up with us we're a match fer any of them lazy buggers in the Rum Corps. And I ain't leavin' the women behind, either. It's time we had our own whores. Even Big John will agree with that. He likes a good lay as well as any man." He guffawed lewdly as the bushrangers began melting into the bush, leaving Artie and Bert to cope with the women.

While Bert and Artie stood arguing and the others quietly scattered, Casey saw an opportunity for escape, albeit a slim one. Grasping Mercy by the hand, she said one word. "Run!" Responding out of pure instinct and the will to survive, Mercy's feet took wing, following closely behind Casey's flying limbs. If they could reach the thicket they had a fair chance of finding a hiding place. Casey's breath grew labored and Mercy's harsh panting sounded like thunder in her ears. The sounds of pursuit grew louder, but Casey dared not look back. Their wild dash for freedom offered their one chance for escape. Directly ahead lay a dense thicket and Casey's heart pounded, her pulse raced, as they sped toward safety. Behind her, already stretched to the limits of her endurance, Mercy stumbled and fell.

"Mercy!" Casey cried, panic a pulsing knot within her. "Get up, please!"

"I can't," sobbed Mercy, gasping for breath. "Save yourself."

"No," Casey refused stubbornly. "Let me help you. You can make it, it's only a few steps into the forest."

Ignoring Mercy's soft pleadings, Casey urged Mercy to her feet, prodding her on despite the fact she could have done much better on her own.

But Casey's innate kindness proved her undoing. Mercy had no sooner gained her feet than Bert and Artie were upon them.

"Ya bitch!" ground out Bert, panting from his exertions. "Did ya think ya could escape so easily?"

Casey flinched, the bite of Bert's fingers on her arms bringing tears to her eyes. When he slapped her, stars exploded in her head and her eyes glazed over. Her senses returned in moments as she renewed her struggles. But this time there was no reprieve as both she and Mercy were dragged deeper into the bush. Behind them the bullock stood grazing contentedly at the tall grass growing beside the track.

Steeped in misery, Casey shivered inside her damp cloak. It wasn't just the chill that plunged her into despair, but the thought of what would happen to them once Bert and his mates met up with the bushranger called Big John. The man must be some kind of ogre to inspire fear in men like Bert and Artie.

Casey was tiring rapidly as she trudged through the woods beside Bert. And judging from Mercy's drooping shoulders she was in no better shape. At least Mercy didn't have the added burden of pregnancy plaguing her. Her unsuccessful dash for freedom had cost Casey dearly, draining her of vital energy. She knew she was quickly reaching the end of her meager endurance and wondered what Bert would do to her when she could no longer keep up with his furious pace. Even now her stumbling drew his anger as well as his cruel prodding, and nausea lurked at the back of her throat ready to gush forth at the slightest provocation.

Just when Casey reached the end of her strength, they came to a small clearing beneath a huge gum tree, and thankfully, Bert halted. "We're here," he announced to no one in particular.

Breathing raggedly, Casey cautiously surveyed her surroundings. Some of the other bushrangers had already arrived and sat on the wet ground, waiting. For what, Casey had no idea. She learned soon enough.

"Where's Big John?" Bert asked.

"He ain't here yet," someone answered.

Casey found herself rudely shoved to the ground. "Rest while ya can. When Big John arrives ya'll have little time fer rest." He laughed crudely.

"Do we 'ave to wait fer Big John?" whined Artie, eyeing the women greedily. "I know ya want the redhead and the blond suits me just fine. I been hard as a rock since I laid eyes on her."

"You'll have to kill me first," Casey challenged with mock bravado.

As badly as he wanted Casey, Bert had decided on something of a more devious nature for her. Since Big John had joined up with them, Bert was rapidly losing control of his band to the huge man's authority, and he didn't like it. Seeking a way to earn the big Irishman's gratitude and make him beholden, Bert thought the perfect solution lay with the women. As much as he detested the idea of giving up the redhead, he intended to offer Big John his choice of the two women and settle for the leavings. One way or another the red-haired bitch would get what was coming to her for his suffering. He still experienced pain where the bullet had been removed from his buttocks by one of his men who knew little about doctoring.

"I've decided to wait fer Big John," Bert said. Keen disappointment distorted Artie's face. "I want that huge bastard in our debt. Doubtless he's as horny as we are, bein' without a woman so long and all. Our 'special gift' ought to please him enough to keep him from breathin' down our necks. Our mates are too impressed with his size and boldness fer my likin'."

"Whatever ya say, Bert," Artie allowed, disgruntled, "but it sure as hell's goin' to be hard to wait. What if Big John wants 'em both? As big as he is he's likely to have a huge appetite."

"Then we take the leavings and don't argue," Bert grimaced. "We do nothin' to anger him."

Casey shivered, her eyes following Bert as he walked away. She and Mercy had been granted a dubious reprieve, but for how long? What kind of monster was Big John, she wondered, to instill fear in men like Bert? Was there the remotest possibility of escape?

"Mercy," Casey whispered, nudging the figure huddled miserably in her wet cloak. "Did you hear what Bert said?"

"Of course," snapped Mercy. "I'm not deaf. I swear I'll not let the big brute touch me."

"I can't see that either of us has a choice," Casey returned shortly. "Unless we think of some way to escape before Big John arrives."

"Do you think we can?" Mercy asked.

"Nothing is impossible, only difficult. If we keep our wits, between the two of us we ought to come up with something. Be prepared to act quickly."

But to Casey's chagrin there was scarcely a moment when they were not under constant surveillance. Toward evening a fire was built to ward off the chill and one of the bushrangers brought them boiled beef, damper and tea. Still there was no sign of the man called Big John. After the meal was devoured, rum was passed around and soon Casey and Mercy were all but forgotten as the men consumed large amounts of the strong spirits. A small smile slipped past Casey's lips as the opportunity she had prayed for finally arrived.

"Mercy, it's time," Casey whispered, rousing Mercy from her fitful doze.

"When?" Mercy hissed, coming instantly awake.

"Now, while the bushrangers are occupied with satisfying their thirst. You go first," Casey directed. "Take off your cloak, it's cold but not freezing. I'll stuff it with grass and make it look like you're sleeping. After you've slipped into the bush I'll do the same with my cloak and follow. If . . . if something should happen and I don't make it, go without me and send help. Burloo is an excellent tracker, he'll easily pick up our trail. Do it now, Mercy, while no one is watching!"

Nodding, Mercy shrugged out of her cloak, shivering but too excited to feel the chill. She spared only a brief glance at Casey who hastily stuffed the discarded wrap with tufts of tall grass, arranging it to look as if Mercy lay sleeping peacefully at her side. It was far from perfect, but passable from a distance to a man in his cups.

Crawling on hands and knees, Mercy covered the short distance without alerting the bushrangers. She was nothing but a shadow when Casey risked a glance in her direction. Satisfied, she began her own preparations. A stroke of bad luck prevented her from following in Mercy's footsteps.

"Are ya sleepin'?" Bert asked, burping rudely. Silence. "Them blokes ain't sober enough to carry on a conversation and I'm in the mood fer companionship." Still no answer. "Wake up, I say!"

Casey groaned in pain as his booted foot connected with her ribcage. Pretending to awaken from a deep slumber, she opened her eyes, glaring murderously at Bert. "Leave us alone. Can't you see we're sleeping?"

"I could care less about the other bitch," Bert slurred drunkenly, "it's you I want. And I'll have ya soon as Big John finishes with ya. I don't want to rile him by takin' my turn first. I just hope the big son o' bitch don't tear ya apart."

To Casey's dismay, he sprawled beside her, resting his head in her lap. Sobbing in frustration, she tried to dislodge him. "Please, I'm tired."

"So am I, wench, so am I," sighed Bert, "and the least ya can do is let me rest my head on yer soft tits. If I wasn't too drunk I'd take ya now and Big John be damned."

For the first time in her life Casey was grateful for alcohol and its devastating effect upon the human body. However, her dilemma still existed. With Bert snoring in her lap escape was virtually impossible. She could do little besides hope and pray that Mercy was able to make her way safely back to the farm and summon help. At least one of them had a chance at freedom.

The moment Mercy reached the protective

cover of trees she rushed through the brush.
Thorns tore at her hair and clothes, but the moon
rose high in the sky, guiding her faltering steps.
She headed in the direction from which they
came, knowing that sooner or later she would
come to the Hawkesbury and follow it home. Her
good sense of direction and keen observation
served her well.

The six men sleeping off the effects of rum in
the small clearing began to stir. During the long
night Bert retained his hold on Casey, and
though she might have harbored a desire to slip
away to follow Mercy, they were soon dashed to
the ground. Not only did Bert's head remain
firmly in place on her breast all night but his large
hand curled possessively around her thigh and
did not let go. His loud snoring and drunken
mutterings allowed her little sleep, and she was
stiff and sore from holding the same position the
entire night.

Now that the camp was coming awake, Casey
braced herself for the ruckus that was sure to
come when Mercy's escape was discovered. She
wondered what Bert would do to her and began
to shake as fearful images built in her mind.

"Jesus, my head feels like someone's been
poundin' on it," Bert groaned, pulling himself
upright. His red-rimmed eyes fell on Casey and
his mouth twisted into a parody of a grin. "Ya
make a passable pillow, wench. Stir yer bones
and hustle up some tucker. Ya'll find the fixings
in my swag yonder beneath that gum tree. Wake
yer friend to help ya."

Casey was torn. Should she do as Bert directed
or remain reclining beside Mercy's empty cloak?

Her body partially concealed the stuffed garment, and Mercy's disappearance had not yet been noticed. The choice was taken from her when Bert rose shakily to his feet, hauling her up with him.

"What's wrong with yer friend? Is she too lazy or too good to help ya?" Curling his lip in a snarl, he raised his booted foot and aimed a vicious kick at the cloak. To his astonishment the cloak flew into the air spilling grass and twigs down on his head.

CHAPTER NINETEEN

Unwilling to admit he had been outwitted by a woman, Bert flew into a rage. "Ya bitch! Where is she?" he roared, backhanding Casey and sending her tumbling to the ground. "Answer me, dammit! How long ago did she leave?"

"Long enough to be far from here by now!" Casey retorted, rallying after the blow Bert dealt her.

"Ya'll pay!" he threatened, sneering. "No woman alive can make a fool of Bert and get away with it. Spread yer legs, wench, me and my mates are goin' to use ya like God intended."

By now the other bushrangers were awake and milled about watching the proceedings with keen interest. When it became obvious what Bert intended, Artie added his encouragement.

"Give it to her, Bert. Give it to her good. After ya finish I'll take seconds. I've been bustin' my britches for two days waitin' fer a piece."

"Don't touch me!" Casey cried, scrambling to her feet. "I won't let you harm my baby."

"Baby!" Bert repeated, momentarily stunned. "Yer breedin'? Which one of the Penrods does the little bastard belong to?" Before Casey could form a reply, he added, "No matter, by the time we finish with ya there'll be nothin' left of the bugger."

Casey's sole thought was taking flight, even if she died in the attempt. Her child's life was at stake. She'd not submit meekly to these depraved thieves and rapists. Death was preferable to being ravaged. And who knows what would happen to her when Big John arrived. Sheer black fright lent wings to her feet as she turned and sprinted toward the forest, the wild Australian bush offering the only hope for survival.

"Come back here!" roared Bert. "Ya'll not get far, not in yer condition."

Casey lowered her head and put on a burst of speed, only to be stopped dead in her tracks. The object she'd collided with was as solid as a stately eucalyptus, and to Casey's horror, nearly as tall.

Two huge hands dwarfed her narrow shoulders, impeding her flight and keeping her upright. Raising startled eyes, Casey encountered a chest as wide and immovable as a wall. Continuing upward, they glided over immense shoulders and bull-like neck to the bearded face of a man like none she had seen before. Limbs like sturdy oaks, arms bulging with corded muscles, the towering giant could be no one but Big John, and Casey sagged in defeat.

Rust-colored hair covered his enormous head and adorned his chin, and his brilliant blue eyes slowly slid the length of Casey's trim form. When he spoke, his booming voice filled the clearing, bouncing from tree to tree.

"What's the lass doin' here, mate?"

"We found her and a companion, another

woman, travelin' alone. Naturally we thought of ya and wanted ya to have one of 'em. But the other woman escaped last night. I was goin' to punish this one fer deceivin' me when ya showed up."

"It sounded to me like you were goin' to rape the lass," Big John accused, his voice laced with contempt. "Would you defile the holy state of motherhood? Didn't you hear the lass say she's breedin'?"

Bert had heard but he wasn't aware that Big John had. "Aye . . . well . . . I don't let a little thing like that stop me. Tell ya what," he said obsequiously, "ya can 'ave her first. I was savin' her fer ya anyways. Me and the boys don't mind takin' yer leftovers."

"I'm takin' the lass back where she belongs," Big John astounded everyone by saying. Accompanying Big John were three of his mates, swelling the number of bushrangers to ten.

"Are ya daft, mate?" Bert bellowed. "Don't be so persnickety. The girl ain't nobody special. We can keep her as our whore and no one will care."

"What about the father of her child?"

"The brat's a bastard. The Penrods will be glad to be rid of her. She can only be an embarrassment to 'em. The older son is already married and she's probably whore to all three of 'em."

From his towering height Big John looked down on Casey. "Is that right, lass?"

Somehow sensing that this giant meant her no harm, Casey gulped back her fear, forcing the words from her throat. "M . . . my baby has a father, one who loves me."

"Then why didn't he marry ya?" goaded Bert cruelly.

Big John's piercing blue eyes cut away the layers into Casey's soul. The question was there but he did not ask.

"You don't understand," defended Casey stoutly. "Dare married Mercy McKenzie for very good reasons, none that would interest you."

"What does it matter?" Bert disputed, growing angry. "The woman is ours now and we want her fer our whore. Right, mates?"

One or two "ayes" led by Artie followed Bert's remark, but Big John was quick to note that the majority did not respond one way or another. Consorting with desperate men like Bert had hardened and changed him. From a rather naive farm lad fighting for Irish freedom, he had learned the hard way to survive along with murderers, thieves and rapists. But he had not forgotten his humble beginnings nor the sacred state of motherhood as taught to him by his sainted mother, God rest her soul.

"I'm takin' the lass back," Big John repeated with unshakable resolve.

Bert's eyes narrowed. He was frightened of Big John but refused to relinquish the girl so easily. Suddenly an idea hatched in his brain, a way to thwart Big John's strange penchant for decency.

"When ya joined up with us, Big John, you and yer mates agreed to majority rule. I say we put it to a vote. If yer word is good ya 'ave to go along with what's decided."

Trapped by his own words, Big John grimaced. Hopefully he could depend on his own mates to vote with him, but not even that was enough. If the lass was forced to become their whore she would surely lose her babe and mayhap her life. Searching the faces of the assorted group of criminals, he reckoned they couldn't all be bad, and addressed his next words directly to them.

"How many of you blokes are eager to rape a lass with a child growin' in her belly? You all have mothers, some of you sisters. Think of them before you vote on the lass's fate."

"I'm thinkin' Big John has a point," one of the bushrangers allowed. "I don't relish rapin' a lass what's breedin'."

"Aye," chimed in another. "Thief and pickpocket I might be, but I don't hold with rape." Several others signified their accord.

Bert fumed inwardly, realizing he was rapidly losing control of the situation. The sheer size of Big John was intimidating enough, but it was downright confounding that the big bastard would possess a streak of decency or speak so eloquently. Previously he had been taciturn and surly, friendly with his own mates but keeping mostly to himself. Though he freely participated in their raids and bailups, Bert feared Big John and the fact that his mates looked to the giant for guidance. But he wasn't defeated yet. No, sir, old Bert wasn't as stupid as everyone thought. The woman might still be good for something even if they couldn't screw her.

"Ya convinced me, Big John," Bert acquiesced ingratiatingly. "In her condition the wench is likely to die on us if we use her like I intended. But mayhap all is not lost. There's another way she can do us some good."

"What are you gettin' at?" Big John asked, his arm tightening around Casey's slim shoulders.

"We should get somethin' out of the girl fer our trouble, seeing as how she is responsible fer the other woman escapin'."

"Go on," Big John said tightly.

"Here's my plan. We send a man to the Penrods askin' fer ransom."

"You're the one who's daft," scoffed Big John. "No one in New South Wales has negotiable cash. And the Penrods are no exception."

"That's the beauty of my plan," grinned Bert, extremely pleased with himself. "We ask fer rum in return fer the girl. Enough to last us a good long time."

At the mention of rum Bert captured the attention of every bushranger in the clearing, including Big John, who knew the scurvy lot well enough to realize the idea would appeal to them. If he had any doubt, the chorus of "ayes" soon disabused him of it.

"We send someone to Penrod station with our demands," Bert continued, warming to the subject. He noted with glee that he was rapidly gaining command of the situation. "We give him a certain time limit to get back to us with the rum before we let the wench go."

"Shit!" grumbled Artie. "How much rum can one man carry?"

"Not nearly enough," allowed a sly, fox-faced man named Dan.

Bert frowned. He hadn't thought of that. Then his frown turned into a smile as a solution came quickly to mind. "We'll be hidin' beside the track at the same place where we took the women. Penrod can load a wagon with rum and leave it where we're waitin'. There's enough of us to carry the rum to our camp. Then the wench can drive the wagon back."

Impressed by his own cunning, Bert took careful measure of each man's face as they mulled over his idea, noting happily their unanimous consent. Big John scowled, unable to do anything until a vote was taken. But even if it went against him, he reasoned, Casey would not be harmed. Either way she would be safely returned to those who loved her.

"Who's to carry the message?" Big John asked, surveying the men. In his opinion not one of Bert's mates possessed the intelligence to undertake the assignment. "And what about the woman who got away? They'll want her back, too."

"The other one is probably home by now," Bert reckoned. "We ain't all that far from Penrod station or McKenzie land. Once they hear the girl's story they'll know we mean business."

Highly satisfied with his thinking, Bert looked pointedly at each of the men gathered around, deliberately ignoring Big John. He knew that none of them had his shrewdness, yet he had to choose one from among them to carry his message. His eyes slid over Artie, who he discarded as being too stupid, and finally settled on a slim, ferret-faced thief with nimble fingers and glib tongue. Quick on his feet and agile of mind, Dan was the perfect choice despite his tendency to arrange things to serve his own needs.

Big John would have liked to be the one to carry the message, but he did not press the issue, afraid to leave Casey unprotected. He waited patiently for Bert to make his choice known. When he did, Big John decided that Dan was no better or worse than any other man in their group.

"Dan can be our spokesman," Bert announced at length. "Are ya willin', mate?"

Puffing out his chest importantly, Dan stepped

forward, his cunning features wearing a pleased grin. "I'm yer man, Bert. Tell me what to say and I'll repeat it word fer word. I'll get the rum fer ya."

As deceitful a man as ever breathed, Dan never did a thing that failed to feed his greed or lust. Born in the stews of London to a prostitute as fond of gin as she was of men, Dan had taken to the streets at an early age, his small size and cunning earning him the title of master pickpocket while still in his teens.

His successful career provided the means with which to indulge frequently in his addiction—women. His need for women was legend, and since his capture and transportation their lack was sorely felt.

After careful coaching by Bert, Dan finally memorized the message he was to deliver to Penrod station, and shouldering his swag he started off on his quest. If he wasn't so frightened of Big John he'd just as soon forget the damn rum and take the woman.

Casey watched Dan slip into the bush, her relief enormous. She was positive the Penrods would furnish the rum Bert requested and she'd soon be free. To her knowledge, Dare hadn't returned yet from his expedition, but Casey fully expected Ben and Roy to come to her aid.

Noting Casey's pensive mood, Big John said, "Don't worry, lass. In a few days you'll be back with your family."

Family. Yes, Casey reflected, somewhat startled. Despite everything, the Penrods *had* become like family. In all of New South Wales they were the only ones who cared what happened to her.

*   *   *

Several long, grueling hours after Mercy slipped away from the bushranger camp, she realized she had been traveling in circles. Dark clouds scudded across the sky and cold rain pelted down on her. Thoroughly chilled and shivering uncontrollably, Mercy had rested but briefly during the interminable night. Thorns and wattle tore at her clothes and hair, now hanging in wet strands down her back.

A feverish flush stained her cheeks and a terrible weakness forced her to halt for a rest. Shaking from exhaustion, she sank down on the damp ground, falling asleep instantly. She had no way of knowing she was close to Penrod station.

Dan whistled a tuneless melody as he followed Mercy's trail. His good sense of direction led him toward the Hawkesbury and Penrod station as he rehearsed the message he was to deliver. Cursing the dampness that dripped from the gum and eucalyptus trees, he pulled up his collar, wishing the sun would break through the clouds left over from yesterday's rain.

His musings led him to the women captives and how badly he has wanted them. Either one, or both, would have suited him just fine. The redhead claimed by Big John was stunning, but the blond who'd escaped had much to commend her. The bulge in his groin strained against his trousers and he rubbed himself, enjoying the stimulation but too pressed for time to stop and relieve the itch that tore at his vitals. He nearly stumbled over the sleeping form huddled on the ground before he realized who it was.

"Blimey," he muttered, his eyes bulging in disbelief. "This has to be my lucky day."

Cautiously he nudged Mercy with his toe, receiving nothing but a groan for his effort. Encouraged, he tried again, this time rousing Mercy from her stupor.

"Wha . . . what!" she gasped groggily, coming out of the fetal position she had assumed to conserve her meager warmth. Prying open her eyes, she recognized Dan immediately as one of the bushrangers traveling with Bert. After all her efforts was she to be taken captive again? "What do you want? Have you been following me?"

Dan laughed, his agile mind working furiously. Would the woman fight if he tried to take her now? Here? He could go ahead and take her against her will, but once she returned to Penrod station they'd likely kill him for what he did before he had the chance to relay Bert's message. Of course, he reasoned, he could kill her afterwards, but somehow killing a woman held little appeal for him. Loving them to death was more his style.

"I'm goin' to Penrod station to deliver a message from Bert," he said. "We thought ya'd already be there by now. But instead I find ya sleeping on the wet ground just a short distance from yer destination."

"So close? I lost my way in the dark. What do you want at Penrod station? Where is Casey?"

"Bert's holdin' the redhead fer ransom. I'm to deliver the message and ask fer rum in return for the girl," Dan responded, leering boldly at Mercy's figure clearly outlined beneath her wet dress.

"They're holding Casey for ransom?" Mercy questioned, dismayed. "I thought Big John—"

"We all did," Dan laughed nastily. "But for

some reason the giant has scruples about
screwin' a woman what's breedin'."

"Breeding!" Mercy screeched, stunned. "You
mean Casey is . . . is pregnant?"

"So she claims. Says the man loves her. Is she
by any chance talkin' about yer husband?" he
asked slyly, watching Mercy's face grow red with
anger.

"The bitch!" she ranted, waving her arms in
the air. "The conniving little bitch! She hoped to
steal my husband but she'll not have him."
Suddenly she turned thoughtful and a crafty
expression transformed her features. "What will
it take, Mr. . . ."

"Dan will do."

"What will it take, Dan, for you to return to
your friends and tell them the Penrods refused
their terms?"

"Blimey, yer a cool one," Dan whistled appreciatively. "If there's no rum to share it will take
more than Big John to save the girl from Bert and
the others. Is that what you want?"

Mercy's eyes narrowed in contemplation. Was
she capable of condemning Casey to a fate worse
than death? Even though it meant destroying
Dare's child? She didn't like the answer but no
other was possible. It mattered little that she'd be
eternally condemned to the fires of Hell, she'd do
anything to keep Dare. Nothing was too vile, too
contemptible, as long as it prevented Casey from
interfering with her marriage. With a baby in the
offing, Mercy didn't trust Casey's promise to
remove herself from their lives. One day Dare
would learn he had a child and all would be lost.

Closing her mind against the evil in her heart,
Mercy looked Dan in the eye and repeated her

question. "What will it take for you to forget about going to Penrod station?"

At first Dan thought Mercy was out of her head from fever. She was trembling violently, her lips blue with cold, her cheeks flushed and voice raspy. From where he stood he could feel the heat emanating from her shaking form. But the cool, calculating gleam in her blue eyes convinced him of her seriousness. Flashing a set of sparse, stained teeth, he asked cheekily, "What are ya offerin'?" His eyes roved insinuatingly over her damp gown clinging enticingly to lush curves, and the ache in his loins grew unbearable.

"I can get money from my father, or rum, if you prefer," Mercy returned eagerly. "I'll meet you wherever you say and give you anything you ask."

"Anythin'?"

"Within reason," amended Mercy, instantly alert. She sensed this cunning individual wanted more than she was willing to give. How far was she prepared to go, she asked herself, to remove Casey from her life and win Dare's love?

Grasping Mercy's upper arms, Dan dragged her forward until their bodies touched; until the feverish heat of her burned his starved flesh; until he would willingly agree to anything to have her nude body sprawled beneath him.

"Ya know what I want, woman," he rasped hoarsely just moments before his mouth smashed down on hers.

Mercy gagged, and not just from the sickness she was slowly succumbing to. Her lungs burned, her throat felt as if clogged with sand, and the pain in her chest intensified with each hard-won breath. If she didn't reach shelter soon she was likely to die from cold and exposure. These past two days had been too much for her. Never having enjoyed robust health, Mercy was fully aware of the danger to her fragile constitution.

Squirming free of Dan's punishing mouth, Mercy fought for breath. "If . . . If I give in to . . . to your demands, will you do as I say? Will you tell the others that the Penrods don't care about the girl and refused to send the ransom?"

The dark slashes of Dan's brows met in the center of his forehead as he carefully considered Mercy's request. Rum meant little to him. He liked it well enough, but he had never craved strong drink. Not only did it confuse the mind, but it decreased his sexual appetite. To Dan, having a woman willingly submit to him meant far more than a bottle in his swag. Another bailup or two might yield them rum as well as other valuables, but not a woman. For him the choice was simple.

"Aye," he grinned delightedly. "Once I've had me fill, ya can go on yer way and I'll tell me mates the Penrods refuse to part with their rum."

"You . . . you promise?" Mercy rasped hoarsely, wondering if she could trust him.

"I said so, didn't I?" he shot back crossly. "Take off yer clothes."

"But it's cold," Mercy protested.

"I'll keep ya warm." When she hesitated, he added slyly, "Ya want the O'Cain woman out of yer hair, don't ya? I'll do my part but ya got to do yers."

Each breath an agony, Mercy quickly shed her clothes, gritting her teeth as she meekly submitted to Dan's prolonged pawing before he bore her to the ground. Spreading her legs, he took her swiftly, much to Mercy's relief. When he finished, he sprawled atop her shivering form, panting heavily.

"Get up, you lout," Mercy gasped, shoving at his chest.

But to her dismay, she soon learned Dan's appetite was insatiable. "I said till I had me fill of ya," Dan reminded her sharply. "I'm already hard again. I ain't had a woman in months."

Dan took her twice more in quick succession, but when he tried again, he failed. Weakened and drained to the point of utter exhaustion, he allowed Mercy to drag her aching and bruised body from beneath him and struggle into her wet clothes. Never was she more aware of the raging sickness that ravaged her body.

"Don't forget your promise, Dan," she cautioned in a raspy whisper as his eyes followed her every move. For the first time in his life a woman had completely satisfied him and he intended to honor his word.

"Aye, I'll not forget," Dan nodded, wishing he had the strength for one more go at her.

Disdaining a reply, Mercy turned and stumbled painfully away from the scene of her shame, not proud of what she had done. But like her father, she thought only of her own survival. She did what her heart commanded. Casey was also a survivor, and Mercy felt no qualms about abandoning her to the mercies of the bushrangers.

CHAPTER TWENTY

Thad McKenzie flew up the steps and barged through the door without knocking, interrupting Ben and Roy as they sat down to supper. He had just learned from Robin, whom he spoke with at the corral moments ago, that Mercy and Casey had taken the wagon out yesterday and hadn't returned. The Penrods naturally assumed the women had remained overnight at McKenzie station due to the inclement weather.

"Thad! What is it?" Roy asked with growing alarm. "Are Mercy and Casey with you?"

"No, and I want to know where they are," Thad said, anxiously tunneling thick fingers through thinning gray hair. "Something terrible has happened to my daughter, I feel it in my bones."

"Calm down, Thad, and tell us what happened," Ben coaxed soothingly. "Martha told us Mercy expressed a desire to visit you and talked Casey into going with her. Had she informed us, someone would have gone with her. We naturally assumed the bad weather forced them to remain overnight."

"They never reached my house, Ben. This

morning one of my convict workers found the
bullock and wagon about two miles down the
track. It never occurred to me that Mercy might
have been driving the wagon until I stopped at
the corral just now and Fletcher told me the
women had taken it out yesterday. Had I known,
I wouldn't have taken my time returning it. Are
you daft, man, to let them go off alone? Where
have they disappeared to?"

Thoroughly bewildered, Roy tried to make
sense of what Thad said. Until this minute he
thought Mercy was having a long visit with her
father. "Tell us again where the wagon was
found, Thad. Did your worker find nothing else?
No clues as to what happened to the women?"

"Where's my daughter, Roy?" Thad asked,
choking on a sob. "She's all I've got. I'll do
anything to get my girl back." Casey was of little
concern to him. Only his daughter mattered. "It's
your fault for allowing her to go alone."

"Sit down, Thad," Roy urged the distraught
man. "Now tell us everything you know. You
realize, don't you, that I'd not let anything happen to Mercy. I have no idea why she decided
against telling us her intentions to leave. Had she
done so, one of us would have escorted her.
According to Martha, she made up her mind
suddenly, after we left for our chores."

Gulping down the tea Ben thrust before him,
Thad calmed down enough to say, "The wagon
was found along that deserted stretch of track
about two miles from my house. It wasn't reported to me until later in the day. I rode out
immediately to investigate. The vicinity yielded
no clues as to who drove the wagon or why it was
abandoned, though I recognized it at once as

yours. Only when I returned it a short time ago did I learn my daughter was somehow involved."

"Did you find anything at all to indicate what might have happened?"

"Nothing," repeated Thad. "But we should organize a search immediately. How soon can you be ready?"

"Do you think that bushrangers . . ." Ben faltered, unable to continue.

"I've deliberately kept my mind from accepting that implication, though all signs point in that direction. Two women don't disappear without rhyme or reason, and bushrangers have been active in the area."

"I'll round up some men," Roy said. "Give me an hour, then be ready to ride."

Chafing at the delay yet powerless to rush Roy's careful preparations, Thad nodded.

Less than an hour later several men, including Burloo, their native tracker, Robin and two trustworthy convicts, prepared to ride out of the yard in search of the missing women.

Hardly had they set out than they encountered a lone figure staggering down the dirt track. It was a woman whose tattered clothes and battered body attested to the ordeal she had been through. Long blond hair hung in snarled strands down her back and her faltering steps and bent shoulders conveyed her exhaustion.

"Mercy!" Thad cried, scrambling from his mount and running out to meet his daughter.

"Papa!" Thad reached her just as her meager strength deserted her and she began a slow spiral to the ground. His arms caught her moments before she hit the ground, looking around helplessly for direction.

"This way," Roy instructed, taking charge. "She looks exhausted, let's get her to bed. I'll get Martha to undress her and make her comfortable."

"She is burning with fever," Thad said with grave concern.

While Roy and Thad fretted over Mercy, Ben and Robin anxiously scanned the track, desperately praying for Casey to stumble forth. Long minutes dragged by. Still Casey did not appear. With sinking hearts they realized she was not coming. Their eyes met in unspoken torment, then both turned toward the house as with one accord. Only Mercy could explain why Casey failed to return. When Ben tried to enter the sickroom to question Mercy, Thad would not allow him access until she was bathed and settled in bed. As yet, no one realized the full extent of Mercy's illness, but it was apparent to all she was gravely ill.

Pacing restlessly outside Mercy's room, all four men started when the door opened and Martha stepped into the hall. "How is she?" Thad asked anxiously.

"Is she coherent?" Roy questioned.

Martha shook her head, her eyes troubled. Though she never liked Mercy, she didn't wish death on her, or undue suffering. "She's very ill, sir. I've done all I can. She can barely speak above a whisper and the congestion in her chest makes breathing difficult. Is there a doctor nearby?"

"There's one in Sydney," Robin offered. "I'll leave immediately if that's your wish, Mr. McKenzie."

"Aye," Thad said. "And pray God it's not too late."

"Can we speak with Mercy, Martha?" Roy asked hopefully. "Will she be able to understand and respond? It's imperative we learn what happened and why Casey never returned."

"She can hear and understand, sir," Martha replied, as anxious as the others to learn Casey's fate. "Whether or not she can answer is in God's hands."

"We'll take that chance," Ben replied, his hand on the doorknob.

"Wait!" Thad objected. "I won't have my girl disturbed. She's sick and needs rest."

"Thad," Roy chided, his patience at an end. "There's another life involved here. Have you forgotten Casey?"

Thad flushed, for in truth he cared little for anyone but his daughter. An ex-convict was beneath his concern. But obviously the Penrods held the woman in high esteem. "All right," he allowed grudgingly, "you can speak to Mercy, but only for a moment."

They entered the room to find Mercy thrashing on the bed. Her face was flushed, her breath harsh and raspy. The shallow rise and fall of her chest was barely discernible beneath the covers. Her head turned at the sound of their entering and she braced herself for the barrage of questions about Casey.

"Mercy," Thad said, brushing the yellow strands of matted hair away from her flushed face. "Roy wants to ask you some questions. If you're too tired, we'll come back, but I'm as anxious as he is to know what happened. Can you talk, darling girl?"

Mustering her faltering strength, Mercy nodded, her voice strained. "It . . . it's all right, Papa, I'll try. I want to tell you everything."

"Where's Casey?" Ben blurted out before Roy could pose his own query.

Mercy's eyes closed as a flash of pain twisted her mouth into a grimace. "Casey is dead," she lied convincingly, her voice the barest whisper. "The bushrangers killed her." Ben's sharply indrawn breath caused her a pang of guilt, but she quickly stifled it when she thought of Dare's child growing in Casey.

"Dead! Are you certain?" Ben asked, thoroughly shaken. "How? How did you manage to escape without Casey?" His tone was bitter with accusation and Thad jumped to his daughter's defense.

"What are you implying, Ben? That Mercy is responsible for Casey's death?"

"No, of course not," Ben denied. "I just want to know how Casey died."

"We were surrounded by bushrangers about a mile or two from Papa's house," Mercy croaked weakly. "They took us with them into the bush, intending to . . . to rape us. They were saving Casey for some man they called Big John. He was expected to join them at their camp. It . . . it was horrible."

"What was horrible? Did . . . did they hurt you?" Thad asked gruffly.

Mercy shook her head. "No. When night fell they began drinking and Casey and I formed a plan to slip away under the cover of darkness. I went first, but when it was Casey's turn, Bert, their leader, prevented her from leaving. He became violent when he found me gone and . . . and I saw him attack Casey. Then they all took turns on her. She couldn't have lived—so much blood. After that I didn't wait around. I didn't stop running until I reached Penrod station."

"Could you have been mistaken?" Roy asked sharply. "Perhaps Casey was only hurt."

"If we leave now, Father, we can easily find the bastards. They haven't a chance with Burloo to guide us."

"No!" Mercy gasped, gathering her wits. "She's dead, I tell you. The last thing I heard was Bert telling his men that Casey was dead. It's useless to go chasing after her." She grew so distraught that Thad put an end to the questions, herding everyone out of the room.

"What do you think, Father?" Ben asked once they were alone.

"Mercy is gravely ill, son. I hope the doctor gets here in time," he added ominously.

"That's not what I meant. I was referring to Casey."

"I know what you meant, Ben, but I'm trying not to think about it. Casey was like a daughter to me. We all loved her. If Mercy swears she's dead it must be true."

"Aye," concurred Ben with quiet resignation. "However, I intend to conduct a thorough search. Robin can join me when he returns from Sydney with the doctor."

Mercy worsened during the night. Her harsh breathing and painful gasps moved everyone to pity. It was obvious she hovered at death's door. According to Martha, who kept vigil at her bedside, Mercy called for Dare with every breath and mentioned her captors frequently during her fevered ravings. Thad was beside himself with grief and could not be coaxed from his daughter's side. Expecting the worst, Roy and Ben remained near the house during the long hours of Mercy's illness.

*   *   *

Later that day as father and son shared a makeshift meal they had prepared themselves, a commotion outside disrupted their morose thoughts. "Robin is back with the doctor!" Ben said, leaping to his feet.

"It's too early," Roy refuted, following Ben out the door. Thad was upstairs with Mercy and unaware of the new development.

A tall, gaunt man, supported by another man equally thin, limped into the yard. At first sight no one recognized the bearded stranger in ragged clothes who leaned heavily on his companion. The men's appearance indicated they had endured terrible hardships and deprivations.

"Jesus!" Ben shouted, trembling with excitement. "It's Dare! Dare has come home, and not a minute too soon."

Sprinting the short distance to meet the two men, Roy relieved the stranger of his burden, assisted by Ben, lending their strength to Dare.

"What happened, son?" Roy asked anxiously. "We expected you home weeks ago, when the first snow fell in the mountains."

"I'm fine, Father," Dare grimaced, belying his words. "I had the misfortune of falling and breaking my leg several weeks into the expedition. Brad Turner, the leader and doctor of sorts, set it and left Milt, here, to look after me until they returned. Only they never came back. I'm afraid they're hopelessly lost somewhere in the mountains. If I hadn't been injured I'd be with them now."

"Thank God you did sustain an injury," Ben returned fervently. "Too many men fail to return from the Blue Mountains. Others have become lost for months, years even. We owe Milt a large debt for caring for you."

"I'm afraid I wasn't too happy about being left behind," Milt admitted, leveling a guilty grin in Dare's direction. "But as it turned out, Dare and I were the lucky ones."

"You're welcome to stay with us for as long as you like, Milt," Roy offered gratefully.

"Thanks, Mr. Penrod, but I'd best return to Sydney immediately and report to the authorities. Perhaps when spring arrives I'll head up a search party for the missing explorers."

"Eat first, and refresh yourself," Roy advised. "I'll have someone take you to town in the wagon."

"I accept gladly," grinned Milt. "I feel as though I've walked enough to last a lifetime."

While Dare and Milt wolfed down their meal, Roy fretted nervously. He hated having to inform Dare of Casey's death. And judging from Mercy's grave condition, she was in danger of succumbing to her illness. It would be a bitter blow, he knew, coming on the heels of his ordeal in the mountains. In the end it was Dare himself who brought up the subject.

"Where's Casey, Father? She's still with you, isn't she?" Dare's biggest worry during the weeks he lay incapacitated was not for his own safety, but Casey's. After their last encounter the night before he left he feared she might have taken it into her head to leave.

The look Roy and Ben exchanged brought a sudden chill to Dare's heart. Sensing a family crisis in the making, Milt excused himself to change into the clothes Ben thoughtfully provided.

Dare's voice cut into the tense silence that followed. "What are you hiding, Father?"

* * *

While Dare was being told of the terrible tragedy, Mercy rallied briefly, realizing with sudden insight that she was dying and that all her scheming had been in vain. Her eyes focused on her father, who kept a faithful vigil at her bedside. "Papa?" she wheezed painfully.

"Daughter," Thad answered, choking on his tears. "I'm here."

"Am I dying?"

"The doctor will be here soon," Thad answered evasively.

"Tell me, Papa, I'm not afraid."

"None of us are God, daughter. If it were in my power you'd not be suffering now. What happened to the warm cloak I bought you? You weren't wearing it when you stumbled in here yesterday."

Utterly drained, Mercy closed her eyes, her guilt enormous. If she was to die she didn't want to go to her maker with sin staining her soul. She had to tell her father the truth about Casey while breath still remained in her body.

"Papa, about Casey—"

"Don't tax yourself, daughter. Tell me later."

"No, there might not be a later. I'm sorry for everything, Papa."

Thinking Mercy referred to her forcing Dare to marry her in return for Casey's freedom, Thad replied, "You did the woman a favor, daughter. She was granted a pardon and knew a measure of freedom before her death."

"No, Papa, she's . . . not . . ." She faltered, the rattle in her chest making speech difficult. If only Dare were here, she thought, her mind already beginning to fade.

Then, by some miracle, her wish was granted

as Dare knelt beside her. He was bearded and dressed in rags, but Mercy would know his beloved face anywhere. If her suspicions were correct her life was slipping away, and she had but a short time to settle things with Dare. He had a right to know about his child.

"Dare . . . you've come . . . back."

"I'm here, Mercy. You must get well," Dare urged, her grave condition moving him to pity.

"I'm . . . afraid it's . . . too late," Mercy rasped painfully. "I . . . need your . . . forgiveness."

"For what it's worth, I forgive you."

"Casey—"

"What about Casey?" Dare asked sharply. "Is there something I should know?"

"For God's sake, don't torment her!" Thad chided angrily. "Can't you see she's—"

"It's . . . all right, Papa. I . . . need . . . to tell Dare . . . Casey's not—"

"Tell me what? Casey's not what?"

"I'm . . . sorry. Go after . . ." Suddenly the breath fluttered in her chest like a trapped bird and words were no longer possible. Only the loud rattle and labored wheeze leaving her blue lips attested to the fact that she still lived.

"What did she mean?" Dare asked, looking at Thad for enlightenment.

"She's out of her head with fever," Thad explained sadly. "I think she's sorry for . . . for insisting you marry her when you loved Casey."

When Roy told Dare all he knew about Casey and Mercy's abduction and the sparse facts concerning Casey's death, Dare refused to believe the woman he loved was dead. Wouldn't he feel it in his heart if his love no longer walked the

earth? His first inclination was to rush into
Mercy's room and shake the truth from her, until
Roy told him how desperately ill Mercy was.
Pneumonia, he suspected, brought on by cold
and exposure. They'd known for years that
Mercy's lungs had been weakened as a child by
constant colds and chest congestion.

Noting that Mercy had lapsed into uncon-
sciousness, Dare reluctantly left the room, but
not before extracting Thad's promise to summon
him the moment Mercy regained her senses. In
the meantime, he bathed, changed clothes and
flopped into bed for a much needed rest. His leg
throbbed painfully from his long trek home and
he knew he still had a ways to go before regaining
full use of his limb.

To Roy's chagrin, Dare adamantly refused to
accept Casey's death, voicing his intention to
search for her after he had rested the night. He'd
take Robin and Ben, if they agreed, and Burloo to
do the tracking. For months he'd thought of
nothing but Casey and how much he loved and
needed her. Their last night together had been
beyond ecstasy, far more sublime than anything
he'd ever experienced or hoped to. He had come
to a decision during those lonely days and nights
in the mountains suffering from pain, cold and
hunger with no one but Milt for company.

He couldn't live without Casey, her love, her
sweetness, her tender care. Even if it meant
leaving Penrod station to make a life elsewhere,
he intended to take Casey away and live with her
outside the bounds of society. Being shunned by
his peers and reviled by Mercy and her father
hardly mattered as long as he had his love beside
him. Perhaps they might go back to England, if

Casey agreed. They could make his home with his grandfather whom he knew would welcome him. His last thought before sleep claimed him was that somewhere Casey was alive and in desperate need of him.

The next morning Robin arrived with the doctor, a ticket-of-leave man who had been transported for performing surgery on a lord of the realm while drunk. The man died and his enraged family had the hapless doctor arrested for murder. His trial was swift, resulting in transportation. He arrived in New South Wales only six months ago.

But despite the doctor's heroic efforts, Mercy died in her father's arms shortly after his arrival, without ever regaining consciousness. Her taxed lungs simply gave out, freeing her from her misery. And with her died the truth about Casey.

Dare was beside himself with grief. Though he mourned Mercy's untimely death, it was concern over Casey that fed his misery. His wife was dead, beyond mortal help. It was Casey who needed him if she was alive as he truly believed. He remained home long enough to see Mercy laid to rest next to her mother on McKenzie station before leaving to begin his search. Ben, Robin and Burloo accompanied him. Roy's best efforts failed to dissuade him to wait until he recuperated fully from his broken leg. Against all odds and arguments, the four men, toting swags on their backs, left the next day, entering the bush on foot near the spot where the empty wagon and bullock was found.

CHAPTER TWENTY-ONE

Casey trembled as she felt Bert's beady eyes settle on her. Soon they would leave to meet Dan and she'd be free of Bert's repulsive company forever. He and Artie were the most despicable creatures she had ever met. She could tolerate one or two of the others but was convinced that only Big John's size protected her from rape, or worse. She had already decided in her mind to kill herself before letting any of them touch her.

Finally the time arrived to leave the rough camp in the clearing and Casey kept close to Big John, surrounded and protected by his mates. It would take nearly a full day of walking to reach the place where they were to meet Dan and take possession of the rum provided by the Penrods. There wasn't a doubt in Casey's mind that she would soon be free. She assumed Mercy had reached home by now and verified Dan's story. Despite her earlier resolve to leave Penrod station, she'd be more than happy to be home again with those who cared about her. If only long enough to bid them a proper good-bye.

"Are you all right, lass?" Big John asked when Casey stumbled over a root.

"I'm fine, Big John. Just anxious to be home. Not that I'm not grateful for your protection," she added quickly, unwilling to offend the gentle giant who watched over her.

"I understand, lass. You shouldn't have been subjected to all this in the beginning. You'll be with your man soon."

"He's not my man," Casey contradicted.

"You're havin' his babe, aren't you? Be patient, lass, things have a way of workin' out."

Casey remained mute, not wishing to disabuse Big John of the romantic fallacy that she and Dare would be together one day. As long as Mercy lived that was not likely to happen.

Abruptly the group halted as Dan burst through the thicket, surprising them. "Dammit, Dan! What in the hell are ya doin' here?" Bert raged angrily. "Yer supposed to wait with the rum till we arrived, not come lookin' fer us."

"There ain't no rum," Dan said sullenly. Ever the actor, he played his role superbly.

"What are ya talkin' about?" Artie asked belligerently. "Of course there's rum."

"There ain't, I tell ya."

"Mayhap ya'd better tell us what happened," Bert ordered, his manner threatening. "And if yer lyin' ya won't live to tell another."

"I ain't lyin'," Dan defended staunchly. "I took yer message to the Penrods only they wasn't interested."

"No!" Casey cried, confused and hurt. "It's not true! He's lying."

"Shut up!" Bert growled over his shoulder. "Let Dan continue. I'll judge if he's lyin' or not. Who did ya talk to, lad? Did ya see the McKenzie woman?"

"I seen her, but it was Dare Penrod I spoke with," Dan said, repeating Mercy's instructions. "The man has his wife back and that's all he cares about. He called the redhead a whore." Dan offered slyly.

"Dare is on an expedition to the Blue Mountains," Casey challenged. "You couldn't have spoken with him."

"He's back," Dan returned, assuming a hurt expression. "And I ain't lyin'. The father don't want ya neither. At least he refused to part with their rum fer ya."

"Did you tell them she's breedin'?" Big John asked, enraged by the Penrods' callous treatment of Casey.

"Aye, I told 'em," nodded Dan, "but it made no difference. They made it clear they'd welcome no bastards in the family."

Casey sagged in defeat, humiliation chilling her blood. She felt a nauseating sinking of despair and her expression was one of stunned disbelief. She felt as if she'd been struck in the face. If Big John's massive arm hadn't been supporting her, her legs would not have held her upright.

"Bloody hell!" thundered Bert, completely unsettled. "Ya mean we ain't gettin' no rum?"

"I started back immediately to give ya the news instead of waitin' until ya showed up at the meetin' place. I knew ya'd be madder'n hell."

"It's all yer fault!" Bert raged, shaking his fist in Casey's face. "Ya'll pay fer this. I shoulda knowed them Penrods wouldn't pay fer a whore. It's time ya repaid us fer our trouble and earn yer keep. I'll take my share now."

When Bert lunged, Big John carefully placed Casey behind him, stopping Bert in his tracks.

"You'll have to get by me first," he challenged, his legs planted on the ground as solidly as twin oaks.

In a burst of anger, Bert's control fled, robbing him of his wit and blinding him to Big John's size and strength. Nothing existed but the need to punish Casey and appease his lust at the same time. He blamed her for depriving him and his mates of a much needed supply of rum and he wanted her to suffer for turning Big John against him.

"Ya can't stop me, ya big bastard!" he grunted, reaching for the knife strapped to his waist. "I ain't afeared of ya."

Shoving Casey rudely to the ground, Big John reacted instantly, incredulous that Bert would deliberately provoke him in the face of over-whelming odds. The man must be demented to even attempt such a foolhardy act.

Casey watched with bated breath as Big John, surprisingly agile for his immense size, nimbly side-stepped Bert's first thrust. Undaunted, Bert lunged again, missing his target a second time. Blinded by rage, Bert roared, drawing back for another wild attack. But his uncontrollable temper proved his undoing as he stumbled, falling flat on his face. Sprawled in the dirt, he lay motionless, his left arm extended outward, his right twisted beneath him.

Scrambling to her feet, Casey would have approached the prone form if Big John hadn't warned her away. "Stand aside, lass, the bloody bloke might be shammin'."

Retreating, Casey doubted that Bert was trying to fool anyone. His anger alone would have brought him to his feet for another attack. Instead, he lay still except for the occasional twitch-

ing of his limbs. With the toe of his boot Big John
flipped him over, and Casey's shocked gasp
brought the others crowding near.

The sharp blade of the knife still clutched in
his right hand had pierced his flesh in the vicinity
of his heart. Dropping to his knee, Big John
pulled the blade free, then stared in dismay as a
steady flow of blood gushed forth to stain the
ground a bright red. Acting from instinct, Casey
ripped the bottom ruffle from her petticoat and
handed it to Big John to stanch the crimson flow.

"Is he dead?" she asked in a hushed voice.

"Not yet but he soon will be," Big John muttered as he helplessly watched the lifeblood drain
from the dying bushranger. With his men looking
on, the last breath left Bert's body in a shuddering sigh.

"He's gone," Artie accused, glaring murderously at Big John. "Ya killed him."

"He brought it on himself," Big John said.

"What are we goin' to do now?" Artie whined.
"Bert was our leader."

"Let Big John take his place," Dan suggested.
"Ain't none of us smart enough to follow in
Bert's shoes 'cept him."

"Aye," agreed one of Big John's mates. "Ain't
no man I'd rather follow than Big John. How
about it, mates?"

Unanimous agreement followed swiftly and
Casey breathed a sigh of relief when Artie voiced
no protest. He wasn't the only one intimidated
by the sheer size of Big John. "So be it," the huge
man intoned tersely. "Let's get this poor bastard
buried."

"What about me?" Casey asked while the
bushrangers scraped out a shallow hole in the
ground with their knives.

"I'm takin' you back where you belong, lass. You'll be needin' care and a father for your babe."

"No!" Casey protested violently. "I'll not return where I'm not wanted. You heard what Dan said. The Penrods don't care about me. My child means nothing to Dare. No, Big John, I'll make a life for myself and my child without the Penrods' help."

"Be reasonable, lass." Big John cajoled. "Sydney is no place for a woman alone, let alone one breedin'. How will you support yourself?"

"I'll manage," Casey contended stubbornly. "I'll not be beholden to the Penrods for my livelihood."

While they argued back and forth, the grave was dug and Bert's body wrapped in the remnants of Casey's blood-soaked petticoat and laid inside. After the dirt was replaced, the area was scoured for rocks to place on top in order to prevent wild animals from digging up the remains.

"I have some money and valuables I've been savin'," Big John said when he realized Casey refused to heed his advice. "You'll be takin' it or I'll go to the Penrods myself and insist they care for you and your child. Mayhap the cash will buy your passage to England or Ireland. Do you have relatives back in the old country?"

"None that I know of," Casey said thoughtfully. "But perhaps it would be best if I left New South Wales. The farther away I am from Dare and his wife, the better off I'll be."

"Then you'll accept my money?"

Casey flushed, thinking of the men he'd robbed in order to accumulate cash and valuables.

"I know what you're thinkin', lass," Big John

interjected before she could form an answer.
"Ill-gotten gains. And you're right. Almost. I
don't rob honest farmers or settlers, if that's what
you're thinkin'. The only bailups I committed
were against Corps members and speculators.
They're the ones with capital."

"I'm glad you told me."

"Then you'll accept my help?"

"What choice do I have?" Casey said with
bitter emphasis.

"Will you go back to Ireland?"

"I . . . perhaps. Or maybe remain in England."

"I'll escort you to the outskirts of town, but
after that you're on your own. I'm wanted by the
Corps and my size restricts my movement. If
there's no ship in port, do you have someplace to
stay until one arrives?"

"No, no one that I can . . ." She hesitated. She
did know someone. Mr. Stanley, Roy's friend.
The kindly elderly bachelor might offer her refuge until she could book passage home. Supply
ships arrived quite regularly now and she
shouldn't have to impose on the man too long.

"Have you thought of someone, lass?"

"Yes, a friend of Roy Penrod. His name is
Drew Stanley and I stayed there once before
when Dare and I . . . well . . . I stayed there before."

"Good, it's settled then," Big John sighed in
obvious relief. His status prevented him from
caring for Casey even if he wanted to.

Bert had been laid to rest and the bushrangers
now shuffled aimlessly about looking to Big John
for guidance. Dan remained well in the back-
ground, poised on the horns of a dilemma. Now
that Bert was dead, should he reveal that he
hadn't actually seen or spoken to any of the

Penrods? He'd be foolish to spill everything now. Big John was likely to be as angry with him as Bert would have been, but for a different reason. Mayhap his mates would retaliate for losing their rum. It was too late now, he decided, to explain his deceit. Besides, the others would most certainly be jealous after learning he'd had the other woman when they got nothing. In the end he decided to hold his tongue. Telling the truth was likely to earn more than a mild rebuke, and Big John could break him in two with one hand.

Casey and Big John walked the entire fifteen or so miles to Sydney. It took them the better part of two days traveling at a leisurely pace for her sake. At the outskirts of town he removed a weighted sack from his swag and placed it in her hand, waving aside her feeble protests.

"What good will it do me out here, lass? The bush provides all I need. Take it and think of me when you're walkin' the auld sod again."

"Good-bye, Big John, I won't forget you," Casey said tearfully, "or what you did for me."

"Take care, lass, and good luck to you and your little one."

Casey watched Big John walk away, wondering if she'd ever see him again. It was unlikely, since she'd not be returning to New South Wales in the foreseeable future.

Casey made her way through town, passing Government House where Governor Bligh had been confined to house arrest. She walked directly to the harbor, her disappointment keen when she learned that no ships were in port. It eased somewhat when she found out a supply ship was expected to arrive sometime soon.

Staring pensively into the churning water,

Casey considered her alternatives. Her previous idea of asking Drew Stanley for refuge seemed the only course open to her. In New South Wales in 1808 there were no inns, no public houses. If one didn't live in Sydney and needed to visit the city, one stayed with friends. Being an emancipist, Casey had no friends in Sydney save for Mr. Stanley. Swallowing her pride, she turned and slowly made her way to the street where Stanley's small house stood. She'd do whatever necessary to protect her child.

Drew Stanley answered the door, appearing slightly frazzled and out of breath. He stared at her through myopic eyes before recognition dawned and his pleasant, lined features creased in a wide grin. "Why, Casey O'Cain, isn't it? Come in, my dear. How nice of you to call. Have you come to town with one of the Penrods? I would have thought they'd be busy with shearing at this time of year."

"I . . . I'm alone," Casey admitted hesitantly.

"Well, come in, my dear, and tell me what brings you to Sydney." Unbeknownst to Casey, Drew Stanley was the only person outside of the Penrods and McKenzies who knew the reason behind Dare's marriage to Mercy.

Seated comfortably in Drew's cozy parlor, Casey saw no reason to prolong her misery. Either he would allow her to stay or he wouldn't. "I've decided to return to Ireland," she began, "and need a place to stay until a ship arrives. I know no one else in Sydney and I . . . I hoped you . . . might—"

"Say no more, Casey," Drew interjected, saving her from further embarrassment. "I'll not ask why you're leaving for I know, and understand perfectly. Dare is my friend and for his sake I can offer you more than merely a place to stay until a ship arrives. I am in a position to offer you safe conduct to England."

Casey frowned. "I . . . I don't understand."

"Simple, my dear. But first let me explain what's been happening here in Sydney. Governor Bligh has already been sent back to England. I've been asked by citizens of New South Wales to go to England and present a true picture of the situation here. Particularly in regard to the New South Wales Corps and their revolt."

"Will the colony be governed by the New South Wales Corps until a new governor arrives? Is John Macarthur still the undisputed leader?"

"Macarthur is a cagy one. He's decided to return to England in an effort to exonerate himself before Parliament. He's preparing to leave on the first available ship. Until a new governor arrives, the Corps is still the ruling force."

"Which means you and Macarthur will be traveling on the same ship," Casey mused, grasping the situation immediately.

"Aye. But with me in England he'll not have things entirely his way. Someone will be on hand to defend Governor Bligh. I will represent the honest settlers and emancipists and present their view to the government. I only hope these old bones can survive the long voyage."

Looking at him, Casey hoped the same thing. Far from robust, it was apparent his best years were behind him. He seemed much too frail to undertake a voyage of long duration. "Perhaps there's someone younger who might go in your place," Casey suggested shyly.

"Alas, most of the settlers are struggling farmers and could not leave their farms for a year or more," Drew explained. "Whereas I am a civil servant with no property or ties, no wife or family. And I also own land and a home in London Town. So, my dear, that's why I'm in a position to offer you safe passage on the crossing. I'm sure the Penrods will appreciate my offer."

Though Casey knew differently, she did not disabuse Drew of the notion that the Penrods cared about her and the child she carried. Instead, she gratefully accepted his offer, telling him she had sufficient funds to purchase passage and pay for her room and board, which he promptly refused.

Though clothing was in short supply, Casey used the time before the supply ship arrived in Sydney to purchase a few items needed for the voyage. In Drew's pleasant company the days passed quickly, but Casey breathed a sigh of relief when he came home one day and announced that the *Southern Cross* had arrived in port. She lived in dread that Dare would come to Sydney and their paths would cross.

Once she left Australian soil all ties with the man she loved would be severed forever. She had been existing in a void since the day she learned how little Dare and his family cared about her or his child. It rankled to think her child would be a bastard while Mercy bore legitimate heirs for the family. How could they be so cruel as to abandon their own flesh and blood?

Why had Dare changed his feelings so abruptly? she wondered despondently. Or had he been lying all along when he said he loved her? He had sounded so sincere, loved her so ardently, she had been totally under his spell. Obviously one woman failed to satisfy his voracious appetite and she had fallen victim to his subtle seduction.

Perhaps it was true that he had been forced into marriage in the beginning, but his reluctance must have evaporated in Mercy's loving arms.

Did Dare ever truly love her? Casey pondered. Probably the only way she satisfied him was in a more basic way; she satisfied his lust, nothing more. If that were so, why couldn't she forget those soul-wrenching moments when his hands and lips claimed her, when her body became his to lead to glory? The answer screamed through her brain. She loved Dare. Arrogant, self-centered, proud, Casey recognized all his short-comings. And loved him still.

Three days later Casey and Drew boarded the *Southern Cross*. Evidently John Macarthur had boarded earlier for he was nowhere in sight. The captain, Chad Bailey, welcomed them aboard, assigned them to two cramped cabins, and informed them no other passengers save for John Macarthur had booked passage this trip. The price of passage left a considerable void in Casey's purse, but if she was frugal she'd have enough remaining to last until her child was born. She adamantly refused Drew's gallant offer to pay for her passage. According to her calculations, she would have a scant month after the *Southern Cross* reached England until the birth of her babe. But she had months yet in which to decide on her future—long empty months to forget Dare and the love they shared.

Burloo, the aborigine tracker employed by Dare, easily located the trail the bushrangers had taken after abducting Casey and Mercy. Struggling to keep up the grueling pace set by Burloo, Dare hovered near collapse, the pain in his leg excruciating. Yet not once did he consider turning back, for in his heart he knew Casey was alive and needed him. And once he found her she would become his wife like she was meant to be before Mercy's untimely interference.

Tracking a short distance ahead of the others, Burloo came to an abrupt halt, kneeling before a small, stone-covered mound as he waited for them to catch up. Dare's heart jerked violently when he saw Burloo examining what looked like a grave. Robin's face drained of all color and Ben cursed, venting his frustration in the only way he knew.

"What do you make of it?" Robin asked, his heart pounding with trepidation.

Beyond speech, Dare stared in horror at the small mound. He didn't want to think what lay buried in that crude grave. Finally Ben gave voice to what each man was thinking. "It could be Casey. We've no reason to doubt Mercy."

"Jesus!" Dare cursed, scrambling to his knees and tossing aside the stones like a man possessed.

"Wait!" Robin intervened, placing a restraining hand on Dare's shoulder. "Let me and Ben do it."

Nodding grimly, Dare moved reluctantly aside as Ben and Robin took his place. When the stones were carefully removed, revealing the mound of dirt beneath, they exchanged meaningful glances. Using their hands, they began the gruesome task of digging while Dare watched from a distance.

"Oh God!" Ben groaned, startling Dare by sitting back on his heels and looking at him with stricken eyes.

"No!" Dare refuted, blanching. "It can't be! Not Casey!" When words failed Ben, he looked to Robin for an explanation. "Robin, is it Casey?"

"I . . . it could be, Dare," Robin choked out. "We've uncovered a woman's petticoat. Do . . . do you want us to continue?"

Steeling himself to face the worst, Dare sucked in his breath and slowly approached the make-shift grave. A flutter of dainty white poking from the dirt brought a wail of despair from the depths of his being. But the evidence was irrefutable. Tears clogged his throat and eyes as he dropped to his knees, in his madness embracing the mound of dirt.

"Do we continue?" Ben asked in a hushed voice. "It's up to you, Dare."

Obviously the white cloth was a woman's petticoat, and Dare stared at it as if it were a poisonous snake. The grave was newly dug, that much he allowed, but did that necessarily mean the body it held belonged to Casey? Perhaps another woman . . . No, he concluded, pain grinding at his innards. He had heard of no other missing woman. The facts spoke for themselves. Mercy hadn't lied. Casey lay in that crude grave and he must accept it even though his own life ended with her death.

"It would serve no purpose to disturb Casey's final resting place," Dare croaked. "Replace everything as it was. Let her rest in peace."

"But, Dare," Robin protested vigorously, "don't you want to know if Casey . . ." His words trailed off but the implication was there.

"I know all I want to know, Robin," Dare said, his voice cracking. "I can bear no more."

"Are you absolutely certain?" Robin probed gently.

"Leave him be," Ben rasped as Dare limped

away. "He's at the end of his tether. He's finally accepted the fact that the woman he loves is dead."

"Which woman?" Robin asked, his voice laced with sarcasm. "He married Mercy and she's dead, too."

Making certain that Dare was out of hearing, Ben thought it long past time Robin learned the truth about Dare's marriage. "Listen carefully, Robin, and I'll tell you exactly why Dare married Mercy." Then he launched into a terse explanation, working as he spoke to put the grave back to rights. When he finished, Robin stared at him in deep remorse.

"Dare made that sacrifice for me and Casey?"

"Aye," Ben nodded. "He loves you both and would have consented to anything to see you freed. He knew what he was doing."

"Did Casey know?"

"Dare thought it best to keep the truth from both of you. He figured Casey's life would be much simpler if she hated him."

"I'm sorry I misjudged, Dare," Robin apologized. "In fact, I don't know how I'll ever live with this guilt. If it weren't for me—"

"Don't even think it. That's the reason Dare didn't tell you. Come on," he said, rising. "Let's go home. I think Dare's had about all he can take."

Six months later Dare still hadn't recovered from the shock of Casey's death. It took nearly that long for his leg to mend, the punishment it suffered had been so great. But to Roy's despair, Dare wasn't the same proud, arrogant man he had been before Casey's death. He racked his brain for a way to bring Dare out of his despondency, but to no avail. Dare became moody, withdrawn and unapproachable. Not even Ben's youthful antics or Robin's cheerful companionship succeeded in rousing him from his deep depression. Then one day a letter from England arrived for him aboard a supply ship. It was delivered by Thad McKenzie who happened to be in Sydney when the ship arrived.

Anthony Winston, Dare's aged grandfather, his mother's father, had died in England leaving his entire estate to Dare. It came as somewhat of a shock, for neither Roy nor Dare thought the old man possessed the kind of wealth he'd left to Dare. Besides a country home and London townhouse, there were several thousand pounds just waiting for Dare to collect. The letter was from his grandfather's lawyer requesting his presence in London to sign papers and collect his inheritance. The astute old man had lived frugally, invested wisely, and accumulated a fortune during the years Roy had lived with his family in New South Wales.

At first the thought of possessing such wealth astounded Dare, for his family, though comfortably fixed, was far from wealthy, particularly in regard to hard currency. Thanks to the Rum Corps, usual payment for crops and mutton sold to the government store consisted of rum, never cash. With the money from his grandfather's estate Dare could purchase his own land. He could also buy pure merino sheep from Africa like John Macarthur and experiment with breeding as he longed to do. With money, anything was possible. Soon someone would discover a route across the Blue Mountains, and he intended to be one of the first to take advantage of the land expansion.

The news brought Dare's spirits soaring, cheering Roy considerably. Thad told them the same ship that carried the letter would remain in port two weeks to sell its cargo. Dare intended to book passage on the return voyage.

The night before Dare's departure, the men sat in the study while Roy urged Dare to call on several old family friends left behind in England years ago. One in particular, Sir Donald Hurley, who lived close by Anthony Winston's London townhouse. Another was Drew Stanley who had left six months earlier to represent the colony in England.

"I know Donald Hurley will welcome you, Dare," Roy said, "and introduce you to London society. If I remember correctly, he has a son about your age and a younger daughter. Also many influential friends."

"I'm not going to London to socialize, Father," Dare replied with a hint of reproach. "This is strictly a business trip."

"It won't hurt to have a good time while you're there," suggested Robin. "It might be your last trip for some time to come."

"Perhaps you'll find a wife," hinted Ben with a twinkle.

"That's highly unlikely," Dare scoffed, a twinge of pain creasing his brow. If he couldn't have Casey he wanted no other woman. After six months her death was still a festering wound that refused to heal. He ate, slept, worked, yet barely knew he existed. The spark had gone out of his life. No woman alive could take the place of his fiery-haired, green-eyed Irish beauty. If by chance he did marry one day it would be only to produce an heir to inherit the empire he hoped to build in Australia.

"Don't close your mind to finding a wife," Roy remarked hopefully.

"Are there any more instructions, Father?" Dare asked, adroitly changing the subject.

"No, son, just enjoy yourself."

"Is there something you'd like, Ben?"

"A pair of boots would be nice," replied Ben wistfully.

"You'll have several pair, the best money can buy. And you, too, Robin, as well as other items not readily available in the colony. And Ben," Dare paused meaningfully, "I intend to share grandfather's fortune with you. There's enough for both of us."

"I . . . I don't know what to say, Dare," Ben choked out, his eyes moist.

"'Thank you' will suffice, brother," Dare grinned, acting more like himself than he had in months. "I'm depending on you and Robin to help Father and take care of things here while I'm gone. Don't fall in love and marry until I return," he teased lightheartedly.

"And you have my permission to marry in England," returned Ben cheekily.

Two days later the *Courageous* sailed from Port Jackson. Standing at the rail watching Sydney disappear over the horizon, Dare wondered what awaited him in England and how long it would be before he saw Australia again.

BOOK THREE

Bold Beginning
1809–1810

CHAPTER TWENTY-TWO

The *Southern Cross* arrived in London Harbor on the same day Dare left Australia thousands of miles away. The first person down the gangplank was John Macarthur. He lingered only long enough to collect his baggage before hiring a hack and making a hasty departure. He didn't bother bidding good-bye to the couple standing on the dock. During the nearly six-months-long journey he had kept much to himself, preparing his defense for his part in the revolt against Governor Bligh.

Whenever they met on deck or at meals, Macarthur was courteous to Casey but studiously ignored Drew, aware of his mission in England.

If it weren't for Drew, Casey might not have survived the long ocean voyage. The weather those first weeks was anything but pleasant. Tossed by towering waves and whipped by virulent winds, the *Southern Cross* bobbed like a cork in the angry sea. Casey met each day as if it were her last, for in truth she seriously doubted she would survive the ordeal. Due mainly to her pregnancy, her stomach gave up its meager contents nearly every day, refusing even water. Drew became most solicitous, caring for her as he would a favored daughter.

But when the storms abated and Casey's illness did not abate, Drew's razor-sharp wits grasped the situation immediately. He waited for Casey to confide in him, and when she did not, he broached the subject himself.

Hanging her head in shame, Casey did not deny the truth, freely admitting she carried Dare's child. "What will you do when you reach England?" Drew questioned with genuine concern. "How will you support your child? Do you have relatives to care for you?"

"I'll manage," Casey returned with a hint of defiance.

"Does Dare know? I'm certain he would have made some provisions for his child had he been aware of your condition. The Penrods are honorable men."

Unwilling to destroy the trusting man's faith in his friends, Casey refrained from blurting out exactly what she thought of the kind of honor that allowed a man to callously abandon a woman to a fate worse than death. It made little difference to them that she carried a child— Dare's child. Swallowing the scathing retort she longed to spit out, Casey tilted her chin at a stubborn angle and said, "My decision to leave Australia was best for all concerned. I'll manage somehow."

"You're a brave woman, my dear," Drew allowed with admiration. "However, I don't believe you fully appreciate the problems you'll encounter in England. The added responsibility of a child is likely to test the strength of even the most courageous."

Deep in her heart Casey knew that Drew's reasoning was sound, but that did not make it any easier. Nothing or no one could reverse her situation. She was pregnant, unmarried, abandoned by her love and set adrift with little or no means of support. Was she capable of facing so demanding a challenge? Capable or not, she would survive, and so would her babe.

Then Drew said something that left her speechless and confused. "Casey, I'm an old man, my health is failing, and I doubt I'll see Australia again."

"Drew, please don't talk like that," Casey protested though she knew his words held a ring of truth. These past weeks he seemed to have aged before her eyes. And the added burden of caring for her sat heavily on his frail frame.

"It's true, Casey. But I'm not telling you this to inspire pity. I've grown to care for you like the daughter I never had. I can't bear to think of you raising your child in shame. A Penrod does not deserve to be labeled a bastard. What I am about to suggest is for my own satisfaction as well as your well-being."

Casey's eyes grew wide with disbelief as she suddenly realized the implication of Drew's words. "Drew, no . . . I . . ."

"Don't interrupt, Casey," he admonished gently. "What I'm offering is marriage. In name only, of course. You are and always will be a daughter to me. I want your child to have a name—an honorable name, I might add. Upon my death all I have in the world will belong to you and the babe you carry. I'm not the wealthiest man in the world but neither am I without resources. Please allow an old man this small happiness, my dear. If you agree, Captain Bailey can marry us immediately."

"I . . . I don't know what to say," Casey stammered, her eyes misty with tears.

"A simple 'yes' will suffice."

"But it's not fair."

"Nor is it fair that you should be denied a father for your child. Had things worked out differently, you'd be Dare's wife and your child legitimate. Many sacrifices have been made, but mine will be a pleasure and an honor."

Put that way, Casey could think of no plausible excuse to refuse. For her, love came only once so there was no question of her marrying for love. Besides, it would be a relief to be taken care of by a man she had grown fond of, a man old enough to be her grandfather, who had no sexual interest in her. Her child deserved a name and loving father for however long God allowed Drew to walk the earth.

In the end, Casey's futile protests were overruled and she and Drew were married later that day by Captain Bailey. If the captain thought the joining of a young girl to a man three times her age highly irregular, he said nothing. A man of wide experience, he had seen stranger things in his day.

After Casey's marriage the sleeping arrangements remained the same, as did Drew's treatment of her. It was exactly as he promised, a father-daughter relationship with the only difference being that she and her child would bear Drew's name.

During the following months Casey recovered from her earlier malaise and seemed to prosper in the vigorous sea air despite the tedious fare offered at meals. As her girth increased, Drew grew more solicitous and careful of her, and Casey had cause to give thanks to providence for delivering her into Drew's tender care.

She tried not to think of Dare living happily, no doubt, with Mercy. But her dreams did not allow her respite. At night Dare's arms held her, his lips loved her and whispered words she longed to hear. Until dawn brought cruel reality, heartbreaking denial—and tears.

Somewhere off the coast of France on a blustery day in late December, Casey went into labor. It wasn't totally unexpected, but both she and Drew had hoped the blessed event would not take place until they reached London. With the help of the ship's doctor, Casey's son came into the world protesting loudly his rude entrance. The birth was not overly difficult, and Casey was able to verbally assure Drew that she and her son would survive when he came in shortly afterwards.

The next day all the ship's officers dropped in her cabin to offer congratulations. Including John Macarthur who felt quite certain that Drew was not the baby's father. It took Casey nearly a week to decide on a name for her son. She finally settled on Brandon. Brandon Stanley. But unbeknownst to Casey, the middle name of Penrod was added by Drew when Captain Bailey inscribed the blessed event in his ship's log. He also prepared a paper, signed by the doctor, attesting to the birth.

Two weeks later the *Southern Cross* entered the

Thames on the journey to London. They docked
in London Harbor on January 7, 1809. Casey
found it difficult to believe she was a married
woman with a child. Never had she pictured
anyone but Dare as her husband. But at least she
had his child, she thought as she lovingly caressed the dark fuzz covering Brandon's head.
His hair held the promise of rich darkness, and
Dare's gray eyes stared solemnly back at her.

A chill January wind whipped at her skirt and
Casey gathered her son protectively closer. Had
not the captain generously offered cloth to make
swaddling clothes, Brandon would have been
virtually naked. As it turned out, he was well-
dressed in soft flannel and wool.

With a proud lift to his step belying his years,
Drew escorted Casey down the gangplank and
into the carriage he had hired. They waited
inside while their baggage was strapped atop the
conveyance, glad to be out of the wind.

"Are you comfortable, my dear?" Drew asked
solicitously. "Is the babe warm enough?"

"We're fine, Drew, truly," Casey smiled fond-
ly, wondering how she and Brandon would have
survived without him.

"I've instructed the driver to take us to the best
inn in London, but we'll stay only until my
townhouse is made ready for you. It's been
closed up many years and I want everything
perfect for your arrival. It's in one of the finer
neighborhoods. Does that please you? I also own
an old family estate in Cornwall but it's far too
remote for my tastes."

"Whatever you decide, Drew," Casey replied.
It made little difference where they lived as long

as her son was with her. She'd endeavor to make Drew's life as comfortable as possible, but the course her own life took was of little importance.

The Red Lion Inn was exactly as Drew described, the best lodging in London. The room engaged for her and Brandon was large, comfortable and scrupulously clean. The commodious common room where meals were served was cheerful, bright and tastefully decorated. The barmaids and chambermaids performed their duties skillfully and courteously.

Because Casey was still recovering from the effects of childbirth, she chose to take her meals in her room, often with Drew in attendence telling her amusing stories. Brandon continued to prosper, and to Casey's mixed heartache and delight grew to resemble his father more and more with each passing day.

Two weeks after their arrival, Drew informed Casey that the townhouse was ready for occupancy. It was on a small street off Grosvenor Square. Their move the next day was accomplished painlessly with little fuss or bother. Drew had hired a complete staff of capable servants, leaving Casey with nothing to do but issue orders. In no time at all she had settled into a daily routine centered mainly around feeding and caring for Brandon.

At Drew's insistence a fashionable wardrobe was purchased for Casey which included a stunning ballgown of green silk shot with silver. Though she knew she would never wear such a beautiful creation, buying it seemed to give Drew so much pleasure she did not have the heart to scold him for his extravagant purchase.

"Drew, you're spoiling me," Casey protested

when a nursemaid joined the staff, relieving her
of much of her duties with Brandon. "There's
nothing left for me to do."

"You're not supposed to work, my dear," Drew
replied with a twinkle. "Just indulge me and
relax. Your life has been far too hard for one so
young. Call on the neighbors, go shopping, em-
broider, do whatever women do in this day and
age."

"Speaking of relaxing," Casey reproved gently,
"you should follow your own advice. You leave
early in the morning and don't return until late in
the evening, drawn and exhausted."

Drew smiled, pleased that Casey cared enough
to be concerned about his well-being. It was true
he had been driving himself of late, but it could
not be helped. Too many people depended on
him. "It's these infernal hearings, Casey," he
said. "The settlers and emancipists are counting
on me to convince Parliament to send a strong
governor to New South Wales and to disband the
102nd Regiment. The Rum Corps has had their
way long enough. John Macarthur's glib tongue
has almost convinced the government that the
Corps revolted against Governor Bligh to keep
him from destroying the colony, and that it was
in the government's best interest to seize control
and arrest Bligh."

"Can you convince them otherwise?" Casey
asked, missing the wild, open spaces of New
South Wales despite her unhappy experiences
there.

"That's the reason I'm working so hard. For
the good of the colony I can't allow Macarthur to
have his way."

"Have they chosen a new governor?"

"It's not certain yet, but I think the honor will go to Lachlon Macquarie. If he's chosen it will be late in the year before he arrives in Australia. In the meantime I must continue to undo the damage John Macarthur has already wrought."

"I'd rest easier if you guarded your health," Casey said, her sincerity genuine.

Drew's eyes grew misty. "You don't know how good it is to have someone concerned over my welfare, Casey. These last weeks have been the happiest of my life. I think of you and Brandon as a cherished daughter and grandson. It pleases me to think he'll inherit all I own after I'm gone."

"Don't talk like that, Drew," Casey chided. "Brandon and I need you."

Though Drew was aware his health was precarious at best, he was too involved in his duties to heed Casey's advice. Not even the painful twinges in the region of his heart or shortness of breath prevented him from performing to the best of his ability. Too many honest men and women depended on him.

The ensuing months were a peaceful time for Casey. Several ladies had come calling, but she had yet to return their visits, preferring instead to spend her days with Brandon, whose feedings still demanded much of her time. Drew remained unfailingly kind if somewhat distracted, but continued to drive himself relentlessly. One day he returned home to announce that Lachlon Macquarie had left England to take up duties as governor of New South Wales. Drew seemed pleased with the choice and told Casey the Rum Corps was to be disbanded upon his arrival. Though the long days of hearings had sapped his strength, he had done his job well. John Macarthur had not come out a clear winner. At long last Drew was able to sit back and enjoy his success.

Governor Macquarie had already left England when Dare arrived aboard the *Courageous* on June 10, 1809. The weather at sea had been mild, with fair winds and favorable tides making the voyage a pleasant distraction. In London, he found his grandfather's townhouse stocked with food and, thanks to his grandfather's lawyer, a staff of servants in attendance.

His first weeks in London were consumed with legal matters, signing papers, inspecting property and transferring funds. When all business had been concluded to his satisfaction, he turned his attention to contacting friends left behind years ago, primarily Sir Donald Hurley. He also wanted to look up Drew Stanley. Perhaps Sir Donald would know something about the old gentleman.

It was several days later before Dare found time to visit Sir Donald's home. He was greeted by a trim maid wearing a crisp black uniform and promptly ushered into the drawing room. A young man about his own age burst into the room while he stood admiring a painting.

"Oh, I beg your pardon," the man said, skidding to a halt. "I didn't know anyone was in here."

Dare smiled, liking the man on sight. "I'm Dare Penrod, from Australia," he replied, offering his hand. "I've come to see Sir Donald at the request of my father, Roy Penrod."

"Penrod! Father speaks often of your family. Pioneers, he called you. I'm Edgar Hurley," he offered enthusiastically, taking Dare's proffered hand. "My friends call me Eddie. What brings you to London?"

"My grandfather's death," Dare informed him. "I'm here to settle his estate."

"I'm sorry to hear about the old gentleman," Eddie offered. "Have you come alone?"

"Aye. Father and my brother Ben are needed to run the farm."

"There's been a lot of excitement involving the colony these days. John Macarthur was foiled in his attempt to put the blame on William Bligh for the problems there. A new governor left to replace Bligh, and the New South Wales Corps is to be disbanded."

"I've heard the good news," Dare said, "and it's about time. The Rum Corps has had things their way too long to suit most settlers. Hopefully things will get better with them out of control."

Dare and Eddie continued to chat in a friendly manner until Sir Donald arrived. Eddie made the introductions and Dare found himself answering numerous questions about Roy, Ben, Governor Bligh and conditions in New South Wales. Time slipped by and Dare was asked to remain for supper. Finding the company congenial, he readily accepted.

The meal proved the first of many he would enjoy with the Hurley family. He and Eddie became fast friends, often visiting Almacks and other clubs to gamble and drink in the course of an evening. And there was Lydia Hurley, Sir Donald's vivacious nineteen-year-old daughter who was instantly smitten with Dare.

Dare had to admit the raven-haired beauty had much to offer, and if he were looking for a wife she would be a perfect choice. She did not lack for suitors, but seemed to prefer Dare who squired her to several parties and found her company invigorating.

The more Lydia Hurley saw of Dare, the more she wanted him. Many men vied for her attention, but none could match Dare in looks or virility. Some were tall, others darkly handsome, but none as intriguing or mysterious with an aura of tragedy lingering about him. Lydia knew he was a widower, for Dare had told her that much. Had he loved his wife so well he could not or would not consider another? Dark eyes sparkling with determination, Lydia set out to ensnare Dare. She knew her father would approve of the match, for Dare was a family friend as well as rich enough to please him.

One day Dare questioned Sir Donald about Drew Stanley, and learned that he had indeed heard of the man. "Stanley has been a busy man since his arrival in England," Sir Donald informed him. "Not only was he instrumental in having the New South Wales Corps disbanded, but his defense of Governor Bligh was outstanding."

"Is he still in England?"

"Yes, he was, the last I heard. The man is unwell. Besides, now that he has a wife and child he might decide to remain in England for good."

"Drew has a wife?" gasped Dare, astounded. "And a child?" Disbelief colored his words. "When did all this come about? I assumed, hell, we all assumed, that Drew was a confirmed bachelor."

"Not much is known about the marriage except that Drew had a young wife and newborn babe in tow when he arrived in England," Sir Donald said. "The babe is over six months old now, and those who have seen her say his wife is a raving beauty."

"Why, that old devil!" laughed Dare, amused and delighted for his friend. "Who would have thought Drew would encounter such good luck in his old age? I must look him up. Where does he live?"

"Not far from here. But why don't you wait a few days? Lydia and her mother have talked me into giving a ball next Saturday and Drew and his wife are invited. I received their acceptance just today."

Dare nodded. He had to leave town for a day or two anyway and would not return until the day of the ball. He had decided to sell his grandfather's country estate and needed to visit the property and retrieve whatever valuables he wanted before the final papers were signed. He rose to leave.

"Dare," Sir Donald began hesitantly. It was obvious he was having trouble expressing himself, so Dare sat down politely to wait. "I hope you won't think me presumptuous, but I'd like to talk to you about Lydia."

"Lydia?" Dare asked curiously. "She's a charming girl, Sir Donald, what about her?"

"You must be aware that she's quite taken with you. She's already spoken to me about you, and I've given my blessing to a match between you if you're willing."

"Sir Donald, I hardly know Lydia, or she me!" replied Dare, dismay bringing an unaccustomed flush to his face.

"Marriages are built on less," persisted Sir Donald. "You could do worse, you know. The size of her dowry is quite generous."

"I'm aware of that, but I don't love Lydia. And she's too young to know her mind."

"I think you misjudge her. She's perfectly capable of making a choice. Was your first marriage a love match?" he asked innocently.

The question so startled Dare that he had little time to arrange his features to disguise the truth. His expressive eyes told a story all their own. Astute as well as sensitive to the feelings of others, Sir Donald had his answer.

"Don't close your mind to Lydia, Dare," he continued when a tense silence ensued. "She's counting on you to escort her to the ball."

"I'll be happy to escort Lydia," Dare allowed graciously. "And . . . and I'll give what you've just said careful thought. But I can promise nothing."

Returning to his townhouse, Dare's mind worked furiously. Was he wrong to reject Lydia? he reflected distractedly. Perhaps, he answered his own question. Only Casey had the power to inspire his love, but a child or children to carry on his name seemed increasingly attractive. Would Lydia agree to live the rest of her life in wild, untamed Australia? Of course they wouldn't have to return immediately. But eventually . . . Perhaps after she'd borne him a child or two.

"My God, what am I thinking?" Dare cried aloud. He wanted no children but those born of the love he shared with Casey, and she was dead. Suddenly a terrifying thought caused a numbness in his brain. What if Casey had been carrying his child when she went to her death? The notion nearly destroyed him. As for Lydia, he would let the chips fall where they may. If it was meant to be, he wouldn't fight it.

"Drew, do we have to go to the ball?" Casey pouted, her eyes pleading. "I really have no desire to attend."

"It's about time you involved yourself in society," Drew chided gently. "You've hibernated within these walls long enough. Brandon is more than six months old and healthy enough to be left in the charge of his nursemaid. Besides, I've not seen you in that beautiful ballgown I purchased."

Drew's arguments finally prevailed, and despite Casey's earlier misgivings, she began to look forward to the party with an eagerness she had not experienced in many months.

The day of the ball arrived with undue haste, and Casey's heart beat like a triphammer as she slowly turned for Drew's inspection.

"You're a vision, Casey," he said with awe. "You'll outshine every woman there tonight."

"You're prejudiced," Casey returned saucily. "I'm certain there will be many others lovelier than me."

Casey did not realize what a tantalizing picture she made in her green silk gown shot with silver. Fashioned off the shoulders with tiny sleeves worn low on her arms, the color enhanced the glowing sheen of her fiery hair and alabaster whiteness of her skin. The bodice molded perfectly her womanly breasts, while the incredibly tiny waist billowed gracefully over gently swelling hips and slender thighs.

Drew thought her enchanting and realized

with a twinge of regret that all her considerable
charms were wasted on an old man. But one day
soon, sooner than he would have liked, she would
be free to find a man she could love. Dare Penrod
might have gained her freedom but his sacrifice
had been in vain. He had ruined Casey for
another man. Though she never spoke Dare's
name in his presence, Drew knew her heart had
been irrevocably lost to the man she still loved
and could not forget. Her son was a constant
reminder of the love they once shared.

The ball was in full swing when Drew and
Casey arrived, and they were soon lost in the
press of people as introductions were made and
belated congratulations tendered. And then
Casey was swept onto the dance floor by one
dance partner after another while Drew looked
on with approval and beaming pride.

Dare made a very late entrance and was immediately claimed by a pouting Lydia, radiant in a
stunning gown of gold tissue. Before he could
protest, she dragged him onto the dance floor,
and after the set ended, coyly expressed her
desire to find a private corner where she might
rest her feet.

"Won't you be missed?" Dare demurred.

"We won't stay long," promised Lydia provocatively. "But I really am tired. You were naughty
to arrive so late. I hated dancing with all those
boorish clods while waiting for you. Please,
Dare," she pleaded, batting long lashes.

"Of course," Dare gracefully acquiesced. Why
not? he reasoned. Lydia was a beautiful woman
and he'd not thought of a woman in a romantic
sense since Casey's death.

"No one will be in the library at this time so we'll be alone," she hinted. Even if it cost her her reputation, Lydia was prepared to go to any lengths to capture Dare's affection.

"But I really do insist we limit our stay, Lydia," Dare cautioned. "There's an old friend attending the ball tonight who I must look up."

"A friend? A . . . female friend?" she asked jealously.

"No," laughed Dare, strangely pleased at Lydia's show of jealousy. "A gentleman friend from Sydney."

Lydia led Dare into the library, carefully closed the door behind them, and seated herself next to him on a small sofa. She sighed in pleasure as she raised her feet to rest on the footstool placed conveniently near. "Oh, that's better," she sighed, allowing Dare a tantalizing glimpse of trim silk-clad ankles and just a hint of delicately turned calves.

Having planned her strategy well, Lydia casually leaned her head to rest on Dare's broad shoulder. Her eyes limpid and melting, she gazed up adoringly and asked, "You do like me, don't you, Dare?"

With her soft warmth pressed intimately against his hardness, Dare did indeed like Lydia, liked her a lot. A surge of desire shot through his body and swelled his loins as he allowed his arms to enfold her nubile curves. "Very much so," he murmured, nuzzling the fragrant softness of her neck. It had been so long since he last felt desire he had forgotten how good it was or how wonderfully comforting a woman's body could be.

"Kiss me, Dare," invited Lydia, recognizing desire when she saw it. She was so close to bringing Dare to his knees she threw caution to the wind and pressed herself into the curve of his body, thrilling in his instant arousal.

Dare needed no further urging as he claimed her parted lips with an urgency that demanded more than innocent kisses. While his body reacted violently to Lydia's subtle seduction, a small voice somewhere in his brain warned him that one did not trifle with a girl like Lydia unless one had marriage in mind.

Whirling in the arms of her latest partner, Casey smiled absently. She liked Sir Donald's young son, Edgar, despite his outrageous compliments. He was a handsome man, she noted, lighthearted and fun-loving, about the same age as Dare. He had been her dance partner twice and each time brought bursts of laughter to her lips. He reminded her of Ben—but that was a lifetime ago. Suddenly Casey recalled Drew telling her Sir Donald had a son and daughter, and she had yet to meet the young lady.

"Is your sister here tonight?" she asked Edgar. "I don't believe I've met her."

"Lydia is here somewhere," Edgar chuckled as if enjoying a private joke. "And I'd be pleased if you'd call me Eddie, Mrs. Stanley."

"Could you point her out to me, Mr. . . . Eddie?"

"That would take some doing, for if I know Sis she has lured her new beau off someplace where they'll be alone. She's hoping for a proposal and I daresay one will soon be forthcoming. Dare seems quite smitten with Lydia and she is crazy about him."

All the color drained from Casey's face as her

heart skidded painfully against her ribcage and her legs turned to rubber. Dare! It couldn't be! And yet, the name was not a common one. Her steps faltered and she would have fallen if Eddie hadn't had a firm grip on her. "Mrs. Stanley . . . Casey, are you ill?"

"N . . . no, forgive me. The name you just mentioned brought back unpleasant memories."

"Dare Penrod? I doubt if you know the man, he's from Australia," Eddie said. "Handsome devil. At least Sis thinks so, and just about every woman who's met him."

Dare, here in England! Assailed by giddiness, battered by emotions she had held under strict control, Casey reeled, her mind spinning crazily.

"Mrs. Stanley . . . Casey, what is it? Have I said something to upset you? You're ill, let me—"

"Yes," Casey gasped, wishing she could turn and flee before Dare saw her. "I . . . I am ill. Take me someplace where I might rest and then please summon my husband."

"Of course," Eddie said, his face puckered with grave concern as he grasped her elbow and carefully guided her through the crush of people. "I'll take you to the library." Across the room he spied Drew turning into the game room with his father but was too late to catch his eye.

They paused at the library door and Casey, still shaken and suffering from shock, said, "I can make my own way inside, Eddie. Please get Drew for me."

Eddie made a hasty departure and Casey leaned her head against the door, her mind whirling with confusion. What was Dare doing in London? How long had he been here? Where was

Mercy and why was he courting another woman? Oh God! She needed to get away from here. She needed Drew. Where was he? Most of all she needed to sit down to gather her shattered wits.

The library door opened on noiseless hinges and Casey stepped inside. The night was cool and a fire burned cheerily in the hearth, filling the room with diffused light. The cozy, peaceful atmosphere beckoned to Casey and she would have collapsed in to the nearest chair if noises coming from a small sofa nearby hadn't caught her attention. She inhaled sharply when she realized she had interrupted a lovers' tryst.

The man, whose face was turned away, held the swooning woman in his arms, lavishing ardent kisses on gleaming white flesh. Devouring was a better word. His large hands roamed freely over her body, and her bodice had been pushed off her shoulders exposing an ample amount of white skin. Her sighs and moans provided the impetus that released Casey's frozen feet, and she would have fled immediately but for one word uttered by the woman in passionate abandon. "Dare, oh, Dare."

The woman's flesh beneath his fingertips was warm, inviting, and oh so willing, and Dare seriously considered taking her there and then on the cramped sofa. Her groans and soft mewlings of pleasure fed his ego and fired his passion. It had been so long—too damn long—since he'd loved a woman, if what he wanted to do to Lydia could be called love. Lust was a better word. Yet something held him back despite Lydia's obvious willingness. When all was said and done, he couldn't take that final plunge from which there was no return. His honor would demand he marry the girl, for she was certain to be a virgin. With a will born of determination and years of self-discipline, he deliberately cooled his ardor, divorcing his mind from the warm, responsive flesh writhing beneath his hands.

If Dare lived to be a hundred he'd never know what made him look toward the door. Some force stronger than life, more powerful even than the lust that drove him and the woman in his arms. A certain magnetism, a special aura that Dare associated to the love he had known and lost. Was his longing for Casey so strong, so compelling, that he felt her presence in this very room while another woman lay in his arms?

Spellbound, speechless, beyond coherent thought, Dare stared at the figment of his imagination so like Casey she could have been a reincarnation. Riveting green eyes looked back at him through a fringe of golden lashes. From the top of her fiery red curls to her tiny feet she was an exact replica of his dead love. Painful recollections brushed against his memory with unseen fingers and brought pictures to his mind he had carefully stored away.

"Dare, what is it?" Lydia asked, suddenly aware of Dare's distraction. When his body grew rigid and began to shake she became alarmed, fearing she had done something to upset him. Little versed in the ways of men, she had been thoroughly enjoying his attentions thus far and didn't want him to stop.

As if in a dream, Casey met Dare's gaze, his eyes changing from shiny silver to smoky mist. "Dare," she whispered, echoing the words spoken by the woman in his arms only moments ago.

With aching slowness Dare's arms left Lydia's

slim body as he reached out to the green-eyed
vision he fully expected to disappear in a puff of
smoke. Abandoning Lydia where she lay in a
froth of gold tissue, Dare rose unsteadily to his
feet. Arms extended in mute appeal, her name
slipped effortlessly from his lips. "Casey . . ."

Though softly spoken the sound was like a
gunshot in the tense silence, inspiring Casey with
the will to turn and flee directly into Drew's arms
outside the library door. "Oh, Drew, thank
God!" she sobbed. "Take me home."

Having already been alerted by Eddie, Drew
had Casey's wrap over his arm, ready to place it
about her shoulders and usher her to their carriage. He knew exactly what ailed Casey. Sir
Donald had just told him Dare Penrod was in
London. In fact, he was attending tonight's ball.
Drew was about to ask for details of his visit and
whether Mercy had accompanied him when
Eddie Hurley rudely interrupted to tell him that
Casey had suddenly taken ill and was waiting for
him in the library. Bidding his host a hasty
good-bye, Drew had hurriedly collected their
wraps and sped to his wife's side. He assumed,
and rightly so, that Casey had seen Dare before
she could be alerted to his presence. He hated the
thought of Casey's heart being broken all over
again and cursed Dare for unexpectedly turning
up in London.

Dare was slow to react. Surely no two women
could be so alike, he reasoned, confusion scrambling his brain. Surely he imagined the similarity
between Casey and the woman who had entered
the library and fled before he could learn her
identity. Suddenly he became aware of Lydia
tugging at his arm. He stared at her, frowning,

scarcely aware of who she was or what he was doing with her.

"Dare, I've never seen that woman before. Who is she and what is she to you?"

"I . . . don't know, Lydia," Dare said in a haunted voice. "But I certainly intend to find out. She . . . reminds me of someone I once knew." He turned to leave.

"Dare, wait! You can't just leave me like this. You owe me more than a rude departure."

"Forgive me, Lydia," Dare said, genuinely sorry. "For a moment I lost my head. You're a beautiful woman but unfortunately not for me. I'm sorry for whatever distress I caused you."

"Dare! You can't . . ." Then he was gone, her faltering words bouncing off his departing back.

No thought existed in Dare's mind beyond finding the red-haired beauty who had just turned his world upside down. He knew Casey was dead but there were still days when he couldn't concentrate at all for yearning for her, remembering her. He still wanted her with a deep, obsessive need that gave him no rest.

Rushing from the library, Dare ran straight into Eddie who had come to see if Drew had arrived to take his wife home. He was terribly concerned for the lovely woman who had become suddenly ill for no apparent reason. But when he observed Dare's white face and shaking hands, he wondered if his friend suffered from the same strange malady and if it was catching.

"Dare, my God, what happened? Are you ill too?"

"Eddie! That woman! Who is she?"

"Woman? Who are you talking about? There are dozens of women here tonight."

"I'm talking about the woman who came into the library a few minutes ago. Red hair, green eyes. Wearing a green and silver gown. I doubt there's another woman here tonight like her. Dammit, man, what's her name?"

"Easy, old man," Eddie soothed, his curiosity piqued. "I know exactly who you're referring to. The lady is the wife of Drew Stanley."

"Drew Stanley! His wife! Quickly, her name. What is her name?"

"Her name is Casey. What's gotten into you? Do you know her?"

"Casey" Dare breathed, shaken to his core. His face was pale beneath his tan. "How can it be?"

"I say, old man, are you all right?" Eddie inquired. "You look the very devil."

"Something strange is going on and I intend to get to the bottom of it," Dare said, coming to his senses. "My Casey would never marry a man old enough to be her grandfather."

"Your Casey?" Eddie questioned sharply. "I thought your wife's name was Mercy."

"One day I'll explain everything," Dare replied cryptically, "but there's still much I don't understand myself. Are the Stanleys still at the ball?"

"No, they tore out of here as if the devil himself was after them."

"Can you tell me where Drew and his . . . Casey are living while in London?"

Eddie hesitated. Did Dare mean the old gentleman or his lovely wife harm? He would never forgive himself if that should happen. The wild look in Dare's eyes gave him little encouragement.

Dare noted Eddie's reluctance and sought to ease his mind. "Don't worry, Eddie, I just want to talk to Casey. I don't intend to do anything foolish. But I have to know what happened."

"Who is this woman? Why does her presence cause you such anguish? Is she someone you knew in Australia?"

"She's the woman I love," Dare shocked him by saying. Then he turned and left so abruptly Eddie was left standing with his mouth open.

Aware of the late hour, Dare went directly home. It was far too late to go calling. Besides, he was in no condition to confront a woman he assumed had been lost to him all these months. To add to his misery, sleep was denied him. His slumber was erotically, provocatively interrupted by the sensuously beautiful woman who invaded his dreams night after night.

As dawn colored the eastern sky an electrifying thought jolted him awake. Sir Donald had told him Casey and Drew had a child over six months old. It didn't take a mathematic genius to figure out that the child belonged to him. Though the woman he loved belonged to another, they had a child to attest to the love they shared. The thought delighted him but offered little comfort.

Eagerly he leaped from bed, ready to face the strange twist that fate had dealt him. By some miracle God had spared Casey. How or why she had turned up in London with Drew Stanley was a mystery he intended to solve in short order. But for now it was enough to know she was alive and had borne him a child.

CHAPTER TWENTY-THREE

Casey wakened early to feed Brandon. When she finished she handed him to his nurse, too consumed with misery to tend to him properly. She had been so distraught when she arrived home last night that she had slept little, pacing the floor into the wee hours of the morning. Her pale face and fatigue-glazed eyes expressed her anguish of the past twenty-four hours. But there was a determination in the set of her lips, dignity in the angle of her chin, and pride in her every movement.

Not even Drew escaped the terrible strain placed upon them by Dare's sudden appearance in London. A tense silence had settled upon them during the short ride home. Lost in her own agony, Casey had no idea Drew suffered right along with her. In the privacy of his room the pains in his chest became unbearable as he thought of the upheaval Dare's arrival had wrought.

Evidently Mercy wasn't with Dare, else why had Sir Donald hinted at a match between Dare and his daughter? Drew wondered distractedly. He hated to see Casey hurt again but knew instinctively it wouldn't be long before Dare realized he had a child and would promptly claim what was his. And where did that leave Casey? Didn't Dare know that Mercy wasn't the kind of woman to accept another woman's child? He had known Mercy McKenzie for years and seriously doubted she had a compassionate bone in her body.

Desperate to save Casey further heartache, Drew pulled his weary bones from bed, dressed, and left the house while Casey was feeding the baby, leaving word that he wouldn't return until evening. His first stop was Sir Donald's town-house, where he cooled his heels, for the man was still abed after last night's ball. After obtaining Dare's address from the blurry-eyed nobleman, Drew hurried off before the thoroughly confused man could question him. It was imperative he find Dare and learn his intentions before he caused Casey further upset.

Mauve streaks still colored the eastern sky when Dare sat down to breakfast. Though he had no appetite, he forced himself to chew and swallow, tasting nothing, well aware it was far too early to barge into someone's home unan-nounced. His departure coincided with Drew's, who exited his own front door at nearly the same moment. Fifteen minutes later Dare stood before Drew's house, his mind a mixture of hope and fear. Why had Mercy told him Casey was dead, and what had happened to bring her to London as Drew's wife?

That question was a stab in his heart. It tore him apart to think that she had chosen to leave the colony rather than tell him about their child.

There was only one way to learn the truth, he reasoned as he set his hand on the door knocker with firm purpose.

A downstairs maid answered the summons. When informed that Drew was out, Dare asked for Mrs. Stanley, his implacable tone brooking no argument. Disapproving of his early morning visit hours before it was considered polite to do so, the scowling maid showed Dare into the parlor while she hurried off to inform her mistress of the rude man demanding her presence.

Casey received the news calmly, already resigned to the fact that Dare would show up today. Only she thought she'd have more time to compose her scattered wits. Strange how fate had intervened, she reflected thoughtfully as she descended the stairs on rubbery legs. She had thought never to see Dare again yet here he was in England, in her own parlor. If only things were different, she mused wistfully. They were married to someone other than each other and their lives had taken them in opposite directions. She prayed desperately for the courage to do what was necessary to protect Drew and her son.

Casey stepped noiselessly into the room; Dare looked up to see her pause hesitantly just inside the door. There was a gentle softness in her voice, an uncontrollable tremor when she whispered his name. "Dare." She had no idea how sensuous her voice sounded to one starved so long for the sound.

A tense interval ensued until his hoarse whisper broke the silence. "Casey . . ."

Shaking herself to break the spell he wove around her, Casey forced herself to speak calmly and coolly despite her rampaging emotions. "Hello, Dare, what brings you to London?"

His answer contained a strong suggestion of reproach. "Is that all you can say, Casey? After I've been thinking you dead all these months, you greet me like an old friend? Bloody hell! Have you any idea how I've suffered these past months?"

At first Casey failed to understand Dare's words, so mesmerized was she by the sight and sound of him after months of seeing him only in her dreams. He was as handsome as ever, despite the underlying sadness and new lines creasing his face. She remembered vividly how it felt to be enfolded in his strong arms, kissed by soft, sensuous lips, loved until her body sang with joy. And then a sudden chill swept through her when she recalled the situation she had found him in last night, on the verge of making love to a woman other than his own wife. How many women did he need?

"Casey, answer me," Dare persisted. "Why did you deliberately let me believe you were dead?" She looked so damn beautiful and desirable standing there that he wanted to take her in his arms, kiss her until she grew dizzy and never let her go. With the greatest of difficulty he forced himself into a calm he was far from feeling. There were still too many unanswered questions between them.

Dare's words jerked Casey back to reality. "What! You knew I wasn't dead," she accused icily. "Ask your wife. I was very much alive when Mercy escaped the bushrangers. By the way, where is Mercy? What does she think of your romancing young girls?"

"Don't you know?"

"Know what?"

"Mercy is dead. She died of pneumonia

brought on by cold and exposure three days after she arrived home."

"Mercy dead?" Casey gasped in disbelief. "Didn't she tell you about me? Was she too sick to explain the dangerous position I was in? Or where I was?"

"Casey, love, my only love." Dare murmured the words with the certainty of a man who had suddenly seen the light after a long period of darkness. "Mercy swore you were dead. She told me Bert killed you after he and his mates . . . after they finished with you. She mentioned someone named Big John. It's obvious now she lied to me. We both know why."

"No, no!" cried Casey, tears blurring her vision. "She couldn't! She wouldn't!"

"I'm afraid we both underestimated Mercy's cruelty," Dare said with terrible sadness.

"But what about Dan?" Casey accused bitterly. "Why did you send him away? You and your family made it perfectly clear how little you cared for me. You wanted me out of your life so you refused to provide the ransom Bert demanded. I would never have believed you could be so cruel—so utterly heartless. If not for Big John I would be dead. And your child along with me."

"Casey, love, I know nothing of what you're saying. Do you truly believe that either Ben, Father or myself could abandon you so easily? I know you never understood about my marriage, but I've never loved anyone but you."

"What was I to think when Dan returned and told us not one of the Penrods cared what happened to me? If not for Big John—"

"Just who in the hell is Big John?" Dare interrupted. "And what is he to you?"

"He saved my life," Casey said, trembling as she explained about Big John, the giant whose huge body harbored a tender heart.

When she finished, Dare said, "If I ever meet the man he'll certainly receive my undying gratitude."

As if coming out of a dream, Casey looked up to find Dare standing only inches away, his gray eyes the color of mist rising over the sea, all soft and hazy. He had resisted the urge to take her in his arms so long he was shaking from the effort. Casey realized what he was going to do but was powerless to resist, her feeble protests paling in contrast to Dare's soaring need.

"Dare, no. I . . . I'm confused. I'm not sure . . . How can I trust you?"

"Perhaps I should explain why I married Mercy—"

"I already know," she shocked him by saying. "Mercy told me. She asked me to leave the farm, hoping if I did your marriage might have a chance to survive."

"My God! It's amazing to what lengths that woman went to get what she wanted. Then you already know I was more or less forced into marriage to obtain your freedom and Robin's ticket of leave," Dare said with relief. He was glad it was finally out in the open. "I didn't tell you before because I knew you'd feel guilty over my sacrifice. I didn't tell Robin, either. It was my choice and I made it with little thought for my own happiness. You and Robin were all that mattered to me."

"Dare, I want to believe you, but when I heard you didn't want me or the child I carried, my world fell apart," Casey said, her expressive eyes conveying her hurt and confusion.

"Not want you? That's preposterous. It was all some kind of cruel plot to keep us apart. But forget Mercy for a moment, love, and tell me about you. About your marriage to Drew," he said, his voice laced with reproach.

Suddenly one of the maids walked into the parlor and Casey moved backwards a step, belatedly realizing how exposed they were to prying eyes and ears. Sending the flustered girl on an errand, she said to Dare, "Let's go into the study where we won't be disturbed. I don't want my past aired before the servants."

Only too glad to comply, Dare followed the seductive sway of Casey's hips until they were behind closed doors where no one dare intrude. They turned to face each other, and found themselves in one another's arms, mouths fused, bodies straining together.

"My love," Dare whispered reverently. "I still can't believe you're alive. It's like a miracle, a dream come true. I want to touch you, feel your heart beating beneath my hands. Oh, my sweet, what I need, what I desperately desire, is to love you."

With one accord they sank to the thickly carpeted floor. Suddenly Casey found herself thrust beyond thought, past protest, her will stolen by the one man in all the world with the power to control her mind and capture her soul. Her one consuming thought was that it had been far too long since experiencing Dare's special brand of love. She needed him, wanted him with a deep, piercing pain felt in every recess of her starved body. She could no more deny him than she could stop breathing.

"Dare . . ." Her soft sigh inspired him with all the encouragement he needed as he gazed at her with incredible love. Each brush of his eyes was like a whisper of fire, making her tremble, searing her skin. Never had he seen a woman so breathtakingly beautiful, so undeniably sensual, so sweetly made.

And then he was kissing her eyes, her cheeks, her mouth, the soft hollow of her neck, burying his face in the texture and fragrance of her hair, holding her and breathing deeply of the heady electrifying sensations. His exploring hands glided beneath her bodice to make intimate contact with her flesh.

"I love you, Casey," he murmured, their warm breaths mingling.

"And I love you. Even when I swore it was otherwise, there must have been a part of me that would not let go, refused to believe you had betrayed me."

"I never betrayed you, love. You must know that now. Fate conspired against us. Fate and Mercy's cruel interference. But forget the past. We're together now like we were always meant to be. Let me love you."

While Dare talked his hands worked agilely at the fastenings of her dress, sliding it down past her shoulders, hips, thighs. Her petticoat left her body moments later, then her shift as Dare tenderly kissed each part of her he slowly and lovingly uncovered. Pleasure radiated upward from some hidden place, and Casey allowed herself to be carried with it, unable to hinder the forward thrust of her own desire lifting her into the turbulent seas of arousal. Boldly he claimed her senses with skill and determination, wanting to be her only reality.

With loving dexterity his mouth followed his hands down her body, fastening on her breast

with a hot wetness that made her cry out and
clutch at him. The insistent tugging at her nipple
reduced her to mindless ecstasy that left her
gasping as his mouth moved over to torment the
other soft peak. Suddenly Casey became impatient with Dare's clothes impeding the meeting of
bare flesh, and she began tearing at the offending
material. A low chuckle rippled from his throat,
and he half rose to aid her in removing his
restrictive clothing. Within moments she felt the
pleasant weight and heat of him searing her skin.

"Is that better, my greedy vixen?" he whispered hoarsely, renewing his passionate onslaught.

His fingers found the velvet of her inner thighs
and stroked higher . . . higher, and a warm wetness melted her core. He was probing inward, his
every movement setting off waves of grinding
pulsations inside her. His mouth sucked and
tugged at the peak of her breast, and she could
feel the long, swollen shaft lying hot and pulsing
against her belly.

"Dare, please . . ."

"Yes, my love, yes . . ."

His possession of her was a sweet desperation
made all the sweeter by the intense longing in his
eyes, the slight trembling of his body. Then the
sweet desperation became a delicious rapture
that grew with the push and withdrawal of each
thrust until Casey knew nothing beyond the
warmth of him, the smell, the taste of him. She
rocked beneath his loving battering, absorbing
his blows and coming back for more, giving as
well and receiving.

In her terrible need she wrapped her legs
around his hips to bring him even deeper, thrilling at the feel of him inside her. Then he quick-

ened his pace, powerfully, skillfully seeking and finding those sensitive areas that sent her moaning in jolt after jolt of delicious agony. Not until the last tremor left her body did Dare release his own tightly leashed passion to join in the upward race to reach the stars.

The peace that descended upon her was greater than any Casey had ever known as she slowly floated down to earth, unwilling to allow reality to intrude too soon. Until Dare's question jerked her startlingly awake. "Do I have a son or daughter?"

"You know!"

"Sir Donald told me Drew arrived in London with a young wife and newborn babe. If I hadn't come to London I might never have known I had a child. You haven't answered me, love," Dare persisted. "Do I have a son or daughter?"

"A son. I named him Brandon. He was born somewhere off the coast of France two weeks out of London."

"Why did you leave New South Wales without telling me of your predicament? Didn't you think I'd care about my own child?"

Sitting up, Casey rummaged around for her clothes. "I was told you wanted nothing to do with us. What did you expect me to do? Come begging? I had nothing left but my pride and wanted to get as far away from you as possible. Big John insisted I use his ill-gotten gains to purchase passage to England and I decided to accept rather than ask you for anything. I still don't understand what Dan had to gain from lying."

"That's something we may never know," mused Dare regretfully. "You can bet Mercy was behind whatever happened. How does Drew

Stanley figure into all this? I never saw two more ill-matched people in my life."

"Don't you dare say a thing about Drew," Casey defended stoutly, struggling into her clothes as she lunged to her feet. "I needed a place to stay until a ship arrived and knew no one in Sydney save for Drew. He asked no questions but took me in, declining payment for room and board. As it happened, he was also planning a voyage to London. He was asked to represent the settlers and emancipists and petition Parliament for a strong governor with the power to disband the Rum Corps. We traveled together, and I don't know how I would have survived without him."

"Why did you marry him?" Dare demanded. "Do you love him?"

"Of course, he's like a—"

"I don't want to hear any more, Casey," Dare frowned, halting her in mid-sentence. "Drew is too old for you. I realize you have tender feelings for him because of all he's done for you, and I'm grateful to him, but you belong to me. I'm leaving England within the month, and you and my son are coming with me. Now," he ordered brusquely, his voice brooking no argument, "take me to my son."

"I can't go, Dare," Casey whispered, choking on her words. Drew was a sick man, not likely to live long though he tried gallantly to hide it from her. He needed her and she'd not desert him despite the love she bore Dare. She would remain and make his last days as comfortable as possible. "I'm a married woman and I won't leave my husband. Where is your gratitude? He married me to give your child a name."

Dare stared at her. "Casey, we love each other. We have a child. Surely Drew won't object, he's a reasonable man, and a compassionate one. Surely a man his age can't . . . that is . . . dammit, Casey, he can't satisfy you the way I do!"

"You don't understand. Drew is—"

"I know he's your husband, and I wouldn't love you half as much if you didn't feel a certain amount of loyalty toward him," Dare persisted doggedly. "I've known Drew Stanley for years. He'd be the first to agree with me. But my gratitude doesn't extend so far as to give him the woman I love and my child."

"Perhaps one day we can be together," Casey proposed stubbornly, "but certainly not while Drew needs me. He has no one but me and Brandon."

"Dammit, Casey, I'm not going to stand here and argue with you," Dare fumed impotently. "When I leave England you and Brandon will be with me. Now I want to see my son. I think I've waited long enough for that honor."

"Why you arrogant, domineering . . ." Casey sputtered, words failing her. What good would it do to try to reason with a man in no mood to listen? Abruptly she turned, heading for the door and flinging over her shoulder, "I'll bring Brandon to you, wait here."

While Dare paced the length of the room fretting and fuming, Casey decided to change Brandon first, allowing Dare to cool his heels in the study. She knew he was capable of storming the nursery if he grew impatient, shocking the servants with his daring.

Drew returned home much earlier than he anticipated. He had waited at Dare's townhouse for over an hour and when he didn't return was struck with the thought that Dare might have gone to see Casey. He returned home, arriving while Casey was still in the nursery with Brandon. A maid informed him that a gentleman waited in the study, and Drew entered the room knowing exactly what awaited him. Dare was alone. "Hello, Dare," he said, his voice laced with sadness.

Dare whirled, his features lifting at the sight of Drew. "Drew, you're just the person I want to see!"

"It's good to see you, Dare," Drew smiled, displaying a multitude of fine lines radiating from around his eyes and mouth. "When I failed to find you at home I suspected you might have come here."

"You were looking for me?"

Wearily Drew collapsed in a chair, the lines in his face deepening into a frown. Dare thought he had never seen him looking so exhausted. "Have you seen my wife?" Though Drew hadn't meant to hurt Dare by referring to Casey in that precise manner, the spasm that contorted Dare's face told him he had done exactly what he hoped to avoid.

Dare stiffened, suddenly, painfully aware that he had just made love to another man's wife. Somehow he couldn't bring himself to think of Casey in terms of belonging to anyone other than himself. "I've seen Casey," he said tightly.

"And your son? I imagine it was somewhat of a shock to learn you were a father."

"It was a far greater shock to find Casey alive after thinking her dead all these months," Dare remarked bitterly.

"What made you think Casey was dead?"

"How much has Casey told you?"

"Not much, really."

"Then perhaps I should enlighten you," Dare

returned. And he did, revealing Mercy's scheming to get rid of Casey. "Mercy died without ever telling us the truth. We all assumed the grave I found in the bush held Casey's remains. For months I was inconsolable, then Father persuaded me to come to England. Thank God I did," he breathed.

"No wonder Casey was so adamant about leaving New South Wales," Drew recalled. "If I had known Mercy was dead I swear I'd never let her leave. And I wouldn't have married her. I did it to protect her and your child. But I truly love her, Dare, like a—"

"Drew, when did you get home?"

The conversation skidded to a halt and both men turned as Casey entered the room carrying a squirming bundle in her arms. Immediately Dare forgot everything but his son; the child born of the love he and Casey shared. He held out his arms, and somewhat reluctantly Casey relinquished her child into his father's keeping. Brandon stared solemnly at Dare through eyes as misty gray as his father's. He must have liked what he saw, for he gurgled happily and broke into a wide, toothless grin, charming his father completely. For Dare it was love at first sight and he knew he'd never willingly part with this tiny part of himself no matter what the consequences.

Drew noted the instant attachment between father and son and realized that they belonged together. His eyes drifted to Casey. She was staring at Dare with so much love in her eyes it hurt to see the three of them together. As much as the thought distressed him, it was time to step aside so that Dare might claim his family. The idea was physically unbearable and his heart spasmed in his breast, causing him to clutch at his chest until the pain subsided and his breath came easier. If only . . . No, he musn't be selfish. He was fortunate to have had Casey to himself all these months and now it was time to step aside. He had been to a doctor and was examined thoroughly. The good man had merely shaken his head and sadly informed him his heart could give out at any time. He was given medicine to ease the pain but little hope.

Dare hated to relinquish his son but finally handed him back to Casey to put down for a nap. The moment she left them alone he turned to Drew. "You know why I'm here, don't you?"

Drew nodded, his gray features drawn into a mask of sorrow. "I'll not keep them from you, Dare, though I must confess it will be like losing a part of myself. I love Casey and Brandon dearly but am willing to do whatever necessary to free Casey. You're aware that it may take some time."

"I thought I made myself clear, Dare. I won't leave Drew no matter what you two have hatched up." Casey stood poised in the doorway, green eyes blazing defiantly. Striding into the room, she knelt beside Drew's chair, placing a small hand on his knee. "You need me, Drew, I'll not leave you."

The intimate gesture sent Dare into a rage, never more aware that Casey belonged to another man. "Drew is in total agreement with me, Casey, and I'll brook no refusal. I need you, I need our son."

"Drew needs us too," Casey insisted belligerently. Was Dare blind? Couldn't he see how sick Drew was?

"Dare is right, my dear," Drew tried to convince her. "I'm an old man. You and Brandon belong with Dare. I'll quietly obtain a divorce."

Drew did not say so but he reckoned he'd be dead long before a divorce could be granted. "You have my blessing to return to Australia. No one need know that you and Dare aren't married."

"No!" Casey resisted stubbornly. "I refuse to consider it. I'll remain with you as long as you need me."

"What about me?" shouted Dare, his temper spiraling.

"Perhaps Lydia Hurley would like to go to Australia," Casey sniffed.

"Perhaps she would," returned Dare angrily.

"Casey—Dare, let's talk about this in a reasonable manner," Drew cajoled, afraid the two headstrong young people might actually come to blows. "There has to be a way to settle this peaceably."

"I don't understand why Casey is so damn obstinate," Dare ground out. "There'd be no argument if she'd let us men handle everything."

"Men, bah! They don't know everything. I don't understand why Dare has to be so arrogant and demanding," Casey rebutted. "Is he so blind that he can't see how much you need me?"

"Ah, Casey," Drew sighed wearily. "Your loyalty pleases me, but we both know our marriage was one of convenience, that we were never truly husband and wife. I love you like a daughter, my dear, and must relinquish you as a father would a bride on her wedding day." That bit of information brought a delighted gasp from Dare's throat.

"You . . . you'd send me away?"

"Send you away? No, never!" Drew denied vehemently. "If you go it will be because you want to. Because of your love for Dare. You do love him, don't you?" he questioned sharply.

The tense silence brought a flush to Dare's

face. "Well, do you or don't you love me, Casey? Whatever your answer I intend to have my son."

"I do love you, Dare," came Casey's whispered reply. "But I also love Drew. Though you are blind to it, he needs me more than you do right now."

"Bloody hell! Stay here with Drew like a dutiful wife. Just prepare my son for a long voyage. I'll not leave him behind." He stormed out of the room, slamming the door behind him.

"I can't force you to leave, my dear," Drew said, his voice resigned, "but Dare is right in believing you two belong together. And should he force the issue and claim his son, I'll not fight him."

"Drew, you're as dear to me as my own father. I know you're ill, you can't hide it from me. Dare is being unreasonable and childish to insist I leave now. Tell me the truth, what is wrong with you?"

"I suppose you have a right to know, Casey," Drew sighed tiredly. "It's my heart. I've consulted a doctor, but my condition is beyond help. It's only a matter of time before—"

"I knew it!" cried Casey, her expression that of mute wretchedness. "I knew you were hiding something from me. I was unable to offer my dear father comfort when his time came, but I'll not fail you. Somehow I'll make Dare realize I can't leave just yet."

"He's a hard-headed, hot-blooded young man," Drew allowed wistfully, perhaps remembering his own wild youth. "But if anyone can convince him, you can."

The following days Dare was too caught up in preparations for his departure and still smarting with anger for another confrontation with Casey. During that time he completed arrangements having to do with his inheritance, turned it all into gold, and packed it for shipment to New South Wales. He bought clothes, boots, furniture and goods still unobtainable or scarce in the colony. But more importantly he arranged for a shipment of pure merino sheep to be delivered to him in Sydney.

Though Dare longed to see Casey and Brandon, he deliberately kept away, knowing his presence would spark another argument. Their love for one another was never in doubt. It was her stubbornness in wanting to remain with an old man and her misplaced sense of loyalty and duty. Astutely he realized that Drew had become a substitute father to Casey, and the man certainly was ill enough to fret over. A woman's sick jealousy had almost destroyed them once, and Dare was determined that nothing or no one separate them again. In his determination he failed to recognize the serious nature of a dying man's illness.

When Dare had everything in readiness for his voyage home, he decided to hire a ship to carry him and his cargo rather than wait for an available supply ship, which might take weeks. He visited the docks several days in a row, seeking the right ship and captain, one capable of getting him and his little family safely back to Australia. Then one day he unexpectedly found exactly what he was looking for.

A tall, barrel-chested man some years older than himself approached Dare while he ambled along the dock looking over the ships, actually considering buying one to transport his goods and his family. The man wore the trappings of a sea captain yet appeared uncomfortable in the shiny new uniform.

"Excuse me, sir," the man said, halting Dare. "Are you the man looking to hire a ship?"

Dare studied the freckle-faced man with light brown hair carefully before replying. His smile was open and friendly, and Dare liked him immediately. "That I am, Captain," he replied with alacrity. "Do you know of a ship for hire?"

"Aye. Captain Jeremy Combs at your service, sir. My ship is one of the finest you'll find."

"Jeremy Combs," Dare said thoughtfully. "Do I know you, Captain? Your name sounds familiar. I am Dare Penrod from New South Wales, Australia." He offered Jeremy Combs his hand.

"To my knowledge we've never met, Mr. Penrod," Jeremy said, wringing Dare's hand.

"Call me Dare. Can we go someplace to talk, Captain? If your ship is for hire I have a proposition you might be interested in."

"My *Martha C* is equipped to take you anyplace in the world," Jeremy beamed proudly, "even Australia, if that be your wish. And Dare it is if you call me Jeremy."

Martha C! The name brought another jolt to Dare's memory.

"The Hart and Horn is not far from here," Jeremy continued, unaware of Dare's thoughtful frown. "It's a decent place and we can talk over a tankard of ale."

"Lead the way, Jeremy," Dare smiled.

Seated at a table in the cheery Hart and Horn, Dare told Jeremy of his need for a ship and his destination. "Are you prepared for a year's absence?" he questioned sharply.

"Aye," said Jeremy with a hint of sadness.

"You have keen eyes so you know I've not commanded my own ship long, though the sea has been my life since I was eight. I was shipwrecked off the coast of South America and it was a year before I saw England again," Jeremy confided. "The only good to come of it was that I returned to England a rich man. We found gold and jewels beyond our wildest dreams."

"I like a story with a happy ending," Dare grinned, unaware of Jeremy's pensive mood.

"I wish it were so," Jeremy sighed wistfully. "When I started that fateful voyage I left a good wife behind. When I finally returned she had disappeared. Her parents were dead and my Martha gone. I've spent months searching for her, but to no avail. I don't know what happened to her after my ship was reported missing. Eventually I gave up the search and with my share of the wealth bought and outfitted a ship. I named her after my Martha. So I'm your man, Dare, if my ship meets with your approval."

Like a bolt out of the blue, comprehension dawned. Martha Combs! Jeremy Combs! Husband and wife. Martha was his father's housekeeper in Australia and he could lead Jeremy directly to her.

"Jeremy," Dare said with a twinkle, "I'm glad you're sitting, mate, for I'm going to tell you something that will knock you off your feet. Your wife is alive, and to the best of my knowledge, well. She's working for my father in Australia."

Jeremy's ruddy face paled, his mouth working convulsively. "Australia, you say? N . . . no, you must be mistaken. What would my Martha be doing in Australia?"

Dare went on to explain about Martha's crime

and transportation to New South Wales. Tears
came to Jeremy's eyes at the thought of Martha's
suffering and deprivation during her incarcera-
tion and long voyage to New South Wales. A
tense silence ensued before he wrestled his emotions under control and coherent speech was
possible.

"I thank God Martha is alive," he said shakily.
"Nothing will prevent me from voyaging to Australia now. Whether you hire my ship or not
makes little difference. If it takes my remaining
wealth I'll free Martha from her bondage."

"I'll help all I can," Dare promised. "And I'll
gladly hire the *Martha C* if we can reach an
agreement."

To that end a fair price was quickly agreed
upon and a sailing date set two weeks hence. "My
wife and infant son will be joining me for the
journey," Dare said with firm conviction. He
decided not to tell Jeremy of the curious predicament he faced in regards to Casey until the
situation warranted.

"You'll have the best cabin, Dare," Jeremy
replied, "and all the comforts I can provide. My
ship is newly outfitted and as seaworthy as you'll
find anywhere."

"I'll arrange for the cargo to begin arriving
tomorrow," Dare informed him, sealing the deal
with a handshake. And whether Casey liked it or
not she would be with him, even if it meant
kidnapping her and their son. "If I don't see you
for a few days, don't worry. I'll be in the country
selecting horses and cattle for shipment to Australia."

CHAPTER TWENTY-FOUR

Drew Stanley died quietly in his sleep of a seizure the day after Dare left for the country. He must have sensed his death was near at hand, for he sat Casey down the day before and carefully listed all his earthly assets which would go to her and Brandon upon his death. She was quite surprised to learn it included a 5,000-acre land grant as well as another 5,000 acres he had purchased to make it one of the largest parcels in New South Wales. Casey suspected his age had much to do with preventing him from farming those acres. Upon his death, Casey could do what she pleased with them whether she chose to return to Australia or not.

One of Drew's last words of advice was to allow Dare to be a father to his son. He cautioned her not to destroy what she and Dare had together, for a love such as theirs came only once. Casey knew Drew spoke the truth but was determined to remain with him as long as he needed her. If Dare returned to New South Wales without her, so be it.

Three days later Drew was laid to rest with only herself and a few old friends present. Dare's conspicuous absence was duly noted and registered despite Casey's grief. Later that day the will was read, but there were no surprises. Everything Drew possessed was left to his wife and son. As easily as that, Casey became a woman of property. And still Dare did not appear to offer comfort or condolences.

Had her continued refusal to leave Drew while he was so ill changed the way Dare felt about her? Casey wondered bleakly. Why was he blinded to her need to make Drew's last days comfortable? He had acted like a spoiled child when things hadn't gone his way. Had he practiced a modicum of patience and shown compassion, he would have gained all he desired in the end. Assuming it was her and their son he wanted.

If Dare truly loved her, Casey reasoned, he would be here now, offering solace. Surely he hadn't given up on her? Dare was not a man to give up so easily, so why wasn't he here demanding she pack up their son and leave with him? When a week slid by with no word from Dare, Casey decided to swallow her pride and visit his townhouse, hoping to discover for herself why he failed to show up after Drew's death, or even acknowledge it. A terrible thought spurred her into action. What if he was sick and needed her? Since Drew had told her some time ago where Dare lived, finding him would present no problem. Leaving Brandon behind with his nurse, Casey walked the short distance to Dare's house, rehearsing in her mind all the things she wanted to say.

*   *   *

Dare was totally exhausted upon his return from the country, but the trip had been thoroughly worthwhile. He had purchased ten cows, two bulls and four blooded bays, the start of a sizeable herd. He had also arranged to ship twenty pure merino sheep shortly after the new year, along with several more cows and another bull. Yes, it had been a profitable trip and he still had a week remaining in which to convince the stubborn vixen he loved that he couldn't live without her. Somehow, some way, she and their son would be on the *Martha C* when she sailed. Even if he had to take Drew Stanley with them.

Halfway through his dressing after he had bathed and changed clothes upon his return today, a maid informed him that a lady waited for him in the parlor. Joy lifted his mood, since he was certain Casey had finally come to her senses. Issuing crisp orders, he instructed the startled maid to dismiss the servants for the day. He wanted no interruptions or prying eyes and ears when he greeted his love.

She was standing in the middle of the room, her hood drawn over her head as if afraid to reveal her identity. But he could understand that. Casey was a married woman and the gossips would have a field day should she be identified visiting the home of a bachelor. "Casey!" His exuberant greeting brought her around to face him. "My God! Lydia! What in bloody hell are you doing here?"

"Eddie said you planned to leave London soon and I couldn't let you go without . . . seeing you again. I waited and waited for you to call on me but you never did," Lydia accused, her full lips quivering. "I finally dragged it out of Eddie. It's that woman isn't it? The redhead. Forget her, Dare. I . . . I've been in love with you from the moment we met."

"You shouldn't be here, Lydia," Dare scolded sternly. "You're a lovely girl and have no need to chase after anyone. Any eligible man in London would be pleased to have you for a wife. I told you before, I'm not the man for you."

Spoiled and pampered, Lydia refused to settle for that which came easily. She wanted Dare. He presented a challenge, one she could not resist. And she actually believed herself in love with Dare. "I've so much more to offer you, Dare, than anyone else."

"I love Casey too much to give her up," Dare admitted, hoping to discourage Lydia without hurting her unduly. She was a beautiful child/woman with the body of a seductress who would one day make a brilliant match. But not with him.

"But you never gave me a chance, Dare," Lydia wailed.

"Are you willing to leave London society for the Australian wilds?" he asked severely. "Can you give up all the luxury you've grown accustomed to? My home is far from sumptuous, the climate harsh and forbidding. There are mosquitoes, floods, droughts, dust and heat so suffocating you can barely draw in a breath without searing your lungs. And London is six months away. Can you truthfully say you'd be happy in such an environment?"

"With you I could," she insisted, her stubborn chin challenging him to prove otherwise.

Dare was about to do just that when a clatter at

the front door announced another unexpected visitor. "Damn," he cursed, exasperated. "Just what I need, someone to find you here alone with me and no servants about. Stay here, Lydia, and I'll get rid of whoever is calling. Don't show yourself until they're gone. You'd best hope it's not your brother."

"But Dare—"

"Obey me in this, Lydia," Dare ordered sternly.

Casey fidgeted nervously, waiting for someone to answer her summons, wondering if she was doing the right thing by coming to Dare. It was what Drew would have advised, but was it worth compromising her pride? She was here, wasn't she? That alone should answer her question. Being with Dare forever was worth any sacrifice. She was more than a little shocked to see Dare himself appear at the door.

"Casey!"

"Hello, Dare," Casey smiled, shifting shyly from foot to foot. He appeared somewhat befuddled, but Casey laid it to surprise at finding her on his doorstep. When he continued to stare at her in a distracted manner, she wrung her hands nervously and asked, "Can I come in?" She was beginning to regret her hasty decision to approach Dare in his home.

"I'm sorry, please come in," Dare said, glancing over his shoulder in a curious manner. "It's . . . well . . . I didn't expect to see you here."

"Did I come at a bad time? If you don't wish to see me, I'll leave."

"No! It's just that I was on my way to see you and my son. I've been out of town and returned only hours ago."

"Then you don't know?" Casey asked. Dare was acting so strangely she assumed it had to do with Drew's death and his failure to attend the funeral.

"Know what?"

"Drew is dead. He was laid to rest earlier this week." The slight tremor in her voice spoke volumes about her grief. Then the thought struck him that he should have been here to lend support and offer comfort.

"Oh God, Casey, I'm sorry! I had no idea. Come in, love, we need to talk." Placing an arm about her quaking shoulders, he deliberately led her away from the parlor and into the study, carefully closing the door behind him. It wouldn't do for Casey to see Lydia. If he was lucky, Lydia would tire of waiting and leave.

It would have shocked and angered Dare to know that Lydia had no intention of following orders or waiting meekly for his return. Hiding behind the parlor door, she fumed with impotent rage when she saw Dare with his arm around Casey, leading her into the study. All she could think of was that Dare was alone with the beautiful redhead who had stolen his love and robbed her of the most intriguing man she had ever met. Suddenly a sly smile curved her full lips.

Behind the closed door of the study, Dare opened his arms and Casey flew into them without reservation. "I would have been there for you had I known, love. I had no idea Drew was so ill."

"If you hadn't been so obstinate you would have known," Casey said reproachfully. "But all you could think of was your own needs, your own selfish desires. Now do you understand why I couldn't leave?"

"I was a stubborn fool," Dare admitted lamely. "I suppose the shock of finding you alive and married to another man robbed me of my senses. Discovering I had a son only added to my confusion. Can you forgive me?"

"People do strange things under the guise of love," Casey said in a husky whisper. "Forgiveness is part of loving. And I do love you. Brandon and I need you. We're prepared to return to Australia whenever you say."

The sweetness of her words filled Dare with joy. How dearly he loved this special woman. "How is my son? I missed him terribly, considering that a few days ago I never knew he existed. We sail in a week, my love."

She gave willingly as Dare claimed her lips, melting into his embrace, tunneling her fingers through thick black hair, caressing his neck and shoulders on their downward journey. The kiss intensified, his tongue plundering between parted lips to sip greedily of her sweet nectar. With a will of their own his hands moved lightly, hungrily, over lush curves, lavishing special attention on the soft mounds of her breasts, the tiny indent of waist and gentle curve of hip and thigh. His touch evoked a delighted moan as her own hands played teasingly over rippling muscles of shoulders and back, settling playfully on tight buttocks which jerked and tautened beneath her mischievous fingertips.

He responded by grasping the delightfully supple twin hills curving outward from her back and pressing her into his hardness, leaving her no doubt as to the state of his arousal. Completely forgotten was Lydia pacing the parlor in a rage. His consuming need for Casey took precedence over time and place as he trailed teasing kisses over her eyelids, cheeks, forehead, neck, and back to her mouth. Just the idea of spending the rest of his life with this tantalizingly lovely and seductive woman fueled his desire until control was no longer possible, or even considered. "I need you, my love."

With mutual consent they began tearing at each other's clothes, both eager to consummate their great love. Given their urgency they would have been stripped nude in moments if the door hadn't burst open.

"Dare, darling, what's keeping you?" a pouty voice complained. "When you left the bedroom you said you'd only be gone a few minutes."

Then, as if noticing Casey for the first time, Lydia's eyes widened with mock innocence. "Oh my, am I intruding? Heavens, darling, you *are* a rogue. Imagine, two women at once. Is that normal?"

Feeling Casey stiffen in his arms, Dare groaned in frustration, cursing Lydia beneath his breath.

"Bastard!" Casey hissed, desire dying a natural death at the sight of Lydia, partially clad and poised in the doorway in delightful disarray. She wore nothing but a thin shift and corset which exposed the tops of straining white breasts down to their pink peaks. She looked charmingly dishabille and invitingly rumpled, leading Casey to the natural conclusion that Dare and Lydia had been intimately engaged before her untimely arrival. Before Dare could utter a word in his defense, Casey turned and fled.

"What in the hell do you think you're doing?" roared Dare, causing Lydia to cower in fright. Perhaps she *had* gone too far. But Dare certainly deserved it. "Put on your clothes, you little hussy, and get out of here. You deserve a spank-

ing, or worse. What would your father or brother
think if they saw you now?" He bent her a chilly
glare, scarcely aware of the charms she so blatantly displayed.

A pang of latent remorse smote Lydia, suddenly realizing what a terrible thing she had done. It
was so totally unlike her she was filled with
shame. Her parents would be mortified should
they learn of her wanton behavior. It certainly
hadn't done a thing to endear her to Dare. He
had expressed nothing but contempt for her
sickening display, making it quite obvious he
cared nothing for her. And if he was telling the
truth about Australia, she would never consent to
live in such an outlandish country. At first it
sounded so romantic, and Dare so handsome,
like a hero in a novel, that she had lost her head
and her heart. It had been fun to be the envy of
all her friends. Now she would give anything to
relive these last moments. She could tell the
lovely redhead meant a great deal to Dare, and
was sorry she had interfered.

Licking her lips nervously, she said in a con-
trite voice, "I'm sorry. I didn't mean . . . that
is . . . you won't tell on me, will you? I did an
awful thing, but jealousy made me forget all I
ever learned about being a lady."

Dare grimaced, wanting to wring her beautiful
neck yet recognizing true repentance. Lydia was
merely a young girl on the verge of womanhood
testing her wings. He had taken her fancy and she
had used her naturally seductive wiles to ensnare
him. And it might have worked if he didn't love
Casey so damn much. Though Lydia didn't know
Casey Stanley personally, she knew she must be
someone special to have captured Dare's affections so thoroughly.

"I won't tell, Lydia, if you promise to behave
yourself in the future," he finally said, easing her
mind considerably. "Now get dressed and leave
before I change my mind and give you the
spanking you so richly deserve. It's time you
grew up and faced the responsibility of your
actions."

"Thank you, Dare," Lydia squeaked gratefully, fully aware that Dare had let her off easily.
"I . . . I wish you well with your lady." Then she
scurried off.

Dare waited until he heard the front door open
and shut some minutes later before leaving the
study. In the face of such condemning evidence,
he realized it was going to be difficult to convince
Casey of his innocence where Lydia was concerned.

Casey ran all the way home, arriving out of
breath as she slammed the door behind her. How
could he? she fumed with impotent rage. How
many women does it take to satisfy him? Obviously he liked them young, for Lydia, for all her
voluptuous curves, looked barely out of the
schoolroom. Had Dare seduced Lydia with
charming words and promises just as he had her?
"How could he love me?" Casey reasoned aloud.
"Or his son. If he did he wouldn't lust after other
women."

When Dare arrived hard on her heels, she
adamantly refused to talk to him. Or allow him
access to Brandon. She knew she shocked the
servants when she stood at the top of the stairs
and shouted like a fishwife, "Go back to your
young paramour and don't try to . . . to seduce
me with false words. Brandon and I don't need
you. Drew provided adequately for our future."

"Bloody hell!" Dare roared, taking the steps two at a time. "You think you don't need me but you do. Just as badly as I need you." He reached her side before the shock of his reaction to her words released her feet, making escape impossible.

"Oh, ma'am," came a frightened voice from below. "What shall I do?"

The young maid who had admitted Dare to the house stood at the foot of the stairs, wringing her hands and wailing in dismay. Casey was tempted to tell her to run for help, but Dare forestalled her, turning to the maid and saying, "I'm Brandon's father and your mistress and I have things to settle between us. No harm will come to her or anyone unless you interfere with something that is no concern of yours. Just go about your duty."

"Mrs. . . . Mrs. Stanley, is what the gentleman says true?" she asked, gawking at Dare as if he were the devil himself.

"Damn you, Dare," Casey whispered for Dare's ears alone. "Did you have to tell her that?" To the quaking girl poised on the verge of flight, she said, "Yes, it's true, Maddie. Go on about your duties, he won't hurt us." She certainly didn't want to involve the servants in her problems.

"Y . . . yes, ma'am," Maddie stuttered, anxious to escape a situation that was proving more embarrassing by the minute. She remained long enough to see Dare sweep Casey off her feet and carry her into the nearest room, which happened to be Casey's, and slam the door.

"Dammit, Dare, put me down! You have no right to order my servants about and act as if you own me."

Smiling with wry amusement, Dare set Casey on her feet, but did not remove his arms from her narrow waist. "I have every right in the world. You belong to me and I want my son to know his father. Do you realize I've barely made his acquaintance?"

"How many women does it take to satisfy you?" Casey sneered.

"Only one, love, only one. I've had no other woman since I met you, except for my wedding night when Mercy insisted we consummate our marriage. Believe me, there was no love involved in that coupling."

Casey found it difficult to believe him. Hadn't she seen Lydia with her own eyes? "You lie very well, Dare," she accused. "You realize, of course, you've compromised a young girl's reputation and her family will expect a proposal."

"You talk too much, love," he chided in a hoarse whisper. "I'd rather continue where we left off before we were so rudely interrupted."

"Have you no conscience? What kind of man are you to hop from one bed to another?" Fury coursed through her like a winter's storm, sharp and icy with a biting sting.

Exasperated, he said, "Things aren't always what they seem, Casey. I told you I never bedded Lydia. She showed up at my door, but her attempt at seduction failed. I tried to send her on her way, but you arrived to complicate matters. Unfortunately, she saw us together and put on an act out of spite and jealousy. Now be quiet and let me make love to you."

"No . . . I . . ." The words died in her throat as Dare captured her lips. What he felt for this green-eyed vixen was more than passion; it was deep and debilitating and obsessive.

His mouth was teasing, caressing, crushing. Casey trembled, buffeted by an onslaught of emotions she had thought lay buried beneath the avalanche of pain she'd suffered at his hands. Roaming her curves at will, he stroked her back and hips as his lips left hers to drop soft kisses over her eyes, cheeks and throat. Then he returned to her mouth, his lips becoming more gentle, more subtly insistent, and she felt his tongue slipping inside her mouth.

By the time he began removing her clothes she had been reduced to a mass of quivering need, powerless to resist. Why did he have such a devastating effect on her? she silently lamented. He had but to touch her and she was his.

She stood before him gloriously nude as he feasted on the lovely sight of long hair fanned about her face and shoulders like a living flame. Gray eyes scanned her face, her slim throat, her creamy shoulders, and locked on her soft breasts, the rosy tips tautening beneath his hot scrutiny. She couldn't think, she could only respond.

Through narrowed eyes she watched him shed his clothes, freeing his manhood which leaped to instant erection beneath her sultry gaze. He pulled her against his eager maleness. Her nipples were hard and stabbing, and between her legs she felt a warm moistness that told her how desperately she wanted him. He swept her effortlessly into his arms and carried her the few steps to the bed. The springs protested loudly as he settled her in the soft folds of the bedclothes, flinging himself beside her.

She sighed and closed her eyes as he kissed each lid, then dropped light kisses across her cheeks and around her mouth, and at last teased her lips with his own. Then his mouth was everywhere, branding her breasts, stomach and thighs with tiny pinpoints of fire. Soft, hot nibbles teased the upward curve of her vulnerable inner thighs, higher, higher, toward the flaming thatch of hair and throbbing moistness that invited his attention. She felt hot breath teasing her downy-soft maidenhair and sighed, squirming, her body writhing with delight. The longer he caressed her there, the more rapture she knew.

Dare feasted greedily on her hidden treasure, sucking the tiny nub into his mouth, creating sheer bliss, all the while his hands stimulating her breasts. "Dare, please," Casey begged, wanting him to claim her fully.

But Dare was in no mood to offer release so easily. "Tell me you need me."

"N . . . no, I . . . can't," she faltered, his mouth and lips driving her beyond mere pleasure into the realm of pain.

Renewing his efforts, he buried his face in the flaming forest, grasping her waist to hold her immobile as his tongue lavished special care on the tender bud and tight slit beneath. Then suddenly it no longer mattered that Dare needed more than one woman to feed his voracious appetite, or that he lied to her. She loved him, needed him, wanted him. If only for the space of this magic moment, she intended to enjoy him to the fullest.

"Dare, I need you!" she cried mindlessly.

Her world tilting crazily, Dare's tongue and lips drove her beyond herself, spiraling her to the top of the highest mountain. Then he was nudging her legs apart and urging his probing manhood into her tight warmth, rapidly entering, withdrawing and reentering. Casey moaned as she surrendered to his demands. She had no idea

her hands were playing in his hair and caressing
his neck and shoulders. Every inch of her responded violently to his touch, craving him,
urging him on with soft sighs and gasps. It
seemed impossible that she could attain rapture
again so soon, but she felt her soul leave her body
and cried out as ecstasy seized her and set her
adrift. Seconds later Dare galloped to his own
victory.

"You're one hell of a woman, Casey O'Cain
Stanley," Dare sighed wearily, rolling to his back
as he carried her with him. "Marriage to you will
never be dull."

"Marriage to you will be impossible," Casey
returned shortly, still trembling with remembered pleasure. "Save your proposal for someone
who will appreciate it. Get out of here." Deliberately she turned away, presenting her back.

Dare grinned with devilish delight at the tantalizing sight of swelling hip and curved buttocks.
She stiffened in indignation when he gently caressed the twin mounds. "Haven't you had
enough? Aren't you ever satisfied?"

"Not with you in my bed." Shifting to his side,
he molded his large frame tight against her curled
body. With a groan of dismay she felt the full
length of his aroused manhood prod her buttocks.

"No!" she protested, aghast. His stamina was
incredible.

"Yes, love," Dare replied hoarsely.

Before she knew what he was about, he grasped
her waist and lifted her to straddle his lean
flanks. Flexing his hips, he slipped easily inside,
and once more she was lost to the spell he wove
about her senses.

* * *

Dusk hovered in gray mists above the ground when Dare finally left. "I'll be back," he promised as he prepared to depart. "Start packing." He thought it best not to tell her the exact day they would leave, for in her frame of mind she was likely to bolt. He still hadn't convinced her he cared nothing for Lydia. So many things conspired against them that Dare seriously considered kidnapping to bring her aboard the *Martha C.*

"How dare that arrogant bastard come in here, make love to me, then issue orders," Casey raged as her legs carried her the length of the room and back. Time and again he had proved he couldn't be trusted. She'd damn well show him she wouldn't surrender to his outrageous demands. She wanted to believe he loved only her but was afraid he would betray her again. There must be some way, she reasoned, to test his love. Some way to put her considerable doubts to rest once and for all. If they were to share their lives, it had to be because she wanted it too, not because Dare demanded it.

He wanted his son, that much was obvious. And he enjoyed making love to her. As well as to other women, she snorted derisively. Well, she'd show him. She'd take her son and . . . and what? The answer jolted through her like a bolt of lightning, and a devious smile curved her full lips. "Watch out, Dare Penrod," she warned. "You're going to learn Casey O'Cain Stanley has a mind of her own. You've had things your way long enough."

CHAPTER TWENTY-FIVE

The next morning Casey arose early, fed Brandon and left the house dressed in a demure gray walking gown and matching bonnet whose wide brim partially hid her face and flaming curls. Because of the distance she needed to travel, she hired a hack to take her to London Harbor. When she reached her destination she asked the driver to wait, set her mouth in determined lines, and stepped down to join the hustle and bustle of the busy port.

Sights, sounds and smells, both exotic and obnoxious, assailed her from every angle. The tangy aroma of salt mingled with the sweetness of spices, but the pungent odor of animals being loaded aboard ships caused Casey to wrinkle her nose. So many ships, she thought, momentarily confused. Hopefully the one she wanted rode at anchor somewhere in the harbor, or if she was lucky, was already being loaded with cargo in preparation for departure.

Self-conscious over the unwanted attention she drew, Casey scanned the area for a likely looking seaman to answer her questions. She knew it was only her ladylike appearance that saved her from the lewd remarks and insinuations being addressed to the dockside whores plying their trade at this early hour. She wanted to complete her business and leave this unsavory neighborhood as quickly as possible.

The sailor she selected to direct her questions to was clean-shaven, neater than most and very young. His vivid blue eyes were mildly inquisitive as he waited for Casey to speak. When she did he was instantly enchanted by her melodious voice and lovely face. When he heard her request he broke out in a wide grin, happy to be of service to so enchanting a creature.

"There's only one ship in port, ma'am, what's sailing to Australia. That be the *Martha C.* She's over yonder taking on cargo right now." The lad pointed to a square-rigged, three-masted sloop rising and falling with the gentle motion of waves slapping her hull. The name *Martha C* was painted boldly in big letters. "That's her captain standing on the quay overseeing the loading. If the *Martha C* don't suit you, another will likely be leaving in a few weeks."

"The *Martha C* looks like a fine ship," Casey commented, "and if the captain is taking on passengers, she'll suit me well enough." Nodding her thanks, she slowly made her way around barrels and crates to where the ship was being loaded with goods of every description.

With pounding heart, Casey approached the captain of the *Martha C,* suddenly in doubt whether she was doing the right thing. Then she thought of Dare's arrogant, demanding manner and it all seemed worthwhile. If Dare really loved her he'd catch up with her in New South Wales.

Of course, once he found her missing, he could decide he liked the diversions offered by London and remain to enjoy them as well as Lydia's ample charms. If her leaving taught him to think of her as something other than a possession, she was willing to risk it.

"Are you the captain of the *Martha C*?" Casey asked of the man standing on the dock issuing brisk orders.

"Aye," Jeremy replied, tipping his hat politely.

"I understand you're undertaking a voyage to Port Jackson in New South Wales, and I'd like to book passage for myself and young child."

Though Jeremy loved his Martha dearly, he'd never seen a more beautiful or appealing woman. Strands of fine red hair peeked out from beneath her gray bonnet and her huge green eyes were two luminous pools in a flawless white face with just a sprinkling of freckles visible across her pert nose. She seemed determined to go to Australia and he hated to disappoint her.

"I'm sorry, ma'am," Jeremy replied, "but I'm not taking on passengers this trip."

Casey's heart sank. Though his words solved one problem they posed another. She learned that Dare couldn't possibly be traveling on the *Martha C* if she wasn't taking passengers, and she need not worry about encountering him. But on the other hand, the captain's outright refusal threw all her plans into disarray.

"Please, Captain, won't you reconsider?" Casey pleaded. "It's imperative I leave England immediately to claim my dead husband's land in New South Wales. I'll pay whatever you ask, within reason, of course."

As much as Jeremy wanted to accommodate the lovely young widow, he could not do so without consulting Dare first. If he approved, room could be made for the lady and her child. Perhaps they'd be good company for Dare's own wife and child, he reflected. But at this time he could offer little encouragement. "Mrs. . . ."

"Stanley, Casey Stanley."

"Though I can promise nothing, Mrs. Stanley, there's a remote possibility that a cabin will be available. I'll know for certain sometime today. Where can you be reached in the event I can accommodate you after all?"

Eagerly Casey gave her address. "How soon will I know, Captain? It will take time to pack."

Jeremy assumed a thoughtful look. Dare had sent word yesterday that he had returned to London and would see him today. He could ask him then. "I might even know today. I'll send word around in the morning."

"Thank you, Captain," Casey smiled charmingly. "Anything you can do in my behalf will be appreciated."

Concealed behind a bale some distance from where Casey and Jeremy stood conversing, Dare watched with a great deal of curiosity. What in the hell is that little vixen up to now? he wondered. He had already been to her house and told she was out. He then insisted on seeing his son and after he assured himself the lad was well he left to tell Jeremy that his livestock would be delivered the next day. He recognized Casey by the wayward strands of red hair the breeze had worked loose from beneath her bonnet. Leaving his concealment only when she was well on her way back home, Dare approached Jeremy as he stood staring after Casey's carriage in a bemused manner.

"What the hell did Casey want, Jeremy?"

"You mean Mrs. Stanley? Do you know her?"

"Aye, I know her," Dare smiled wryly. "What did she want?"

"To book passage to Australia for herself and young child."

"What did you tell her?"

"Nothing, really, except that I wasn't taking on passengers."

"Did you mention my name?"

"No, should I have? I thought, though, after I conferred with you, it might be possible to accommodate the young widow."

"Entirely possible," grinned Dare wickedly. "I think the time has come for you and me to have a long talk, Jeremy."

In the privacy of his cabin, Jeremy was bemused by all that Dare told him about Casey and their volatile relationship. "The two of you certainly have led a . . . er . . . rather complicated life," he said dryly. "What are your intentions?"

"Send a message to Casey tomorrow saying a cabin has been found for her. Tell her when to come aboard and leave the rest to me. If my lovely little vixen wants to play games, she'll find herself pitted against a master. I love her too much and have come too far to lose her now."

"Are you sure, Dare? It's a nasty trick to play on that nice little lady."

"No more nasty than what she intended for me. Do as I say, Jeremy. I give my word all will turn out well. Oh, and Jeremy, I hope you know how to perform a marriage."

"Blimey!" Jeremy beamed importantly. "It'll be my first."

When Casey received Jeremy's message she burst into a frenzy of activity. She hadn't seen Dare all the previous day but thought surely he'd show up today, and she didn't want to alert him to her imminent departure. When Dare finally did arrive, his arrogant manner infuriated her.

"I'm waiting for a ship, Casey," he said, "to take us to Australia. It could arrive any day now, so be prepared to leave at a moment's notice."

"What makes you think I'll go with you?" Casey retorted belligerently.

"I'm a determined man, love. I claimed you long ago and you belong to me. When I leave London you and our son will be with me."

Casey smiled a secret smile but said nothing to contradict his erroneous belief. "What about Lydia? Won't she miss you?" she taunted.

"Perhaps I'll bring her along," he teased with wicked humor.

"Damn you, Dare! Is everything a joke to you?"

"Who's joking?"

She looked so adorable with her green eyes spitting fire he couldn't resist pulling her into his arms and kissing her. She stiffened. Feeling the hesitation in her lips, the reluctance in her body, the way she held herself, he sighed regretfully and loosed her from his apparently unwelcome embrace. He wouldn't force her response. Not now. Once she recovered from her anger over Lydia she'd be more receptive to him. She was being stubborn and evasive and he allowed her her little secret, for one day soon she would be totally and irrevocably his.

After cuddling his son for a time, he left, informing Casey he had business which would occupy him for the next several days. Casey welcomed the news, for it fit in perfectly with her plans. The *Martha C* was to sail in three days on the noon tide and if her luck held she would be gone before Dare returned. Of course she would tell Drew's lawyer where she had gone, in the event Dare wanted her badly enough to come after her.

Three days later Casey was packed and waiting for a dray to arrive to take her and her baggage to London Harbor. Fortunately she had had sufficient time before her departure date to purchase necessities to make her voyage comfortable as well as stock up on much needed items of clothing for her and Brandon. Luck had been with her these past three days. True to his word, Dare did not appear to badger her. It was just as well, for she'd not had to put up with his arrogance or impossible demands. Nor did he have the opportunity to wear down her resistance or persuade her to change her mind. It was embarrassing the way he had only to touch her and she was reduced to a blubbering idiot. She wanted Dare, but not at the expense of her own independence. She was a person in her own right, not an extension of her husband, should she eventually marry Dare. She also needed proof that Dare loved only her; loved her enough to want her no matter how angry he was with her.

The dray arrived and while it was being loaded Casey left instructions to the servants for closing up the house. If she decided later to sell it she would write Drew's lawyer outlining her intentions. And then all was in readiness and

Brandon's sobbing nursemaid reluctantly handed her small charge to his mother. But before the driver whipped up the horses, a small, raven-haired woman hailed Casey. She recognized Lydia immediately. At first she considered ignoring the woman but thought better of it and instructed the driver to wait.

"Mrs. Stanley, I'm glad I caught you," Lydia said breathlessly as she drew abreast. "I learned your address from my brother. Can you spare a moment for me? I'm Lydia Hurley."

"I know who you are," Casey said coolly.

Flushing guiltily, Lydia replied, "You have every reason to dislike me. I . . . I made a fool of myself over Dare. What you saw the other day was none of his doing."

"Why are you telling me this?" Casey asked curiously.

"Because I'm ashamed of the way I acted. And besides, Eddie told me how much Dare loves you. And all the trouble you two had finding one another," Lydia revealed, her voice laced with remorse. "I'd never be happy in Australia no matter how romantic my fantasies made it sound. And that's what it was, pure fantasy."

"You don't have to tell me this, Lydia," Casey said, feeling more kindly toward the young woman.

"Yes I do," she persisted. "If you're leaving because of me and what you thought you saw at Dare's house, you should know the truth."

"What is the truth?"

"The truth is that I arrived that day only moments before you did. Dare resisted my attempts at seduction, calling me a spoiled child. A name I richly deserved. Then you arrived and he asked me to wait in the parlor, unaware it was you at the door. I couldn't stand the thought of another woman having Dare. Without considering the consequences, I partially disrobed and . . . You know the rest. Dare was totally innocent."

"What made you decide to come to me now to tell me this?"

"It took a while to summon my courage," Lydia admitted sheepishly. "That and what Eddie told me about the two of you."

Suddenly Brandon began fussing and Lydia's attention was drawn to the dark-haired infant in Casey's arms. She stared intently at him a few moments, then smiled. "He's Dare's child, isn't he?"

Casey nodded, seeing no harm in admitting the obvious. Brandon was a tiny replica of his father.

"I . . . I wish you both well," Lydia offered with a wistful sigh.

"Thank you, Lydia, for being honest with me. It won't change my immediate plans but it might alter my future. You're a lovely young woman," Casey allowed generously, "and one day the right man will come along. Just as it did for me. I think I loved Dare from the first moment I laid eyes on him."

Casey stood at the rail of the *Martha C* watching London disappear in the distance. She didn't exactly regret leaving London behind. Since living in the wild, untamed beauty of Australia, neither England nor Ireland held any appeal for her. She was astute enough to know her future lay in the new, unpredictable land she had come to love, and so did Brandon's. Thousands of acres of rich land in the region of the Hawkesbury belonged to her. Should Dare decide he no longer wanted her, Drew had left her secure enough to make a life for herself and her son. She was young and strong and capable of forging her own destiny.

Casey seriously doubted that Dare would choose to remain in England once he found her gone. He loved her, she always knew that. Besides, she had no reason to doubt Lydia's version of what happened in Dare's house that day. She realized he would be raving mad when he learned what she had done, but perhaps it would teach him not to take her for granted as he was inclined to do. Or issue orders without asking her opinion or taking her needs into consideration. She wanted to be more than a possession; she wanted to be Dare's partner and have an equal say in all things.

From his position on the bridge Jeremy watched Casey as she stared pensively into space, wondering if she was thinking about Dare. He chuckled to himself, glad he wasn't in Dare's shoes when his lady discovered him aboard the *Martha C.* From Dare's description, Casey wasn't some meek miss to sit back and let others decide her future. Give him his own sweet, uncomplicated Martha any day, he thought wistfully. Though she was no great beauty, she suited him just fine.

Casey felt Jeremy's eyes on her and turned to smile at him. With a start she realized she was sailing on his ship and had never bothered to ask his name. She saw him making his way toward her and decided to rectify that oversight at once.

"Captain," she greeted cheerfully, "here I am aboard your ship and don't even know your name."

"Combs, Mrs. Stanley. Jeremy Combs at your service."

"I have a friend in Australia named Martha Combs," Casey mused. Suddenly comprehension dawned. "Oh, no, it can't be! I know the name but it's too much of a coincidence. Surely you're not the husband my friend Martha thought dead all this time?"

"Aye, ma'am, I be Martha's husband," Jeremy admitted, grinning. "I just recently learned what happened to my Martha. I'm off to Australia now to set her free, if that be possible."

"I . . . I can't believe it," Casey gasped, her green eyes wide with wonder. "Martha spoke of you so often I feel I already know you. She thought you were dead."

"I'm pleased to meet a friend of my wife's," Jeremy said sincerely. "It's no wonder Martha thought me dead. I was shipwrecked off the coast of South America for over a year before I saw London again. How was my lass when last you saw her?"

"Very well, Captain Combs."

"Call me Jeremy. Any friend of Martha's is a friend of mine."

"Only if you call me Casey."

"Agreed. Tell me about Martha. She must have suffered terrible hardships."

"Martha is working for the Penrod family and is happy enough. They treat her well and she's changed dramatically since arriving in New South Wales. You may be surprised when you see her."

"I hope she'll be glad to learn I'm alive and that she still loves me," Jeremy said with a hint of trepidation. Then duty called him away, leaving Casey to ponder the strange workings of fate.

Casey's cabin was more spacious than she would have imagined. From the generous proportions and comfort it offered she assumed she had been given the captain's cabin. And wonder of wonders, a cradle appeared as if by magic. Even more astounding was the fact that fresh milk would be available for Brandon during the entire voyage. That bit of information was welcome, for he was of an age to be weaned. Little did Casey know that these amenities were due to Dare's foresight and thoughtfulness in providing for the comfort of his small family.

Casey retired early that night after a solitary meal in her room. She had mashed up some of her own food for Brandon, nursed him and put him to bed. At nine months he craved more than just milk, demanding solid food as well, which she gladly provided. Soon she could stop nursing entirely. Her son now slept peacefully in his cradle, looking so like Dare she had to catch her breath to keep from crying out his name.

These next months without Dare would be the longest and bleakest in her life, Casey thought with a shaky sigh. With no other passengers aboard, she could expect little companionship other than what Jeremy could spare during the limited time away from his duties. Once in New South Wales there would be Roy and Ben and Martha to provide the friendship she needed. And eventually she'd have Dare. She knew him well enough to realize he'd never allow his son to slip from his life without a fight.

The night was extremely warm and Casey wore her thinnest shift to bed. In England it was midsummer, and when she reached Australia it would be summer again. Strange, she mused, drifting off to sleep dreaming of the man she loved. She was confident that when they finally came together it would be forever.

Lost in the throes of a dream so real she could hear the rasp of Dare's warm breath in her ear, Casey imagined she felt his touch sliding across her heated flesh. The lips that whispered erotically across her cheeks were full, velvety soft and oh so tender. The hands that explored beneath her shift were teasingly gentle yet roughly demanding, and highly arousing. Her phantom lover kissed her closed eyes before claiming her mouth, at first softly and then hungrily. Fulfilling her fantasy, she opened her lips, allowing their tongues to touch, savoring the taste and texture.

Casey's head shot backwards as her dream lover's mouth wandered down the silky column of her neck. His teeth nibbled gently at her collarbone, and his tongue played in the hollow of her throat before his tantalizing journey was halted by her single garment. Then abruptly the dream became reality as Casey felt the shift leave her body. Her eyes flew open but the night was very dark. A quickening wind had driven heavy clouds in from the north, obscuring the pale light of the crescent moon. A promise of rain hung heavy in the night air. She could just make out the menacing shadow hovering above her.

"Who . . . who is it?" Her voice cracked with

fright yet she resisted the urge to scream for fear
of awakening Brandon. If he set up a racket her
intruder might harm him.

No answer was forthcoming as the man captured her lips, gently covering her breast with a
warm palm. His tongue invaded her mouth,
savoring its sweetness while he caressed the
fleshy mound and tenderly thumbed the taut
bud. With loving care his lips trailed down her
throat and closed over an erect nipple. His
tongue circled and flicked over the aroused peak
while his hands claimed other treasures below.

The moment he released her mouth, Casey
whispered his name. No other man had the
power to capture her senses so thoroughly.
"Dare . . ."

"Did you doubt it, love?" he chuckled in wry
amusement.

His mouth returned to hers and greedily
feasted there as he settled down beside her on the
spacious bed. Casey gasped, his hot flesh like a
branding iron against her nakedness. She had
been so enthralled by his kisses she hadn't known
when he removed his clothes. His passionate
onslaught continued unabated as Casey buried
her fingers in his hair and drew his lips downward to where her breasts begged for further
attention. She jerked in response as his hand
touched the incredibly silky curls which guarded
her womanhood, gently parted her downy maidenhair, and found the satiny folds which were
burning with inner heat yet damp to his touch.

The tiny peak he discovered was hot and hard,
eager for his attention. Very carefully, aware of
the sensitivity of this aroused bud, he massaged it
until she began to vibrate, driving her to a frenzy

of yearning. His hands were bold, yet gentle and skilled. As his tongue plundered the taut crests of her breasts, pleasure spiraled in her belly and swept over her body like rolling thunder. His right leg slipped over hers and now rested between her thighs, and his thick shaft lay hot and stiff against her hip. With exquisite torment Dare's tongue loved Casey's breasts, assaulting their tender peaks with shards of delight, his hands stroking her from her firm mounds to the downy triangle between her legs. Gently he nudged her thighs apart and, enticed by the warmth and softness of her, thrust one finger deep into the tender crevice to roam its silky valley and taut peak.

Casey moaned softly as she surrendered willingly to his demands, every inch of her responsive to his touch, alive and craving him.

And then he was inside her, sliding full and deep, moving, slowly at first, feeding the fire that licked at her vitals, destroying all but the power to respond. She accepted him greedily, urging him on with words that made little sense.

"I love you, Casey, only you," Dare rasped in a voice made husky from passion and need. "You are my life, my love, my very soul. Without you I am nothing. Come, my love. Let us take this journey together."

Whether he was talking about the voyage to Australia or their erotic journey, Casey never knew for at that moment her whole world centered at that place where he labored so lovingly. Then coherent thought was no longer possible as they achieved the reward they strained toward, yearned for, the experience so shattering it left them breathless with wonder.

Casey was the first to find her voice.

"How did you know where to find me?" She spoke in a whisper so as not to awaken Brandon who had slept blissfully through their rather vocal lovemaking.

"Did you think you could escape me so easily?" Dare chuckled, lightly stroking her breasts. "I don't give a damn about Lydia or any other woman. It's you I love. You and my son."

"I know," Casey agreed sweetly.

"You know? You believe me?"

"Of course."

"Bloody hell! Do you realize what you've put me through? Why were you so set on leaving me if you were aware of my feelings?"

"Dare, please be quiet," Casey cautioned. "Fortunately Brandon is a heavy sleeper but if you continue like this he'll soon be yelling his head off."

"Sorry, love, but you must admit I have just cause for my outburst. Will you kindly answer my questions?"

"I had a visitor before I boarded the *Martha C.* Lydia called on me and explained everything. She even apologized for her brazen behavior."

"Well, what do you know, there's hope for her yet. Why, then, were you going to leave me?" Dare accused. "You continue to puzzle me, woman."

"Would you have me any different?" she teased, her fingertips playing on the furred roughness of his chest, then trailing down his lean flanks.

"Stop that, you little hussy, or I'll never hear your explanation. Now, tell me why you were leaving me when you knew I loved you."

"Because of your domineering and overbearing manner."

"What? Me domineering? What in the hell are you talking about?" Dare exploded. Nearby in his cradle Brandon stirred and Dare lowered his voice to a hoarse whisper. "Explain yourself."

"By leaving I hoped you'd realize I'm more than a possession. You can't order my instant obedience as if I were a simpleton. Did you ever once think to ask me what I wanted? No, you ordered me to return to Australia with you without considering my feelings."

"Dammit, Casey, we love each other. I have only your best interests at heart. You should want the same things I do."

"Typical male thinking," snorted Casey derisively. "I have a mind of my own, a brain to use as I see fit. I . . . I knew you would follow me. I expected it, really. But by then I hoped you'd come to realize I should have a say in how or where I want to live my life."

Slowly, carefully, Dare digested all Casey said, agreeing with her in principle but reluctant to admit it. He wanted her so badly he thought she had wanted the same thing. To spend the rest of their lives together, to raise their child, or children, with love and affection. And that's exactly what he told her.

"I do want the same things, Dare," she admitted, swallowing the lump forming in her throat. "But I also want to be your partner, with a say in everything that concerns us or our children. If you can't understand that—"

"I understand, love, it will just take some getting use to. I suppose I was rather . . . er . . . forceful in my dealings with you. But the thought of losing you again was more than I could bear. If I promise never to take you for granted, will you forgive me?"

"That's all I ever wanted, to be thought of as something other than someone to satisfy your sexual appetite and bear your children."

"Any woman would do if that's all I wanted," Dare said reproachfully. "I've never thought of you as a sex object, though I must admit you fill the roll admirably," he leered. "You're everything I've ever wanted in a woman despite our rather dismal beginning."

"And you're all I've ever wanted or needed, Dare darling. But you still haven't explained how you knew I'd be aboard the *Martha C* when you've been conveniently absent for days."

A low rumble escaped Dare's throat. "Some weeks ago I met Jeremy Combs by accident and hired his ship to take us to Australia. When I realized who he was and told him about Martha, he was more than eager to strike a bargain with me."

"And I played right into your capable hands," Casey giggled. "How had you planned on getting me and Brandon aboard ship if I hadn't proved so obliging?"

"I would have kidnapped you, of course," Dare revealed, his tone light and teasing yet tempered with steel, leaving Casey no doubt that he would have done exactly as he said without a smidgeon of remorse.

"You're an arrogant rogue, Dare Penrod, but I wouldn't have you any other way."

"And I'd take you any way you'd let me," Dare replied playfully. "In fact, I think I'll have you now."

"Again?"

"Again and again and again—"

"Not if I have you first," she murmured, her small hands playing artfully over his body until his breathing grew ragged and his manhood hardened with anticipation. He jerked spasmodically when her fingers grasped his rigid manroot and stroked in a back and forth motion, driving him wild with need.

Her lips tasted the slight saltiness of his skin, explored the thick ropy muscles banding his chest and rippling across his flat abdomen. When her mouth found him he nearly arched off the bed, shock and pleasure snaking through him. It never occurred to him that Casey would want to pleasure him in the same way he sometimes pleasured her. That she did was highly erotic and arousing. But he did not want the night to end too soon, so he reluctantly dragged her upward until she was lying atop him and eased inside her. "Witch," he growled, abruptly reversing their position, assuming the dominant role as he took them both to glory.

CHAPTER TWENTY-SIX

A rather bored and somewhat sleepy Brandon, held lovingly in his father's arms, yawned throughout the brief but moving ceremony uniting his parents in marriage. At the end he protested vigorously as Dare planted a possessive kiss on his mother's smiling mouth, which Brandon assumed belonged exclusively to him. He wasn't entirely happy about sharing his mother, but he appeared enthralled by the large man who showered him with tenderness and love. He failed to understand why his wonderful mother sometimes, but not often, neglected him whenever this man called Papa put his arms around her. Usually, after such an outrageous display, they ended up romping in bed. He couldn't see what they were doing but the noise they made clearly indicated they weren't sleeping. Perhaps, Brandon's childish mind concluded, if Mama was so taken with Papa the least he could do was give the man a chance. Gurgling happily, he rewarded them with an enchanting grin, in his own way bestowing his blessing upon their union.

During the following six months Brandon

learned to love his mama and papa equally. He also learned to walk, keeping his parents occupied with preventing him from toddling into places considered unsafe. Though he loved his mother's soft arms and pleasant smell, he adored his papa's rough play and underlying tenderness. When the *Martha C* docked at Port Jackson, Brandon delighted them both by speaking his first word. Naturally it was "Papa."

A hot sun glared down on them as they stepped ashore on January 10, 1810. They had been gone over a year and a definite change had taken place in the colony. More buildings crowded the harbor and everywhere Casey looked new roads were being constructed by convict labor. Several ships rode at anchor in the harbor, including English, Yank, and French, most either supply ships or convict carriers.

"I'll take you to the house Drew left you, love," Dare said once they had debarked. "It will take several days to unload my cargo and arrange for the animals to be taken to Penrod station. Thank God we have a place to stay. Even with all the building going on, inns still appear to be in scarce supply."

The house was much as Drew had left it, and Casey began the process of settling in for a few days. The servants had been let go and no food remained in the house, but Dare assured her everything would be taken care of. True to his word, two convict servants arrived an hour later carrying supplies from the *Martha C* as well as from the government store. Dare returned at dusk, anxious to impart some of the news he had heard during the day.

"Governor Lachlon Macquarie reached New

South Wales late last year," he informed Casey as
they ate their supper. "He brought his own
regiment with him to the colony and disbanded
the Rum Corps. Most have already been removed
to England, although a goodly number who purchased land remained."

"Thank God they're gone," Casey said.

"I also learned that Macquarie was not too
happy to find a select group of pure merinos in
dominent economic and social positions. He's
sworn to change all that."

"It's difficult to change a way of life overnight."

"But it's a start. Macquarie has plans to use
convict labor to build public buildings and con-
struct roads, establish a bank, and introduce
currency to take the place of rum. If his plans
materialize, we'll soon have a hospital, convict
barracks and church. I have every confidence
that one day soon we may know what lies beyond
the Blue Mountains."

Several days later they began their trek to
Parramatta and Penrod station, both anxious to
see Roy, Ben and Robin. Jeremy Combs accompanied them. Some of the supplies Dare purchased in England were packed in the back of the
wagon that accompanied them aboard the *Martha C*. Jeremy drove the wagon with Casey and
Brandon on the seat beside him while Dare rode
one of the bays. The other three horses followed
behind, hitched to the back of the wagon by a
leading rope. No one interfered with their passage this peaceful day, allowing Casey ample
time to admire her surroundings.

She had forgotten just how awesome the Australian bush was with its majestic eucalyptus

trees, wattle, profusion of colorful blooms, kangaroos, cockatoos, parrots and the laughing jungle cry of the kookaburra. She drank eagerly of the familiar sights and sounds, while Jeremy appeared stunned as well as highly impressed.

But then nothing could dampen Jeremy's spirits, for during the week spent in Sydney he was granted an appointment with Governor Macquarie and, after much cajoling and arguing, obtained a full pardon for Martha. It was a hard-won victory but well worth the time it took waiting for an audience with the much beleagered governor. No matter if Martha still loved him or not, she would have her freedom.

The wagon departed from the dusty track and entered the farm yard. To Casey's eyes it looked as if nothing had changed, for the same dogleg fences surrounded the yard and the same gum tree provided shade to the house. No one but a few convicts hard at their chores were on hand as the party pulled to a stop before the front door. Cautioning the others to remain outside so that he might cushion the shock of both Casey and Jeremy returning from the dead, Dare entered the house to find Ben and Roy eating supper. On this night, as on most others, Robin had joined them. Upon seeing Dare, all three leaped to their feet, greeting him like a returning hero. None of the three men knew exactly what to expect, for Dare had left Australia a man burdened by sorrow and heartache.

"Dare, welcome home!" Ben whooped excitedly.

"It's good to have you home, son," Roy added his own sentiments. "God, we've missed you."

"We've all missed you," Robin chimed in,

pumping Dare's hand and slapping his back. "Did you have a pleasant voyage?"

"How was your stay in England?" Ben interjected, eager to hear all the details.

"My stay in England was productive beyond my fondest dreams," Dare grinned cryptically. "And the voyage home was wildly pleasurable."

"Sounds like the old Dare," Robin said happily. "The trip must have done you a world of good."

"More than you'll ever know," Dare agreed. His next words shocked them to silence. "I took your advice and brought back a wife. I'm also the father of a young son."

Rendered nearly speechless, Roy was astounded by the change in Dare. He had left a bitter, withdrawn man who had just lost the love of his life to return happy and obviously cured with a wife and son in tow. It was a miracle. Whoever the woman, Roy was grateful for her positive influence on his son.

"I'm more than pleased things worked out for you, Dare," he said. "After you lost Casey I feared you'd never love again."

"Casey is the only woman I'll ever love," Dare revealed, producing a second shock as great as the first.

"Dare!" admonished Roy sternly. "Are you telling me you married a woman you don't love? That's not like you and certainly not fair to your wife."

"Believe me, Father, I love my wife dearly."

"But you said—" Ben protested with a puzzled frown.

"That I'd never love anyone but Casey, and I meant it."

"Dammit, Dare, you're not making sense," Roy returned, certain that Dare had lost his senses.

"I think it's time you met my wife," Dare grinned roguishly. "Then you'll understand. First, you'd better all sit down."

He left the room with six pair of eyes staring at his back as if he had lost his mind. He returned a few seconds later with Casey and Brandon.

"Jesus! She looks just like . . ." Ben's words fell off as he gawked rudely at the flame-haired beauty standing beside his brother.

"By God, it is!" Roy shouted gleefully, astounded. "I don't know how, but somehow, some way, Dare found Casey alive and made her his wife. No two women could look so alike. And that's my grandson she's holding!"

"Bloody hell!" Ben gaped, using Dare's favorite expression. "You're right, Father. Only Dare could manage the impossible."

Robin said little. He could only gaze at Casey, his expression soft and tender.

Casey giggled, thoroughly enjoying the sensation she caused, a position quickly usurped by her son.

"Do either of you want to tell me how all this was managed?" Roy asked, his eyebrows raised inquisitively. "We were led to believe you were dead, Casey."

"It's a long story, Roy," Casey laughed, "and one worth telling, but there's another surprise in store for you."

"My God! I don't think I can stand another," gasped Ben, clutching his chest in mock dismay.

"This surprise involves Martha, is she in the kitchen?"

"I'll get her," offered Robin, still choked up over Casey's return.

While they waited, Brandon began an exploration of the room, ending up being saved from disaster by Ben who whisked the youngster off his feet and onto his shoulder amidst squeals of delighted laughter.

During the interim Dare explained about Jeremy Combs. Then Robin returned with Martha. Having learned about Casey's miraculous return from the dead from Robin, Martha hugged Casey exuberantly and made a great fuss over Brandon who was now being dawdled on his grandfather's knee.

"Robin said you wanted to see me, Dare," she said, looking at him curiously.

"It's about Jeremy, Martha," Dare began hesitantly.

"My husband Jeremy? He's dead, sir, I thought you knew that."

"He's very much alive, Martha," Casey said gently. "He was shipwrecked and returned to England a year later only to find you gone. But we'll leave the telling to him."

"He's here? In New South Wales?" cried Martha, her eyes huge, her face drained of all color.

"Aye, he's right outside the door," Dare smiled. "I thought you'd want to welcome him privately."

Martha stared at the door for a long, tense moment before floating through it as if in a dream.

A short time later a beaming Martha returned with an ecstatic Jeremy in tow, arms linked like lovers, features flushed. After Jeremy's story was told and Martha informed of her pardon, the joyous couple excused themselves and disappeared into the privacy of Martha's room.

Then Dare launched into a detailed explanation of Casey's ordeal, leaving everyone stunned over Mercy's deception. "I recommend we keep the truth from Thad McKenzie," Roy suggested thoughtfully. "He doted on the girl."

"I have no wish to dredge up old hurts," Casey said. "With Mercy dead it would serve no earthly good."

"I'm sorry to hear about my old friend Drew Stanley," Roy added. "He was a good man."

"The best," Casey agreed, smiling through a mist of tears. "I don't know what I would have done without him."

"Nor I," Dare added emphatic agreement. Suddenly he yawned hugely. "It's been a long day and time we put our son to bed. There's still much Casey and I want to tell you but it will have to wait for tomorrow."

Sleeping peacefully in one of the spare rooms in the cradle brought from the *Martha C,* Brandon was unaware that he had become an instant sensation at Penrod station. The exuberant lad had quickly captured the hearts of everyone in the house.

In the bedroom across the hall Dare pressed Casey into the softness of the mattress, his fully aroused body hot and hard, hers arching upward, melding them together. Her eyes were luminous green, her face flushed; a fine sheen of perspiration dewed her flesh. Small gusts of breath escaped her parted lips inviting further exploration.

Dare's hands, mouth and tongue worked dili-

gently and lovingly to bring her to the highest
peak of arousal. Flexing his hips he entered her
easily. Casey moaned mindlessly in joyous welcome of the steely length and silken strength that
brought her such piercing pleasure. They moved
together as one; one body, one mind, one accord.
Fullfillment washed over them in turbulent
waves, setting them adrift in a storm-tossed sea
of pure passion. Afterwards they floated to shore
in peaceful contentment.

"I love you, Casey. You'll never leave my sight
again," Dare promised, playfully nipping at her
ear. "You're my life, I am nothing without you."

"What makes you think I'd want to leave?"
answered Casey lazily. "I've not looked at another man since I met you. I love you, Dare."

"You're a woman of property now, love. What
will you do with all the land Drew left you?"

"Settle on it as soon as a house can be built. It
belongs to you as well."

"Are you certain?"

"Absolutely. We'll breed our own flock with
the pure merinos you purchased in England. And
children. We'll raise lots of children."

"Do you think we made one tonight?"

Casey giggled, as if finding Dare's words worthy of ridicule. He bent her an austere glare.
"Why do you find that amusing? I gave it my best
shot."

"Even if you made love to me every night for
the next six months you couldn't make me pregnant."

"Casey!" Dare gasped, properly affronted. Was
she insinuating he wasn't man enough to make a
baby?

The clear tinkle of Casey's laughter dispelled

some of the outrage her words inspired and he allowed the stiffness to leave his spine. "What in the hell are you up to, woman?"

"Girl or boy?"

"What?"

"Would you like another son or a daughter?"

"You mean . . . you're already . . ."

"Your virility was never in doubt, my love. We've been together night and day for six months with little to do but care for our son and make love. Surely it can't come as a surprise that we're to have another child," Casey teased, twining her arms about his neck and drawing his lips to hers.

"Nothing you do surprises or shocks me, vixen," Dare said, grinning roguishly as he accepted her invitation.

Dear Readers,

Governor Bligh, John Macarthur, Lt. Colonel Johnston and Governor Macquarie and the events surrounding them all happened as described on the dates mentioned. All other characters and dates are fictitious and could have occurred but are figments of my imagination. If you enjoyed my story, or any of my other works, I would love to hear from you in care of my publisher. I answer every letter I receive. I write primarily for the entertainment of my readers and enjoy knowing I please them.

Exquisite tales of love that recapture a more romantic age.
By Connie Mason

AUTOGRAPHED BOOKMARK EDITIONS

Each book contains a signed message from the author and a removable gold foiled and embossed bookmark.

PASSIONATE INDIAN ROMANCE
BY MADELINE BAKER

"Madeline Baker proved she knows how to please readers of historical romance when she created *Reckless Heart* and *Love In The Wind*." —*Whispers*

LOVE FOREVERMORE. When Loralee arrived at Fort Apache as the new schoolmarm, she had some hard realities to learn . . . and a harsh taskmaster to teach her. Shad Zuniga was fiercely proud, a renegade Apache who wanted no part of the white man's world, not even its women—but he couldn't control his desire for golden-haired Loralee.

_____2577-9

$4.50 US/$5.50 CAN